I0600882

Cover Design and Interior Format
© THE KILLION GROUP INC.

SATING EMBERMOON

CARA CRESCENT

PROLOGUE

London, England
January 12, 2009 AD 3:02 AM

TODAY, HE WAS SIXTEEN. SIXTEEN years, one day, six hours, and two minutes old, to be exact. If he were honest, he'd lived six months, twelve hours, and twenty-one minutes too long.

Harrison Cayce gripped the blade in one hand and covered his privates with the other. She always stared at his junk and he hated it. Hated her. Hated this place. Truth be told, he hated himself.

Muscles trembling with weary anxiety, he braced for the coming onslaught. His toes curled into the ash beneath his feet. He stood alone in the small, dark arena, but he wouldn't be alone here for long.

The arena hadn't been used in centuries. It was about thirty feet in diameter, with viewing booths high overhead, and walls of solid slabs of curved cement, moss covered and stained with a substance he didn't want to contemplate. Three large, stone gates were spaced around the circular arena. They were closed for now. There were no monsters on the other side of those gates. They were boys. Hungry, naked, scared, and all bolstered by the insincere promise of release. Those boys would do everything they could to destroy him.

And he meant to let them.

Adia triggered the gate mechanisms. A startling bang boomed

through the arena before the scraping of stone-on-stone overwhelmed the echoes.

He didn't want to live. Hadn't for the last six months. He'd held onto hope for a while, but now he'd been transformed. There would be no going home. No growing up.

There was just Adia and her sick desires.

Size made the gates sluggish, but as they rose, he could make out his opponents' pacing feet. Could hear their thundering hearts over the scrape of the rising stone slabs.

This was her way of bringing him around, but he wouldn't break. He'd never be hers. The smell of fresh blood overwhelmed each breath—she'd cut them. But he would not break. He would not feed, nor fight.

He turned his face to the high booths above. Adia stared back through almond-shaped brown eyes surrounded by flawless ebony skin. She had high cheekbones and a narrow chin. Slim and curvaceous, she could've been a model, but behind the façade of angelic beauty breathed the essence of true evil.

He threw down the blade.

Adia laughed.

For the first time since entering the arena, doubt crowded his determination. As he stared at his nightmare, the scent of blood grew stronger, mingling with the stench of sex and dirty bodies. The pounding of their hearts amplified. The boys crawled under the gates, impatient to collect their prize.

One of them grabbed his shoulder, spun him around.

He held no rational thought after that.

She'd been right.

The vampire drive took over. He had the vague impression of screams. Warmth splattered his body, sticky and sweet-smelling. It filled his mouth, spilled over his chin, and dripped down his chest.

In the aftermath, he cried. They'd been boys. Just like him.

He glanced at his watch, the only thing she allowed him to wear. She wanted him to feel the passage of time. Wanted him to feel his humanity slipping away with the same persistent measure of the second hand ticking away time. He was sixteen years, one day, twelve hours, and forty-two minutes old. He'd lived six months, twelve hours, and forty-two minutes too long. The last of his innocence was gone. Harrison wiped the backs of his hands over his eyes and stood, glaring at his creator.

The bitch would die.

Adia must have seen his intent in his expression. She recoiled, shouting for her guards.

When they arrived, he let his vampire instinct take control again. With each step, he allowed a perfect duplicate of himself to split off until his copies outnumbered Adia's guards. While he might be a neophyte, he was small and slippery and quick as hell. So were his copies. It didn't take long to kill the guards, nor for Adia to call for a Guardian to come and put him down.

The Guardian could try.

He took solace in Adia's shouts of displeasure and the fear lurking behind her eyes. Had she truly believed he'd return to her willingly? Never. It was unfortunate he couldn't get to her now, but he would. Eventually.

He was sixteen years, one day, six hours and fifty-eight minutes old, and he wouldn't rest until she was dead.

CHAPTER 1

Seattle, Washington
October 8ᵗʰ, 3 AA 10:42 PM

*I*F YOU WOULD LIKE INFORMATION *on Harrison Cayce, meet me at The Knot Works in Fremont at 11:00 PM. Present this note to the bouncer at the door.*
    Adia

Being out after dark wasn't only dangerous, it was a federal offense.

"You getting out, lady?"

Ember Moon huddled in the back of the cab, a picture of her high school sweetheart clutched in one hand, staring at the daemon driver. "Meter's running, right? What's it to you if I want to pay to sit here?"

He snorted and faced front again. He looked as human as she did. The only reason she knew he wasn't was because the sticker on the plexi-glass partition separating them said so. Daemons were required by law to make it known what they were.

Daemons had become a part of life since the world's brush with Armageddon three years ago. In fact, society had changed so drastically all over the world that a new date stamp had been developed—AA: After Armageddon. There had been a time, before the daemons arrived, that humans hadn't expected to survive the Nephilim. Almost two-thirds of the global population had perished. What was left of humankind owed their existence to the daemons, but that didn't mean they trusted them.

She turned her attention to the activity outside the window. The driver had stopped right in front of The Knot Works and humans comingled with daemons, talking, laughing, and moving to the deep bass spilling out of the club. The line to get in wound around the block.

As a social worker, she'd always been careful to obey the laws and stay well away from daemon kind. In her line of work—placing children in foster care—it was of the utmost importance that she maintained a squeaky clean record.

But someone had information on Harrison.

Butterflies swarmed in her belly. Eight years had passed since she'd seen Harrison. She thought of him often. Every day. When they were sixteen, he'd gone with his parents for a vacation in England and while his parents had returned, he hadn't. He'd disappeared.

With one finger, she traced the outline of the awkward teenage face on the photograph. God, had she loved that boy.

They'd grown up together in Tucson. His parents both worked at University of Arizona and owned a beautiful home at the edge of the Sonoran. Her stepfather, a drunk bastard, lived a quarter mile from their place in a rundown trailer. Back then, there had been times when things got so bad that she wasn't so sure she wanted to keep living, but Harrison always managed to bring her back into the light.

They'd met at school and he had taken her under his wing almost immediately. The other kids tormented her over her stepfather's drunken antics; Harrison, though, had always protected her. He became her best friend. Funny, sweet, protective Harrison. She'd fallen hard and fast in love with him. He and his parents had been responsible for saving her from countless drunken tirades. They'd brought her along on trips, nights out, and kept her over for dinner until she wasn't quite so skinny. The Cayce's had been her family even then. After Harrison had disappeared, she'd moved in with the Cayce's and then they'd been her family for real. Except it never felt quite right without him there.

She needed to know for herself what had happened to him but would also love to give something back to Nancy. Harrison's mom had opened her home to Ember, had taken care of her, and she'd never found a way to pay back that kindness. If she could find out what happened…maybe even discover if he was still alive…

First, she needed to get out of the cab.

"Okay. What do I owe you?" She paid the fare, got out of the cab, and wiped her sweaty palms on her slacks. Dressed in a bright blue, conservative suit, she didn't fit in with this crowd. The women were scantily dressed, ready for a night of revelry. The men carefully put-together to exude nonchalance in their attire.

With a quick glance around, she made a bee-line for the bouncer, lifting the note for his inspection. He waved her in.

Ember paused inside the club, giving her eyes a moment to adjust to the flash of strobe lights. Humans and daemons lingered in a long hallway with neon lights highlighting the entrances to alcoves. Bright strobes flashed in the darkness, distorting everything and the music blared so loud it affected her equilibrium.

Slowly, she moved deeper inside, trying to look everywhere at once. Inside the first alcove, a naked woman had been strapped onto a large vertical wooden X. Little silver weights hung from her nipples, and her mouth had been stuffed with a ball-gag. A huge man held a vibrator to the apex of her thighs while she writhed and twitched, her face contorted into an expression that could as easily be pain as pleasure.

What the hell was this place?

Clutching her purse tighter to her body, she walked farther in, trying to ignore the scenes of twisted debauchery playing out on either side of her. The last alcove was empty. Almost. Someone had hung a banner that read: Welcome, Ember Moon.

Her stomach sank. She wasn't going to find out anything about Harrison here. Someone was messing with her. With a hasty glance around, she turned to head back toward the front door. If she hurried, she'd be back home before curfew.

"Miss Moon!" A teenage girl with shiny yellow hair, dressed in a baby-doll dress stumbled through a doorway at the back of the alcove and fell to her knees.

For a heartbeat, she didn't recognize her. She didn't know any teens that would wear something like that, much less have their hair plated into two pig-tails with big bows at the ends. Then she realized who she was looking at.

"Oh, my God, Madison?" Heart stuttering in her chest, she stepped into the alcove. Madison—one of her clients, a child she was in the process of finding a home for—shouldn't be anywhere near this place. Why was she dressed like this? She looked like a baby-doll going to her first communion. Ember glanced around. Was this a set-up? Was a parent of a child she'd removed from a home trying to get revenge? Maybe, but how would they know about Harrison Cayce? How had they gotten hold of Madison?

She crouched and helped Madison to her feet. "Are you okay?"

Madison nodded, her big blue eyes filling with tears. She leaned close to her ear. "He's watching."

Who? She'd ask later, right now... "We're leaving. I want you to close your eyes real tight—" The girl didn't need to see anything going on in this club. She stopped when Madison shook her head. "Why not?"

Again, Madison leaned close. "The ghost man won't let us."

The hair on Ember's nape lifted. "Ghost man? Who's that?"

Madison's eyes jerked to their left.

Ember looked, but didn't see anything. There was just the wall. She squinted, trying to see past the strobe lights.

A black wall, painted in great whirling strokes.

"There's nothing there. We have to go."

Madison's hand tightened on her arm. Again, her eyes jerked to their left. And again. The girl held her whole body rigid, tense, as if she feared by moving, she'd catch unwanted attention.

A shiver stepped up Ember's spine, raising the hair on her arms. She had to look again, to put the girl at ease, but now she didn't want to. This was like when she was a kid and would accidentally see a preview for a horror film on T.V. She'd get just a brief sense of something terrible and then for days after would feel it stalking her. See it from the corner of her eye. Sense it trying to sneak up on her.

There never had been anything there, of course, just like there was nothing here.

Still, she stood there staring at Madison, with her heart pounding in her chest and her breath catching and she *didn't want to look again.*

The tendons in her neck had become so tight, she could feel them creak as she turned her head. A tremor ran through her. There was something about those swirls on the wall. Some of them almost looked like knots in a tree . . . or eyes. Now that she'd noticed them, the rest of the features were obvious—nose, wide chin, broad shoulders—obvious, but oddly shaped. Flat. Stretched and distorted. As if someone had carefully cut away the skin on a face and flattened it between the pages of a book like she used to do with flowers.

Disturbing. Awful. For several deep beats of the music, her fight or flight instincts failed her. She stared like a jaywalking animal caught in headlights. Was it an illusion? A trick of the light?

A daemon?

Oh, God. She pulled Madison back.

The eyes blinked open and the creature peeled himself away from the wall, becoming three-dimensional as he did.

"Run." Her grip tightened on Madison's hand, and she broke into a sprint, dragging the screaming teen with her.

They didn't even make it out of the alcove.

Thick, muscular arms wrapped around them, squishing them together. The air, her body, turned frigid as ice.

He was trying to separate them. She tightened her grasp on Madison's hand, grabbed hold of her wrist with her other hand. "Madison! Hang—"

Madison's hand slipped from hers.

No. *No!*

The cold was so deep she began to shake. Flailing out with her arms, reaching for Madison. "Madison!"

"Miss Moon?"

The daemon released her.

Ember stumbled back, staring at her new surroundings.

Where had the club gone? The Ghost-man?

She stood in a room. Maybe at a hotel, but if so, it was a strange one. Everything was red and black and on either side of the satin-clad bed stood two towering black statues of Anubis. Handcuffs dangled from one of the Anubis statue's mouths. Her belly twisted and though she wasn't cold anymore, her shaking increased. What was going—?

Madison!

Ember swung around and came face-to-face with three people she'd never seen before—two rough-looking males and a female. The woman couldn't be more than twenty-five, her ebony skin as flawless as her svelte figure. The men were older. One was tall and sleek with long white hair—almost elegant. The other was thick and rough-looking, like a fighter who didn't win very often.

Ember reached for her purse, her cell phone, but it no longer hung from her shoulder. Had she dropped it? Had the Ghost-man taken it? "Where's Madison?"

The woman gave her a tight-lipped smile. "Safe. My associate took her back to Washington."

"If you hurt her, I'll—"

"I'm not interested in the child." Adia scoffed. "You can have her back after you help me."

"Then why involve her? You could have grabbed me any-where." That daemon . . . he could've hidden anywhere.

"Yes, but then you wouldn't know about the Knot Works and you wouldn't have a reason to do what I need you to do."

That didn't sound good. "Where are we? Who are you?"

"Vegas."

Ember's mind spun. A moment ago, she'd been in Fremont, a suburb of Seattle, Washington.

"My name is Adia." Her lips curved in a thin smile. "You help me get what I want and then you and the child can go your merry way."

Right. Easy. Except she must want her to do something horrible if she planned to use Madison against her. From the corner of her eye, she saw the door. Started edging toward it on legs that trembled. "Why should I trust you?"

Adia's smile grew. "You shouldn't. Never trust anyone, my dear. That's the first rule of survival." Adia sighed. "I wasn't sure until you arrived, but it seems you and me, we have the same weakness for the same man. My Harry, he's been . . . trouble-some, of late. I need you to bring him to me."

Ember froze, glomming onto the most important part of what

Adia had implied—Harrison was alive. He must be alive if he'd been causing trouble. "I don't . . . I don't know where he is." She hadn't seen or had news of Harrison in years. How had he gotten mixed up with daemons? "I came because I thought you could tell me about him."

"I can." Adia flung her arms out to her sides with a flourish. "Soon, he'll be right here in this room."

Everything spun a little. She'd always hoped . . . but she hadn't been sure . . . "He's alive."

Two quick steps brought Adia right in front of Ember and before she could jerk away, Adia clasped Ember's chin between her fingers. "Now, listen close. If you're still alive come morning . . ." Her lips twisted into a cruel smile. " . . . which I seriously doubt, you'll bring Harry to the Knot Works."

Holy shit, this woman was crazy. Whatever Adia wanted with him, it couldn't be anything good. "Why not just talk to him when he gets here?"

"Oh, no." Adia pursed her lips. "That would never do. He must come to me. He *will* come to me."

Ember took a step back, closer to the door, shaking her head.

Adia's arched brows lifted. "You'll sacrifice the girl for him?"

Ember blanched. Sacrifice? Was someone going to die? She'd never sacrifice one of her kids. At the same time, what was she supposed to say to Nancy—So, sorry, I discovered your son was alive but I had to sacrifice him for the safety of a kid? Thanks again for letting me live with you those last couple of years of high school. Gotta run.

"I thought not. Don't give him another thought. A woman like you wouldn't want anything to do with him. He's a child-killer, you know."

"He wouldn't." Tears pricked her eyes. She didn't understand what was happening, *why* this was happening, but she damned well knew Harrison. She shook her head. Not Harrison.

Adia shrugged. "Murdered nine boys in cold blood. Tore. Them. Apart." She glanced back at the men. "Gastov, bite her."

Heart pounding in her chest, she ran. Shook so hard by the time her hand wrapped around the door knob, she almost couldn't turn it. She flung open the door.

She was free!

She opened her mouth to scream for help and . . .

"He's a child killer you know."

Ember blinked. She stood facing Adia. An overwhelming sense of déjà vu washed over her. Something just happened. Something . . . "He wouldn't." She touched her forehead which had started to ache. She'd said that already, hadn't she?

Adia shrugged. "Murdered nine boys in cold blood. Tore. Them. Apart." She glanced back at the men. "Gastov, bite her."

Heart pounding in her chest, Ember turned to run and smacked right into a solid chest. The man with the long white hair smiled. "This will only hurt a little." His hands clamped around her arms as the other man came up behind her.

Gotta get out. Gotta get free. She lifted her leg, slamming her foot into his knee cap. *Call the police. Get help.* The brute's grip lessened and she broke free, running two steps before she was tackled to the ground. She skinned her knees on the rough carpet, slammed her chin into the floor so hard she saw stars.

"No!" The denial was guttural as it tore from her throat. She clawed at the plush carpet, trying to drag herself free.

Strong hands dug into her flesh, pressing her shoulders to the floor. She couldn't even drag in a deep breath with her face smooshed to the carpet and his weight bearing down on her back. Another hand dragged her hair away from her back, baring the nape of her neck. *Oh, God.* Were they vampires? Did they plan to kill her? "What are you?"

The white-haired man—Gastov—brought his face close to hers, his hot breath blasting against her ear. "I'm an Incubus, love. After I bite you, you'll crave sex like an addict craves heroine. I almost envy how much fun you'll have. You know, right up until you die."

No. No, this wasn't happening. This couldn't be happening.

He moved out of her line of vision. His breath brushed over the back of her neck. His lips parted over her skin.

Ember Moon screamed as he sank his teeth into her neck.

CHAPTER 2

Las Vegas, Nevada
October 9th, 5:39 AM

THERE WAS A NAKED WOMAN chained in his room.

Harrison Cayce Sinclair blinked.

Not a stitch of clothing graced her luscious curves, nor were any lying about the ostentatious hotel suite. Just ball-gag in her mouth and a thin golden chain wound round her waist with what looked like a note attached. Or maybe a price tag.

Her shackled arms stretched high overhead, the chain linking them threaded through the jaws of a gaudy statue of Anubis. For a breathless moment, Harrison did nothing but stare while she writhed against the stone, her large breasts thrusting out with each movement.

His cock perked with interest.

Then, reality intruded with the force of a thunderclap, recalling him to who and what he was.

He withdrew his sidearm, stepped deeper into his hotel suite, and locked the door.

What in the hell was going on?

George, his minion, jumped from his preferred spot on Harrison's broad shoulders to roll on the floor. Not much larger than a ferret, pearly white scales protected his back from nose to alligator-like tail. Tufts of midnight fur stuck between his scaly armor and covered his belly, which he currently offered for a rub. George glanced at Harrison through his large inky eyes as if to ask, "What's the hold up?"

Damn minion. He wasn't any help.

With one eye on the blonde, Harrison searched the room, checking the bathroom and closets for other intruders. Nobody else was around. Not so much as a hand towel hung askew, nor had George given any indication of danger.

Was this another of his partner's practical jokes? With the Department of Daemonic Control still understaffed, their boss had asked Julian to book the room for Harrison's trip and the jackass had chosen this overly done daemon suite at Treasure Island. Julian must've had a long, hard belly laugh picturing his reaction. The ceiling-high Anubis statues on either side of the round, satin-clad bed were hideous. The bright red carpet brought to mind a thick pool of blood, while the black-lacquer furnishings were just plain depressing. Where did humans get the idea daemons would appreciate something like this? They'd had three years to realize daemon's tastes didn't deviate this much.

Yeah, Julian was probably still laughing with the other guys at the precinct over the room and the woman. Maybe some high-end hooker Julian thought would be funny to tease him with.

The woman's eyes opened long enough to turn heated as her gaze roamed his length. She arched her back as her lids slid closed, trying to get closer.

He'd ash the bastard next time he saw him. First, he needed to send his uninvited guest on her way.

George approached the blonde. He took a few sniffs of the woman's leg before rubbing his diamond-shaped, scaly head against her and then trotting off to the bathroom.

Well, if the minion thought she was okay, he'd trust him. George's instincts had saved him on more than one occasion. He strode over and ripped the small square of paper off the belly chain and unfolded it. Instantly, he recognized the sprawling script as Adia's and his gut rolled into a tight knot.

Dearest Harry,

I've had enough of your interference. You've proven a constant irritation. Lucky for you, I'm a benevolent lady. I've left you a gift. This is Ember Moon.

His attention shot back to the woman. *Dear gods.* Ember? He cupped her head, holding her still while searching for traces of his childhood friend in her features. She had a pale, round face with a narrow chin and a wide, sensual mouth. A small contusion peeked out from her hairline near her temple and a rug-burn reddened her chin.

"Look at me."

Her tawny lashes snapped open to reveal unfocused emerald jewels that sucker-punched the breath right out of him. Eight years had passed since he'd last seen her. He'd never met anyone with that same shade of green in their eyes, but . . . . He removed the ball-gag, wiping the saliva at the edge of her mouth with the side of his hand. "Em, is that you?"

"Please help me." She rubbed her cheek against his hand.

"Answer me. What's your name?"

"Ember Moon."

His first instinct was to pull her down, her arms had to be numb, but he'd learned long ago never to make rash decisions where Adia was concerned. There were always repercussions. "Where did you grow up?"

"Tucson." She was slurring her words, barely staying awake. What the hell was wrong with her?

More. He needed something only Ember would recall. "When you were a kid, you explored a dry riverbed with your best friend. You remember?" He gave her a little shake.

"Mm-hm."

"What did you find?"

"Trouble."

"What kind?" He rubbed his palm against her feverish cheek to rouse her.

"Javelina." She wet her lips. "Whole family."

Yeah, she'd been tough as nails while they ran like hell from those pigs and once they reached safety, she'd laughed right by his side about their near miss.

"What's wrong with you? What'd they do to you?"

Her head lolled back against the statue, her eyes fluttered closed.

Shit. His attention returned to the now crumpled letter. He tossed aside the ball-gag and scanned to where he'd left off.

Do you remember her? Tragically, an incubus bit her last night at around 11:00, and she has not yet been sated. That gives her until about 7:00 AM before she expires.

He closed his eyes. That meant she was a succubus. Succubi were insatiable until after their first mating, when they claimed their mate for life. And if he didn't mate her? He'd witnessed the death of an unsated succubus once. The woman had been abandoned in a sex house he'd busted and they'd had no recourse but to witness her demise. They'd been too late to locate a mate for her, and with no known cure for the bite of an incubus, they could do nothing but watch her burn from the inside out and listen to her screams. He glanced at his wristwatch: 5:50 AM. He didn't have a whole lot of time left. He continued reading.

I do hope you've arrived in time. Then again, I've heard you've become something of a monk, so perhaps you can't help her. Either way, she's fucked. Whatever you decide, enjoy.

Adia

P.S. You'll drop your ridiculous harassment and come to me willingly or I'll take everyone you've ever loved and when I return them they'll be in pieces or corrupted beyond redemption.

Whatever he decided? As if she'd given him ample time to mull things over. Either he sated Ember, thereby becoming her mate, or he stood by while she died a horrible death. Only Adia would consider this a choice. He couldn't allow her to die, but he wasn't sure if he could have sex with her, either.

For a moment, he was right back in that old arena, trying to resist something much larger than him under Adia's careful scrutiny. No, he wasn't a kid anymore. He was stronger now. He'd sworn to himself he'd never get caught in Adia's games again.

And the bitch knew it.

She'd concocted a new game. A game where, if he refused to play, an innocent life would be lost.

He paced away a few steps, dragging his hand through his hair. How did this happen? He had the whole department searching for Adia and she'd waltzed into his hotel room? What next? Adia found Ember, she must also know where to find his parents. His friends. His daemon family.

He'd been so fucking careful for the last eight years. He never visited or called, refusing to lead his enemies to his family and friends. He hadn't even sent a letter home telling his parents he was still alive.

What if Adia went for his loved ones now, after ensuring he was busy with Ember?

The note crackled in his shaking hands. Gods, had all the air been sucked from the room? He couldn't seem to drag in a decent breath. He shut his eyes and forced his mind to focus on his breathing, to block out his chaotic thoughts.

Everything's fine. It will be okay.

Breathe in. Breathe out.

You're overreacting. Send a protection detail to your parents and then sort out Ember.

He sent a quick text to Julian, his partner at the DDC, instructing him to send a squad out to his parents' house to protect them from Adia, adding that he'd explain everything later. He had no doubt Julian would take care of everything, even without the details. That was one worry he could set aside for now.

Once he felt more centered, he returned his attention to Ember. Something about this wasn't right. Adia didn't do simple. She never showed her hand. A hidden viper lurked somewhere in this whole scenario, some sick twist that would completely flatten him when revealed. The fact that he knew it was there but couldn't find it was making him half-crazed.

What? It's not enough Adia's transformed Ember? True, her life would never be the same. Her human friends and family would shun her. She'd lose her job. Her home. Gods forbid if she had kids, the government would take them from her, too. *This is my fault. Adia went after her because of me.*

Still, his gut told him he was only seeing the smoking gun. Not the bullet that was still whizzing through the air searching out a target.

Was this a trick? What if Adia had found out about the Javelina? They'd both been chatty kids. Had they told anyone stories of their adventure? What if this wasn't Ember but some imposter? He wracked his brain trying to remember an identifying mark, a birthmark, a mole, something. *The cross.* She had five freckles in the center of her back that made a perfect crucifix.

He turned the woman around and froze. Adia couldn't have known he'd remember the marks, nor would she have taken the time to put this much detail into her game. Would she? With an unsteady hand he touched the freckles. Dampened the tips of his fingers in his mouth and tried to rub them away. Her skin turned red where he scrubbed, but the freckles stayed.

This was Ember.

"How long have you been here?" He turned her around; he cupped her face in his hands.

Her eyes opened and slipped closed again and she arched forward, attempting to rub against him.

"Ember." He shook her. "How long?"

"Forever." She moaned. "Please. I ache everywhere. Touch me."

He released her, searching her body for a bite mark. What if Adia lied and had only given Ember a drug to make her behave this way? He searched every exposed inch of her lovely body and only found more bruises on her shoulders and thighs, and a wedding band. "Were you bitten?"

Her head lolled to one side, eyelids fluttering. "My neck."

He lifted her blonde locks with unsteady hands. There, right below her hairline, he found the mark. He released her hair and stroked over the palm-shaped bruises on her shoulders with his thumbs. They must have restrained her while the incubus bit her. Ember would've fought like hell, she'd always been tough.

He let his forehead rest against hers, forcing himself to stay calm. There would be nothing he could do for her if he panicked, but this was his fault. By refusing to return to Adia, he'd made Ember a target. "I'm so sorry, Em."

How would he get them through this? Until three years ago at the age of twenty-one, he'd been stuck in his sixteen-year-old body. Oh, his mind had aged. He'd matured, but his body hadn't. Not until three years ago when the Grigori coven's superb spell craft had aged his body into adulthood. Unfortuantely, not even their Magic could fix whatever was broken inside him. The first time he'd tried to have sex . . . . As soon as she'd started pawing at his pants, his cock, he'd panicked.

Very sexy. So manly.

Ember arched forward again, moaning when her nipples brushed his shirt.

"I know, baby. I'll find a way to ease you, I promise." She might hate him for it tomorrow, but he wouldn't let her die. Not like this.

Ember's skin was already unnaturally hot. He glanced at the clock: 6:12 AM.

"Sh." He angled her for a kiss, praying the small act might revive her a little. He pressed his lips to hers, easing her even as he struggled with his own inner turmoil. How would she react to being stuck with him as a mate? What if she was in love with someone? He didn't look anything like he did as a kid. Did she even recognize him? "Do you know who I am?"

A smile played around her lips and her eyes had cleared a little. "I always feared it'd be awkward when we met again, Harry."

Yeah, this was his Ember. He allowed himself a small laugh. "No worries on that count. Nothing awkward about this."

"Good, now do what you need to do to make this stop." She paused to let out a low moan. "I'm burning up."

Okay, he had consent. Sort of. Maybe. Did she even know what she was saying? His gaze flashed to her hand. "You're wearing a wedding band, Em. You married?"

"No."

"Engaged?"

"Good God, Harry! No. No boyfriend. No nothing. No one ever quite measured up."

He wanted to ask who she measured them to and how he might weigh in by comparison, but now wasn't the time. "Why the ring?"

"To keep people from bothering me. Touch me, damn it."

Her gaze was glassing over again. He let his hands travel from her face to her breasts and when she sucked in a hard breath, his erection went from interested to fuck-me-now in a heartbeat.

She strained, arching into him. Afraid she'd hurt herself, he leaned into her, pushing her back against the statue. He pressed his leg between hers and grabbed her by the ass, sliding her forward until she straddled his thigh.

"Your skin is cool," she whispered. "I want more."

That was easy. He could give her that. He put a hand on his collar and pulled his shirt off in one swift motion. A shiver ran along his spine as her hot flesh pressed to his, as her hardened nipples stabbed into his chest.

"Harry." She moaned. "The pants. Now."

He grimaced against her neck. "No, Em. Not yet. It's been a hell of a long time for me, and I'll never outlast you, not in your current state. Relax. I'll take care of you." He cut off her protest with an open-mouthed kiss. At the taste of her, his balls tightened. He massaged her breasts with his hands while she rocked herself against his leg. "That's it, baby." He kissed the arch of her throat, testing the tight tendons with his teeth before easing away any hurt he caused with the flat of his tongue.

Ember's breath came in short little gasps. Her heart pounded loud enough for him to hear. Her wet heat soaked into his pant leg. Gods, she smelled of vanilla and aroused woman and her scent was making his mouth water.

He wrapped his arms around her. His hands on her shoulders adding force to every thrust of her hips against his jeans-clad leg. *Come on, baby.* She cried out, shuddering with release. He held her through the tremors, caressing her back and dropping kisses on her cheeks. He slipped his thigh from between hers.

For a moment, her eyes cleared and she stilled. A pretty blush bloomed over her features and she pressed her body to his, not to urge him on, but to cover her nakedness.

He cupped her face and forced her to meet his gaze. "This is gonna be a long morning. I need to know if—"

"No. No, I'm fine now." Her gaze slid away. "I'm not sure what happened. I'm so sorry."

"This isn't your fault and it's not over." He pulled her close, her cheek against his chest. "I promise I won't leave you until you're sated." He paused. "If you want me to stay."

Ember nodded.

Then the moment was over and he still hadn't told her what this meant for her. Hadn't explained what he'd become. Where he'd been. Nothing. He couldn't. He couldn't bear her disgust.

"Harry." She moaned and with her pressed against him, the increase in her body temperature was obvious. She needed more.

"I know, love."

Gods, did he know. What he wasn't sure of was whether he could continue. Consummate their mating. His body was ready, like any male, he craved sex. It was his mind giving him problems: He hated being touched, and refused to allow anyone close enough to hurt him again.

But this was Em. When they were kids, he'd never considered the possibility of growing old with anyone but her. Never wanted anyone the way he'd wanted her.

Ember rubbed her breasts against his chest.

He unlatched one of the cuffs and stepped back out of reach. "Touch yourself, Em."

"I want *you*."

"Then you'll do as I say." As hard as he was, he'd never outlast her. If he came before he sated her, her demon would take over and the morning wouldn't end well for either of them. He closed his eyes, trying to regain some control over his pulsing cock.

"Watch me."

Her tone was full of sultry allure and his gaze darted back with a will of its own. Was that her demon speaking or her?

She trailed one slender hand over her chest to pluck and pinch at her hardened nipple. She rolled the tight bead of flesh between her fingers, tugging. *Gods help him.*

"Lower." His voice turned rough as wet gravel.

Her hand skimmed over her gently rounded belly to sink into the thatch of blonde curls. She came almost immediately, crying out, her hips thrusting and her sex-slicked thighs trembling.

"Gods, yes, Em. Again."

He watched her bring herself to fulfillment, almost coming himself when she cried out in ecstasy.

When her eyes cleared again, he needed to explain as much as he could before her need consumed her again. "An incubus bit you."

"That w-woman, Adia." She covered her breasts with her free arm. "Her name was Adia, she ordered that b-bastard to *bite* me." Her gaze slid away. "Said I would become a succubus." Her eyes filled with tears. "This is insane."

Shit. A shuddering breath wracked through him. What the hell else had Adia told her? He forced himself to a calmer place so he could focus on the current problem. "Did she tell you what that meant for you?"

"I'll be addicted to sex." Her cheeks flamed.

"Until you're sated. When you're first bitten, you have to take a mate. Do you understand? Part of taking a mate is having sex with them. After today, you'll be the same as always." Almost. "The thing is, while you can still have sex with other people," he nearly choked on the words, "you'll only find fulfillment with your mate."

"What if I don't choose one?"

"You'll die."

She closed her eyes, biting her lip. "I don't want that."

"If there's someone else you'd prefer . . . ." He let the offer hang in the room. Hating himself for being kind enough to ask and hating himself more for needing her to say no.

A smile ghosted over her lips. "You'll do."

Something in him eased, but something else tightened. She deserved better than him, someone clean and whole. A male who could truly enjoy his role as her mate. "Em, I'm not the same."

"No, you outgrew your awkward stage." She gave him a shaky smile.

He couldn't help but return the gesture. "I, uh. . . ." *I'm sorry, this is entirely my fault. I'm not human anymore. I'm sorry, I—*

"Thank God you still have the habit of rescuing me."

"I'm no hero." *Not even a little bit.*

"You are to me." She shook her head. "I don't believe anything she said about you."

He looked away, unable to meet her earnest gaze. She should. He was a killer, a vampire. He had been a sex slave. For years now, he'd failed to stop Adia's growing underground sex trade. "I'm a lot of things." He wet his lips. "But that isn't one of them."

Ember's eyes clouded with need again. "Undo the other cuff."

His chest squeezed. He couldn't do that. She already had one hand free. Things were going all right so far, but he didn't want her pushing him, trying to control him. *Touching him.* He shook his head. "Later."

She looked up, reaching for the clasp.

Harry pulled her to him, dragging her free arm around his neck as he kissed her, plundering her mouth in a siege for dominance. "If you want me to continue, you'll do as I say."

"Okay." She gasped as he dragged the bulge of his erection against her heated flesh.

His cock throbbed with the need to sink deep into her heat. Instead, he drew one tight little nipple into his mouth.

"Harry."

He soothed her with a few swipes of his tongue, before letting his teeth graze the sensitive bud. His hand caressed across her hip, over her sex-dampened thigh. A shudder ran through her when he brushed past her nether curls. He thrust his fingers deep inside and she came again. Her inner muscles squeezed and sucked at his digits while he devoured her breasts.

"More, Harry." Her hips rotated, pressing to his hand. "Please, I need something more."

He found her hard little clit and rubbed his thumb against it. She gasped, trembling as he kissed his way along her belly.

She'll hurt you and laugh. Bite you and— No. This is Em. Sweet, sweet Em. The litany played in his head, over and over until it overwhelmed the ugly voice reminding him of pain and humiliation. *She can't hurt me. She's restrained.* Her scent filled his nostrils and he inhaled. *Sweet Em.* He kissed her thigh, then dragged the flat of his tongue across her mound. She tightened around his fingers again, the deep pulse squeezing and releasing as moisture covered his hand. He swiped through her damp curls. Focused on the hard nub that would give her the most pleasure, he licked her, suckled her. He drank in her passion as she writhed above him.

This is Em. Sweet, sweet Em.

Her whole body convulsed, his name spilling from her lips like an invocation.

He stood, guiding her hand to her slit.

"Keep going."

He walked over to the dresser and ripped the shade off the lamp. The bright light behind him would prevent her from seeing too much, help hide his scars.

As he undressed to his boxers, his attention remained on her. On the rapid little flicks of her wrist as she stroked herself off, her nipples hard and straining. Gooseflesh spread over her skin. Her head tipped back and her long blond hair brushed against her ass. Her whole frame shuddered again.

Never had he seen anyone so beautiful, so fucking erotic. He approached, held her gaze as he lifted her and forced her legs around his hips.

"Em, are you sure? You'll be bound to me after this."

She nodded, her eyes clear. She was sure. With her unshackled hand, she cupped his cheek. "It really is good to see you, Harry."

He grinned. "I didn't think you'd ever forgive me."

"I'll always have a bit of forgiveness for you."

His smile faded. Gods, he hoped so. Eventually, she'd find out everything. Then he'd need her absolution more than ever.

In an awkward maneuver, he reached under her legs, slipped his boxers off, and stepped out of them. Later, getting back into them without her seeing the mangled mess he hid would be an even bigger trick. She'd be disgusted. Or worse, she'd pity him.

She leaned in and kissed him, chasing away his worries. Her tongue dragging over his bottom lip before sinking deep to tangle with his. The reality of Ember exceeded any fantasy he'd ever had. He'd always imagined her skinny with small breasts and an innate shyness. The reality of her was curvier, fuller, warmer, and sweeter than a ripe peach on a humid monsoon evening.

His aching cock found her center, dipping into her. Harry held her there, the head of his cock breaching the tight ring of her entrance and dropped his hand to her clit, stroking her off again. At the first pulse of her orgasm, he withdrew.

———◆———

Good God, did he intend to torture her to death?

Ember needed the deep fullness that came with intercourse and he seemed determined to give her everything but. Being on her own as long as she had, she wasn't used to ceding to anyone and she'd promised herself she'd never be at anybody's mercy ever again. Like a leaf in the wind, she fluttered between Harrison's will, that bitch Adia's demands, and the mercies of whatever she was becoming. Had anyone but Harrison walked through that door, she might have opted for death.

After the incubus bit her, something ugly and frightening had begun to grow in her belly, writhing in anger. Its agitated, serpentine movements radiated heat until she thought she'd burn from the inside out. The entity had eased when he'd arrived, purring at the sensations his hands and mouth invoked. Now, his teasing caused the ugly something to grow restless. *It* needed. She *needed*.

"Harry, you're killing me here." Another moan escaped her lips. If she hadn't been so out of her mind with need, she'd be mortified by her behavior. Tomorrow, she wouldn't be able to look him in the eye, but right now, none of that mattered. In this moment, all her energy focused on slaking her lust.

Pure unadulterated pleasure shot from her breasts to her clit as he suckled and tugged her nipples. Her thighs tightened around his narrow hips and her fingers sank into his shoulder muscles. He was hard as hell everywhere.

The broad head of his prick pushed into her. *Yes.* That was what she wanted. She'd clobber him if he stopped again. This time, he drove deeper. Afraid he'd pull away, she eased her grip with her legs, lowering herself.

Ah, yes. So full. Stretched. His hands settled on her ass. Raising her up. Pushing down. Lifting. The width of his cock rubbed mercilessly against that sensitive spot deep within her and she began to tighten around his hard length.

His mouth tugged at her breast sending shockwaves straight to her clit.

Her inner muscles tightened to the point of pain.

Another orgasm quaked through her and he withdrew.

That strange entity writhing inside her screamed in outrage.

Ready to yell at him, her eyes flew open. His face was contorted into something that looked like pain. He forced his breathing into a slow, deep pattern. He struggled, his muscles bunched tight around her.

"You all right, Harry?"

His eyes opened, spearing her with their electric blue brilliance.

"Harry?"

In response, he winked. His hips flexed and he sank his cock deep within her again. She gasped at the fullness, her gaze never leaving his. In that moment, she knew everything she needed to know about Harrison. Despite all the nastiness Adia had spewed, the kid Ember grew up with was still in there.

Somewhere.

He set a slow pace. A frustrating pace. With one wrist shackled overhead and her other arm and legs wrapped around his hips, she couldn't force the rhythm she wanted, the hard, deep thrusting the entity inside her needed. A slow buildup of tension wound in her core. One that had her squeezing her inner walls to keep him buried deep inside, attempting to swallow his dick whole to maintain the fullness she craved. And, though they spoke no words, a wealth of communication traversed between their gazes. She felt bonded to this man, once familiar but now a stranger, which was both frightening and exhilarating.

His gaze trapped hers, commanding her to rise to the challenge in his eyes, compelling her to meet him thrust for thrust. Demanding submission.

As her passion climbed higher her head tilted back, her eyes closing.

He shook her, forcing her eyes to his. "You'll know who's taking you. You'll see me when you come."

She stroked her hand over his neck, across his cheek, hoping to soothe him. This must be hard for him, too, being ambushed with a woman from his past. She couldn't imagine how he felt or what he thought of all this, but his need to gain control was real and reasonable under the circumstances.

She leaned forward and kissed him, maintaining his desire for eye contact as she did. "Anything, Harry," she whispered against his mouth. "You're in charge. Tell me what you want."

Her belly clenched tighter and her womb cramped as the tension wound higher. She squeezed her inner muscles, dragging him deeper.

"Come." His breathing turned ragged. "Come for me."

She did.

As he slipped right out from between her grasping slit.

The entity growing inside her twisted in rage, wanting out,

demanding control.

"Harry! I need you with me."

"Soon." He sealed his promise with a kiss. A hand caressing her chest. He didn't push back into her until her body had calmed once again.

"Now." She swallowed hard, unable to explain her fear that the entity within her might hurt him. "Come inside me this time."

His back bowed when he entered her so he could take her breast in his mouth. He tugged her nipple, suckling. Biting and then sweeping the rough pad of his tongue across the rigid tip. Licking his way up her chest, he nipped at her neck, marking her with his bite. All the while he drove into her with unwavering, impaling thrusts.

Those gorgeous blue eyes stared into hers. "I want to feel your nails, beautiful Em."

She eased the grip she had on his neck, flexing her fingers and dragging her nails down his chest, leaving red marks in their wake.

His eyes rolled back and his head tipped back on a moan. She dipped with him, as his knees bent and he thrust hard and deep. She had never felt more powerful than she did right then. That such a simple act of submission on her part made this big man lose a little control was a heady sensation indeed.

The entity coiled, ready to strike if he tried to tease them again.

When his gaze returned to her, the intensity in his eyes was almost frightening. "Ride me, Em."

She wound her bound hand in the chain of the shackle for more leverage and her other clenched in the soft curls at his nape. She rode him, tightening and releasing her legs around his waist. Her inner muscles squeezed him in time to her flexing thighs. Raising. Lowering. A deep thrust. A shallow, teasing one.

His breathing grew erratic. His cock thickened, pulsing within her.

Yes. She had to make him come this time, had to protect him. Leaning forward she took his bottom lip between her teeth and tugged. Rubbed the tight points of her breasts against his chest and sank her nails into his neck.

"Gods, Em, yes."

His rocking, pivoting hips met each of her thrusts. Faster. Harder. Deeper.

His eyes glazed. It was time. She quickened her pace, and even as her insides tightened to a painful knot of need, she worked him, rotating her hips with each gliding movement, heightening their pleasure. She was there, tipping on the precipice and he was, too. "Come with me, Harry."

He gripped her ass, adding force to every thrust, slamming her onto his cock, pressing himself deeper with each joining. The slap of flesh hitting flesh filled the room. The musky smell of sex hung in the air. His brilliant blue gaze remained intent on hers.

She gasped, unable to wait any longer. Intense brilliance shook her to her core, and she raked her nails down his chest, right over his taut nipple. His knees buckled and he thrust hard, deep. His embrace secure, he shuddered around her.

The entity settled within her.

After a moment, Harrison pulled away enough to give her a lazy kiss. His fingers slid through her hair, smoothing her locks back from her face. "See. No awkwardness."

She laughed, cupping his cheek in her palm. "It's over."

He covered her hand with his and squeezed, drawing it away to lace his fingers with hers. Almost like a gentle rebuke.

A bright light flashed to her right as something tightened on her upper arm. She flinched, trying to get away, but couldn't. The light faded, leaving behind a golden band, melded into her flesh. Another light flared to her left and a matching armband locked around his bicep.

What was this? The equivalent of daemon wedding rings? Her questioning gaze searched his.

"It's your Magic. The bands bind a succubus to her mate." He stroked his knuckles across her cheek. "We're mated now, Em. I swear I'll do good by you. I'll do my best to make you happy." He glanced at his watch and gave her a kiss.

She swallowed hard. Happy? So far he'd made her delirious. God help her, she wanted nothing more than to do the same for him. She craved to ease the tenseness from his shoulders and chase away the haunting darkness lurking in his eyes. Oh, yes, she desired to bring this man joy above all else.

Which meant she was in a whole lot of trouble because if she ever wanted to get Madison back, she had to betray the man who'd just saved her life.

CHAPTER 3

October 9th, 8:36 PM

EMBER WOKE WITH A START, sitting straight up in bed. Disoriented, she glanced around the darkened suite, noting the Anubis statues, the cuffs, the man snoring softly next to her.

It wasn't a nightmare. Her whole life had changed.

She forced her breathing back into a steady pattern, stretched her aching muscles and snuggled back into the satin sheets. She'd have to figure out what to do soon, but for a little while, she wanted to continue to pretend. To imagine herself nothing more than a woman lying with her long-lost love. She wished she still possessed those idealistic, loyal, trustworthy qualities she valued yesterday morning when she'd never betray a stranger, much less a man she knew.

That version of her had had to die once Adia kidnapped Madison.

Not only was it her moral responsibility to protect the child, it was her job. She'd removed Madison from one unhealthy environment and now she was in another—scared, alone, and facing an uncertain future.

Unless she did what Adia demanded and lured Harrison to the Knot Works.

This was a nightmare. She'd worked hard to get where she was in life. She'd worked two jobs to put herself through college, and while it had taken her twice as long as most because of her lack of funds, she'd graduated top of her class. She was respected for her hard work and her unwavering loyalty to her client's needs. She had to get Madison back.

But what would that mean for Harrison?

Ember rolled over and contemplated her sleeping lover. How many times had she dreamed of this? She still couldn't believe this gorgeous man was her childhood friend. His thick blond hair curled at his shoulders; he had hard, chiseled features and a body to die for. She couldn't believe he'd acquired such a muscular build after being the scrawniest kid in school—he didn't look like his father at all.

Oh, God, what was she thinking? She couldn't betray him, and she couldn't leave Madison's fate to Adia. What was she going to do?

Harden yourself to him. He left you to your stepfather's mercy.
And he's saved my life twice now.

It wasn't Harrison's fault her stepfather had gotten to her. He'd disappeared long before then. Those had been bad days. She'd been shocked when the Cayce's hadn't returned home on schedule, but when they'd arrived home a year later without their son, she'd been horrified. It was the worst day of her life. Nancy had taken her aside and explained that while she needed to tell everyone Harrison died, he hadn't. For the longest time, she thought Nancy was delusional, but while she refused to explain, she said she hoped that someday Harrison would return.

Finally, he had.

Sort of.

The boy she'd known was in there. She'd caught glimpses of him in his self-mocking grins and in the way he put her at ease this morning.

Except the old Harrison hadn't been a control freak, nor would he have participated in any activity that might leave the kind or amount of scars this man had on his body. He wouldn't be so demanding or forceful or have such a bone-weary, seen-way-too-much pain in his beautiful blue eyes.

Now Adia wanted her to hurt him some more.

Distance yourself and think of Madison. Think of the children Adia said he murdered.

Her gut soured.

No, he'd never hurt a kid. You can't trust Adia.

Harrison rolled over and grabbed a remote from the nightstand. The lights clicked on and he turned to her. "Morning, Em."

She forced a smile in greeting. "I think it's evening." *Was it still the same day?*

"All a matter of perspective, I suppose." He stretched with the grace of a tawny lion. "Did you need anything?"

What, like more sex for the nymphomaniac? Her face flamed.

"Gods, I didn't mean—"

"It's all right."

"Please don't be—"

"I'm fine." She sat up, pulling the sheets with her which made them slip low on his waist. He gripped the comforter tight, hopping out of bed in a swirl of material, wrapping it around himself. His wide shoulders tapered to slim hips with a vast expanse of sleek skin pulled taut over rippling muscle in between. She drew in a sharp breath.

"Uh, Em?"

She jerked her gaze from the dusty trail of blond hair disappearing under the comforter and back to his face. He wore the shiest smile she'd ever seen and the expression tugged at her heart.

There was no way she could betray Harrison. She couldn't choose between the two of them. She'd have to go after Madison on her own and find a way to keep them both safe.

"I, uh. . . ." He paused, chuckled. "Funny how this morning wasn't as awkward as tonight."

She laughed. He'd always put her at ease. "Thank you for everything, Harry."

With a shake of his head, he turned away, dragging a hand across his neck. "Listen, I need to get back to work and we should talk about what happened, so why don't we dress and I'll order you some breakfast."

Good. A little mundane conversation would soothe her nerves. "Where do you work?"

"Seattle."

"Seattle?" Nancy had sold her house and moved to Washington three years ago—at the time, Ember hadn't understood the abrupt move. She'd been so worried, she, too, had moved to be closer to Nancy. Now, she had to wonder, had Nancy found out Harrison was in Seattle? Had she moved there to be closer to him? The question burned on her lips, the only thing keeping her from asking was that she didn't want Nancy to get caught in the middle of this whole debacle.

"Yeah, I'm late and there's gonna be hell to pay." He glanced at his watch. "I also need to try to hunt Adia while I have a hot trail."

Ember turned away. Wait, did he say he meant to hunt the bitch? She swung around. "What did you say you do for a living?"

"I work at DDC Headquarters."

A knot began to form in the pit of her stomach. The Department of Daemonic Control was the daemon equivalent of the FBI. Maybe even more powerful these days with the Nephilim still on the loose. A vampire by the name of Julius Crowley had brought the Nephilim—animalistic creatures of insatiable appetite—to Earth three years ago and released them on humanity. Humans couldn't fight them without adding to the Nephilim's army—one bite and the human turned into one of them. Daemon kind had revealed themselves and offered to aid people against their common enemy and as a result, society had become dependent on daemons for protection.

Wait, Adia said if she involved the authorities she'd kill Madison. If Harrison worked for the DDC, wasn't *he* the "authorities"?

Ember pulled the sheet tighter around her. "Uh, yeah, that sounds good. I live near Seattle, too. I should get back to my job." Her clients needed her. Madison. . . . Oh, God. She was a daemon now. They wouldn't let her associate with kids. She couldn't be a social worker in foster placement anymore. What would happen to her clients?

"Are you kidding?" He scrubbed his hand over his face. "Em, you're going to have to stick with me. For a while, at least." He glanced away. "Look, maybe I didn't make myself clear enough this morning—"

"I can't come to fulfillment with anyone but you." Her heart rate increased. Shit, she didn't even understand what she was anymore. "Believe me, I'm used to going unsatisfied."

"Em, you're a daemon now, a succubus requires sex like food."
He sat at the edge of the bed and took her hand in his. "You'll
change if I don't sate you on a regular basis. You'll kill to get it
and then you'll die."

He was talking about that ugly something she'd felt writhing
inside her body last night and she had no doubt about its ability
to kill. "You said I wouldn't be addicted."

"Not like this morning. As long as you have access to your
chosen mate."

"Right." She turned away, panic welling like steam from Old
Faithful. Who the hell was Adia? How was she going to go after
Madison if Harrison was with her all the time? Her hand shook
as she brushed her hair from her face. This wasn't supposed to
happen. None of it. She shouldn't even be here, she should be
getting Madison settled into her new foster home. Damn it, she'd
made a good life for herself.

And Harrison . . . while she appreciated what he'd done for her
this morning and while she did still care for him, if only for their
history together, if she were honest, he made her a little nervous.
He wasn't the same as she remembered. Hell, neither of them
were. Eight years was a long time and now he was talking as if
they were going to have to be together, forever?

Maybe she'd been hasty in her decision to take him as mate this
morning. All she'd been able to think about was the need overwhelming her. She'd made an impulsive decision under duress
and... No, damn it. That wasn't fair. He'd been ambushed the
same as her. He'd done his best to explain and she'd made the
best decision she could with the information she'd had.

Should she call someone? Who? Her human friends? Her
human coworkers? None of them would give her the time of day
now. She could lie . . . maybe. She might get away with passing
for human for a while. Then again, she wasn't sure exactly what
she was, or how that might manifest. If she got caught lying
about being human, they'd send her to prison. She couldn't risk
it. In one night, she'd lost everything. How could that be?

"Em, I'm real sorry about all this. I promise I'll keep you safe."

"Like last time." An old rage she'd thought long dead welled
up. *You're being unreasonable.* Harrison had been a kid when he'd
promised to protect her from her stepfather but she'd still felt

betrayed when he didn't return from England. Now, seeing him so hale and healthy, acting like eight years hadn't passed since he'd made that promise infuriated her. "Yeah, heard that before, cowboy. Thanks, anyway." She scooted to the far edge of the bed and wrapped the sheet tighter around herself. "I'll figure something out."

No matter how much she wished things could be otherwise, she couldn't act the part of a newlywed with him. She didn't know him anymore.

Two hundred pounds of angry man blocked her path. "You'll stay with me. I won't watch you go homicidal-suicidal now. Not when I can keep you safe."

What was he even talking about? Was she dangerous? To herself or others? Damn it, she didn't want to know. Couldn't handle any more bad news. Tears burned the backs of her eyes and she wanted to scream. "You can't save me. No one can." Not when she was a kid. Not now. She'd have to figure this out on her own. She tried to walk past him.

He blocked her way. "Hit me."

"What?"

"I let you down." His eyes were more intense than ever. "If I had a choice—damn it, Em, punch me."

Wary of his mood, desperate for escape, she backed away.

"I promised you I'd be back. I left you alone with that bastard."

"Don't."

"What happened?"

"Nothing." *Everything.*

"Did he touch you?"

She clutched the sheet tighter, pacing, searching for a way past him, but he blocked every attempt at escape. "Stop it."

"Did the son of a bitch hurt you, Em?"

No one had called her Em since she'd left Tucson. She leveled him a glare. "Shut up, Harry."

"Yeah, bet you'd like that. Let's sweep the whole mess under the rug like we did when we were kids. Sorry, not happening."

Her fists clenched. Why did he insist on taunting her? She was starting to *want* to hurt him. "I'm warning you."

"Hit me." He stepped closer, angled until she couldn't avoid him. "Did you curse me when he finally got to you?"

Her scream of fury filled the room as she launched herself at him. They tumbled to the floor and she pounded her fists into his flesh with every ounce of strength she had. She punched his arms. His chest. His face.

"That's right." He took each blow, unflinching. "Hit me. I know you hate me. Get it out."

Her fury fizzed as fast as it flared. She grabbed fistfuls of his hair and collapsed against him. Her tears pooled on his chest as anguish replaced anger. "I never hated you. I wanted to, but I never did. I didn't have any left for you."

———◆———

Harrison's gut twisted.

He enfolded her in his embrace. Held her tight while she cried. All those years ago, he knew the whole time that he lived through his hell, Ember was likely enduring her own. Now his worst fears were confirmed and she'd get to experience a whole new kind of hell with him.

I didn't have any left for you. It wasn't that she thought he didn't deserve her hate—she didn't even have that to give him. That was okay, he had plenty of hate for himself.

Her sobs subsided and he handed her the edge of one of the blankets to dry her tears with.

"You're such a man." She grumbled something incoherent while she dabbed the material to her face. She pushed off him and slouched back against the wall.

He rolled to his side, reached out and captured her foot in his hand. He squeezed, stroking his thumb on her arch. "Everything's gonna be all right."

Her mouth wobbled as she fought off fresh tears. "What do you do for the DDC?" She leaned her head back, staring at the ceiling. "Are you a cross-over consultant?"

He'd hoped she'd assume he was a human who worked in an advisory position for the DDC. The organization was new and with all the other societal changes taking place, human cops, psychologists, social workers, and a slew of others consulted with the DDC to help ease the transition. Unfortunately, she'd now asked a direct question and he refused to lie to his mate. "I'm a detective."

Her brows pulled together. "For Seattle PD?"

Damn. "For the DDC."

Her eyes widened. "You'd have to be a—"

"Daemon." He nodded. "That's why I couldn't come back from England. Humans didn't know about us yet. It wouldn't have been safe for you. For my parents."

"What are you?"

Her suspicious gaze killed something deep inside him. Humans had taken a crash course in daemon kind. From Valkyries to Dybbuks, Oni to Gallu, daemons had become a fact of life in the last few years.

He gave her a rueful smile. "Me? Oh, I'm the worst of the lot."

She stood, sliding her back up the wall, and pulling the sheet a little tighter. His sweet Ember looked like she wanted to disappear right into the plaster. "Vampire." Then louder. "You're a fucking vampire?"

Though he wanted to plead with her, to make her remember this morning, he said nothing. He held his lips in a stiff line, nodded. "A Guardian raised me; you have nothing to fear." He couldn't tell if she'd heard him. His comment should have reassured her, the Guardians were a sect of vampires who had maintained balance between humans and daemons for millennia. Most humans gave the Guardians the same cautious respect they gave DDC agents.

"You scabbed where I scratched you." She pointed at his chest.

He glanced at his chest to the reddened nail marks. A few tiny scabs dotted the lines where she'd managed to break the skin a bit. His cock jumped at the sight, not caring about the other tension between them.

"You're bruising."

"I fed this morning before I came back to the room." At her horrified expression, he added, "In the restaurant." She still looked unsure, so he gestured around them. "Didn't you notice the ostentatious, yet slightly creepy décor? We're in the daemon section of the hotel."

Her eyes darted around the room, resting on the giant Anubis statues, the red-and-black color scheme, the metal shades covering the windows for total black out.

He reached for her. "You're safe with—"

She flinched away.

Hell, this wasn't going well. He dropped his hand and gave her some space. She needed time. A lot had changed for her in the last twenty-four hours. "Why don't you take a shower? I'll call the concierge for some clothes for you. What size?"

"Twelve." She sped past him, adding over her shoulder, "Size seven shoes. 36D."

Yep. She was luscious. And completely out of his reach.

⸻

Ember closed the bathroom door with a click and shifted the lock into place. *Holy shit, I've mated with a vampire.* Did Nancy know what her son had become?

Vampires possessed frightening powers. Some projected a person's desires, others sapped energy from those around them, and others shape-shifted, or turned ghostlike. Vampires always inherited their talents from their originator and conspiracy theorists all agreed they only knew a sliver of the existing Vampiric talents.

And those were only the vampires. Daemon kind consisted of all sorts of creatures.

A handful of humans accepted daemons, taking them in as friends. A few businesses and restaurants catered to their needs. The majority of humanity shunned them, considering them a necessary evil. She was sure the government-imposed curfews separating the two races were the only reason no infighting had ever occurred.

She hadn't given much thought to daemon kind. Her life and her job had always been removed from the conflict. She didn't know any daemons. Had only seen a few in person since she abided by the curfew laws and most daemons only came out at night.

Now she'd mated one. She *was* one. *Now what?* She'd also never paid much attention to daemon laws before. Where was she allowed to go? When was she allowed out? How would she make a living? She sucked in a shuddering breath. "You're a smart cookie, damn it."

She needed to get a grip. Everything would be fine.

Somehow, she'd figure out a way to get Madison back without putting Harrison in Adia's way. Then she'd focus on Harrison.

They'd been close once. She'd loved him back when they were kids. Surely, they could find that same affinity again now that they were stuck with each other.

Sweeping the shower curtain aside, she reached in to turn on the water and was greeted by a scaly creature with a wide, toothy grin who already occupied the tub. Armored scales covered its diamond-shaped head and continued down its back to its squared-off tail. Its oversized, inky eyes fixed on her. The thing gurgled. With a scream, she flew out of the bathroom and right into Harrison's arms. She didn't stop. Oh, hell no. She climbed straight up him.

The low rumble of his laughter slipped past her panic and triggered the rational side of her brain. She stopped her struggles, arms wrapped around his neck, one leg slung over his arm, the other around his waist. Her sheet twisted and pulled, leaving parts of her exposed that she'd rather have covered.

His laughter shook them both.

Was he nuts?

She glanced back over her shoulder—no small feat in her current position—to see the creature lounging in the bathroom doorway. It seemed to be laughing as well. "What the hell, Harry?"

"I'm . . . gods, I'm so . . . sorry."

"I might take your apology more seriously if you'd stop laughing."

"That's George." His big, strong arms wrapped around her so he could double over with his laughter. "You should've . . . seen . . . your face."

She slipped out of his embrace and whacked his shoulder. "It scared the crap out of me. What the hell is it?"

George, as he called the thing, slunk past her and walked up Harrison's leg as if its dainty feet had suction cups on them. It didn't stop until he perched on one wide shoulder. A paw landed on Harrison's bedraggled hair as if to say, "Mine."

Harrison sobered a bit, though his smirk suggested he could break into peals of mirth at the slightest provocation. "This is George. He's with me."

"But what is it?"

"He. *He* is a minion. George sort of . . . adopted me a few years back and he's saved my life more than once."

She raised a brow. Okay, maybe the little beast wasn't so bad.

Harrison patted George. "Yeah, George has a sixth sense for ferreting out lies and zeroing in on bad guys."

She stared at the thing in horror. Would George give her away? "He's been in here all day?"

His lips twitched in amusement. "You're still alive. He didn't even try to taste you."

She gave the two of them a narrow glare before turning on her heel, marching back into the bathroom, and locking herself in. Seconds later, hating herself a little more, she threw the door wide. "Is there anything else in here?"

The two of them laughed in her face.

Closing the door again, she leaned against it.

Madison was out there someplace, sixteen and likely terrified, waiting to be rescued from God-only-knew-what. She felt bad enough Adia wanted her to manipulate Harry. The *idea* practically killed her. The reality *had* almost killed her.

And now she had a lie-detecting minion to add to her growing list of challenges. Perhaps she should've told Harrison to let her die after all. Her future wasn't looking all that bright.

It was bad enough she'd withheld information from her mate, that wasn't the most auspicious way to start a relationship, but she'd withheld information from her mate, DDC Agent Harrison the Vampire.

It was foolish.

Dangerous.

"Hell, it's another goddamn Federal offense."

CHAPTER 4

October 9th, 10:15 PM

CLEAN AND DRESSED IN THE clothes Harrison had gotten for her, a pair of Calvin Klein jeans, a tank, DC sneakers, and a hoodie, Ember was ready to take on her new life—for however long it lasted.

She stepped out of the bathroom and straight into a crime scene. Four men in full DDC-issued black fatigues combed the room, bagging items, and dusting for fingerprints. One agent glanced at her as he bagged the handcuffs and her cheeks heated.

Frozen with the thought of being surrounded by daemons, she stared, studying them. If not for the uniforms, she wouldn't have known they were daemons. They looked as human as her. Well, as human as she was yesterday. Learning about the different daemon races became a requirement for all State and Federal employees—part of the immersion program—but before this moment, she hadn't realized she might have interacted with any number of daemons without ever being the wiser.

Harrison took hold of her arm and led her out of the suite, his tone clipped. "Come on. Plane's waiting."

"Plane?" She let him tug her along, keeping her eyes locked on the creature riding his shoulder. George's long, forked tongue swept out of its mouth and swiped over one unblinking eye.

"Seattle, remember? I told my boss we're on our way and the company jet is waiting."

She pulled away. "It's dark. We can't go outside."

Though the threat of Nephilim attacks were lower now, for humans, going out at night after the government-imposed curfew was a Federal crime and she already had two of those on her docket.

"I'm a vampire, Em." He sighed and ran a hand through his hair. "You're a succubus."

Yeah. She kept trying to forget those facts. "Right, so I guess we don't have much choice." Another thought occurred to her. "Can I go out in sunlight?"

He shook his head. "Sunlight won't hurt you but you're under daemon curfew now. Come on, we'll be in Seattle before you know it."

Seattle was closer to home than Vegas. Closer to Madison. "How will you find out if they discover something?"

"They'll send the evidence to the Seattle office. They'll find any clues she left behind."

"But—"

He hit the elevator button and turned to her. "Everything's going to be fine. I need to close out my last case and file a report on what's happened with you. I'll get you registered so you don't have to worry about any legal issues. We'll go through whatever evidence they find here and start the investigation. We'll get her, Em."

Unable to do anything more than nod, she turned away. She was pretty sure the only clue Adia had left behind was her.

❦

Once settled in the small private plane, she took a deep breath and forced herself to relax. Harrison had kept to himself on the ride over, maybe giving her a chance to come to terms with everything. *You wanted to find him, you've found him, you should at least talk to him.* He sat across from her with George curled like a cat in the seat next to him.

"Why were you in Vegas?"

"I hadn't planned to be. I was in Phoenix for a DV—domestic violence—case; a wife hired a hag to curse her husband."

"Does that sort of thing happen often?"

"Nah, most humans are too frightened of daemons. This woman is mean as a rattlesnake, though. She didn't give a shit as long as her spouse suffered. She wanted him out of the house."

"Why?"

"She'd met someone else, but the husband wouldn't sign for a divorce. They have a three-year-old son. So, the wife decided to force the issue."

She pulled a face. "By cursing him? Did the curse kill him?"

"Might've been kinder." He stroked his hand over George's back. "The hag cursed him with lycanthropy."

Daemons weren't allowed to be near human children. The State would force the divorce and ban the husband from access to his child.

"That's caused by a curse, not a bite?"

"Yeah. Unfortunately, it's incurable."

The whole situation must be horrifying for the father and she couldn't imagine what the child must be going through. "Why did they call you in?"

"The father took off with the boy."

"Oh, God, he changed him into a werewolf, too?"

"Nah." He dragged his hand across his face and leaned forward, bracing his elbows on his knees. "Dad ran with the boy to his mother's place in Vegas. He thought his son would have a more nurturing environment with the grandmother. I placed Dad with a local pack. The Lycan agreed to take him in, teach him about his new life. The wife is now in prison for soliciting Magic with malicious intent." He shook his head. "You know, the only thing humans focus on is the physical change. They see the monster and assume the daemon transforms psychologically and emotionally into monsters, too." His jaw flexed. "How different do you feel from the way you did yesterday?"

"I'm scared. Confused. Upset about the enormity of the life changes I'm facing."

"You're not focused on visiting friends and family and finding out how much you can fuck up their lives now that you're a daemon?"

She gasped. "Don't be ridiculous."

"Aren't you plotting who you're gonna eat? Oh, wait, you're a succubus—which man you'll fuck?"

Her jaw clenched. "I get it, Harry. Daemons were all regular people like me at one time."

"Like you *still* are." He pointed to his chest. "I may be a vampire, but I'm also that kid you used to build forts with."

She must've hurt his feelings when she had her little breakdown. "I'm sorry. I know you are." She'd seen glimpses of the old Harry, but he was buried behind the new one. The darker, mysterious Harry. "But I know nothing about you anymore. Where have you been? How did you become a DDC agent? A vampire? How do you know Adia?"

His eyes narrowed. "Speaking of, how do *you* know Adia?"

Shit. She looked away. "I don't, not really."

"Ember." His tone was full of warning.

She had to tell him something. If she stuck close to the truth, maybe she could avoid telling him everything. "I got a note yesterday telling me that if I wanted information about you to go to a club called the Knot Works in the Fremont district of Seattle and ask for Adia. So, I went."

"Why the hell would you do that?" He dragged his hand through his hair. "Gods, Em, she was fishing. She had no way of knowing if you were the right woman. She had no way of knowing if you would even remember me." He cursed. "I disappeared, Em. Didn't it occur to you that going might be dangerous?"

He was right. All of this was her fault. If she hadn't gone to that damned club, if she hadn't been so curious to find out where he was, if he was even still alive, none of this would've happened. Now he'd die . . . or Madison would. Guilt choked her.

"What the hell were you thinking?"

She blinked back the tears, but couldn't keep the tremor from her voice. No, she shouldn't have gone to the club, but . . . "Didn't it occur to you I might have questions? That I might need some kind of closure? You were alive all this time. Why didn't you contact us? Why didn't you warn us? Does Nancy even know?"

"No. I didn't—" He blew out a deep breath and when he spoke again his tone was softer. "I didn't think Adia would find any of you as long as I didn't lead her to you." This time, he looked away. "What happened when you went to this club?"

"I thought they wanted to meet there because the club was

in Fremont. The neighborhood is still ultra-liberal, it's the only place I know of where humans and daemons mingle freely, so human police avoid the area. When I arrived, I discovered The Knot Works was a sex club."

He closed his eyes, letting his head drop back on the headrest. "You should have left right then." He clenched his jaw tight as if restraining himself from rehashing his earlier lecture. "Why didn't you leave?"

"I . . . ." She shook her head. She didn't dare tell him about Madison; Adia had been very specific about the repercussions of doing so. If Adia found out, she'd be signing the child's death warrant. "I was going to, but I saw something on the wall. Kind of like the image of a man. Next thing I knew he peeled himself off the wall and grabbed me."

"A wraith. They're called wraiths." He leaned forward. "That's how she got you to Vegas?"

Ember nodded. "I didn't realize where I was. When he let go of me, I was standing in the hotel room where you found me. The wraith had disappeared. He left me there with a woman, Adia, and two men. One of them held me, the other bit it me."

"Can you give me a description?"

She didn't dare tell him anything else. "I-I was scared. I don't remember. Everything happened so fast and I blacked out when he bit me. I wish I could tell you more." She wished she could tell him everything.

He pressed his lips into thin line. Though he didn't appear happy with her story, he seemed to accept it. "I'm sorry as hell this happened. I'm sure the last thing you wanted was to be turned daemon."

No, she couldn't say 'become a daemon' had been anywhere on her bucket list. "What am I, Harry? The things they say daemons can do. It terrifies me. I am a daemon now, right? I don't know much about daemons. I don't know what I can do or how to control it. Do you even know?"

"Yeah." He stared out the window at the darkness beyond. "Look, in the beginning, there were angels and there were humans and for a time, we all got along until two hundred angels fell from grace. They created the first daemons."

"The fallen angels, you call them the Watchers."

"Yes, most of us. Some of the old-timers still call them the Grigori. The Watchers were banished to a world called Machon to prevent them from destroying the humans."

She'd heard stories of Machon. "Have you been there?"

"Machon? Yeah." His head tipped from side to side. "It's . . . beautiful in its own way. For daemons, there are portals between the two worlds. I'll show you one of these days."

"So the Watchers came first. . . ."

"Yes, and they created the rest of daemon kind. There are three types of daemons. Witches are human, but still considered daemons because they're gifted with the Magic of the Watchers. The second type, Nephilim and vampires, are the only true daemons. We're biological descendants of the Watchers. Well, and creatures like George, that are native to Machon." He stroked his hand over the minion's pearly scales. "Daemon animals are true daemons. The rest of daemon kind are either blessed or cursed with a demon: A separate entity living inside in a symbiotic relationship. Most of the time the demon lies dormant, but you can call the entity forth when you need aid. In weak moments, the demon will overpower and control you."

Right. That's what terrified her. "That's what I have? A demon inside me?" She shivered, remembering the something moving beneath her skin. It hadn't been her imagination.

"Yes. Demons have no conscience. They're completely nihilistic. It's the host's responsibility to stay in control."

Great. No pressure. "What else can you tell me about being a succubus?"

"Everything's going to be okay, Em."

He wasn't telling her everything. "What else?"

"Succubi are rare." He scrubbed his hand over his face. "We've started seeing an outbreak in the last couple years, but we don't understand much about them yet."

This time she turned to stare out at the night sky. "How can you not know much about them? If an outbreak happened, there must be a lot of us running around."

"I'll take care of you, Em."

He'd avoided her question. Why wouldn't he answer? What did that look he was giving her mean? Had they locked the others away? No. If imprisoned, the DDC would've studied them. Her stomach clenched. "They're all dead, aren't they?"

He wouldn't meet her gaze.

"Why?"

"Some never mated. Others . . . ." He shrugged. "Maybe their mates died or left or their mates couldn't take care of them. I'm not sure. Like I said, we're still learning about them."

She stared. *Maybe their mates died?* "They died because their mates died?"

"Yeah, but nothing is going to happen to me. Your situation is different. Everything will be fine."

She wanted to ask how. How was their situation better? Had the others also been hoisted off onto men forced to decide between watching them die and sacrificing themselves in exchange? The full reality of the responsibility he'd taken on hit her. If anything happened to him, she'd die, too. If they separated, she'd perish without access to her mate. Wasn't Adia clever? If she decided to betray Harrison and deliver him to Adia, she'd be committing suicide.

They spent the rest of the ride in silence, leaving her too much time to think. George remained curled next to his master. Harrison spent the time working on a small laptop and she wracked her brain for a way out of the current situation.

Maybe she could sneak into the club and kidnap Madison back. Her mind reeled as she contemplated everything that could go wrong with such a scenario. She needed more time. The answer would come.

After they landed, the drive from SeaTac to DDC headquarters took fifteen minutes. George clung to the ceiling of the car, staring out the windshield upside-down, his thick tail never still. She spent the ride plastered against the passenger door to avoid getting whipped.

DDC headquarters was situated near the waterfront in the old city courthouse where Julius Crowley—they called him the Harbinger of Armageddon—had been assassinated three years ago after he'd released the Nephilim on earth. The structure had an imposing aura at several stories high; like any federal building, its architecture was designed to intimidate. Harrison parked the rental car in the No Parking zone out front.

Four bright lights lit the flagpole that the crowd had hung the

Harbinger from. A mob of humans milled about close to it in front of the building with picket signs. Some read *Go Back to Hell*; others, *Daemons Have No Place on Earth*.

"Why does the DDC let them stay out here? It's past curfew."

He stared out the windshield. "Who, the human bait? Takes too much time every night to lock them up. Instead, we've reached an agreement of sorts with them."

That was surprising. "You guys got them to talk to you?"

He grinned. "It was all done through bullhorns." The hand he rested on top of the steering wheel pointed straight ahead. "You notice the cages?"

Three cages the size of small U-Haul trucks were placed at intervals around the front of the building. "Yeah."

"If the sirens go off, they've got a choice. They either go inside DDC or they lock themselves in the cages."

The sirens he spoke of were the city's Tsunami warning sirens. Nowadays they used them if Nephilim were spotted in the area. The creatures created portals allowing them to travel from place to place, avoiding sunlight while searching for food. The best humans could hope for when confronted with a Nephilim was death. If the Nephilim didn't kill them, they transformed, adding to the Nephilim's numbers.

"Have they ever gone inside your building?"

"No. Well, this group hasn't been tested yet. The protesters who came before, they chose the cages."

"They aren't big enough. The Nephilim could still reach them."

"The government won't give us more money." He shrugged. "Some DDC stations don't even have this much. We happened to have the cages. Makes for easy clean up. They're bitten and transform but are locked inside until the sun comes up."

Easy clean up, indeed. She pressed her hand to her belly. "It's a different world from when we were kids, isn't it?"

"It'll get better. Some day." He opened his door. "Come on."

He walked her through the picket lines where the human bait touted their beliefs and through the front doors of the building.

Beyond herself with curiosity, she tried not to stare at the wide array of daemons and humans working inside. Creatures she'd never seen before. A daemon with mottled red skin and tiny horns poking out of his skull greeted them from behind the front desk—an Oni. "Detective Sinclair, you're late."

"I know. Deno, this is my mate, Ember."

The devilish daemon gave her a once over with his yellow eyes and smiled. From what she understood, Oni fed on strong emotions. If that was true, this one must be feasting on hers. "Ma'am." She nodded in greeting and he turned back to Harrison. "Your partner's getting antsy."

"Antsy, Deno?" He raised an eyebrow in question. "What's with the PC shit?"

Deno cleared his throat. "Fine, he's being a right fucking bastard is what he's being."

"When isn't he?" He shot back with a grin. "Get someone to return the rental, will you?" He tossed the keys to the daemon, guided her to the elevators, and punched the button.

"You have a partner?"

A human-looking woman passed by. She flipped her long brunette hair over her shoulder, smiled at Harrison, and gave George a pat. "Hiya, boys. You're late. Jules is fit to be tied."

"Hey, Kara. Yeah, I heard." He ushered Ember into the elevator and the doors slid closed.

"Jules?" Something close to jealousy slithered through her at the thought of a him having a female partner.

"Yes, his name is Jules."

His? "What kind of name is Jules?"

The elevator doors slid open at the next floor. "It's short for Family Jewels." He shot her an evil grin. "As in, he's a real prick."

CHAPTER 5

October 10th, 2:48 AM

HARRISON SAID THE LAST WITH a nod toward a man waiting in the elevator lobby. Tall, with broad shoulders and a narrow waist, he didn't look a day over twenty-one. If not for the wicked scar running from the inside of his brow to his ear on one side, or the piratical eye patch he wore, she might have called him handsome. Except he looked too damned mean for that moniker.

"He's a lying bastard." The pirate folded his arms over his chest. "Don't trust anything he says. He's just jealous of the size of my dick."

She stared. "You're Jules?"

"Julian Elisha Crowley at your service." He swept out his arm and bowed.

She paled at the surname. *My God, this must be the Harbinger's brother.*

"Don't worry, sweetheart." He took her hand and pressed a kiss to her knuckles. "I may resemble my twin, but on the inside, we're as different as two males can be."

Harrison snorted. "Keep your lips to yourself, you damn fool, or I'll be having a long talk with Kat."

Julian dropped her hand. "Leave off, pup."

"Oh, for fuck's sake." Harrison's face twisted in disgust. "Deno's right, you are being a right bastard today."

Ember studied Harrison. Did he have a hint of a British accent to his voice? She hadn't noticed before; it was so faint. He had disappeared while he was vacationing in England. Had he been there the entire time?

"You're late." Julian narrowed his eye. "I've been stuck in this hell-hole for two days."

"Something came up." He glanced at Ember.

Julian stared at Harrison for a long moment before his gaze dropped lower. "I bet it did."

George chortled. Her cheeks caught fire.

"Not now." Harrison lowered his voice. "We've got a bit of a problem, one we don't need to discuss out here, so quit being a prick and help me out."

Julian's attention flashed back to Ember. "You want a drink? Food?" His one eye narrowed. "What are you?" He cocked his head to the side. "You don't smell human, but you have a heart-beat."

"Damn it, Jules." Harrison twisted away, his hands raising as if he wanted to pull at his hair.

"What are you?" This time when Julian spoke the words were soothing, alluring. They seemed to bounce around in her head. *What are you? Tell us what you are. Trust us.*

She couldn't resist answering. "Succubus."

"My, my." Julian turned to Harrison. "We have been a busy boy."

"Move it." He grabbed Ember's hand and shoved Julian back. "Interrogation room A. Move your ass or I'll leave your black hide here for the next month."

With a growl, Julian led them down the hall and into an inter-rogation room.

Ember glanced around the sterile room. Aside from one chair and a built-in bench, the room was empty. "Why here? Am I being interrogated?"

"No," Harrison said at the same time Julian asked, "Should you be?" *Do you need to tell us something? Trust us. We'll share your burden.*

"Yes." She jerked and clapped a hand over her mouth. *Why did I say that?*

"Stop it." Harrison shoved Julian. "No more mind tricks."

Oh, God, Julian had done something to her, forced her to tell the truth.

"She said 'Yes,' partner."

Harrison froze and hurt flashed over his face. The creature, George, flattened himself out on his shoulder, nuzzling under his chin. His inky stare fixed hard on her.

"Yeah, I'd love a drink." She wet her lips. "Whatever's on hand?"

No one moved.

Julian nudged Harrison. "She yours?"

He nodded.

"Then go get her a drink."

"No—"

"You've got no perspective on this." Julian folded his arms over his chest. "I'll take care of her. Now get out."

The door swung open and another man popped partway into the room. Older, with gray streaking his dark hair, his assessing brown gaze flicked over her before landing on Harrison. "Sinclair, now."

Cursing under his breath, Harrison left, slamming the door behind him.

"Sinclair? Didn't he mean Cayce?"

Julian smirked. "What? Didn't you two even exchange surnames before you got biblical?"

Ember turned away from the pirate. Julian scared the hell out of her. She didn't like him and couldn't lie to him.

"Look at me, Ember."

Was that how he made her tell the truth, eye contact? She kept her face turned away.

"What's your name, sweetheart?"

"Ember Moon."

"You acquainted with our boy for long?"

"Since we were kids."

"Really?" Surprise laced his voice. "He was a homely son of a bitch, wasn't he?"

She whirled around and caught herself before she lifted her eyes to skewer him with a glare. Damn, he was good. "He was sweet." Her tone non-negotiable, she sat on the built-in bench lining one sterile white wall.

"You relocated to Washington from Arizona three years ago. Why?"

They'd run a background check already? She shrugged. "I got tired of the heat. A friend of mine moved here and I didn't want her to be alone. I told Harry about what happened."

"And now you're gonna tell me. See, I've got a problem, sweetheart." He dragged the sole chair in the room over and straddled it with his arm slung across the backrest. "I'm hoping you can help me out."

"Oh, yeah?"

"Yeah, see, our boy Harry? He saved my sorry hide. While I will never admit this to his face, I owe him and for some reason I'm getting a bad vibe off you."

The trembling in her hands transferred to the rest of her body. She was screwed.

"Yep, I've gone over the evidence from Vegas and this all seems a little too convenient." He paused. "You gonna look at me?" *Look at us. Look us in the eye.*

Now that she had a grasp on what he was doing, she found his suggestions easier to resist. Still, she worried that if she met his gaze, she'd be fucked. She shook her head, keeping her eyes locked on his black boots and the gleaming silver edge of a hidden blade visible under the toe. Not the sort of weapon she'd expect a law enforcement officer—even a DDC agent—to wear. Apparently, Julian had no qualms about fighting dirty.

"I know you don't lie. Not well, at least. You didn't resist me." He leaned forward, edging into her line of sight. "You didn't expect me to distrust you, which tells me you're used to dealing honestly with others. What do you do for a living?" *Tell us what you do.*

"I'm a social worker." She folded her arms over her chest.

"In what capacity? Research? Vagrant placement? Reassimilation? DV? Foster placement?" She remained silent. "Ah, foster placement. That's tough."

Again, she almost looked up. What had she done to give herself away? "I worked hard to get where I am. I love my job."

"Shitty pay." He scoffed. "Long-ass hours filled with dragging kids away from crappy parents and then checking and double-checking that the foster homes you put them in aren't ten times worse. What was I thinking, who wouldn't love a job like that?"

"I'm starting to understand now." She nodded.

"What?"

"Why everyone keeps referring to you as a bastard."

He had a deep laugh, almost hoarse as if it didn't get dusted off and used often. "I like you, Emerald Eyes."

"Yeah?"

"Oh, yeah." *We like you. We'll help you. Tell us your secrets.* "I think my mate will like you, too."

She snorted. "Am I gonna meet your mate, Jules?"

"If I'm right about you." He folded his arms over the back of the chair and rested his chin on them. "This is what I'm thinking, because of your job you somehow got caught in a shitting contest with Adia."

She schooled her expression. Maybe Julian would be more willing to talk about Adia than Harrison had been. "Oh, and who's Adia?"

"Tall, bad-ass black bitch."

"Can't accuse you of going overboard on the PC lingo."

"That woman doesn't deserve any consideration. She's a viper. As sneaky and manipulative as they come. Look at me." *Look at us. Trust us.*

She shook her head, smoothing her sweaty palms over her jeans. "How did you meet her?"

"Oh, we go way back." He tried to angle into her line of sight again. "You said you moved because you were tired of the heat. You referring to the sun, or Adia?"

"My decision didn't have anything to do with her. I didn't even know she existed."

"No? You happened to relocate here three weeks after the DDC opened. Three weeks after Harrison arrived."

She closed her eyes. Nancy, Harrison's mom, had been frantic to move to Seattle. To Ember her decision had seemed like a random, overnight whim, but now she suspected Nancy had somehow found out her son would be here. Ember had been worried and dropped everything to stay close to the woman who'd been like a mother to her. Didn't that look bad for her right now. She could end that line of questioning by telling him that she'd followed Nancy here…but she couldn't repay Nancy's kindness by dragging her into this mess.

Confide in us. Talk to us, Ember Moon.

"Do you think Harry will be back soon?" She glanced at the door. Her will to remain silent was weakening; that sneaky voice in her head stripping away her concerns bit by bit.

He sighed. "I'd wager our boss has him pinned with three or four agents on the other side of that mirror right about now."

She glanced over at the mirror and her reflection stared back. *Just* her reflection. So, Julian was a vampire, too. She crossed her legs, folding her arms over her chest. "That's a very specific guess."

"Well, maybe less of a guess and more of a plan. We daemons tend to be a might protective of our mates and I didn't want him interfering."

What if she got Harrison in trouble? "He hasn't done anything wrong."

"Didn't expect he had. I don't think you have, either. Yet. What did Adia ask you to do?"

"Why would you assume she wanted anything from me?"

"We're talking about Adia. Nothing about her is random. She knew who you were and that Harry knew you." He drummed his fingers on his arm. "I can see your aura, sweetheart. Maybe you can hide your secrets from your mate, but not from me. Did she take one of your foster kids? Ah, yep. That's what she's got on you."

How the hell did he do that? She took a deep breath, fighting the sudden burn of tears. She hated keeping secrets, but she couldn't fail Madison. "Weren't you going to get me a drink?"

The chair scraped across the cement floor. Julian knelt in front of her, clasping his hands around hers. "Soon. We're gonna make this real painless; I need you to look at me." *Now. Look at us now. You're safe with us, Ember Moon. You can trust us.*

Resisting his suggestions became more difficult. Her gaze kept tugging toward Julian and she kept dragging it away. Her eyes ached. Her sinuses, too. Was he getting tired of waiting? Leaning on her harder with his talent? She had to resist. To think of Madison. "Why are you doing this?"

"I need to see your eyes, sweetheart." His tone turned so kind she almost lifted her gaze to make sure the pirate was still in the room. How did he make his voice so innocent and sweet? "That's all. Help me help you tell the truth."

"What if the truth gets someone killed?"

"I thought you heard. I'm a right bastard." He startled a shaky laugh out of her. "When I'm around the only ones getting killed are those I want dead. Now, let's see your pretty green eyes." *We'll make everything all right. Trust us. Help us help you.*

God, she wanted his help. Harrison's help. Part of her was certain they'd find Madison and bring her back, but maybe that was just Julius making her feel so hopeful.

"You make it feel too easy, Jules." That was the truth. She'd been with him maybe ten minutes and all she wanted to do was spill her guts, meet his gaze. Never mind Harrison sat listening on the other side of the mirror. Forget the fact he now knew she was hiding something from him after he'd bound himself to her. This must be killing him. How would they ever build a relationship with this sitting between them? Would he ever forgive her? What would happen to Madison if she told the truth? "I need more time to think about this. I'm sure I can fix this on my own."

"The problem is, even though I'm pretty sure you're innocent, I'll need to put you in a cell until I know everything you do."

Adrenaline spiked through her, leaving her with the sensation of ants marching under her skin. "You can't." She'd never get Madison back.

"I will. I can't take the risk you'll hurt Harry. Lead him into a trap or something."

She squeezed her burning eyes shut and covered her face with her hand. What now? If they locked her up, she'd never complete the mission. Harrison would be safe, but Madison would be lost forever.

We'll take care of all your problems. Look at us.

Julian pulled her arm away. His thumb caressed her cheek, wiping away a tear. "Bet this is the first time you've seen one agent play both good cop and bad cop."

She laughed, losing even more tears. "God, I hate you right now."

"That's okay. I'm used to it." He forced her chin up. "Come on, Emerald Eyes, look at me." *We'll take care of everything. Talk to us. Trust us. Look at us.*

Overwhelming hopelessness filled her, but knowing Harrison and Julian were her best chance at saving Madison, she did as he asked.

George growled low in his throat, pacing across the table in front of Harrison's face. His dark fur jutted between the scales covering his back.

"Get off me, man." Harry bucked under Scott and two other agents' combined weight. They had his torso pinned to the table. It was fucking embarrassing. As soon as Scott told him the plan, he'd tried to return to the interrogation room, but Scott had two agents waiting for him.

"Are you gonna behave?" For a human, Scott Mason, DDC's director, was a strong son of a bitch. Had to be to maintain control among the denizens of the DDC.

George apparently had had enough. He snarled, getting into position to pounce.

Scott leaned on him harder. "Call off your minion."

Harrison slapped his free hand against the table. "George, heel."

George sat back, but still growled, making sure everyone understood he didn't like obeying.

"Now get *your* fucking minions the hell off me." Scott's weight and the weight of the others lifted from him and he pushed himself off the table. His gut twisted as Ember met Jules' gaze. "This is bullshit. She's innocent, you'll see."

Scott glanced at the other two agents. "Out." The burley daemons left with a glare.

He flipped them off and turned to the viewing mirror.

Julian was speaking to Ember. "Good girl. Now, what did Adia want you to do?"

"I'm supposed to bring Harry to a club called The Knot Works in Fremont."

Harrison's face burned. How could he have been taken in so completely? He knew what a conniving bitch Adia could be.

"Relax, son." The older man put a hand on his shoulder. "Let's find out what else she has to say before you go off on her."

"I'm not angry with Ember." He paced away, out of reach. "It's the situation. Adia will never quit."

In the other room, Julian tucked Ember's hair behind her ear. "Why?"

Ember spoke in a dull monotone, completely under Julian's mesmerist talent. "I don't know. She indicated Harry was being troublesome."

"Okay, okay. You're doing real good, Em." Julian rubbed his hand over hers. "How did she find you?"

"I don't know. I got a note saying if I wanted information about Harry to come to the Knot Works, which I did. Once I was there, I got scared. I was going to leave, but then I saw Madison, she's a foster kid I'm trying to place. I couldn't leave Madison there."

"Did she say why she picked Madison? Was there anything different about that client?"

Ember shook her head. "I don't think so."

"Nothing in your home, your car that might make someone think Madison was special to you?"

"She gave me one of her school pictures with a homemade card. I have it on my refrigerator."

Shit. Adia had been inside her house. She could've killed Ember at any time. He rubbed at an achy spot on his chest.

"Okay. All right." Julius glanced at the mirror and nodded. "Adia was waiting for you at the club?"

She shook her head. "A wraith grabbed us and took us to the hotel room where Harry found me. Adia was there with two men, but the wraith disappeared with Madison."

Harrison dragged his hand down his face. Gods, Adia must have better surveillance than the DDC. She knew where to find Ember. She knew he had gone to Vegas last minute. She'd set them up together when he was away from anyone he trusted.

"And the incubus?"

"Gastov. Adia ordered him to bite me. The other one restrained me. Adia promised to return Madison once she had Harry."

"That seemed a fair trade?" For the first time since entering the room, Julian's voice got hard.

"Of course not. I'd already decided I could never betray Harry.

I've been trying to think of a way to get Madison back without getting Harry involved. Adia said I couldn't talk to the authorities, and then Harry told me he was DDC. I couldn't risk Adia finding out if I told him. I didn't want anyone to get hurt. I planned to sneak back into the club and try to slip Madison out unnoticed."

Julian's mouth quirked. "Yeah, that's a shitty plan, Emerald Eyes."

Yeah, it was. The tension eased out of Harrison once again. She hadn't planned to sacrifice him. She was another victim in Adia's twisted games.

He glanced at Scott. "We're good. You got what you needed, now let me out."

"Glad everything worked out the way it did." Scott slapped him on the shoulder. "We'll get the girl back."

"Yeah, we'll find Adia this time. She's getting sloppy, leaving witnesses." Still, something niggled him. This seemed too easy. Where was the hidden viper he'd been waiting for? "Did you send a crew to check out Adia's old hidey-hole in London?"

Scott nodded. "The tunnels were clear. The team found an inch of dust covering every surface. No one has been there in a long time."

He'd known it was a long shot. Adia hadn't returned to her old stomping grounds since they'd defeated the old Vampiric Council and cleared all the tunnels three years ago. Still, it was the only place he knew for sure that she was connected to.

"What else did Adia say?" Jules asked in the interrogation room. "Now, Ember, you've been doing so well. Don't resist."

Harrison's attention returned to the scene in the interrogation room. What now? He stepped around the table, trying to note the tells Julian saw.

"You can tell me anything, sweetheart."

Ember struggled against speaking, but Julian had her in his mesmerist's grasp. Her whole frame shook as her face turned away, but she couldn't break eye contact, not until Julian decided to release her.

Harrison moved closer to the glass. A drop of blood trailed from Ember's nose.

"Tell him to stop." He didn't check to see if his boss left to do as he asked, he couldn't.

"Talk to me, Emerald Eyes. I can tell it's hurting you." Julian stroked the back of her hand. Easing her. Calming her. "I'll share the burden with you. We'll work it out together."

Her eyelids fluttered, her eyes trying to roll up in her head, she strained against Julian's talent so hard. Whatever the secret, she sure as hell didn't want to speak it.

"Come on, sweetheart, let it go. Everything will be easier once you tell me."

The words burst out of Ember's mouth like cannon fire. "Harry killed a bunch of kids."

When both Julian and Ember's heads jerked toward the mirror, he realized he'd slammed his fist against the glass. He turned and walked straight out of the room. Right past Scott's commiserating gaze. Julian and Scott knew all about his past.

Somehow, he'd hoped Ember never would.

———◆———

Harrison had heard everything.

Ember stared at her shaking image until the glass smoothed out to reveal her shocked expression bisected by a crack in the mirror. Blood trickled out her nose.

Julian handed her a handkerchief. "He doesn't like anyone to know."

She wiped the blood from her face. "It's true?"

"We're daemons." Julian moved back to the chair and slumped into it. "We've all got deep, dark secrets. Do yourself and him a favor and reserve judgment."

Anger burst from her. "They were kids."

He jerked forward until they were nose to nose. "So was he."

That gave her pause. She hadn't considered that possibility. Harrison disappeared when he was sixteen. Had he been transformed then? Vampires were notorious for killing indiscriminately during the first few hours after a transformation.

No, that was impossible. Vampires didn't age, so he must have been transformed as an adult.

"Don't do your head in trying to puzzle it out." Julian shook his head. "You're too sweet to even begin to tap the depth of Adia's depravity."

"Adia transformed him?"

"She kept him as a slave." Julian lowered his voice to a whisper. "She'd gotten bored with the lot of them. They were hungry husks of the boys they once were. She gave them all weapons and locked them—"

The door flew open, bouncing off the wall. "You two finished?"

Startled, they both turned. Harrison stood in the doorway, his face unreadable. George had wrapped himself around one of his hips, and peered out at them from under his arm.

Julian rose. "What's our next step?"

Surprised, yet grateful they weren't going to discuss what happened, she got up, too. "We should go to the Knot Works."

"Soon." He focused his attention on Julian. "Did you get a team over to my parents' place? Adia's letter threatened everyone I care about, and now we know she's serious."

"We're searching for them. They moved."

Harrison's gaze zeroed in on her. "Where are they, Em?"

Oh, God. He didn't know. Where should she start? "Your mom lives here in Washington, Harry. On Mercer Island." She paused to find the rest of the words she needed to say.

His expression turned inscrutable. "And Dad?"

Ember approached him. Vampire or not, killer or not, this was still Harrison. "I'm sorry." She went to wrap her arms around him, but he captured both her hands in his and held them. George sniffed her and she had to fight not to react.

"When?"

"Five years ago now."

His grip tightened as a tremor swept through him.

"It was his heart."

He swallowed. Nodded. "Thank you for telling me."

"Nancy's been waiting for you. Your mom never lost hope."

He released her hands and backed away a step. "She would've stayed in our old house if she wanted to be found." He glanced at Julian. "Jules, get the address and send a team."

Then he was gone.

What happened? Didn't he want more information? Wasn't he going to go see his mother? How did he disconnect from everything like that? "He's not going to go visit her?"

Julian guided her out of the room, an arm across her shoulders. "You don't understand. It's tough for us. He has no guarantee of how his mom will react to him. He's different now."

Most days, Nancy didn't speak of much else beside her son. She and Harrison's dad had both blamed themselves for his disappearance, but they never lost hope that he'd come home someday. She'd reminisce about how he'd been. Wonder what kind of man he'd become. Nancy would accept her son any way she could get him. "She'd never reject Harry."

"He has no assurance of her reaction. In his mind, it's better to keep the memories he has of her than corrupt them with ones of her rejection or fear."

How could she argue? Hadn't her first reaction been fear? Her insides went cold. If what Julius said was true, she'd basically turned one of Harrison's nightmares into reality. "I should be beaten." She stopped walking.

"Into kink, eh?" Julian winked. "You should talk to your mate about that."

She rolled her eyes. "This evening, when I found out he was a vampire, I overreacted."

Julian sighed. "Jesus, you're stacking the marks against yourself, aren't you?"

She rubbed her forehead. "He's been so nice and instead of trying to make this work, I keep putting more space between us. I need to try to fix this." They were mated now. They could be happy together—they'd been friends once, she'd loved him at one time—but they'd never find happiness if she kept screwing things up.

He forced her to look at him. "Look, you do it or you don't, but if you're just gonna try, you'll hurt him worse than you already have."

She forced herself to nod. She still didn't know if she liked Julian, but she didn't doubt his loyalty to Harrison.

"That goes for George, too." He tugged her into motion again. "You want on Harrison's good side, you'll make nice with his damned minion."

CHAPTER 6

October 10th, 6:34 AM

"THIS ONE IS BROKEN!"

Adia screamed her complaint, ensuring her assistants heard. They would find another. Pacing, her unbelted silken robe swirled around her. She planted her palm on her naked hip and glared at the bed, at the body lying motionless on the pink satin sheets. Blood smeared his ruined face. His big blue eyes stared at her over his damaged nose.

She couldn't bear to look at him anymore. Didn't he understand how much she loved him? How much she needed him?

"He's broken. Broken, broken, broken. Broken!" With each word her voice raised in pitch and volume. The small tantrum helped relieve the emotions twisting inside her.

This one could have been *the* one. But no. He wasn't strong enough. Nor willful enough. He wasn't enough. Her heart ached. After all the time and the energy she'd sacrificed to instruct him. To love him. To mold and train him to be her mate, he broke. Like all the others. Every fucking one of them.

Except Harry.

Harry never broke. He matched her. He'd been perfect until he'd forced her to call the Guardian. She'd mourned for him. Hadn't taken another boy for years after she'd lost him. But the

Guardian hadn't destroyed him. She couldn't believe her eyes when she ran into him again. She'd been in the process of escaping the Vampiric Council's prison when she ran into the control room and there he was, sitting at the computer, assisting Duncan—the Guardian that was supposed to ash Harry all those years ago—in finding Trina. Harry hadn't been half as happy to see her as she'd been to see him.

True, the Grigori coven had aged him which was disappointing. She'd changed him to a vampire to preserve him in that perfect stage of male adolescence. That brief time when a male begins to blossom sexually, but still lacked the stubble, the bulge of muscle and strength that went hand-in-hand with maturity. When they were still malleable.

Despite the fact he was grown, she still wanted him. He was trained. He wouldn't break. She could love him to her heart's content, and he'd never break.

But the silly male was holding a grudge. What had he expected? That she'd sacrifice herself after he'd lost control and disappointed her? No, he never expected her to do such a thing. He'd never want her to get hurt. Harry loved her too much.

He was playing hard to get. That's what this was. He wanted her to prove her love before he submitted.

She walked over to her dressing table, opened the small box of treasures she kept there and pulled out the 5X7 photo. A young Ember Moon smiled back at her. Harry had often cried out for the girl in his sleep while he was here. The silly boy had thought he loved her.

And Ember must still hold some tender emotion for Harry. She had, after all, come to the Knot Works to find out what had happened to him.

Adia scoffed. By now, Ember Moon was dead. She took a deep, cleansing breath and grinned.

Oh, she'd kept a close eye on Harry since discovering he was alive. He'd never had sex with anyone else. All these years, he'd stayed true to her. Pined for her. He wouldn't be able to sate Ember Moon because he only wanted *her*.

And with her out of the way, he'd have no reason not to come home.

Harrison was still ignoring her.

Ember had stayed with Julian most of the night while he'd secured a team for Nancy, and Harrison finished his reports from his last case. By the time Harrison arrived in Julian's office he appeared wrung out and yet her whole being reacted to him. Dark circles smudged under his eyes, his shirt was rumpled, and stubble peppered his jaw, yet he was still sexy as hell. She couldn't refrain from letting her gaze rake over every inch of him. Physical attraction wouldn't be an issue for them, at least not on her side.

Not sure what to say or how to alter the mistakes she'd made, she asked, "Are we going to Fremont now?"

He shook his head and turned his gaze to Julian. "I think we have enough time to get home before dawn. You ready?"

Julian got to his feet. "Yep."

Harrison left. He hadn't even glanced at her once. This was not going well. She needed to make amends, but how could she if he wouldn't acknowledge her? Her body was demanding to be sated again, but that wasn't possible as upset as he was. Hadn't he said she wouldn't need sex as often after that first time? Why then was everything in her urging her to go wrap her body around his? Why had she gotten wet as soon as he'd walked into the room?

She stood on shaky legs and Julian motioned for her to precede him out the door and then walked next to her. With a wink, he put his arm over her shoulders.

"Get your paws off her or I swear, I'll leave your sorry ass here."

George growled from his master's shoulder.

"See." Julian grinned. "He's paying attention."

Thank God, because pretty soon, she'd need all of Harrison's undivided attention. "Why does he keep threatening to leave you here?"

A dark scowl flashed across Julian's face. "Don't wanna talk about it."

The three of them made their way through a maze of corridors before taking the elevator to the lobby. Harrison stopped at the front desk. "I'm checking Jules out, Deno."

With a twitch of his lips, Deno pushed a log book across his desk and Harrison wrote in it.

Ember glanced at Julian. He stood ramrod straight, his arms crossed, and though unsure of what was going on, her heart went out to him.

"You have a good day," Deno called out as they left. "Don't you be giving your partner a hard time, Jules."

Julian turned and growled at the Oni. "One of these days I'm gonna shove that fucking log book right up your ass, Deno."

Once outside, they walked a block and a half in silence. The men strode down the street with calm, easy strides. George flattened out over Harrison's shoulders, his head hanging over his arm, reminding her of a bear rug.

How could they be so calm?

Her heart thumped against her ribcage and her gaze darted from one dark corner to another. "Don't you two worry about the Nephilim?"

"Nah." Julian shrugged. "The Grigori witches alert us if Nephilim are in the area."

"How?"

"Harry there has a direct connect in his head to Trina, one of the witches."

"I told you a Guardian raised me." Harrison shrugged. "Duncan, he mated a Grigori witch named Trina and they both tend to worry to death. Trina is telepathic and she raises hell inside my mind if Nephilim are anywhere near me."

"And me—my better half, who is also a Grigori witch, keeps me on speed dial." Julius lifted his phone. "Never leave home without it."

Ember took a calming breath. So, they weren't as blasé as they acted. Knowing someone would alert them if Nephilim were nearby did settle her racing heart. Still, her gaze darted from shadowy doorway to dark alley. Daemons were everywhere, and not all were as tame as these DDC agents.

The sky began to lighten, but the surrounding skyscrapers prevented any light from touching more than the tips of the structures. Still, they were pushing the boundaries of the curfew laws.

Finally, Harrison stopped in front of a brick building with

limo-grade tint on the windows. He punched in a code. The door clicked and he opened it, motioning her in.

The lower floor of the chic building was empty. Marble floors gleamed under the fluorescent lights. A sitting area with comfy club chairs sat off to one side, a bank of snack machines on the other. The elevators were straight ahead—one that required a code for residents and one for visitors—with a large packing box next to it.

Julian held out his arm, stopping them both. He pressed a finger to his lips.

Something was wrong.

Harrison swept the area with his gaze. Held two fingers to his eyes, then pointed to the box sitting by the elevators.

Julian nodded.

Harrison motioned for her to stay put, stay quiet.

Her heart hammered in her chest. A bomb? A trap? She had no idea what to expect but both daemons were all business now. The two of them made their way across the marble floor, approaching from opposite sides of the large package.

The box shifted.

Her hand flew to her mouth. She scanned the room, but no one else was around.

Julian bent and placed a hand on either side of the box. Harrison got ready to pounce. Even George hopped to the floor, circling the box with a twitch of his reptilian tail.

Why didn't they draw their weapons?

In one swift motion, Julian jerked the box up and away and Harrison dove in to grab whatever hid underneath.

Someone dressed in black jumped out from under the box and the two men were a blur of motion as they wrestled with them in a barrage of cuss words—some from them, some from their attacker. He was shorter than Julian or Harrison, with long straight black hair that whipped wildly around his head as they grappled with him.

Harrison locked his arms under the attacker's arms and then behind his neck in a double-nelson.

A kid. A kid dressed in baggy black jeans, untied florescent blue sneakers, and a Call of Duty tee.

Julian hauled back his arm and threw a punch at the kid's stomach. She almost screamed, slammed her hand over her mouth as she realized Julian stopped just shy of actually hitting him.

Still, the kid did a dramatic buckle forward and grunted as if he'd taken the punch.

Julian rolled his eyes.

For God's sakes, they were playing. A breath shuddered out of her.

Harrison lifted the teen off his feet while holding him in a double-nelson and then shoved him to Julian, who put him in a choke hold.

George pranced between the men, trying to join the fun.

"I almost got you." The teen's laughter filled the room and a reluctant smile tugged at her lips. She was furious with them for scaring her, damn it, but they were kind of cute—the big tough DDC agents playing.

"You wish, brat." Julian put his knuckles to the kid's head and scrubbed hard.

"Okay, okay." The teen was shouting every word, laughing so hard he couldn't catch his breath. "Mercy, you rat bastard."

Harrison chuckled. "You kiss your mom with that mouth?"

The teen tried to buck forward, to break Julius' hold.

"You gonna quit lurking in dark spaces, Lucas?" Julian pushed him away and glared.

His scowl had zero effect on Lucas. He grinned. "Maaaaybe."

"What?" Harrison bent over, his shoulder to Lucas' stomach, hauled him up in a fireman's carry and did something to the back of Lucas' knee that had the youth in stitches all over again. "What's the right answer?"

"Put me down, you mangy crapbag!" He thumped his fists on Harrison's back. "You've got bony shoulders."

Julian threw his head back and laughed.

"Nope. Not even close." Harrison went after the back of his knee again.

"Yes. No lurking. Okay, okay. I gotta take a piss."

Harrison dropped the kid back to his feet. Going off his movements and language, he was older than she first thought, maybe fifteen or sixteen, but on the small side. Asian, with big chocolaty eyes and thick black hair.

He grinned at the two daemons. "Where you guys been lurking? It's been *days*."

"Had a long case." Harrison crossed his arms over his chest.

Julian shrugged. "I got stuck at headquarters."

Lucas planted himself in front of Harrison and folded his arms over his chest in such a perfect imitation it made her smile. "Did you think about my offer?"

Harrison sighed. "Dude, we've been over this—"

"Yeah, but I could help out. Maybe keep an eye on Julian. Tidy your place—"

Julian cuffed the back of Lucas' head. "You're not old enough, for one thing. I could take down you with one arm tied behind my back."

"You wish." Lucas snorted. "I've been working out."

They both made a big show about squeezing Lucas' biceps, somehow coming across both teasing and encouraging.

Ember made her way over to where the three of them chatted. What did Lucas want? As young as he was, he must be human. He shouldn't be in this building.

Harrison patted his thigh and George scurried back to his perch. "Being a daemon isn't all that great."

"You got decent jobs." He planted his fist on his hip. "A nice place." He glanced at Ember. "Both of you have a woman now."

Harrison turned his face away, but not before she caught his amused grin.

"Yeah." Julian kissed his teeth. "But we got no HMO."

"That's true." Harrison punched the button for the elevator. "We get sick, we're screwed."

Lucas' face scrunched up. "Who the hell needs an HMO? It's all about the ACA, man."

"Daemons don't get citizenship, man. No ACA. We're stuck getting our own insurance." Julian shook his head. "They claim vampirism as a pre-existing condition. Can you believe that shit?"

"Yeah." Harrison scratched George under his chin. "It's pretty damn bad when they won't even insure immortals."

The elevator pinged and the doors slid open.

Lucas narrowed his eyes. He pointed at the men. "I've been thinking about this a lot. We can start an Explorers program. I'm sure I can find more people to join."

Ah. Several of the local police departments had programs for kids that were 'young officers in training' programs. They even got to go to the police academy for a week a year. Lucas was dreaming, though, the government would never allow the DDC to have such a program.

"All right. You have a good day, Lucas." Harrison put a hand to her lower back and ushered her into the elevator. She wanted to ask about Lucas—why he was here and how they got away with associating with him, but she didn't dare. Not after all the other mistakes she'd made tonight.

As the doors closed Julian added, "Say hi to your parents for us."

Lucas waved them off and headed for the front doors.

"She's getting better." Julian tipped his head toward her. "She didn't scream."

"Her heart damn near jackhammered through her rib cage."

"The two of you should have warned me." She pinned her fist on her hip. "I didn't know what was in the box. You scared the crap out of me."

The corner of Harrison's mouth curved. "Fair enough, I guess."

Her lips twitched. "No HMO?"

Julian nodded. "I think we should strike."

Harrison scoffed. "Hell, even if we had insurance—no doctor would treat you after what you did."

"What'd you do?" She quirked her brow.

"When the DDC first started, management wanted daemons to go through the same exams as humans." Julian rolled his eyes.

Harrison grinned. "As soon as the doc walked in with the rubber gloves and tube of lube, Jules there had the doc giving himself a prostate exam."

She stared at him with wide eyes, her hand flying to her mouth to hide her grin. "Oh, no."

Julian shrugged. "Early detection saves lives."

"That's evil." She giggled.

The elevator opened into a spacious apartment. Windows surrounded the room, but were shuttered in preparation for dawn. The rest of the space was tasteful, if a bit masculine. Decorated in earthy tones, with large pieces of furniture and a wall dedicated to all types of electronics. The whole place screamed man cave.

Julian made a bee-line for the couch, snapping a remote from the side table as he went. The TV clicked on, but instead of the expected ball game, "Downton Abby's" opening theme played. "Dude, you guys wanna watch?"

Ember's lips parted. "I'm afraid I'm gonna have to revoke your 'scary daemon' card, Jules."

An overstuffed pillow sailed over Julian's shoulder, which she dodged. "Tease me all you want, but shush."

With one last disbelieving glance at Julian, she turned to Harrison. He stood closer than she'd realized, leaving her staring at his throat. She lifted her gaze over the corded muscle in his neck and his sharp jawline to the brilliant blue of his eyes. Her demon shifted as desire wracked through her. She forced the need away, tried to focus on the here and now. "What's his mate like?"

"Kat?" He shrugged. George leapt from his arm and wandered into the kitchen. "Smart, beautiful, sweet to his sour."

She laughed, her voice huskier than usual. "I'm starting to think he's not so bad."

Hurt flickered over his features.

"Listen, Harry—"

"Quit yapping." Julian shot her a glare. "You made me miss Thomas' line."

With a roll of her eyes, she took Harrison's hand and led him to the first door she spotted, which turned out to be a bathroom. She pulled him in. He flicked on the lights, but not before she gasped at the sight of his glowing eyes.

He jerked away and opened the door. She slammed it shut, putting herself between him and the exit. It took all her willpower to keep from tugging him into a passionate embrace. She shoved her hands into her pockets. "You need to give me a chance to get used to things without getting upset every time you surprise me."

"Is that what you call it?"

"I thought you were human all these years. I never imagined you'd be anything else. I'm sorry I overreacted."

Still, he wouldn't look at her.

"A lot has happened in a very short period of time." She shifted, pressing her thighs together in effort to dull the needful ache. "My entire world has changed and I have to alter many of my preconceptions about daemons as a result. All I'm asking for is some patience while I work everything out and for you not to be so damned sensitive."

He nodded, his face still turned away.

"We could at least be friends, right? We used to be the best of friends."

His lips curved into a semblance of a smile. "We've always been friends. I never forgot you."

Every nerve in her body stood at attention, focused on her mate. This was a terrible time. He was angry and hurt, but she couldn't wait much longer.

"How often is this going to happen?" She tried to keep her voice steady, but the end came out as a moan.

His gaze snapped to hers. Then he checked his watch. "Now?"

"I didn't plan for this to happen," she whispered through her teeth. "I've been ignoring it all morning but now that you're so close, I can't anymore."

His lids narrowed. "You were with Jules all morning."

"Yeah, and thinking about you." She covered her face. "Ever since I told him I needed to be beaten—"

"You said what to him?"

Great, he sounded outraged. "I told him I should be beaten for how I reacted to finding out you were a vampire. I felt horrible. I intended no sexual innuendo."

"Oh." He rubbed his hand across his neck.

She put her palm on his chest and leaned forward.

He backed away. His Adam's apple bobbed as he swallowed.

God help her, she must've really screwed up. He didn't want her.

"I'll be right back, Em."

———◆———

She needed sex. Again. Now.

Harrison closed the bathroom door behind him. *Shit.* Not only did he feel a panic attack coming on, but he was pretty sure he'd hurt her feelings in the process of trying to leave.

Julian rose from the couch and crossed to the kitchen. "You're white as a fucking sheet, man."

He glanced back at the door and drew in a deep breath. Gods, he wished they were still in Vegas. Here, not only would Ember know if he freaked out, Julian would, too.

Julian paused, a stupid grin on his face. "She's in the bathroom, isn't she?"

"None of your damn business."

With a shrug, Julian disappeared around the corner. The fridge opened and he returned with a bag of blood. "I know you don't want to talk about this."

"Then don't."

"Seems to me you were fine yesterday."

Harrison paused, halfway to telling him to fuck off, but, yesterday he had been okay—when she'd been chained. He didn't have any shackles or cuffs now.

As if he'd spoken his thought out loud, Julian added, "We've got some zip-ties in the cabinet."

Harrison's face flamed and he took a deep, bracing breath. Julian must've seen the cuffs in the evidence box.

"I could always mesmerize you."

"Fuck off." Harry turned around and opened the door.

Ember splashed cold water on her face, pausing when Harrison entered and the lock clicked into place. She glanced into the mirror as she dried off, forgetting for a moment he didn't cast a reflection. She jumped when his hand spread over her belly.

"Harry." She tried to turn in his arms, but he stopped her.

His warm breath fanned her ear. "Be still, Em."

In the mirror, the buttons to her jeans seemed to undo themselves. Her shirt bulged around an unseen hand slipping underneath to cup her breast. It was disconcerting. Unreal. Except his hands on her skin felt tangible enough as did the warmth of him at her back. His calloused fingers almost tickled when he skimmed them over her flesh and her nipples tightened into hard buds.

Reaching behind her, she pulled his face to hers. He was aggressive. Possessive. He made her feel delicate and feminine. His breathing grew harsh, labored. His mouth skimmed away from hers, dancing across her cheek, sucking at her ear lobe. "We're going to play a little game."

"I don't want—"

"First rule, no talking unless it's 'more, please,' or 'leave.'"

"What do you mean?"

"Tell me to leave if you want me to stop." He nuzzled the side of her neck, and one hand slipped into her jeans, her panties, to stroke her clit.

They needed to talk about this, but she couldn't think straight while he was doing that. "But—"

He pulled his hand from her jeans and she cried out.

"Remember the rule, Em." He nipped her shoulder. "What do you want?"

Didn't he understand she needed him? Part of her was pissed as hell at his game, another, darker part shuddered in anticipation. "More."

Calloused fingers slipped past her waistband, into her panties, and deep between her damp folds.

"Second rule." He kissed her shoulder, sending shivers down her spine. "Your eyes stay on the mirror."

"Is this some kind—" She stopped when his hands left her, then once again ground out, "More, please." Silently, she added the endearment, *You control freak, bastard* to the end of the sentence. She wanted to see his face, his expression, as she pleasured him, too. How would they ever build any kind of intimacy if he wouldn't allow her to try? Part of her wanted to end the game now, to stop and talk about this, but her demon was restless, yearning, and her arousal was near overwhelming. She forced her eyes to the mirror, squelching her frustration.

Both his palms slid up her sides, taking her shirt with them. In the mirror, the garment seemed to jump to the floor with a will of its own. Her bra followed.

He placed her hands on the countertop. "Gods, you're beautiful, Em."

In this position, all the blood pooled in the tight tips of her nipples. Her breasts grew heavy, full, and when he cupped them, she moaned. He pinched each nipple lightly, giving one a tug that sent bolts of delight straight to her pussy. She arched back, pressing her bottom to the hard line of his cock, pleased when he, too, moaned.

Anticipatory heat gathered low in her belly and resonated between her thighs. She opened her mouth to tell him to take her now, but at the last moment, remembered his damn game.

"More."

His voice was deeper. "More what?"

"More, please."

He dragged her jeans and panties off. Kissed her hips, nipped her rear, licked her thigh. He lifted each of her legs, removed her shoes, socks, and the pant leg, his mouth skimming over her sensitive flesh the whole time. No man had ever taken such care. She felt desired. Sacred.

When he placed each of her feet on the ground, he spread them wider, forcing her legs back until she bowed forward, horizontal from the waist up, with her arms resting on the counter, her ass level with her head. His tongue made a wet trail from her knee to her pussy. His shoulders brushed the back of her thighs. Hands cupped her bottom. She wanted to watch him, but if she dared glance down, she'd be looking right into his eyes.

The heat of his breath beat against her mound and she tensed, strung tight from waiting. What was he doing? His breath had grown erratic. She could feel his body trembling against her legs. "More, please."

His teeth scraped her mound, causing her pussy to clench, forcing a startled half-scream of pleasure from her mouth. Tension wound deep in the pit of her belly.

He slipped a couple fingers inside her. His tongue delved between her folds, stroking her while his fingers plunged in and out, twisting as they went. Her breasts jiggled, sweeping across the too-cool marble countertop.

The dam burst inside her, making her knees buckle and forcing her even deeper onto his hand. Her whole frame shook with the force of her orgasm. His tongue swiped across her one last time and then he shifted positions, his fingers twisting as he did. He kissed the backs of her thighs, her bottom, her back as he rose behind her. His fingers slipped from between her wet folds and traced a line straight along the center of her backside, pausing for a moment to press on her pucker.

Her breath caught. His damp finger pressed to her virgin hole sent dark sparks of pleasure racing through her. Made her inner muscles clench in anticipation. Her whole frame froze as she waited to see if he'd push farther.

He moved his hand away. With a pang, she realized he must of have been waiting for her prompt. He had her playing the submissive, but she held all the control.

"More, please." She needed him deep inside her.

Behind her, his clothing rustled as he stripped and then the length of his naked masculine shape curved around her. Lips skated across her neck, hands played with her nipples. In a matter of seconds she was gasping, ready.

And he was shaking. With need? With excitement?

She pushed back against the hard length of him, begging without words.

"Gods, Em." His cock nudged between her slick folds, pressing in, stretching her. Her body opened for him, grasping at each sex-slicked inch as he pushed into her. In this position, his cock seemed even larger and she lifted onto her toes trying to accommodate him.

"Relax, honey." His hands went to her hips and coaxed her back onto the flats of her feet. "Spread your legs a little more." She did, and slid even farther onto his thick length. "Oh, yeah, Em. Tip your ass back." She arched her spine which allowed her to lift her bum higher and he sank the rest of the way in. Her slit was flush with his pelvis, his sac brushing against her clit and, dear God, she'd never been so full.

She moaned and rotated her hips to grind against him. He clutched the curve of her waist in his large hands. Directed her to do so again. With one hand, she reached between her legs and cupped his balls.

He jerked a little. Groaned. He swallowed hard enough for her to hear. "No. Hands on the counter."

"I want to touch—" She gasped as he withdrew and she slapped her palm on the counter. Damn him. "More."

She closed her eyes to hide her hurt as he slid back in. Why did he keep rejecting her? *How* could he reject her while balls deep inside her? Tears of frustration threatened to spill through her lashes and she lowered her head.

Seated inside her once again, he embraced her in a gentle hug—one arm fitted around her belly holding her close, the other crossed between her breasts, his hand cupping her cheek. "It's not you." He kissed her back. "I just can't."

"You hate me." He must. He didn't want her to touch him.

Didn't even want her looking at him.

"No."

"You hate that you're stuck with me."

"Damn it, no." He sighed. "I never wanted anyone to touch me. Not like I wish you could . . . but I can't let you."

What was he talking about? He wasn't even making sense. Was he lying to make her feel better? "This seems so cold. I want to pleasure you. Hold you, too."

His lips danced across her skin. One arm unwound from her. "Take my hand, Em."

She opened her eyes. His big hand lay palm up on the counter next to hers. The offer wasn't what she wanted. It wasn't enough. Behind her his body tensed, his breathing labored and his fingers trembled as he waited. For whatever reason, this small concession cost him.

Maybe he'd explain to her later, or perhaps she'd find another way to show him affection.

She slipped her hand in his and his fingers closed around her. Stared into the mirror, hoping she was looking into his eyes and said exactly what was in her heart. "Love me, Harry." He didn't move, wasn't even breathing, and she realized her mistake. If he couldn't stand her touch, why would he want her emotion? That, and she'd forgotten his damn rules. She swallowed past her hurt. "More, please."

———◆———

With a start, Harrison set his body back in motion. What had he thought she'd been asking? They didn't know each other well anymore. Why the hell would she be interested in anything more than a good shag?

He ignored the pang in his chest. Their relationship would be better this way. She made him feel too much and that was dangerous. She brought all the emotions he'd buried closer to the surface.

Her fingers clasped tight around his. A secret part of him wished she was squeezing his hand to hold him, but after everything that had happened, maybe she just needed to hold on to *someone*, anyone. He eased out of her slick passage and thrust back into her heat. Her skin was like warm satin on the front of his thighs. His balls tightened as they slapped against her wet slit.

"More, Harry." Her voice had turned husky. Breathless. Would she chant his name again when he made her come?

With his free hand, he stroked the curve of her spine. Cupped her ass. Teased the cleft between her cheeks.

"Yes. More."

Gods, yes.

He withdrew long enough to slip his fingers in her wet heat. As he slid his cock back in, he circled his slick fingers around the rosebud above. He liked the idea of possessing her in every conceivable way. Would crawl underneath her skin, if possible.

She ground her hips back, pushing against his hand. *Fuck.* The tip of his finger slipped past her tight outer ring and she sucked in a hard breath, shuddering. Damn. He didn't want to hurt her. Shouldn't have—

"More."

Oh, damn that was hot. He pushed deeper, past his knuckle. Shivers spread across his lower back and gooseflesh rose on hers. Her inner muscles clasped and pulled at his cock and his balls drew tight. He pistoned his hips against hers, sliding his finger partway out, plunging back in.

"Oh, Harry." Her whole frame jerked with the force of her orgasm. "Harry." Her body milked his cock, pulsed around his finger and he couldn't hold back. "Harry."

He shuddered, his knees going weak as he thrust one last time into her warm depths. He clung to her as the rush of release washed over him. He slipped his finger out of her and wrapped his arm around her belly. He kissed her back, content to stay connected to her while they waited for their breathing to slow. "You okay, Em?"

"Amazing. You?"

"Oh, I'm fine." He nuzzled her neck. "You *are* amazing."

"Can I hug you now?" His insides went cold at the thought, even as his heart leapt a little. "I . . . I need a hug."

She started to turn, and his grip on her tightened. Gods, he didn't want her to see him. The scars. She'd be disgusted. Wouldn't let him touch her anymore. "Give me a minute, Em." He gritted his teeth as he pulled his over-sensitized cock from her and, keeping one hand on her back, bent to grab his boxers.

He slipped them on. Covered now, he nudged her up. "Come here."

Ember straightened and turned. Her gazed darted over his chest, glanced at his boxers and her brow furrowed. "Why—"

He opened her arms, forced a grin. "You wanted a hug, right?"

Her emerald eyes filled with tears and she dove into his embrace. Surrounded him. Caged him.

Breathe in. Out.

Gently, he put his arms around her. *This was Ember. Sweet, sweet Ember.* Her tears fell warm on his chest, tickling as they ran down his skin.

Relax. Breathe.

The chaste hug wouldn't kill him. He didn't like the idea of anyone feeling they had the right to access his body, but this was okay. Should be okay. She'd asked. He'd given her permission. This time. Just once.

Focus, Sinclair. Help the distraught woman and quit freaking out.

"Em, are you okay?" He eased her long, silky, blonde locks away from her face. "Did I hurt you?"

"No." Her voice trembled. She sniffed. "I keep hurting you. You've been nothing but kind and I'm scared and worried about Madison and I don't even understand what I am or where I'm supposed to go, or what the new rules of my life are, or how you fit into it." She took a deep, shuddering breath. "Do you even want to fit into my life? 'Cause you don't seem like it. I know you're still mad at me for freaking out when you told me you're a vampire, and I'm sorry I overreacted, but, I mean, what happens now? Am I supposed to go home? Am I living here, and if so can I go home and get my stuff? Do succubus's—"

"Succubi."

"See? I don't even know what the plural of what I am is. Do succubi live here or in that daemon world, Marchon?"

"Machon."

"Yeah, that one. Are you going to help me find Madison?"

He took a deep breath. "Okay. Yeah, that's a lot." He'd been so focused on his own shit he hadn't stopped to consider what she must be going through. "You're going to stay here where Jules and I can keep you safe. I sent a crew to your house to get your clothes and bathroom stuff and they delivered it to your room here. We'll go to Fremont tonight and yes, you'll come. We'll check out the Knot Works and try to find Madison."

"You don't think we're going to find her."

He rubbed his chin on the top of her head. "I think Adia did whatever she's going to do with Madison."

"Oh, God." She pressed her face to his chest.

He tightened his embrace. "Which is nothing. Madison's a girl. Adia has no interest in females." Likely, Adia would be too busy with whatever boys she had in chains to be bothered with a young female.

"So, we'll find her?" She tipped her face to his.

He stared right into her luminous, emerald eyes and prayed he spoke the truth. "Yes, and she'll be fine."

She nodded and snuggled close.

CHAPTER 7

October 10th, 8:52 AM

"COME ON. LET'S GET YOU to bed. This has been a hell of a long day."

As soon as she eased her grip, he got out a couple washcloths and dampened them with hot water. They both cleaned up and dressed and he ushered her out of the bathroom. "Are you hungry?"

She shook her head.

Julian didn't so much as glance away from the TV. "I ordered her a pizza while we waited for you at headquarters."

"Thanks, man." *He* should've made sure she'd eaten. He hadn't been thinking. "You can help yourself to anything in the kitchen."

She shot the kitchen side-eye. "You have regular food?"

He grinned. "Yes. I asked housekeeping to stock regular food before we even left the hotel in Vegas. Your clothes should be in your closet, as well."

"Thank you."

"Jules and Kat live on the far side of the apartment." He motioned across the living room. "We're on this side. The rooms in the middle are common areas."

"Where is Kat?" She slipped her hands into her back pockets.

"She's a member of the Grigori Coven. Each of the witches take turns monitoring the Nephilim and helping the DDC pinpoint their location."

Julian glanced in their direction. "She'll be back in two more days."

"Do you know them, too? The Guardians?"

Julian grunted. "Oh, yeah. We're all great friends."

Her questioning gaze shot to Julian's.

Surreptitiously, Harrison flipped Julian the bird. As badly as Ember took the news that he was a vampire, the last thing he needed was to try to explain that his partner was *actually* the Harbinger and not the Harbinger's brother as everyone knew him. She'd never understand. "Let's go get you settled." He prodded her toward the hall. "We'll have plenty of time to chat later."

"All right." She slipped her hand into his and his breath caught. She was warm and silken and the urge to wrap her in his arms and bury his face in her hair almost overwhelmed him. His chest tightened at the thought. *Breathe, damn it.* In time, he'd get used to her. Until then, he needed to keep his shit together—act like everything was all good—because he did *not* want her cluing in on how fucked up he was.

He led her down the hall and stopped in front of the spare bedroom. He opened the door. "This'll be your space."

She stepped in and glanced around. "It's nice."

Once a guest room, it had been decorated in beige and blues. A queen-sized bed had been centered along the back wall, with a dresser on one side and closets on the other.

"All your clothes should be in the closet and drawers."

She moved around the room. Opened the closet and pulled out a pink silk nightgown. "Where's your room?"

He nodded across the hall. She slipped past him, opened the door and walked in. "I like this better."

Why? His room was dark, with heavy cherry furniture and maroon-and-gold accents. At least housekeeping had tidied up.

"It smells like you in here." She tossed the gown on the king-sized bed and explored his space.

How was it possible for his chest to puff with pleasure over her words at the same time his gut knotted? She couldn't mean to sleep in here. Not with him.

She glided her fingers along the dresser and picked up his cologne, then put it back and lifted his spare Guardian blade. She withdrew the knife from the sheath, running her finger along the cut-out design in the center. "This is pretty."

"Uh, it's a Guardian knife. The metal is silver so it works well on Lycan, but there is also a strip of wood in the center of the blade." Jesus, was he babbling?

She pulled it closer to her face. "I see it through the cut-out design."

"It works the same as a stake on vampires."

"Ah." She returned the blade to its sheath and set it back on the dresser before making her way across the thick, beige carpet and opening the door to the connected bathroom. "Towels?"

"The ones on the rack are clean."

She turned to him and smiled. "Do you mind if I take a shower?"

In here? He shook his head.

The door clicked closed behind her and he exhaled the breath he'd been holding. Well, hell. Now what? She must intend to sleep in here, otherwise she would've used her own damn bathroom. He could ask her to go back to her own room . . . except he didn't want to disappoint her. *Shit.*

What if he used his talent? Maybe split off a copy and left *him* with Ember.

He moaned, covered his face with one hand.

Had he sunk that low?

"Come on, Sinclair. Quit being a fucking coward."

It was 9:15 AM. They'd been mated one day, two hours and fifteen minutes and he was about to sleep with his mate in his home for the first time.

Stop with the OCD shit already.

He waited until Ember finished and went to shower. When he returned, she lay still and quiet and he thought her asleep. George pawed at the door, so he let the minion in.

He turned out the lights, trying to ignore the fact that his whole damn body shook and got into bed.

———◆———

Start out how you mean to go on.

A couple weeks ago at her friend's wedding shower, someone had given the bride-to-be that advice. It might be illegal for daemons to marry, but she'd use the advice for herself and Harrison anyway. They were mated and they should sleep together.

Ember opened her eyes and stared at the darkness above her. She didn't know what she wanted to prove, but she'd be damned if they slept in separate bedrooms. That reminded her too much of her mother and stepfather.

Besides, if they wanted to make a go of this, they needed to get to know each other again and the intimacy of sleeping together would foster closeness during waking hours.

She hoped.

She couldn't figure him out. Having some idea what his life had been like since she'd last seen him would help. Pieces of that time were coming together. A woman had kidnapped him—Adia. She still didn't understand his transformation. Julian indicated he'd been changed while still a kid and as a result killed other kids that Adia had in her custody. But had that been true, Harrison should still have the physical body of a sixteen-year-old. Whatever. Somehow, he'd been transformed. He must have escaped from Adia. Harrison said a Guardian had raised him which explained his desire to be in law enforcement. He seemed to be dedicated to his job, although she didn't know what type of agent he was. She suspected, if Harrison was anything like her, his job description would fall right in line with whatever had happened in his past. She'd found a job that allowed her to help children neglected or abused by their families. So maybe his job had something to do with finding missing children.

"Harry?"

"Mm."

"What do you do at the DDC? You mentioned you're an expert."

He drew in a deep breath. "Jules and I are the resident experts on human trafficking and child sex tourism."

"What? But the case you told me about wasn't much more than a domestic dispute with a parental abduction."

"That's not how it was reported." He sighed. "Most of the cases we get involve adults or children who are kidnapped, transported to a different country than the one they were abducted from, and sold into prostitution or slavery. My job isn't nice, but I never considered doing anything but this."

No! For a moment, she thought she'd shouted the denial, but he didn't react. *Human trafficking and child sex tourism.* He'd gone missing while he was in England—in her line of work she knew what happened to kids who went missing. She'd never imagined him as a victim, much less a victim of a sex-related crime. After what Nancy had told her, she'd always thought he'd been put into protective custody or something. No. Her initial assessment was wrong, that's all—his job didn't have anything to do with his past.

It couldn't.

He showed appropriate bonding with his partner. Interacted well with others. He gave his pet attention and affection. Nothing she'd seen indicated he'd ever been subjugated to abuse of that magnitude. He'd been kind and tender with her. He seemed to enjoy sex, although . . . .

Although he wouldn't let her touch him. Refused to allow her to give him pleasure.

Ember swallowed past the growing lump in her throat. What had he said earlier? That Adia wouldn't bother with Madison because she was a girl? "Harry? If Madison were male, what would Adia do to him?"

"Depends."

"On what?"

"Lot of things." He cleared his throat. "What's Madison like? Cute? Ugly? Fat or skinny? How old?"

"Your average kid. Sixteen, skinny. She'll be beautiful some-day, but right now she's in an awkward stage. Kind of a late bloomer." He remained silent so long she'd thought she'd over-played her hand. She hadn't described Madison, after all, but a young Harrison.

"She'd play with him." His voice was little more than a whis-per in the darkness. "She'd chain him to her bed. Tease him. Gain his trust and fuck him." Even though his voice didn't raise in volume, the intensity of his words sent a shiver over her skin. "When he couldn't control his body's response, she'd berate him. Hurt him. Degrade and humiliate him until—"

His passionate tirade ended abruptly. She wanted to coax him into finishing. Needed to know everything, but she didn't trust her voice.

"And when she brought other boys in, she'd make him school them."

Oh, God. She closed her eyes. Her heart breaking. Shattering at what he told her.

The effort needed to hold back her anguish made her break out in a cold sweat. Tears rolled down her face in itchy trails but she dared not wipe them away, nor did she try to breathe through her congested nose. He'd know then. He'd never tell her more. She forced slow, deep breaths through her mouth.

She strained to hear him, his voice dropped so low. "If he refused, she'd destroy him. She'd eat away at every redeemable quality he had until he'd sink so low death would be his only out. Thing is, she'd also force upon him a survival instinct so strong, so insidious, that he couldn't even die to escape. See, he'd never be free. She'd infect every nuance of his life until no matter where he turned, he couldn't see anything but her."

The bed moved under his weight as he rolled over. Away from her.

Because Adia and her twisted games had infected *her.* There would be no chance of happiness for them. No opportunity for love to grow. She was tainted in his eyes. No wonder he didn't want her to touch him, they were together because of Adia. She probably reminded him of Adia. Ember buried her face in her pillow. That's what she got for trying to find the light at the end of the tunnel—utter darkness. Her lungs protested the breath she held. Her muscles ached from suppressing her sobs. Oh, God, never had her heart hurt so much.

"You don't have to stay."

She peered in his direction, though she couldn't even make out his outline in the absolute pitch darkness of the room.

"I'd never turn you away when you need me, but you don't have to associate with me once we get Madison back."

A tiny spark of hope ignited. What if she was reading him wrong? He almost sounded like *he* couldn't imagine *she'd* want to be with him.

Oh, this wouldn't be easy, but maybe he wasn't rejecting her. Perhaps he was mitigating further damage to himself because he expected her to shun him. She'd felt like that after her step-father had raped her. Dirty. Damaged. She'd had a hard time relating to her peers, but worse, she'd gotten it into her head that her presence would taint them. Harrison's parents had helped her to see how wrong her thinking was with their patience and affection.

She slid across the bed. When she spooned herself around his hard, broad frame, his whole body jerked, but he didn't pull away. His hair was damp from his shower, but he wore jeans and a belt. That couldn't be comfortable. Why had he gotten dressed?

Then again, he'd probably told her a fraction of what happened. Of what his female assailant had done to him. Of course he was wearing pants to bed. He was sharing his bed with a woman. Was planning to sleep which would leave him completely vulnerable. That was that. No more sex. Not until he had time to get used to her presence and got comfortable with her. She'd never get past his shields if she kept forcing him past his comfort zone.

His flesh cooled her overheated skin and she slid one arm over him to rest her hand over the spot his human heart had been. She kissed the back of his neck. Maybe he didn't have a physical heart anymore, but that was okay. She'd have more room.

One way or another, she'd fill that spot in his chest near to bursting with love. With self-respect. With hope. They'd loved each other once and she had no doubt they could love each other again now that they were mated. Oh, yes, she'd fill his metaphorical heart with so much fucking joy he wouldn't be able to resist her.

But not today. She couldn't seem to find much joy at all today.

━━━◆━━━

Harrison stared into the darkness. What the hell was wrong with him? The last thing she needed to hear was the truth about how sadistic Adia was.

He couldn't relax in her embrace. His body had learned the hard way that the worst pain came after the gentlest moments. But this was Ember, damn it.

The same person who'd spent almost an entire week at his house, teaching him to cook breakfast, lunch, and dinner when both his parents had shingles. The same person who'd helped him nurse a roadrunner with a broken wing. Who had cried in his arms when the time came to set the wild bird free. Who held his hand as they'd jumped from the 51/50 ledge at Canyon Lake even though he'd teased her all day.

His mate was hurting. Oh, she was trying to be damn quiet about it, but her heart hammered away in her chest every time she held her breath. She shook. His back was growing damp where her cheek pressed to his skin.

He got out of bed and retrieved some toilet paper from the bathroom while making a mental note to tell housekeeping to stock tissue and all the other fripperies a woman would need. He got back into bed and put his arm around her. Fuck's sake he felt like a sixteen-year-old again—awkward and inept. He handed her the toilet paper. "Come on, Em. I swear it's not as bad as all that. Adia doesn't mess about with girls." His comment didn't help. Now she didn't even try to hide her tears. Great wrenching sobs tore out of her.

"I-I-believe you."

"I've got patrols watching the club. If anyone matching Madison's description enters or leaves they'll grab her."

"I-I-trust you." She blew her nose and settled back in his arms to cry some more.

She was killing him. He had no idea how the hell to fix this. "Are you still worried about your future? I promise everything will work out." He smoothed her hair away from her face and kissed the top of her head. "I swear I'll always be around for you no matter what you decide to do."

"I'm n-not crying for m-me. I'm cr-crying for you."

"For me. Why?"

"Because I d-don't think you ever cried for yourself."

What the hell did he need to cry for? He stayed awake for a long time trying to puzzle out the answer. Wasn't like he could sleep. Not with Ember plastered against his side. He kinda liked the feel of her, the warmth, but he couldn't get his body to relax. Couldn't silence that nagging little voice in his head that urged him to guard himself.

Pain always followed the gentlest moments.

CHAPTER 8

October 10, 10:00 PM

HER ASSISTANTS SAID THEY'D SEEN Harry last night. Walking home with Ember Moon. How could he mate her? She hadn't thought he would. Assumed he'd return to her, defeated. But no. No, he'd fucked Ember Moon and taken her home.

She may have lost her temper.

Used this boy harder than she should. Depression had overwhelmed her, and she hadn't even bothered disposing of the body before she went to sleep. Adia pushed aside the cold, stiff corpse of her latest attempt at training a suitable mate.

A knock captured her attention.

A new suitor?

Butterflies danced in her belly. She flung open the door and frowned. The hall was empty. She leaned out the doorway, glanced both ways, but none of her assistants were around. As she stepped back to close the door, a small cage on the floor caught her eye.

The shapeless creature inside writhed within the confines. She lifted the offering, closed the door and brought the six inch by six inch cube-shaped cage to her vanity. The creature had oily, midnight skin. The thing had no face. No arms or legs.

She went to her bookshelf and retrieved her Bestiary. The

creature must be a minor demon, but what kind? As she paged through the book, she'd glance over now and again, admiring the way the light glistened on the creature's skin when it flexed and stretched into different shapes.

On page 364 she found the reference she sought with a picture of a beast resembling the one in the cage.

Cuero — Shapeless, squid-like daemon. Re-uses features of creatures consumed. Skin can become shadowlike. Tamable with music. Prefers human meat.

Adia's mouth quirked. She sang a few bars of "Hush, Little Baby."

Eyes of all shapes and sizes emerged from the cuero's body. Each moved independently, taking in its surroundings. She stopped and all but one of the eyes disappeared. When she sang again, they returned. Fascinating. The cuero responded to stimulus, going dormant in the absence of sound and movement.

She went to the door. "Assistants."

Three male daemons came scrambling into the hall. Two chrono-deviants, dark-haired twins, pleasant-looking but plain, and one big, burly, bearded redhead. They'd been with her for decades, these three. The chrono-deviants had the power to stop time, rewind or freeze it and the wraith, well, he was her special pet. She focused on the large one, the wraith, meeting his small, black eyes.

"Why have you brought me this creature?"

The wraith stepped forward. "Well, Mistress, since the succubus is still about, I thought you might want to keep an eye on your gentleman friend 'til 'e comes around."

She eyed the small creature. "The cuero will help me do that?"

"Oh, yes, Mistress. Me mum gave me one when I's a lad. If you cut the beast in 'alf, you can keep one and plant the other in 'is quarters. It'll show you everythin' 'e sees and 'ears."

Her gaze shot back to the little creature. "Keep talking."

"You need to feed the cuero before you send it, otherwise the creature'll search out food instead of doin' yer biddin'."

She didn't want the cuero eating Harrison. The other two could become food, though. "How often?"

"Once a week or so, for a bit this size."

"And it eats humans?"

"Yes, Mistress. Daemons, too, if 'ungry enough. That corpse'll do if you want to save yerself the trouble of disposin' it."

She retrieved the cage from the vanity, set it next to the corpse, flipped the lid, and jumped back.

The cuero didn't move.

"Nothing's happening."

The wraith shifted from one foot to another, knotting his fingers together. "Give the wee beast a minute, Mistress. Cuero's are shy at first. Maybe if you sing."

"Hush, little baby. . . ."

Eyes popped up, glancing about before zeroing in on the body. They seemed to widen a fraction and then they disappeared. The cuero changed shape, shortening its mass and producing several long arms. Creeping up and oozing out of the cage, the cuero's movements reminded her of an octopus. It crawled onto the body.

Hundreds of tiny mouths appeared on the creature's oily skin. Opening, closing, tearing through flesh as the cuero devoured the boy. The thing had doubled in size by the time it had finished eating.

She glanced at her assistant. "Divide it."

"Sing some more, Mistress, to distract the wee beast. It's easier when it's calm."

She sang.

The wraith pulled out a long blade and set to work slicing the creature in half. The twin chrono-deviants leaned in the doorway, watching. He returned one half to the cage. The other he held out to her.

She shook her head. "Go. Release the cuero in Harry's home."

"Yeah, all right, then."

Her assistants left and she sat on the bed and cradled the cage to her chest.

She'd see Harry soon.

———◦———

Harrison parked a couple blocks away from their destination and they walked the entire length of the warehouse-style building housing The Knot Works. From the outside, the club didn't seem much different from any of the other nightclubs in this area of Fremont aside from its size.

Despite being well past curfew, both humans and daemons milled about. At The Knot Works, a bald, husky bouncer stood at the front door checking IDs and shooing off the riff-raff. He turned away two beautiful women and, because of the way he inspected them, she suspected he denied them access because of their jeans, hoodies, and sneakers.

Since she'd had an invitation last time, it hadn't occurred to her the club might have a dress code. She glanced at her two companions—Julian in his signature black attire and Harrison in jeans and a blazer. Both would pass muster even with George perched on Harrison's shoulder, but not her with her causal jeans, sneakers, and sweater.

"Come on." She grabbed Harrison's hand to tug him along the sidewalk. Julian followed behind.

Despite the late hour, daemons and humans strolled through the trendy shops and boutiques that catered to daemons during the night. They walked past a Haagen-Dazs, winding their way through the crowded patio seating area and a Blues Bar spewing sad saxophone music. A few shops later she found what she needed—The Mod Hatter Boutique. She hoped they carried something bigger than a size 4.

Harrison squeezed her hand. "Where are you going?"

She paused. "We want in without raising suspicion, right?"

He gave her an expression that stated, "*Well, yeah—duh.*"

She gave the same expression right back to him. "Then I need appropriate attire."

Pulling him behind her, she walked into the trendy shop with far more outward confidence than she was feeling. She hated shopping. Especially when she had two gorgeous men in tow who must be annoyed with the delay.

Both Harrison and Julian shocked the hell out of her. Once they entered the shop, they spread out and began searching through the racks.

The sales lady—okay, she'd say it, the sales *girl*—swept past her and zeroed in on Harrison. Flipping her long, dark hair over her shoulder, she smiled. "How can I help you?"

He didn't even glance up. "Find my mate something suitable for clubbing."

The girl's shocked gaze landed on Ember, slipping from her eyes down the length of her body.

Ember smiled. "Got anything in a twelve?"

"Uh, yeah. Toward the back of each rack."

Like most clothing stores, the smaller sizes for each article of clothing faced outward with the larger sizes hiding behind. Ember found a top right away. With the current styles, shirts were easier to find than bottoms.

"Check it out, Emerald Eyes." Julian lifted a leather mini-skirt with stretchable sides and waist. Hot damn.

"Got some boots over here." Harrison held up a pair of knee-high fuck-me boots and winked.

She grinned. "I'm never going shopping without the two of you again."

"You can thank Kat for the training." Harrison laughed. "Come on. Go change."

Amazingly, everything fit. Hell, she even felt kind of sexy in the clothes. The skirt fit like a second skin, but the shirt was low-cut and blousy enough to camouflage the bits she liked to hide. She stuffed her other clothes in her bag and emerged from the dressing room to playful whistles and cat-calls from her companions. Harrison paid and they went straight to The Knot Works. George slunk under Harrison's blazer and flattened himself out. Had she not seen the minion crawl under there, she'd never have known. He took her hand as he slowed his pace.

Julian strode to the front of the line like he owned the place.

"Where the hell do you think you're going?" The bouncer's eyes narrowed. "I need to see your IDs and membership."

The only reason they'd let her in last time was because she had the letter. At least this was a different bouncer who wouldn't recognize her.

Harrison squeezed her hand.

Julian never spoke a word. He folded his arms over his chest, rocked back on his heels, and emitted a little sigh of annoyance, but he never said anything. Ember tried to get closer, wanting to talk to the bouncer, but Harrison pulled her back.

That's when she noticed the bouncer's expression, head tipped to the side and eyes glazed. The whole thing was over and done within ten seconds or so.

The bouncer stepped back, shaking his head as if to clear it. "Yeah, all right. Go on in. Have fun."

Julian was scary as hell with that talent of his. If she hadn't known about his mesmerist ability, she wouldn't have realized anything had happened. Maybe that's why the DDC wouldn't let him out on his own. That had to suck.

Harrison's palm settled low on her hip as they walked inside behind Julian. Music thrummed so loud the bass vibrated through her body. The black walls and floors combined with the strobe lights had a disorienting effect, giving the hallway the illusion of being wide-open yet making her worry she might walk right into a wall without seeing it. Neon lights outlined alcoves to either side, highlighting the activities within.

To their left, a naked woman hung suspended from the ceiling by a harness of intricately woven knots. Her eyes rolled back as her partner flogged her with a multi-strand leather whip.

On their right, a dominatrix spread her thigh-high leather boots, twisting her lithe body as she swung a wicked-looking cane. Bound on his knees, a ball-gag secured in his mouth to muffle his shouts, a naked man received the punishment.

At the end of the hall, the building opened into the main warehouse portion of the club. The dim lights, erratic strobes, and colored lasers created an aura of anonymity. Scantily clad patrons writhed and jerked to "Closer" by Nine Inch Nails on the crowded dance floor. Couples and groups drank and made-out in the high-backed booths surrounding the dancers. Some, less self-conscious, were doing a lot more under the intense stares of others. One couple rose from their seats, and made a bee-line for a staircase leading upstairs.

Julian noticed, too. He turned and jerked his chin up.

Harrison nodded and tugged her off to the side to an empty booth. "Stay here. We're going to check upstairs." He had yelled, but even then she had to read his lips. He glanced around and frowned.

Was he worried about leaving her alone? "I'll be fine."

He stepped to the side and left an exact replica of himself where he'd been standing. She let out a gasp, stepping back, and bumping into someone. Harrison took her arm to steady her. "Sorry about that. I'm a splitter. My copy will stay with you. I see what he sees. Yeah?"

Her gaze locked on the copy. *Holy shit.* She nodded.

Harrison nudged her into the booth and the copy followed, crowding her farther along the red vinyl seat.

Despite being faced with Julian's talent from day one, she'd never thought to ask about Harrison's. Now, she had a thousand questions. Did splitting hurt? What happened if a copy got wounded? How many could he make? How did he control them? Or did he? Her mind spun.

Ember touched the copy's cheek with the tip of one finger. His skin was smooth and warm to the touch. The copy wasn't an illusion. Sliding closer, she nudged him until he turned to her. She couldn't tell the difference. Even the copy's eyes were that amazing shade of crystal blue. His clothes were the same as what Harrison wore. The only thing missing was the minion.

The copy leaned in until his nose touched hers. "Quit looking at me like that."

She shrugged. "I can't help it."

The copy's eyes narrowed. "It's distracting."

"Fine." She turned away and scanned the crowd. As her gaze landed on a familiar face, her eyes widened.

The incubus.

—◆—

Harrison and Julian went separate ways at the top of the stairs and searched each of the private rooms, meeting at the far end of the hall. The rooms weren't much bigger than closets fitted with couches or armchairs, leaving no hiding places. None of the patrons were young enough to be Madison.

Harrison gripped the railing and stared into the sea of writhing bodies below. When they'd arrived at the club, they'd walked the entire length of the building on the outside. The warehouse must run damn near a quarter block, but this wasn't that big.

Julian joined him. "Anything?"

He shook his head, leaning an elbow on the rail. "There's a lot of floor space not accounted for."

Julian's gaze darted around the club. "You're right." He shrugged. "Might be another business on the far side of the building."

"Maybe."

Julian's attention fixed on something over his shoulder. George crawled out from under Harrison's jacket and growled from his perch. Harrison stiffened, but forced himself not to react. "You ever seen one of Adia's clubs as clean as this one?"

Julian kissed his teeth. "Haven't even seen any drugs. It's a little disappointing. Almost like they knew we were coming." He thrust his chin forward to indicate Harrison should turn around.

Two big brutes closed in on them. Big being the operative word. They looked like they could've eaten the bouncer at the door without breaking a sweat.

He tipped his head toward Julian. "You want to do the honors?"

"Been trying." Julian cocked his head to the side, raising his voice. "Either they're immune to my particular charms or they have no brains for me to meddle with."

One of the hulks grinned, showing off his gums. "Adia warned me that you'd be sniffin' 'round."

Julian snorted. "Jesus, he sounds like Daffy Duck."

The big brute might not be the brightest, but he understood when someone was poking fun at him. His expression darkened.

Well, shit. He shot Julian a glare. "I'll take toothless." George gripped his shoulder, hissing. He lifted his hand to stay the minion.

"Guess that leaves me with The Lump."

He did resemble a lump. Bald and muscular, he resembled a whole lot of lumps.

"They're not vampires, Harry."

Maybe not, but they were daemon if they worked for Adia. "What do you think?"

"You're not gonna like what I think."

Toothless jerked his head to the side, cracking his neck. His features shifted.

What the fuck? "Jules?" What were these things?

Julian had a second talent. Such things weren't common, but he'd been wounded badly enough at one time to make mesmerism impossible and a second talent had emerged, one that remained even after his mesmerist talent returned. He could read auras and garnered quite a bit of information from them.

"Black Tamanous."

Harrison stared at Julian. "You're cracked."

Julian jerked his chin toward the two meatheads. "So are they." His eyes widened a fraction. Oh, hell. They were in deep shit. He backed away.

The two Black Tamanous were changing. Their skulls splitting like the lobes of a Venus-fly trap, revealing rows of jagged teeth. Each fold held an eye, half a nose, and half a mouth creating a gruesome illusion of terrible wounds when parted and a normal human when the halves melded together. Cannibals, the Black Tamanous fed on both human and daemon.

Their arms elongated, snapped, and cracked as the joints moved. The legs did the same until the males stood at least nine feet tall on four, thin, multi-jointed legs, their cavernous, toothy maws yawning.

Julian nudged him. "You still want toothless?"

Harrison glanced at Julian. In unison, they both turned and ran like hell.

"Get out!" Harrison shouted over the music. "Run!" The humans didn't hear, but the daemons did and when they saw the Black Tamanous they reacted, hastening those around them toward the exits.

Julian took off down the stairs, half sliding on the curved railing.

The floor shook beneath his feet; the creatures were gaining. If he veered over to the stairs now, he wouldn't make it.

He palmed the rail overlooking the dance floor, vaulting over the edge into the crowd below.

✦

Tall and wiry-thin, the incubus stood out amid the other patrons, making him easy for Ember to spot when he paused to talk to a buxom blonde near the table she shared with Harrison's copy.

People rushed passed, but her focus remained locked on the daemon who'd turned her life into chaos. She didn't realize something was wrong until Harrison's copy grabbed her arm.

"Get out!" The copy yanked her out of the booth and she stumbled straight into the incubus. The copy jerked her back against his chest. "I need you to run."

A high-pitched screech forced her to put her hands over her ears. Speaker feedback? No. That didn't explain the terrified wave of clubbers racing past and ramming into them. Her gaze darted around, lifted to where Harrison and Julian had gone.

Something big and spider-like dangled from the balcony. Seemed to hang suspended before two of its segmented legs hit the dance floor. Its mouth parted, not up and down, but side to side and another horrendous screech accosted her ears. The crowd separated for a moment and she spotted Harrison long enough to determine the fool man had positioned himself to fight the creature.

The copy jerked her into motion, guiding her to the door, but she yanked out of his grasp.

The incubus!

He fled deeper into the club, fighting against the human tide. Ember followed.

"Ember!" The copy shouted for her, almost caught hold of her again, but thanks to the crowd she darted out of his grasp.

Madison might be here and she refused to leave before finding out for sure.

The incubus went through a nondescript black door near the bar.

Had she not seen him open it, she would've missed the door. Even the knob had been painted black, making the handle almost invisible against the midnight walls.

She waited a couple heartbeats and glanced around. Harrison was unloading his weapon into the creature dangling from the second story by its hind legs. The sound of the gunfire was almost drowned out by the pulsing music. A second creature crouched near the staircase, as if it had someone cornered between the wall and the spiral metal rails. Julian? She hesitated. Maybe she should try to help.

No. She'd get in their way. She should leave, Harrison would be pissed if she didn't. She just couldn't live with herself if she left and found out later Madison was here.

Ember wiped her sweaty palms on her skirt and followed the Incubus.

A fleeing club patron rammed into Harrison and he went down in a tangle of limbs. He freed himself, George jumped back onto his shoulder, and stood. Fired again. Silver bullets wouldn't kill the Black Tamanous but if he put enough bullets into the daemon, they'd slow it down. He unloaded the magazine and grabbed his spare.

The creature's rear legs hit the dance floor, its snapping, snarling mouth coming closer. The club's patrons ran in full retreat now. Screams overtook the pulsing music. Bodies slammed into him as they fled, making him miss his target.

The creature came at him with jerky, unnatural movements that were both strange and beautiful. Almost mesmerizing. The curious part of his mind wanted to stop and stare, study how the Black Tamanous moved on its segmented spider legs. The sane part of his mind just wanted it dead.

The creature paused to seize a club patron in its jaws. Three bone-grinding bites and the woman disappeared as the muscles around its mouth flexed and stretched like a snake swallowing its prey. Lifting its head, the bulge of the woman slid through the creature's throat until there was no sign of her. There had hardly been any blood, just a muffled scream as the Black Tamanous shoved her headfirst into its gaping mouth.

Harrison unloaded the rest of his magazine into the Black Tamanous' face. One round hit the eye, rupturing the membrane and spilling a thick black goo. It roared, pawing the ground with its thin, spear-like legs.

He drew his Guardian blade. The wood worked between the silver blades wouldn't bother this thing, but if he could mortally wound the creature it would have to return to human form to heal.

The music muted as Ember shut the door. She was in a storage area filled with bottles of liquor, plastic straws and glasses. Where the hell had the incubus gone? She wandered the small room until she found a metal door behind one of the large wine racks.

The music blasted behind her as the door opened and then muted again as Harrison strode in and slammed it shut. No, wait. George wasn't with him. This was the copy. "I want you out of here now." Odd. He spoke in first person, but he wasn't really Harrison, was he?

"I found the incubus. We can't risk losing him, he might lead us to Madison." She didn't wait for his argument, but pushed the door open and darted inside.

"Ember!"

Padded bucket seats lined a large viewing window in the small, dark room. On the other side, an orgy played out.

At least that was her first impression. Four couples were in various stages of intercourse in different parts of the dimly-lit room. It wasn't until one of the women opened her eyes that Ember realized this wasn't a normal, consensual, sex club amenity.

The young woman's dead stare fixed on Ember. Her skin was slack, ashen. Her dry, cracked lips parted and formed one silent word. "Help."

Her belly twisted and bile shot up to sit at the top of her throat. Oh, God. She had to get them out. She had to—

"Em, come out of there. I'll handle this."

"No." The women all looked sick. Too thin. They all wore golden arm bands like hers.

Harrison's copy's hand wrapped around her arm, tugging her back. "You don't need to see this, honey. I'll get them—"

She pulled away. They were succubi, like her. This is what Harrison wouldn't tell her on the plane—the reason all the succubi died. Her fists clenched at her sides. She needed to be inside that room with a weapon. If she got in there, maybe she could save them. "How can their mates treat them this way?" Were those even their mates?

"Their mates are dead."

Ember and the copy both swung around to face the new voice. The incubus came through a door on the far side of the viewing room, lifting one thin, arched brow. His lips curved into a smug grin. He held two long, curved blades, one pointed at the copy, one at her.

The copy stepped between them, his arm held out, warning her to stay back. *I see what he sees.* Harrison would come. He'd burst through that door any second now.

"How could you? Those women are sick. They need medical attention." A dark rage twisted inside her. *Save them.* Ember stiffened. What was that voice?

The Incubus inched closer, trying to edge around Harrison's copy. "Nothing can help them. Their chosen mates are dead. I'm giving them an opportunity to slake their growing, consuming need so their demon doesn't take over right away."

The copy paced him, keeping himself between the Incubus and her.

Deep inside, her demon shifted under her skin, as if woken by her anger. "You can't tell me this is anything other than rape."

Save them.

That voice didn't have the same sneaky quality of Julian's talent.

"Better than them going on a killing spree trying to get what they crave."

Her eyes narrowed. Her whole body shook. "Am I supposed to believe you had nothing to do with their mate's demise?"

He chuckled. "You are a smart one. It's what I do. I create the succubi. Wait until they mate and then I kill the male." He nodded to the couples in the other room. "They're so much more cooperative than human sex slaves."

Of course they were, they needed sex the same way a human needed food. *Let me free. I'll kill them. End the succubi's suffering. Destroy the men dishonoring them.* No, this wasn't Julian. This voice was angry. Insistent. Inside of her.

The incubus' gaze flashed to Harrison's copy and back. "You've made this way too easy. I didn't expect you to hand deliver your mate to me. Yet here he is. Unarmed."

An acute wave of fear shot through her, making the room spin. Was this Adia's plan all along? Was all this an elaborate trap to kill Harrison and use her? She'd walked right into it.

The room blurred and turned red. Her skin prickled as something slithered inside her. She looked at her hands. At the pale blue glow enveloping them. Oh, God, what was happening? Was the incubus doing something to her? Was this her demon?

I'll destroy him. Make him suffer.

Ember relaxed into the rage building under her skin. "Yes. Suffer."

"Did you think Adia would allow you to walk away? You're mine. You still crave sex. Your mate hasn't sated you. I'll make sure you get all you want." He grinned. "With each partner, your need will increase. Without your mate, you'll fuck yourself to death."

He drew his arm back.

The copy pushed her out of the way as the incubus released the scimitar with brutal strength.

The copy jerked, as the tip of the sword burst through his chest, propelling him into the wall and pinning him there.

She grabbed one of the chairs lining the back wall. Raised the piece of furniture with an unfamiliar ease, as if playing a lion tamer to his lion. All the rage, the fear and pain, burst out in a war cry worthy of an Amazonian Princess.

"Suffer, you bastard." She rushed the incubus.

<hr>

Harrison backed away from the Black Tamanous while he loaded a fresh magazine. He'd blinded the creature in one eye; if he could get the other he was gold.

The visions coming from his copy were distracting, though. The scene played out like a movie in the back of his mind. The women being used in the back of the club. The absolute devastation on Ember's face.

He took aim at the Black Tamanous, stopped his retreat and fired. In his mind, he could no longer see what was happening. His copy was pinned, facing the black wall. Even twisting his copy's head he could only catch glimpses. A male screamed. Glass shattered, tinkling on the cement floor. Half-naked men, scurried for their clothes.

Damn it.

The Black Tamanous reared back, lashed out one of its muscled legs and knocked him from his feet. George leapt free. His gun slid across the floor, well out of reach. He still had his knife clutched in one hand, and another on his thigh.

Gods, he needed to get her out of that room. He tried again. *"Ember? Where are you?"* Was she hurt? Is that why she didn't free his copy?

The Black Tamanous stomped forward, forcing him to dodge

its spear-like legs. Beneath each thundering stomp, the concrete floor shattered like glass. He swung out his arm and sliced one of the legs with his blade.

It roared. Another of its legs stomped, pinning him by his shirt and jacket to the floor. Gods, that had been close, a millimeter to the left and that leg would've pierced his arm.

George leapt over him and jumped onto the leg, biting and clawing.

The Black Tamanous' gruesome jaws lunged and he stabbed it. He grabbed his other blade and when the creature dipped his head again he used both blades to slice into the two lobes of its face. Black blood gushed from the wounds and he twisted, trying to avoid it.

George pounced, disappearing over the thing's shoulder.

In his mind, the men in the other room shouted, lunging for the door and then cowering in the back corner of the room. Gods, what the hell was going on in there? "Ember!"

Nothing.

Shit.

Harrison kept one blade in the Black Tamanous to try to keep the thing still. He used the other to stab the hell out of it. He clenched his jaw tight at the feel of the blade puncturing, sliding in, withdrawing and puncturing again. Black blood spattered him.

The Black Tamanous shook its head, rearing back. As soon as it lifted its leg, Harrison jumped to his feet, rammed one of his blades into its underbelly and dragged the blade down. *Gotta get to Ember.*

Black goo oozed out of the creature as it staggered back. Thrashing, it sank back to the ground as its legs shortened back into human-like limbs, the whole mass shuddering and twitching. Unwilling to give the daemon a chance to heal, he leapt on the shrinking form, sinking his blade deep into the Black Tamanous' neck, dragging his blade across until the creature moved no more.

He took two running steps toward the back room, slipped in the Black Tamanous' blood, and landed flat on his back.

Fuck. Way to be a hero, dumb ass.

He sat up, shaking his head to clear it. George ambled over, his mouth covered in black goo, and climbed Harrison's arm to his perch.

"Are you two done screwing about?"

He glanced at Julian. "You look like hell." Black Tamanous blood coated Julian's hair and face.

"Right back at you, asshole." He held his hand out.

Harrison took Julian's hand and he hauled him to his feet. "Ember's alone with the incubus."

CHAPTER 9

October 10, 10:33 PM

HARRISON RAN THROUGH THE BLACK door and into the storage area, flung open the door to the viewing room and froze.

Whoa.

Julian plowed into his back and cussed.

Harrison took in the entire scene at once. His copy faced a corner, pinned to the wall. A thick, curved sword had gone through his chest, pinning him in place. He recalled the copy, taking its energy back into his own body.

A moan drew his attention to the opposite side of the room, where a chair pinned the incubus to the wall. Two of the metal legs had speared straight through him, one in his chest, and the other in his abdomen. The other two legs had sunk deep into the dry wall, holding him in place. Good, the fucker could hang there for a while.

But damn, the strength required to do that . . .

George hopped to the floor and paced below the struggling incubus, growling.

Straight ahead, the glass viewing window had been shattered. Four men huddled together, one was still jerking on his pants. Their wide-eyed stares focused on Ember. Or rather, on the demon in control of her body.

Julian glanced around. "Ho-ly shit."

Ember's blond hair had turned a deep violet. Her clothes, gone. Glittering, violet scales covered her luscious body. Long black nails tipped her fingers. With a sensuous sway to her hips, she made her way around the room, stopping next to one of the bound women. "No more pain." She leaned down, cupped her face and kissed the woman's forehead. She lay the woman's head back on the bed, and moved on to the next. "You're free now."

A small smile graced the woman's chapped lips, but the light had faded from her unblinking stare. Dead. That maybe for the best. He'd heard what the Incubus said, that their mates were gone. Better that they go now, than to go through the slow wasting away. The burning from the inside out.

Still, he didn't like his mate so close to those men. "Em."

Julian pulled him back. "Don't. Not while her demon is in control."

Maybe. He wished he knew more about succubi. About their demons. Once the succubi were taken care of, would she come back to herself?

When she'd finished with the last of the succubi, she turned her focus on the cowering men. Her legs merged into a serpentine tail and she slithered closer, glass tingling under her body. "You dishonored my sisters and your punishment will fit your crime." Her scale-clad breasts heaved as she blew out a long breath, exhaling across the group of terrified men.

What the hell was that? He glanced at Julian who shrugged.

One dark-haired man tried to run. Her arm shot out and she grasped him by the neck, lifting him off his feet. He clawed at her hand with both of his, then held them to his face, staring at his bloody hands. Her scales must be as sharp as tiny blades.

She tsked. "You can't leave. I interrupted your fun. You haven't come yet."

As a whole, their terrified expressions eased. Blissed out. One man with a Borat style mustache, shivered. He looked at the front of his pants as his brows snapped together. A dark, wet spot spread on the front of his trousers. His gaze widened, shooting to Ember.

Harrison's brows snapped together. She was making them

come? They weren't touching themselves. She wasn't touching them.

"Mm. You're just men. I know you can't help yourselves." She grinned. "Again."

The men came, their mouths parting on moans and groans.

"You have no control over your bodies when a beautiful woman is near." Her voice turned hard. "Again."

Concern began to etch into some of their brows, even as their hips jerked and their frames shuddered. The man she held aloft clenched his teeth and this time his moan didn't sound blissful. His muscles bunched as he pulled up his knees and he clutched at his groin as if in pain.

"Jesus." Harrison took a step back. He wasn't certain what she was doing to them, but he didn't want any part of it.

"Again." Her voice was a gunshot echoing in the small room. She dropped the blond male. He curled himself into a ball on the floor, crying.

They were all crying. Clutching themselves as if they could shield their peckers from her wrath. Leaning on the wall. Crumpling to the floor. Screaming.

Harrison's balls tingled. His cock perked to life. Gods, whatever she'd breathed into the room was starting to affect him, too. His gaze shot to Julian. "Get out."

They turned to the exit.

The door slammed shut in their faces. The lock clicked into place and wouldn't budge when he tried. His cock grew hard. Straining. She may not have acknowledged either of them, but Ember's demon knew they were there and didn't seem keen on them leaving. He shared a worried glance with Julian.

He drew in a hard breath and his throat closed, refusing to release it. *Fuck.*

Borat was rocking himself on the floor. Around where his hands put pressure on his groin, the wet splotch on the front of his khaki pants turned a deep maroon. His face twisted into a mask of pain.

Breathe, damn it. Half a breath shuddered out of him and he sucked in a new one.

"Again."

Harrison cupped his hard-on, trying without success to block her spell which seemed to be growing more powerful with her anger. They were trapped. He grit his teeth as the first orgasm rocked through him. He couldn't breathe. Couldn't—He closed his eyes. Pushed out half a breath and sucked in a new one too quickly. His lungs burned. Ached.

Beside him, Julian gasped. Punched him on the arm. "Stop her."

Focus. Breathe.

The men writhed in agony on the floor. All but Borat who stared unblinking at the ceiling. The others were probably wishing they were dead, too.

Harrison took a couple steps toward her, his groin muscles straining with the effort. Drew in air through his nose. Expelled half that though his mouth before he was inhaling again. His whole body started to shake. He wiped the sweat from his brow with his sleeve. His chest ached, his lungs throbbing from the strain.

"Ember, look . . . at me."

Her demon whipped around, those violet locks swinging out in a wide silken arc. Even in demon form she was gorgeous. Sensuality personified. Her long muscular tail flexed as she slithered closer. Her beautiful face didn't fill with recognition, but twisted in rage. Her torso thrust through the viewing window frame, her tail curling over its lip behind her.

Though she no longer spoke, her spell continued, the three remaining men screaming and clutching at themselves.

Breathe.

Her malevolent gaze moved from his to Julian's before dismissing them and locking onto the incubus'. "You don't deserve to live. You don't deserve to be called a male. You're vile."

The incubus' jaw clenched, holding tight to the chair pining him to the wall, his body jerked as blood blossomed on the front of his trousers. Below him, George continued to pace, growling every time the incubus moved.

"Show her the mating band." The incubus shuddered, his voice strained. "Remind her who you are."

Right. Good idea. He got his jacket off but then had to reach out and grasp her arm to steady himself as another fierce orgasm shook him. *Fuck's sake, this was insane.* He jerked his hand away from her razor-edged scales. "Em, you're . . . destroying us, too."

Her eyelids narrowed.

He spoke through a clenched jaw as another malicious orgasm built. "I'm . . . your mate, damn . . . it." He could barely get the words out. Felt like he was suffocating.

She ripped his sleeve off. Her gaze locked onto the golden band on his arm and she reared back, eyes widening.

"You'll . . . destroy . . . yourself, too." He bent forward, mouth open on a silent shout as a horrible release broke. "Ember!"

Breathe. Don't pass out. Not now.

When he looked up, Ember's eye color had changed, returning to their familiar green. "Don't." She gasped. "Don't hurt him." She struggled, her whole body shaking, her hands fisted at her sides. "I'm in control. This is my body."

Her serpent-tail spit into to shapely legs.

The black pointed nails became more human.

A full breath finally shook from his lungs, allowing them to fully deflate before he drew in another breath.

The scales faded until nothing was left but a blue aura. Then, that too, disappeared. Her demon's spell released them from its grasp. A shudder ran though him as his body became his own again. *Breathe.* The air came in and out easier now, but he was winded. He retrieved his jacket from the floor and wrapped the garment around Ember's bare shoulders. Once she was covered, he braced his hands on his knees and focused on regulating his breathing. Damn, that was close. He didn't like how difficult it had been for her to regain control and now she seemed dazed, as if just waking. He untucked his shirt, letting the tails fall over the front of his pants. He straightened and cupped her face in his hands. "You okay, honey?"

Her brow furrowed in confusion and her gaze kept sliding to where the incubus was pinned to the wall. "W-what happened?" She shook, her teeth chattering.

He cupped her head in his hands. Kissed her forehead. "Your demon took over."

"The women." She swung away from him and he drew her back. Pulled her into his embrace. She didn't need to see what her demon had done.

"They're at peace, Em. We'll have a team come put them to

rest." George growled deep in his throat, drawing his attention to the incubus who still writhed where her demon had pinned him to the wall. His features were contorted in agony but Harrison had no sympathy for the bastard. "Where's the girl? Madison?"

When he didn't answer, Julian pulled away from the wall he was leaning against, strode over and angled a punch through the chair legs right where that bright red splotch blossomed on the front of his trousers. The incubus howled. Julian wiped his knuckles on the incubus' shirt. "We can make the pain last as long as you want, dickhead."

The incubus tried to speak but couldn't; tears flowed down his face.

Julian lifted his Guardian blade. "I'll make it quick. You know you won't get such an offer from Adia. She'll make all this seem like a walk in the park. Where's the girl?"

"We don't . . . don't deal in girls. Mistress' rules."

Ember stepped out of his embrace. "Adia took her. She said she wouldn't give her back until I brought Harrison here."

The incubus smiled. "You're gullible. We returned her. The little brat was more trouble than she was worth. She's snug in her new home by now."

"He's lying." Ember lunged out of his arms, angling for the incubus.

Harrison pulled her back. "We've got this, Em." He had no doubt the son of a bitch was lying. "You expect us to take your word for it?"

"Adia wanted her." The incubus' pain-filled gaze flicked to Ember. "Wanted to use her to torture you. That's all. You know how she likes her mind games. She has no interest in girls. They can't be changed to succubi and they're too temperamental and unpredictable to control." He sneered at Harrison. "Boys are easier, aren't they?"

Harrison's gut twisted. "Where's Adia?"

The incubus shook his head. "I know when she's here, not where she goes when she's not. She's got a hard on for you, though. She's gonna destroy everything you ever loved."

Julian made a threatening gesture with his blade.

The incubus laughed.

Harrison glanced around at the destruction. "You think this is funny?"

"No. What's funny is that you two don't have a clue what you're in for." He nodded toward Ember. "She's not fully sated. Before too long, she's gonna tear you two into pieces." His gaze toggled between him and Julian.

Bullshit. The bastard was useless. Harrison turned away, pulling Em along with him. "Ash him, Jules."

━━◆━━

"She's gotta be here!" Ember slipped out of Harrison's grasp and crawled through the window frame, pausing to stare at the destruction in the room.

"Damn it, Em." Glass crunched behind her as Harrison followed.

There were more doors. More rooms. She wasn't leaving unt—

The women were dead. The men—they didn't look like they went as peacefully as the succubi. The succubi died smiling, whereas the male's bodies were contorted. Their faces twisted into masks of pain.

Dear God, had she done this? She remembered the rage building inside her when the incubus attacked Harrison's copy, but none of what came after. She remembered wanting them to suffer.

She spied her purse, which seemed to be all in one piece. Oh, thank God. She grabbed out her jeans, pulling them on under Harrison's jacket, turned her back on the men and dragged her sweater over her head.

Harrison took her hand, his expression full of concern. "Em, come out of there. We'll search all the rooms."

"No." She stepped out of reach, trying to block out the destruction around her as she dusted off the bottom of her foot and pulled on her shoe. She had a job to do. "I don't trust him. She's here." She put the other shoe on and glanced around.

There were two other doors in the room. She went to the closest, but before she opened it, he stopped her.

"Let me. If she's in there. . . . there might be a guard."

A guard? No, he was worried about the condition they'd find Madison in, not a guard. Still, a fissure of apprehension slid through her and she nodded, motioning him in ahead of her.

He opened the door, sweeping the room with his weapon. Something out of her line of sight captured his attention. He glanced at Ember, his expression inscrutable and he put his gun in his holster. Checked the time on his watch. When he faced forward again, he plastered a smile on his face. "Hiya, honey."

"Who are you?"

A breath shuddered out of her. She recognized that voice and the relief that roared through her left her light-headed. She braced her hand on the doorjamb. "Madison."

He touched Ember's arm, leaned close, and whispered in her ear. "She's still human."

Something eased inside her. She nodded, blinking back tears. *They found her. She was safe. She was alive.*

"Stay put until I clear the room." He moved deeper into the room and Ember, too impatient to wait poked her head around the doorframe to peek inside.

The small space was decorated for a princess with pink walls and swirls of rainbow-colored glitter. A daybed covered in pristine white ruffles filled one end of the room. Stuffed animals and dolls crowded together on the plush bed. Madison sat at a table, dressed in that same creepy dress—the one that reminded her of a first communion gown. Her hair had been brushed and divided into two neat pigtails. She appeared clean—immaculate—and, if the small feast in front of her was any indication, she'd been fed well, but this whole set-up was creepy as fuck. She was used to seeing Madison in torn jeans and concert tee-shirts with her hair loose and messy around her shoulders.

"How are you, Madison?" He leaned against the wall, as if they were having a normal conversation in a normal setting. She loved how calm he was. It couldn't be easy.

"Who are you?" Madison gave him a side-eye look.

"My name's Detective Sinclair. I'm a policeman and I'm gonna get you out of here, okay?"

Madison wasn't softening, so Ember stepped into the room. "Hi, Madison. Remember me?"

She let out a sigh and slumped in her seat. "Miss Moon? They told me you died." Tears welled in her eyes.

"Nope. I'm fine, honey."

At the sight of her tears, some of Harrison's calm façade cracked.

He straightened. "Did they hurt you? Do you need—"

"No, they left me alone in here except to bring me food. They're all freaking creepy, though."

The girl looked good. Healthy. Just uncomfortable, whether because of where she was, the dress or a combination of the two. Ember smiled. "That's quite a look for you."

"I hate this." Madison tugged at the high neckline of the dress. "Can I get my clothes back?" Madison sniffed and her voice quavered. "I really want to get out of here."

"We're going." She glanced at Harrison and nodded. "Just think, you've got your new foster parents waiting for you. I'm sure they've been going out of their minds."

Madison nodded. Her lips wobbled and she put her hand in front of her face. "I don't even know them well and I've been missing them."

Harrison dropped to his haunches in front of her. "If you'll trust me, I'll carry you out." He nodded toward the door. "There's lots of glass and stuff out there."

Ember's gaze dropped to the floor—Madison's feet were bare.

When she nodded, he scooped her up and stood. "Good job. Now, I'll need you to keep your eyes shut real tight."

Madison looked at Ember with hesitation. Poor girl, it'd be a while before she trusted people again.

"You can trust him. He's a good guy."

The girl shut her eyes and Harrison strode past with Madison.

Ember glanced around the room again trying to figure out why the decor creeped her out. There was nothing bad here. Everything looked and smelled clean. It was perfect. Like a dollhouse for a small child.

She shivered.

CHAPTER 10

October 11, 6:47 AM

IT HAD BEEN A LONG, emotional night. She spent a long while with Madison, chatting. By the grace of God, despite the creepy room and weird clothing, Ember didn't see any of the tell-tale signs that anyone had touched or harmed the girl. Madison was shaken and upset, but she'd work thought it. They'd handed Madison over to Seattle P.D., and Ember had spoken to her boss—ex-boss now that she'd disclosed she was a daemon—and updated him on the case. By this time tomorrow, Madison would be with her new family.

And, she'd learned a valuable lesson tonight. If her daemon took over, whatever she was wearing was toast. She was going to have to start carrying extra clothes, at least until she figured out how to control her demon.

When they returned home, Lucas was sitting on the stairs, his big brown eyes widening when they walked through the door minutes before dawn. "Dude, did you guys get in a fight?"

Harrison chuckled. "Yeah, kid."

Lucas' gaze raked over the three of them. "You lose?"

The three of them did look like hell, covered in cuts and bruises and glass. Ember chuckled.

Julian shook his head. "Nah, you should see what's left of the other guys."

Ember smacked him on the shoulder. "Don't encourage him."

"You should take my offer." Lucas hopped to his feet. "I can keep an eye on your place while you get some rest." Lucas held his hand out to her. "They've been being rude. I'm Lucas."

She grinned as she shook his hand. "Hi, Lucas. I'm Ember."

"You need help taking care of these two?" He glanced around her to the men again. "Or giving George a bath?"

He was sweet, always trying to help. "I think we're going to be all right. Thanks for the offer, though."

"What's that black shit?" Lucas scrunched his face. "Should he be eating that?"

She followed them into the elevator and glanced at George. Sure enough, the minion had curled himself on Harrison's shoulder and had a rear leg stretched out while he licked the black daemon blood off his scales. "He'll be okay."

The doors were sliding shut, when he blurted out, "A daemon came earlier."

Harrison's hand shot out and stopped the doors from closing. He got out of the elevator, tugging her along with him. "Who?"

Lucas shrugged. "He's never been here before. Doesn't live here. He's not part of housekeeping."

"Can you give us a description?" Jules folded his arms over his chest. "You're sure you didn't see Scott or Duncan or one of the males from DDC?"

Did he think this was connected to Adia?

Lucas snorted. "Nah, nobody that's been here before. This guy wasn't a vampire or an Oni." His brow furrowed. "I'm pretty quick at identifying daemons; you guys taught me some good tricks. This guy, he was real big, like a pro wrestler, with red hair and a ZZ Top beard. He spoke like your father does when he's getting pissed." Lucas directed the last to Harrison, and Ember tucked the snippet of information away for later.

Julian leaned back against the elevator doors to keep them from closing. "He's a Cockney, like Duncan?"

"Think so." Lucas' studied the ceiling while he thought. "Dropped some of his letters when he sang."

The men exchanged a glance. "He was singing?"

"Yeah. Yeah." Lucas appeared ready to bounce out of his socks, despite the topic he seemed excited to have the men's attention. "He got in the elevator, but he never went anywhere. Weird, right? The numbers never changed. He stayed in there about fifteen minutes and then the doors opened and he left."

"Anything else?" Harrison took Lucas by the shoulders. "This is important."

"He had a box with him, or maybe a cage."

"What did it look like?"

"I didn't see much. Small, like this." He held his hands out to indicate a box about six inches square. "Covered with a white cloth." Lucas frowned. "I messed up, didn't I? I should have gotten closer."

"Nah, man." Harrison slapped him on the back. "You did excellent. Agents need to balance safety with surveillance. How 'bout you come by Friday night and we'll watch a movie, okay?"

Lucas grinned. "Yeah? What are we going to watch? Can we have popcorn? Pizza?" His face fell. "Oh wait, you guys don't eat."

"I do." Ember piped up. "I love popcorn. With lots of butter." She winked. "You and I can share."

His cheeks tinted pink. "Yeah, all right."

"Think about the movie, Lucas." Julian ruffled his hair. "You did real good. You should pick."

"Cool. I've been wanting to see that new Stephen King flick." He started to walk away, then turned to walk backward. "You all be careful, okay?"

Julian rolled his eye. "Don't worry, man. We won't get ourselves ashed before Friday. You make sure it's okay with your parents. They're welcome to come, too."

"They've been busy, so they probably won't come, but they won't mind if I do."

The elevator doors slid shut and Ember looked at Harrison. "I didn't realize Seattle offered mixed-living units." In some places across the country there were buildings where both humans and daemons could live together in the poorer areas where not everyone could afford the rent in an exclusively human or daemon building.

He shared an inscrutable glance with Julian and looked away. "They don't."

Then how was he here? "Is he always hanging around?"

"Yeah."

Neither of them would look at her.

It didn't seem right for Lucas to be roaming at night and hanging around with daemons. The only reasonable explanation was that his parents were daemon. If his parents had been transformed and the State found out, they'd remove Lucas from the home. Considering he hung out in this building every night, it seemed a likely scenario. Another thing to add to her overwhelming list of depressing revelations for the evening. Legally, it would be their responsibility to notify the authorities. However, now that she'd spent time in the company of daemons, she wasn't so sure anymore that doing so would be morally right.

"Look." Harrison sighed. "The company that owned the building sold it to the DDC. What they didn't mention is that the humans that provided the maintenance for the building owned their apartment."

Julian leaned against the elevator wall. "The Zhang's are good people. They're not prejudice against daemons. Didn't have any qualms about working for the DDC."

Thank God, at least they were human. "So Lucas' parents work for the DDC and live here?"

"Yeah. Lucas' dad does all the maintenance in the building. His mom cleans. The DDC made them sign all kinds of hold harmless agreements, but since there currently aren't any laws against humans and daemons working together—or humans not getting the same benefits packages as a daemon would..." He shrugged. "So far, they've slipped under the radar.'"

"Then again," Julian shrugged, "they may just not have noticed the Zhang's are here with a kid."

Harrison wet his lips. "I'd appreciate it if you didn't say anything."

Her lips parted. He thought she'd turn them in? She shook her head. "I wouldn't. He's a great kid." She had to look away from the suspicion in his gaze. Why shouldn't he be? A week ago, if she'd found out about Lucas, she'd have done everything in her power to get him and his parents out of the building—she'd been ignorant. Had believed all the government's anti-daemon propaganda like a good little sheep. "What about the daemon he saw?"

Julian shrugged. "Could be nothing. A friend or relative stopping by to visit someone in the building." He kept his tone casual, but the look he shared with Harrison suggested he didn't trust the stranger's appearance.

Once upstairs, they both pulled out their sidearms. "Wait here, Em. Let us check the place out."

She waited by the elevator with George for protection while they searched the apartment and with nothing to do, her mind returned to the back room of The Knot Works. She kept picturing the incubus pinned to the wall. The men, lying motionless on the floor. Those poor women.

She didn't remember allowing her demon to take over, just the rage, the feeling of impotency. She kind of remembered a voice. The writhing entity in her belly. Now she had to live with the fact that she'd killed. Tremors wracked through her. She didn't want anyone to see her like this so she headed straight for the shower in Harrison's room and scrubbed herself until her skin turned pink. Then she scrubbed some more until the water turned cold.

She dried off, got dressed, and then sat on the closed toilet, staring at the towel hanging across from her. Part of her wanted to cry, but the tears wouldn't come, which made her feel worse. Why couldn't she cry? What was wrong with her?

She was thrilled to have recovered Madison. Depressed that she'd lost her job just because she was a daemon. Then again, she supposed her termination was justified. She'd lost control tonight, killed a room full of people and didn't even remember. What if she'd hurt Madison, too? Or Harrison. Or Julian. She shivered. This time, the shakes stuck. Her whole body trembled and her belly roiled.

Still, the tears, the remorse she should feel, wouldn't come. Just the empty knowledge she *should* feel those things.

Worse, her body was primed for sex despite all that had transpired, despite the shakes. She shifted, crossing her legs and pressing them together to try to sooth the building ache. She hated this. Despised the fact she had so little control over her libido. Would that ever change?

"Em?" Harrison rapped on the door and then cracked it open. "Ember?"

He must've used the bathroom in the spare bedroom because he was bare-chested and his hair was damp. Despite the colorful bruises he sported, he looked good enough to eat. Her breast tingled, her nipples tightening into hard little nubs against her nightgown.

"We searched the house. Nothing's here." He tipped his head toward the bedroom. "I've got some tea for you."

"Mm, thanks." She combed her fingers through her hair. "You should warn your neighbors about the intruder."

"Jules is taking care of that." He opened the door wider and leaned against the doorjamb. "You expended a lot of energy this morning. Do you need me?"

God, yes. At his offer, the tingling heat changed into a deep throbbing need. How easy would it be to pretend she hadn't killed those people and lose herself in pleasure? Too easy. Except her heart and mind didn't agree with her body. Not after what happened. Not knowing how difficult Harrison must find this whole situation. He didn't trust her yet. She needed to give him more time.

She shifted, trying to alleviate the ache between her thighs. "I murdered nine people this morning. I'm not in the mood."

"Eight. Jules destroyed the last one."

She glanced away.

He came in, picked her up, and carried her to the bedroom without a word. She leaned her face against his shoulder, breathing him in, a heady blend of Calvin Klein and Harrison's own unique scent.

"You'll be okay, Em." He paused long enough to pull back the covers and deposited her in bed. He drew the sheets around her, and knelt on the floor as he checked the time on his watch. "Killing is never easy, whether they're human or daemon, good guys or bad."

"How do you live with it?"

"I try to think of killing as a necessary evil." He inhaled a deep breath and let it out slowly. "I can shoulder the burden of taking that one life, or accept responsibility for all the lives they might ruin."

She nodded. His answer was logical, but too simple to quell the emotions whirling inside her.

He cupped her cheek in his big hand. "I know that's not a perfect answer, but it's the best one I've got."

She pressed deeper into his palm. "I didn't have control. I felt as if someone else managed my body."

"Your demon had control. She was stronger than you."

"What if she takes over again?" She gripped his wrist. "What if I hurt you or Jules?"

He tugged out of her grasp and took her hand into both of his. "Neither Jules nor I would do anything to trigger your demon. Based on what I witnessed tonight, your demon protects women. So do we. Both of us have dedicated ourselves to preventing human trafficking and child sex tourism. I can't imagine she'd want to stop us from continuing our mission."

A simple answer. One she wasn't sure she agreed with. She wasn't sure her demon would be so logical. "I don't even remember. I saw those women and I was furious. The incubus said he wanted to destroy you and make me like them. He attacked your copy, pinned him against the wall. That's it. Next thing I knew you were there. What did I do to them?"

His gaze slid away. "It doesn't matter." He took a steaming mug from the nightstand. "Drink some tea." He held the mug out to her.

As she brought the cup to her lips she inhaled the sharp scent of spirits. "What kind of tea is this?"

"Earl Grey." The corner of his mouth tipped up. "With a healthy dose of rum."

She sipped from the cup, wincing when she swallowed. "Trying to get me drunk?"

He smiled. "I was aiming for calm. I thought the rum might help you sleep today."

Sleep would be long in coming. They still had so much work to do. They were no closer to finding Adia. "What about Adia? The incubus gave us nothing."

"I didn't expect he would. The DDC is going over the club with a fine-tooth comb. We'll find something. She'll have left a clue behind. She wants me to find her."

The resignation in his voice bothered her. "Why?"

"I never let her break me." He gave her a forced smiled. "Drink more."

When she put the mug to her lips, he tipped it with his finger. She glared at him while taking a healthy gulp and then grimaced.

He grinned. "You're tired." He tucked her damp hair behind her ear and stroked his knuckles along her jaw. "I want to make sure you rest."

She leaned into the caress trying to ignore her body's heightened state of arousal and focus on the comfort he offered. "I like when you touch me."

His Adam's apple bobbed as he swallowed. What was she doing? Even that little compliment made him uncomfortable. She pulled away.

"Are you sure you don't need me?"

God, yes. She wanted his arms around her. To feel him deep inside her. She needed him to love her until he erased all the ugliness she'd seen.

Her demon pressed against her skin, seeking a connection with him. Needing him.

But his hand was shaking as he took the mug and set it on the nightstand.

"I'm all right. I'll be fine after I sleep."

A little sigh escaped him. "How about some food first?"

"No." She smiled, though all she wanted to do was cry. "Only sleep."

CHAPTER 11

October 11, 11:18 PM

EMBER STOOD WITH JULIAN IN a long corridor at the DDC, while Harrison knocked on Agent Scott Mason's door. George clung to his back like one of those character backpacks some of her young clients liked to wear. "You wanted to see me?"

"Yeah." The DDC director's voice was brisk and all business. "Is your mate with you?"

Harrison nodded.

"Bring her and Jules in here and shut the door."

Oh, God. Were they in trouble? Was he upset she'd gone with Julian and Harrison to The Knot Works?

Harrison gave her hand a reassuring squeeze and motioned for them to precede him into the office.

The room was large enough for a more casual sitting area off to one side, as well as a couple chairs facing the overcrowded desk. The man sitting behind the stacks of files and papers scribbled notes on a legal pad. He was the older man she remembered from before—the one who'd pulled Harrison away while Julian questioned her the first morning. He finished and set his pen aside.

He stood and extended his hand to her. "You can call me Scott."

Straight to the point. She liked that. She shook his hand. "Ember."

"You can call her Em." Julian nudged her. "Or Emerald Eyes."

Scott smirked. "Glad the three of you are getting along." He motioned to the sitting area. "Why don't we have a seat?"

Harrison sat and pulled her down next to him. "Are we getting backlash from the Fremont case?"

Scott shook his head. "For what? Taking care of what Seattle PD didn't?" He sat with a sigh. "No. We've got other problems."

"What?"

"I wanted to chat with your mate first." Scott smiled at Ember. "I heard you're a social worker. Is that true?"

She folded her hands in her lap, forcing herself not to fidget under his stare. "Yes. I work with foster placement." She shook her head. "*Worked* with foster placement, I should say."

"Have you done any other work?"

Why was this starting to sound like an interview? "I did my internship at a women's shelter."

"What kind?"

"Domestic violence mostly. Sometimes we'd get rape victims who needed a place to stay until they got comfortable with the idea of going home."

"Thank God." He sat back in his chair. "So you've done some counseling?"

Harrison leaned forward. "What's this all about?"

"Couple things. First, we're getting a lot of heat right now with the picketers out on the street. Now that the threat of Nephilim attacks are lower, they're starting to think they don't need us."

That wasn't anything new. For months now, the news had been reporting about groups lobbying to have the DDC shut down.

"All the DDC branches are getting picketed." Julian snorted. "They'll stop as soon as we get hit by a group of Nephilim again and they're forced to remember why they need us."

"I agree." Scott steepled his fingers. "Thing is, our lucky little department is getting national coverage."

Harrison and Julian both swore.

In the past, when the press singled out a specific DDC office, it was to report on corruption within. Was this department corrupt? "Why?"

"Does she know?" Scott jerked his chin toward her, but his gaze remained on Harrison.

Ember's gaze flew to Scott's. Then to Harrison and Julian, who both shook their heads. "Know what?"

Harrison cleared his throat. "She's still acclimating to her new status. Give her a little time."

"You're right. I spoke out of turn." Scott smiled at her before turning his assessing gaze to Julian and jerked his head toward the window. "They've noticed your presence here."

Ember shifted in her seat. "Why would they care? Is this because his brother was the Harbinger?"

"You're a smart lady." Scott nodded. "Because a human child was associated with the case last night, the human authorities demanded to know who from our department was involved in the rescue." His gaze bore into Julian's. "Your name caught someone's attention and they went straight to the news stations. They've guessed your talent based on your brother's."

Always living in the shadow of his notorious brother must be miserable. "That's not fair. He shouldn't be held accountable for what his brother did."

Scott shrugged. "Sometimes perception is everything." His attention returned to Julian. "Right?"

Julian leaned forward. "Jesus, Scott, don't bench me." He raked his fingers through his hair and slouched in his seat. "I'll go out of my fucking mind."

"I'm not benching you, but people higher on the food chain want to cover their asses. They want a second set of eyes on you. If I want to keep you, I have to make them feel safe."

Julian let his head drop back onto the edge of the couch. "This is getting ridiculous."

"They wanted Deno."

Was he nuts? That was the Oni at the front desk that was always razzing Julian. Nothing good could come from him being assigned to Julius.

"Hell, no," Harrison said at the same time Julian burst out with, "No fucking way."

"I suggested due to the nature of your current caseload, adding a trained social worker to your team might be more of an asset. She can assure them Julian isn't using his mesmerist talent outside an official capacity and assist with the victims you come across in your investigations."

Harrison's hand landed on her knee. "I don't want her involved."

She scoffed. "I already am."

"You have a job." He frowned.

Had he not been paying attention? "They fired me."

His lips parted. "Why?"

"Daemons aren't allowed to work with human children in any capacity, remember?" She had to make a living somehow. She couldn't pass by this opportunity.

He lifted his hand and raked his fingers through his hair. "Yeah, but they could've kept you on in another capacity. You could've done paperwork or parent advocating or something."

Scott cleared his throat. "Son, the thing is we found something in the Fremont club—a couple invitations for a very exclusive auction on Camano Island."

Harrison's gaze sharpened. "The auction? You're gonna let us go after them?"

The older man nodded. "Depending on what you find, Ember could help you out."

They seemed to be speaking a different language. Were they planning on explaining? "What auction? How could someone with my training help?"

Julian leaned forward. "It could be nothing more than a swinger's club, but we have intel they're auctioning off humans. We've been itching to bust this place for a while."

"Exactly." Scott pressed his fingers together into a steeple. "The women I suspect we'll find will be traumatized. They'll need someone to talk to. It's the one thing we're lacking in the DDC—trained counselors."

Okay, that was different than what she'd done, but she liked the idea. "Would this be a paid position?"

Scott grinned. "Oh, yeah."

She liked the idea of having a purpose again. Of having a job. Maybe her training could still be put to use after all.

"If the incubus had an invitation, you can bet they're selling humans and you can bet Adia's involved." Harrison sat back in his seat. "He struck me as the type to be selective in who he chose to transform."

"I'll take the job." She turned her attention to Scott. "When do we leave for Camano Island?

Harrison's hand tightened over hers. "Ember—"

"Her or Deno." Scott winked. "Your choice, son."

Julian scowled. "I'm not working with Deno, Harry."

"I spoke to Ember's boss. She'll be perfect for this."

She met Harrison's gaze. "I can do this. I want to do this."

He released a heavy sigh. "Guess that's settled." Harrison glanced at his watch. "When do we go?"

Her and Scott shared a victorious grin. She was employed!

"Tomorrow night." Scott pulled the invitations from his pocket and handed them to Harrison. "Take tonight to get a plan together and head out at dusk tomorrow. We'll have an extraction team nearby just in case."

The men started to rise, but Ember wasn't finished. "Wait, what about the humans? Have arrangements been made for them?"

Scott raised his brow in question.

"Beds in a local shelter. Human councilors. Translators. Food, clothing, and medical, if needed. Maybe packs with toiletries—nothing expensive, but something that they can hold onto, something that's theirs to keep. That's important."

"See, Sinclair. She's what we need." He nodded to Ember. "I'll have Deno make the arrangements."

She smiled. For the first time in days, someone needed her.

⬥

On the walk home, Harrison and Julian briefed her on what to expect at the auction raid and some of her excitement started to fade. What they expected to find in that place was awful. Going there, witnessing people selling other human beings . . . There would be an emotional toll from doing this kind of work.

"Remember none of the women being sold will leave with their buyer. They'll leave with us." Julian shrugged. "Remembering that helps."

"I'll get you a weapon." Harrison glanced at her. "Have you ever done any target practice?" He shook his head. "Of course you haven't."

Now who was making assumptions? "I have. Some of the places I had to go were pretty rough. First day on my own I walked into a house where a father was holding his wife and son at gunpoint. I've had a carry concealed permit ever since."

He grinned. "You any good?"

She lifted her chin. "I'm a fair shot."

Julian's phone rang. He dug the device out of his pocket while they walked and answered. "Hello?"

A woman's voice yelled through the phone.

Julian stopped.

At the same time Harrison's hand flew to his head. He doubled over for a second. "Okay. Yeah, got it, Trina. Get the hell out of my head so I can think."

Ember froze. That first night Harrison had told her that Trina was Duncan's mate—the witch. If she was setting off the alarm in his mind, it must be something bad. Her gaze darted around the deserted street.

He straightened, his attention focused on the shadows around them.

Julian lowered the phone. "Get her away from the buildings."

Harrison backed into the center of the street, his arm extended and pushing her back, too.

She fisted her hands in his jacket. "What's wrong?" She didn't know why she asked. She knew. The Nephilim were coming.

"We need to get home." Harrison turned and gripped her hand in his. His gaze met hers. "Run."

He broke into a sprint along the center of the street and she had no choice but to follow. Julian hung back a little, then caught up, pacing her on the other side. "She should have a blade, Harry."

"I know." But Harrison's attention stayed on the darkened entries and alleyways.

She squeezed his hand. "The Nephilim are coming, aren't they?"

The city's tsunami alarms wailed. Lights flicked on in the darkened windows around them as people came to their windows.

Behind them, something snarled. She tried to turn and look, but Harrison jerked her arm. "Don't."

"Pick up the pace, guys."

Ember pumped her legs as fast as she could. She wasn't used to running and was losing steam. Her breath came in hard gulps. Her heart tried to pound free of her rib cage. Not far, now. She could see the building.

Up ahead, outlines of what looked like a group of very large people came into view.

Harrison's pace slowed.

Stopped.

They were between them and the building. They couldn't make it.

They needed to get inside. Like vampires, Nephilim couldn't enter a dwelling without express permission. She glanced around at the windows. The people staring down at them. "Can we go in one of these other buildings?"

Harrison met her gaze. Shook his head.

Of course not. They were daemons and the humans watching wouldn't risk themselves to help.

Next to her, Julian spoke into his phone. "We're surrounded, Kat. Two blocks from DDC on First. Yeah, we can see the front door to the apartments from here. Love you, butterfly."

Harrison pushed her behind him and Julian covered her back. They drew their blades.

"Duncan is on duty. They're sending him and a couple of witches."

"Good. How long?"

"They're using the Travelers' spell. Five minutes, tops."

It was too dark to see anything more than the outlines of the Nephilim, but their animalistic snarls, grunts, and snorts made gooseflesh rise over her skin.

Harrison nudged her and she looked down. He handed her his gun.

"I got one over here."

She turned, looking around Julian's shoulder.

The creature came into view under a street lamp. Human at one time, the Nephilim looked stretched—its body bulked with unnatural muscle mass. The Nephilim stared at them through yellow eyes, sniffing the air.

"Ember." Harrison's back brushed against hers. "If we get bit, you know what to do, right?"

One bite and the victim would become a Nephilim—a corrupted daemon with no conscience, only an insatiable desire to feed.

Her hands began to shake. "I'll use your blade on you, Harry." Because no one wished to add to the Nephilim's numbers. No one wanted to become like them.

The Nephilim standing beneath the streetlight opened its mouth and let loose a war cry.

She clicked the safety off on Harrison's gun. Bullets wouldn't destroy these creatures, but she might slow them a bit.

It loped forward with an uneven gait.

Behind her, Harrison tensed, reminding her of the group of Nephilim he faced. They must be coming, too.

When the Nephilim got close, Julian ran toward it.

A scream built in her throat.

At the last second, Julian turned, bringing his blade around and sinking the knife into the creature's shoulder. It dissolved into ash.

Behind her, Harrison jerked away.

She turned. He ran into the midst of a whole pack. As he neared the first, he threw his blade.

The Nephilim he hit dissolved to ash.

Without pausing, he somersaulted on the ground, grabbing the blade and sliced into another creature's leg.

He moved fast, but there were too many.

Ember lifted the gun, aimed at the closest Nephilim to Harrison and fired. Took aim at another and—

A bright light drew her attention. She looked over as a woman appeared. Another flash to her left delivered a man. Then, another woman.

Armed for battle, they joined the fight.

Help had arrived.

Bolts of fire streaked across the sky as the witches cast their spells. The fire balls exploded on contact with the Nephilim, setting them aflame.

"Get to the apartment, Em." Harrison shouted the command.

"I don't know the damn code." She aimed the gun and hit another Nephilim sneaking up on Harrison.

"Good shot." Julian stuck something into her jacket pocket and ran into the melee.

It was his sidearm and extra ammo.

Slowly, she walked toward the fight, her heart hammering in her chest. She must've lost her mind. That was the only reason to get closer to those things. She kept her sights trained near Harrison, taking shots at anything close to him. Lifted her arm long enough to wipe the sweat from her brow and aimed at another Nephilim.

As she began to pull the trigger, George leapt onto the thing's face. "Shit."

George kept it blinded, covering its eyes, while Harrison stabbed it.

Behind her, something growled. She spun, but the creature was almost on top of her. It knocked the gun from her hand and she scrambled backward. In her haste to get away, she fell.

A daemon tackled the Nephilim, sinking his blade into the creature's skull. It dissolved into ash before they even hit the asphalt. The male hit the ground, rolled, and got to his feet. He walked over, and gave her a hand to her feet. "Gotta watch your back, love."

He ran off, too, into the midst of the fight.

You almost died.

Shaking so hard she feared falling, she pulled Julian's gun from her pocket. She aimed for the first Nephilim her rescuer would encounter. Shot the creature in the head, giving him an extra second or two to ash it.

He turned around and winked.

While she reloaded, she walked forward, keeping her gaze on Harrison. He was nothing short of amazing. He showed no fear while he fought, his movements graceful and deadly. The Nephilim seemed to notice, too.

They swarmed around him, clawing and snarling.

She lifted her weapon and fired at the creatures, buying him more time.

There were fewer now. The man who'd helped her went to Harrison's aide. He ashed two Nephilim and when Harrison swung around to confront who was at his back, the man scowled. "Get her in the flat, pup. We got this."

Pup?

Harrison glanced over his shoulder at Ember, motioned for her to come. She ran, but her gaze locked onto the other daemon, trying to get a better look. He must be the one who'd raised Harrison. He dropped some of his letters, just the way Lucas had said. Cockney.

He grabbed her hand and ran with her to the apartment building. Lucas waited inside and opened the door. His eyes widened as they closed the door behind them. "You guys were slick as shit. That was fucking insane."

Harrison cuffed the back of his head. "Watch your mouth."

George stood on his shoulder, his paws braced on his head. He leaned forward, watching the action outside, his tail twitching in agitation.

"I wish I could kill the Harbinger all over again." She stared out the window, her heart in her throat as Julian narrowly avoided one of the Nephilim's claws. "What the hell was his brother thinking to release these creatures on Earth?"

"It wasn't Julius."

She swung her head around to gape. He was going to defend the Harbinger? Even Lucas dragged his gaze from the window to stare.

"It wasn't. Julius was possessed by a being much stronger than him. You know what that's like, Em."

"That's not what the news said." She shook her head.

"Of course not." He dragged his hand through his hair. "You want to know what happened? A Watcher—one of the two hundred fallen angels—who happened to have a vendetta against mankind *possessed* Julius Crowley. The sick twist in all of this is that he couldn't have succeeded in creating the Nephilim without the aid of a human bio-weapons lab. The DOD hid that little fact real quick. After the first week, any mention of the lab disappeared. They blamed the whole thing on the biggest victim in the whole scenario—Julius. Daemon kind stepped into the fray because humans couldn't handle the Nephilim. In return for allowing us to help, the government demanded Crowley's ash. They didn't give a shit that he was innocent, they just wanted to show they were in control."

She wet her lips. She didn't want to believe him, but God knew the government was quick to cover their own asses. And being possessed . . .? She understood the sense of helplessness that accompanied that. What if what he said was true? Had they sacrificed the wrong man? "Now Julian suffers for it. Is that why you have to keep an eye on him?"

Tight-lipped, he turned away. There was more to this, she was sure. If she hadn't freaked out upon learning he was a vampire, this might be easier. Now, though, he took everything she said as prejudice. So why would he want to trust her with his secrets? Or Julian's? He probably feared she'd judge him, like she had everything else.

"He's coming. Don't say anything about this around him."

"I won't." She shook her head, her chest aching a little that he thought she would. "I didn't know. I'd *never* say anything to hurt Julian." Or you. God, if she knew more about them, if he'd *talk* to her, she might have half a chance at not sticking her foot in her mouth again.

He searched her face and nodded. "Thanks."

Only a couple Nephilim were left when Julian walked to the building. She pushed the door open.

"Thanks, Emerald Eyes." He looked at Harrison. "They're wrapping up. Duncan will come up in a minute." He walked to the elevator and punched a button.

Harrison took her hand and followed. "Lucas, you wait until sunrise to go out. Do you need to stay with us until then?"

The kid shook his head. "I'll head upstairs in a minute after I let Duncan in."

"Okay. Be safe."

They all got into the elevator.

She looked at Harrison. "Is Duncan the one who raised you?"

"Yeah. He's—"

Julian nudged her with his elbow, grinning. "He's the big dog."

Harrison's lip curled. "Fuck off, Crowley."

Ember looked over each of them. Julian had claw marks on his neck. Harrison's jaw had been nicked. Both of them were covered in ash.

She put her hand on his arm, trying to offer a little comfort, but he captured her hand in his. He wasn't ready to accept even that tiny physical contact. "Can I do anything for you?"

He shook his head. "Itches more than anything. Once I clean up, it'll be fine."

She looked away. Of course he didn't want her help. He'd be required to suffer through her touch. She didn't want to push him, or cause him more pain, but how would she ever get him to trust her, when he couldn't seem to lower his guard long enough to give her a chance?

When the elevator doors opened she was the first out. She took a seat at the kitchen counter and lectured herself. She needed to be patient. To show him through her trust, he could trust her, too.

Both men entered the kitchen. Julian opened a cupboard and took out a jar. Harrison grabbed a couple towels out of another and tossed one to Julian. She blanched when Harrison turned around to wet his towel in the sink. His jacket and shirt were both shredded.

Ember skirted around the island and approached him. "Harry, take off your jacket."

He glanced at her while he rubbed the soapy towel against his jaw.

"Can't you feel your back? At least let me look." She took the towel out of his hand and swiped the clean edge over his jaw to wipe away the soap.

With his jaw clenched tight, he pulled off his jacket and winced. "Didn't notice before. I guess I'll need some help after all."

She smiled. "You must have a lot of adrenaline pumping through you."

He took off his shirt and gave her his back. She gasped. Four long, deep slashes crossed his muscular back from shoulder blade to hip. "This might hurt a bit."

"Better than having it itch. Clean it out good, Em."

As she cleaned the wound Julian came around to have a look. "Damn man, you're losing your touch."

Harrison snorted. "Like you came out of this one unscathed."

Julian scoffed and walked away. "I'd better go call Kat and let her know everything's good."

"You're being too gentle, Em." Harrison glanced at her over his shoulder. "The Nephilim are dirty. You have to scrub hard to get the grit out, otherwise those wounds will itch even after they heal."

She wet the towel some more and scrubbed harder, clenching her teeth and shuddering as she did. "God, I'm so sorry. This must hurt like the devil." She couldn't imagine how much this must hurt. His hands clenched the edge of the counter until his knuckles whitened, but he didn't make a sound. "You can cuss if you need to."

His chuckle was strained. "You're making enough noise for both of us. If I didn't know better I'd think it was your wound being cleaned."

"I can't help it." She rinsed the towel and wiped the soap from his back.

Harry handed her the small jar Julian had taken out earlier. "You mind putting some on?"

She opened the jar, wrinkling her nose at the pungent odor, and dabbed a liberal amount on her fingers. While she applied the gel, the elevator pinged.

The man who'd helped her earlier strode into the room, took in the scene with one glance and scowled. This must be Duncan—the big dog. His hair was clipped close to his scalp. He had a square jaw and a crook in his nose. He looked mean as hell.

Harrison looked over. "Hey."

"What the hell happened?" He walked around to stand next to her. "Doesn't look too bad. Should heal by tomorrow."

Not too bad?

Harrison nodded. "Figured."

"All done." She turned the water on to wash her hands, keeping her gaze on the newcomer.

Harrison turned to Duncan. "Thanks for your help."

Duncan pulled him into a hug. Harrison not only allowed the intimacy, but returned it. "Anytime, pup." He pulled away and grasped Harrison by the neck. Rested his forehead against his. "Jesus, you scared the hell out of us tonight. When Trina told me—" He wrapped Harrison into another hug, then thumped him on the shoulder and pushed him away.

She couldn't take her eyes off them. Nor get over how comfortable Harrison appeared with accepting affection from this man.

Duncan's attention landed on Ember next. "And who's this?"

"Ember."

His eyebrows raised high on his forehead. "*The* Ember? Ember Moon?"

Harrison nodded, scrubbing his hand over the back of his neck.

A broad grin broke out on Duncan's face. "Well, I'll be damned." He pulled her into a hug that swallowed her whole. "Duncan Sinclair—Harry's dad for all intents and purposes."

When he pulled away he gripped her arm right over where her succubus band wound around her arm under her sweater. He squeezed, his brow furrowing as his gaze traveled from her to Harrison's band and back. His grin faltered. "I see." He nodded and looked at Harrison. "You're mated, then."

"Yeah."

Duncan's arm snaked around her shoulder. "Seems you and me have some catching up to do, love." He guided her over to the sofa and they both took a seat. She wiped her damp palms along her thighs. "Why don't you go get showered and dressed, pup, while we have us a chin wag."

She smiled. Now she understood why Harrison got so upset about Julian calling him pup. He was teasing him about Duncan.

"Thanks for your help tonight." She pressed her hand to her belly. "There were so many of them and that one was behind me before I realized it."

Duncan sat back against the cushions and spread his arms out over the back of the couch. "Jules and Harry would've handled them. They've got plenty of experience under their belts." She strained to make out the words past his accent. "It's easier, though, when the numbers are even."

"I wasn't sure. They seemed like they knew what they were doing, but neither used their talent."

Duncan shrugged. "Jules' talent don't work on Nephilim and Harry's woulda been suicide. 'Sides, Kat told Jules we were coming."

"How? Harry's a splitter, he could have evened the numbers by himself."

"True, but when a vampire uses his talent, love, he pays a price. If he splits off one copy, his attention is divided between the two. When outnumbered by Nephilim, that ain't wise."

"I wondered how it worked."

"Vampiric talents are tricky. Some, like Jules' talent, take little energy. He could be on death's door and still use his talent. However, it's a defensive ability, for the most part. A shifter like me or a splitter like Harry can't do that. If we attempted to use our talent when wounded, we'd risk getting stuck inside the confines of our talent."

What? "I don't understand."

"Say I've taken a mortal blow and I shift into a bear. I'm leaking energy from me wound and I'm expending a lot more to use me talent. Me consciousness could shift to the form where I'd pushed me energy. I could get stuck as a bear, unable to stop expending energy to hold the form. I'd perish."

How horrible. "I'd read that vampires don't use their talents when wounded, but I didn't realize why." She gave him a lop-sided grin. "Thank you for explaining. Harry doesn't talk much."

"He's being shy, eh?" He grinned. "How'd you find Harry?"

Her smile faded. "I didn't."

One of his dark eyebrows rose. "He finally went and found you?"

His question gave her pause. "Did he want to?"

Duncan sat back, his bottom lip popping out in a thoughtful expression. "He's always talked about you and he never put much heart into chasing after anyone else. Guess I assumed he planned to find you eventually."

"Oh." That was . . . surprising.

His brows furrowed. "How d'ya say you met?"

He wasn't going to let it drop. "Adia. She had me changed to a succubus and left me for Harry to find."

Duncan leaned forward and put his big hand over hers. "You okay?" His gaze traveled to the hallway where Harrison disappeared. "How's he handling all this? I mean, I don't need the nitty-gritty, but how'd he take your, uh, condition?"

"Yeah, I'm okay." She nodded, looking everywhere but at his kind eyes. "Harry's been good to me."

"You ain't got the look of a woman in the throes of new love."

She forced a smile. "Everything is going to be fine. Growing up, I always hoped we'd be together someday. We need time to get to know each other again, that's all."

"Good attitude." He leaned back. "Arranged marriages were all the rage when I was human. The couples who went into such contracts with open minds and hearts at least found a companionable match. Those who didn't, they never had much to smile about, yeah?"

She stared into his piercing hazel eyes and gathered her courage. "Could I ask you a personal question about you and Harry?"

He grinned. "Might not answer, but I won't hold asking against you."

"How did you get Harrison to trust you enough for him to let you hug him?"

"Oh. I see." His smile faded. "Took a long time, love. Five years of me finding bizarre ways to show him affection." He shook his head. "When he was a lad, I think sometimes he'd attack me just to get me arms around him."

Her heart sank. Five years was a long time and Duncan had the advantage of being male. "I understand."

"No, love. I don't think you do." He leaned forward a bit. "I was supposed to destroy him."

"What?"

"After Adia transformed him, she lost control of him. See, right after a vampire is transformed, they're starving. They'll take blood any way they can get it. Add that to the trauma he'd gone through and, well, Harry was beyond reason. Adia called me in to ash him. I arrived expecting the usual gig—rogue daemon or something—but no. I walk in to this ancient underground arena and the whole damn place is deserted except for one skinny little lad covered in nothing but blood." He shook his head. "He was too young to be transformed. I knew he wouldn't physically age. Vampiric law demanded I destroy him." He shrugged. "Couldn't do it. I wrapped him in a sheet and took him home. Took me over a year to even get him trust me enough so I didn't have to keep him locked in a cell. You understand? He was feral. Then, when I could trust him enough to give him free run of me place, he didn't allow outright affection. Not for years. The only time he'd let me touch him was when we were training. Didn't let me hug him for the first time until about three years ago when all hell broke loose. It was right after the Grigori coven aged him."

"So, Adia did transform him when was a kid."

"Yeah. The bitch. It's against our laws to transform children. He matured on the inside—" He pointed to his head. "—in his mind, but still looked sixteen until three years ago."

Ember swallowed hard. What Adia had done was beyond twisted.

"Jesus." Duncan sat back and scrubbed his hands over his face. "I kept promising him somehow we'd age him and had no idea how. He'd still be stuck if not for the Grigori coven. See, I got sent to kidnap one of the witches—another assignment I gladly botched. I mated her, instead." He shot her a wink. "Trina and the rest of the coven fell hard and fast in love with Harry. They wouldn't rest 'til they found a way to age him into the man he should've been."

How had she thought Duncan looked mean? Now, seeing how much he cared for Harrison and how concerned he seemed for her, she felt like an ass for her unkind thought. "I'm glad he had you, Duncan."

He rubbed the back of his neck in a gesture she recognized from Harrison. "And I think it's good he's got you now."

Harrison walked into the room. "How's Trina?" He slipped onto the couch next to her.

"Good. She's going to take over teaching daemonology at the school on Machon."

Harrison laughed. "I wouldn't want to be one of her students. They'll never get away with anything."

Duncan chucked and glanced at Ember. "Me mate's a Grigori witch; she reads minds."

"That must make it difficult to keep secrets."

He appeared taken aback. "Ain't got any from her."

His complete lack of guile charmed her. "No, I mean if you try to surprise her with a gift or something. Don't you miss surprising her?"

He grinned. "Oh, well, still do. I sing "John Jacob Jingleheimer Schimdt" in me head. She hates it."

Ember couldn't help but return his smile. His happiness was contagious.

"You should bring Ember to Machon. Trina is going to want to meet her."

"We'll come. I need to finish this case first."

"I'd like that." She stood. "Right now, I think I'd like to clean up, too. I won't be long."

As she made her way to the bathroom she caught herself humming "John Jacob Jingleheimer Schimdt."

CHAPTER 12

October 12, 1:57 AM

"WHAT'S GOING ON, PUP?"

Harrison slumped in his seat. Duncan had always been the one person he couldn't fool. "Adia is threatening everyone I care about. You and Trina be careful. I ordered patrols to watch my mom's place, but that can't go on forever."

Duncan cleared his throat. "You seen your mum?"

"No."

"Seems to me if she's living here in Washington and you're here, why not?"

He tensed. Had Ember told him? "I didn't say where she lived."

"I thought maybe . . ." He grimaced. Swore. "Trina keeps saying I need to come clean with you. Guess now's as good a time as any."

He couldn't remember ever seeing Duncan squirm before. "What did you do?"

"Your parents would've stayed in England searching for you, Harry. I lost a son. I know what it's like and I couldn't carry on as if I didn't care what they were suffering."

Harry fisted his hands and he wanted nothing more than to hit him. "You spoke to my parents?"

"Yeah. I made sure they knew you were safe. Kept in touch

over the years, sent them updates on your progress."

"Is that why my mom moved here three years ago?"

Duncan winced. Nodded.

Harrison stood and paced away. "What did you do, tell her I'd come visit?"

"No. I'd never make promises on your behalf. Shouldn't have interfered, but I couldn't stand by and say nothing."

The hell he couldn't. "Why didn't you tell me before?"

"I didn't want to cause you more pain, pup. You'd done your mourning for them. Made your peace. Your mum understands. That's why she hasn't come to you. She's waiting until you're ready. If you ever are."

He wasn't sure what to think. On the one hand, he understood—morally, Duncan felt obligated to try to ease the situation. On the other, he couldn't stand the thought of his mom knowing about him. "She knows everything?"

Duncan shook his head. "Told her you're alive and that I'd keep you safe. Explained that you had . . . special needs they couldn't accommodate. That you wouldn't be accepted among your kind anymore. I let her and your dad see me eyes glowing so they'd understand what you were involved in was out of their league. That's all. Once the existence of daemon kind became common knowledge she put two-and-two together and I told her you'd been stationed in Seattle. The rest is for you to tell, or not. I told you before, pup, no one ever needs to know anything else. I don't think burying your past is the best choice, but that's up to you." He wiped a hand over his face. "How aggravated are you with me?"

He paced away again and raked his hand through his hair. "I wished you'd told me sooner in some ways, but maybe it's best the way things are. It always bothered me that they thought I had died." He returned and slouched into his seat. "You know, I didn't need this on top of everything else going on."

"What else?" He leaned forward, resting his elbows on his knees. "Ember said Adia brought you two together." Duncan's troubled gaze met his. "How you feeling 'bout that?"

A riot of conflicting emotions boiled to the surface and it took every ounce of determination he had to tamp them back into place.

"Ah." Duncan nodded. "Figured it must be hard."

"Ember's great." His breaths came too fast. His chest started to burn. "She's sweet."

Duncan took a slow, deep breath, holding his gaze, like he used to do when Harrison was a kid. Never said anything, just showed him how to be. Gave him the example to follow.

Harrison fought the burn behind his eyes and breathed slower, deeper. "I loathe that Adia's sitting between Em and me. I don't know how to deal with that. Every time. . . . It's always in the back of my mind. I feel like shit because it's there and it's not Em's fault. So I keep pushing it down, forcing it away." The whole time he spoke, Duncan listened, nodding his head. "What?"

"How's she treat you, pup?"

"Em?" At Duncan's nod, Harrison sat back. "Like she's trying to figure me out, and—"

"And you don't like the idea of her seeing you clear."

No. He didn't want her to ever see what he was. "She'd treat me different."

"You are different." Duncan shrugged. "There was this lad once. Mop-headed, foul-mouthed little shite, he was." He leaned forward again and took a deep breath.

Harrison followed suit.

"Jesus, he was a mess. Didn't know what to do with him and, see, he reminded me of me own lad with those big blue eyes of his. Tore me up. I couldn't destroy him, but all the pain from losing Charlie sat between us. For the longest time, I couldn't open up and the mop-headed little shite kept getting worse."

He swallowed past the tightness in his throat. He didn't want to hear this.

Duncan took a long deep breath and waited until he did the same.

"One day, this lad gets hold of some electronics I had stashed in a closet—to this day, I haven't a clue what he was trying to do."

Harry winced. "It was supposed to be a Taser."

"Damned near burned my place to the ground right around his own ears. I got so damn angry that he'd almost ashed himself, I couldn't see straight. All the shite I'd buried about losing Charlie came rolling out of me in spades. Once the door opened, I couldn't shut it, which pissed me off even worse."

That's what he feared. There was too much there. Ignored. Festering. He couldn't let all his pent-up emotional shit out.

"I was a fucking mess, you remember?"

Harrison nodded. It had been the one time he'd ever feared Duncan. Not because he thought Duncan would hurt him, but because he was afraid Duncan might hurt himself. He'd been terrified the asshole he'd come to rely on would suddenly be gone.

Gods, he didn't want to hear this. He pressed his fist to the ache in his chest.

"All of the sudden, everything started to make sense. The crap I used to do, the risks, the women, the constant focus on the job—I was running. Proving my fucking manhood." Duncan paused again and took a breath.

Harrison shook his head. That wasn't it. It wasn't the same. He stood. *Fuck.* He couldn't. . . . His hand went to his throat as if he could open the airway manually.

Duncan rose and grabbed him by the nape—put his forehead to his and those familiar hazel eyes filled Harrison's vision. Duncan inhaled.

"Stop." Harrison sucked in a breath.

"When you pushed me and I lost it, I found meself, pup."

He clenched his jaw until his teeth hurt. "I can't." He couldn't let all that shit out. He couldn't do what Duncan did.

Duncan took a deep breath and waited for him to do the same. "I traded all the shite I'd been holding on to for a relationship with you. Best damn deal of my life."

He fisted his hand and brought it down on Duncan's shoulder. Christ, he was suffocating.

Duncan inhaled.

Harrison did, too. "I'm not you."

"No, but you're mine. I raised you. I know what you can and can't do."

"Then you know this is a lost cause."

"Nah. Quit hoarding your shite, pup. Make room for your something beautiful."

His something beautiful. That's how Duncan always spoke of Trina and their relationship: his something beautiful. Gods, what he wouldn't give to have the same with Ember. "But Adia—"

"My guess is, Adia set you up expecting you to fail. She expected

Ember to be dead by dawn. You rose above. You opened your heart a little and mated Ember. Now you need to finish the job, pup. Open your heart the rest of the way. Accept your something beautiful and as a bonus, it's a big 'ol 'fuck off' to the great black cunt."

Gods, he wanted it to be that simple. "Yeah, okay."

"Damn it, Harry. Look at me." Duncan's hand tightened on his nape. "You can do this. I know you can do this because I did. And you are so much better than me."

———◆———

When Ember returned, Harrison was telling Duncan about their case. Both men grinned at her when she entered and Harrison motioned her over.

"They've given us the green light to bust the auction over on Camano Island."

"Island?" Duncan frowned. "You need to go in a boat?"

Harrison shook his head. "No. No boat. We'll go across by bridge."

"Thank God."

Ember looked at Duncan. "You don't like boats?"

"Water. Vampires sink like stones when we hit the water. Don't like the idea of Harry being near water when going after Adia, that's all." He kissed his teeth. "When is all this happening?"

"We're going in tomorrow night."

"You and Jules?"

"And me." She fought the urge to squirm under Duncan's considering stare. She put her hand on Harrison's knee. His fingers entwined with hers, but he moved their hands to rest on her leg.

Duncan's gaze followed the silent exchange before rising to meet hers. "Scott's got his claws in you, yeah?" He shook his head and looked at Harrison. "That lad don't miss a punch, does he?"

Harrison chuckled.

Lad? Did he not like Scott? "Why 'lad'? Scott's older than all of us."

Harrison laughed harder. Her cheeks flamed as she realized her mistake. Daemons stopped aging once they were turned.

Duncan smiled. "I'm not disparaging Scott. He's all right, if a bit of an opportunist, but you can't make assumptions where daemons are concerned. I'm well over three-hundred and Jules, he must be double that."

Wow. Okay, then.

They chatted for a while longer before Duncan rose. "I better get back before Trina sends out a search party."

She stood and smiled. "I enjoyed meeting you, Duncan." Had it only been an hour ago she thought he looked mean? Now she thought him one of the nicest men she'd ever met.

"And I enjoyed meeting you." He wrapped her into another embrace, this time whispering into her ear. "He's a good lad. Don't give up on him, yeah?"

She nodded against his shoulder.

No. She wouldn't ever give up on Harrison.

She just hoped her demon was of the same mind.

CHAPTER 13

October 13, 1:11 AM

CAMANO ISLAND WAS QUITE BEAUTIFUL even when shrouded in darkness. The air, cool on her skin, smelled of brine.

The three of them were decked out to the nines and armed from tips to tails. Harrison supplied her with a small 9mm fitted with a magazine of silver bullets, plus a spare, now both in her purse.

She and Harrison traveled separately from Julian and tonight was the first night she'd ever seen Harrison leave George at home. The minion had carried on so much, she'd begged on the small creature's behalf, but minions were rare and he'd be easy to distinguish with George perched on his shoulder, so the minion stayed at the apartment.

"Are you comfortable with your role, Em?" He covered her hand with his.

She repeated what they'd told her. "I'm your wife and I like to keep an eye on the business. If I left things to you, we'd never have a decent variety for our clients."

He nodded, but his features pulled taut with concern as Deno drove them through the front gates. "We're here."

A manor home deep in the interior of the island hosted the

auction. A solitary structure centered in acres of woodlands and wetlands. Despite the modern security, the stately house was reminiscent of bygone eras. The clapboard siding, portico, and columns had been painted white, and the bay windows, dentils, and trim a pale blue. An antique weather vane topped the turret room's roof. Flower beds bloomed all along the drive and a porch swing hung on the portico. The whole property looked so picturesque, she had difficulty believing something as ugly as selling human beings might be happening inside.

Occasionally, Harrison nudged her knee to point out guards and cameras. The closer they got, the tighter the knots in her belly wound. Why had she thought this was a good idea? She was a freaking social worker, not a cop.

"Relax." He squeezed her fingers. "Remember, Kara and Jules are here, and Scott and the others are standing by. We won't ever be on our own, okay?"

The car stopped and Harrison stayed her when she reached for the door. "Let Deno."

The Oni walked around the front of the car and opened her door. She took his red-mottled hand and stood on shaky legs. "Thanks, Deno."

"Miss."

Harrison put his palm on the small of her back, guiding her up the steps and into the home.

The manor appeared even more impressive from the inside. Marble pillars and gold-tiled floors accented the two-story foyer. Colorful blooms burst from huge Grecian urns. A string quartet played from somewhere farther in.

Harrison handed their invitation to a shady character dressed in evening finery. Ember slid her gloved fingers along the sides of her ankle-length red-velvet gown. Adrenaline pulsed through her, feeling like thousands of ants crawling beneath her skin, urging her to run away from this place.

When Harrison returned his hand to the small of her back, she jumped.

"Easy, Em."

She looked into those blue eyes of his and got a little lost for a moment. It should be a crime for him to be so handsome. She forced a brilliant smile. "I'm good." As hard as this was, she'd have to grow accustomed to the nerves associated with under-cover work. She imagined the alternative—staying home and worrying—would be a million times more difficult.

"Come on, we'll get you a drink." He ushered her through an archway and into a ballroom bursting with well-dressed patrons. The crowd of cultivated occupants were so far removed from what she'd expected the whole scene seemed surreal. "I'd assumed there'd only be a small number of buyers here."

"There are. The rest of these guests help provide cover and anonymity."

She slid him a side glance. "How?"

"None of us know who will stay at the party and who will be shown to a buyer's booth. I'd wager half of these people don't have any idea what goes on in the back rooms."

"Ah."

A liveried waiter passed and Harrison plucked a champagne flute off his tray. "Here. It'll help take the edge off."

She took the glass and sipped the liquid while she glanced around. "This is a beautiful house." Berber carpet surrounded a sunken wood dance floor. Large columns of marble stood spaced around the room and sitting areas had been set between each. The atmosphere was festive, but more along the lines of a cor-porate mixer. The music played loud enough to dance to, yet remained unobtrusive to those chatting or making new connec-tions. "How do we know where to go?"

"Let's dance." He led her onto the dance floor, leaving her no time to set aside her drink. When he pulled her into his arms, she rested her wrist on his shoulder, letting the glass dangle. He took her other hand in his and she felt his touch all the way in the pit of her belly. "They'll come get us when they're ready."

Damn, he smelled good. Her insides tightened with need. She took a long sip of champagne. "How do they know who we are?"

A small smile played on his lips. "Didn't you notice the mirrors in the foyer? When I handed over our invitation, he held it to the mirror so the person on the other side could make a note of us."

"Of course." She had no idea what he was talking about. She'd noticed a lot of things, but hadn't seen any mirrors. She caught sight of Julian across the dance floor. "Jules is by the bar."

Harrison's grin grew. "I nodded to him when we walked in."

She blew out a frustrated breath. "You're taller."

He chuckled. "I see well because I'm taller?"

"People were blocking my view." She sniffed, playing offended. "That's all."

"And the mirrors?" His eyes crinkled at the corners.

She leaned closer. "I think you're making stuff up."

This time he laughed loud enough to draw interested glances from those around them.

"People are looking."

"Good." He skimmed his lips along the curve of her neck, making her shiver. Her nipples grew taut. "Wouldn't want them to think we're trying to hide."

When he straightened, his blue eyes still glittered with mirth, reminding her of the boy he'd once been. Teasing her. Loving her in his own way. And oh, God, did she want him. Right then. Right there.

She forced her urgent need aside. Smiled. "I'm glad you walked in that hotel room, Harry."

He winked. Honest to God, he looked so damn sexy right then she could hardly stand him.

***

Julius Crowley leaned against the bar, watching Harrison and Ember dance. He'd been a little concerned for them the last few days, but if the two of them kept looking at each other the way they were right now, they'd be fine.

He just hoped that when Ember realized he was the notorious Harbinger that it wouldn't screw everything up for Harrison. He had no doubt it would be a tough conversation for Harrison to have with Ember—explaining that the Harbinger wasn't dead and they were actually sharing living space with him. Hell, most of daemon kind didn't even think he was real—they all assumed Kat had been so brokenhearted after watching him die that she'd used her Vampiric talent to create a projection of him. The humans, they all assumed he was his brother. One of these days he'd get found out and all hell would break loose. Until then, he was enjoying life. Enjoying his mate and his job. He owed Harrison for the life he had now—couldn't be easy playing babysitter twenty-four-seven. After everything Harrison had done to help him and Kat have a somewhat normal life together, the last thing he wanted was for his past to mess with Harrison's future.

He turned away, scanning the crowd for Kara. She should've arrived before him, but he had yet to lay eyes on her. He was about to send her a text when someone tapped him on the shoulder.

A tiny Asian woman, slim and curvy, pouted at him with her full lips and sultry brown eyes. Her pale-blue, floor-length, sequined halter dress had a high neck-line that seemed almost too prim for this place. She smiled. "Sir, if you'll follow me?"

Ah, time to get to work.

"Yeah, sure, honey." He straightened and followed her. In the back, her dress pooled low on her hips, allowing teasing glimpses of the curve of her waist. He wouldn't mind seeing Kat in a dress like that. His gaze locked onto the tattoo that scrolled down her back. The two large Chinese characters inked parallel to her spine seemed familiar, but he couldn't quite place them.

She led him through a security entrance and into a dim corridor bordered by nondescript black doors. His attention traveled back to the tattoo and gooseflesh spread over his skin.

Woman Who Eats. Yeah, the first character represented the phrase: Woman who eats. What the hell did the last character mean? He should know this—he'd seen these symbols before.

She stopped by a door and motioned for him to precede her.

Julius paused in the entrance. "Your tat, what's the second symbol?"

The woman's mouth stretched impossibly wide. Her teeth elongated, becoming thin, pointy and canted like the teeth of an angler fish. "Everything."

Julius stumbled back into the room and went for his blade. She was a fucking Diwe.

A dark sackcloth dropped over his face.

Jesus. Not again. He clawed at the material, overwhelmed by the stifling sensation. Why did they always use a fucking hood? He made out four auras through the thick fabric. He pulled his blade and slashed out at the closest.

Someone punched him in the back. Sharp pain shot up his spine, the intensity paralyzing.

He lashed out with his knife and this time, his Guardian blade sank into flesh. One bastard's aura winked out.

One of the others kicked the weapon out of his hand.

Julius got a couple solid punches on him, but there were three of them, if you counted the Diwe and it didn't take long before they wrestled him to the ground and had him pinned.

"You missed a leg." Julius kicked out and connected with the smallest aura—the Diwe.

She gasped as her ass hit the hardwoods. Then her aura began to grow.

"Don't hurt him."

That wasn't the Asian woman. Julius cursed as a new aura walked into the room.

"Hello, Mr. Crowley." *Adia.* He groaned. "Don't worry. We have no intention of destroying you, Julian. At least not before Harry has front row seats."

"You want him on the catwalk?" one of the males asked.

"No." Adia slid her palm down his chest. "Use the female we captured for that."

What female? Did she mean Ember, or did they have Kara? Adia's hand traveled south, approaching Kat's private property, making his skin crawl. "What's up, sweetheart? You getting curious about men now?"

Adia jerked away. "Why don't you take Mr. Crowley to visit the tank? He's a slippery little bastard. I think he'd like to swim with the fishes."

Julius struggled against the restraining hands.

"Now, now, Mr. Crowley. You wouldn't want to upset the fun I've planned for your partner, would you?"

CHAPTER 14

October 13, 1:41 AM

AN ASIAN WOMAN TAPPED HARRISON on the shoulder. "Sir? Would you and your companion follow me, please?"

He nodded. "Lead the way."

Ember put her hand in Harrison's and his fingers squeezed around hers. The woman they followed was dressed in a long, pale-blue evening gown that pooled on the ground behind her. The back dipped so low, the tip of the crack of her ass was visible. A tattoo of Chinese writing scrolled down one side of her back, moving with each swish of her hips. Despite a slight limp, the woman moved with elegant grace. She used a key card to open a security door and led them through a dark hallway lined with doors. She paused about midway in the corridor, opened a door, and motioned them inside.

The room had two high-backed chairs angled toward a viewing window. A low, round table sat between them with two glasses of champagne and a small box with a green button on its top.

The woman cleared her throat. "When you see something you like, press the button. In cases where more than one buyer shows interest, the auctioneer will call." She motioned to a phone on the wall. "All your bids are held in strict confidence."

He gave her a curt nod. "Thank you."

She bowed before she left, closing the door behind her.

Ember glanced at Harrison. "What—"

He shook his head. "Not now, love." He winked at her and took a sheet of paper from one of the chairs so he could sit.

Right. He'd told her the booths would be monitored.

Curious, she moved to her own chair and picked up the paper lying on her seat. She sat, crossed her legs, and scanned the paper.

It was a menu.

Twenty-six women would be auctioned today. Their vital stats were listed next to the number representing each woman—weight, height, hair and eye color, nationality. A single letter had been typed at the end of every row. Some had a V, some an M, and others an E. "The letters?"

His jaw flexed. "Virgin, mother, or experienced."

Considering the pricing differences, she expected those listed as "mother" were *not* single purchases, but rather mother and child together. Ember's gut rolled. God, she was going to be sick. She counseled herself: Remember, none of these women will leave with their buyer tonight. They're all coming home with us. Her daemon writhed under her skin, wanting free. She inhaled a deep breath, picked up her glass and took a sip. *Stay calm.* The viewing booths were monitored. She had to keep her cool.

The lights in their booth dimmed and those on the other side of the window brightened, showing a narrow hallway with a catwalk. Light came from above as well as from round lights built into the center of the floor, spaced every four feet or so. Across the catwalk from them, there was another mirror the same size as theirs.

Everything would move fast once Julian and Kara sent Harrison texts that they were in position. She rubbed her sweaty palms on the arm rests and took a slow, deep breath in attempt to slow her heart.

The first woman walked into their line of sight. She wore nothing but a camisole and panties. Her skin had been scrubbed clean and her long, black hair plaited into a braid. Her dark eyes were dazed. She paused in front of their window and faced them. After a moment, she turned around, giving them a view of her from behind.

As she moved farther along the catwalk, her keeper came into view, a large man wielding a police baton. He remained just far enough behind to stay out of sight from those viewing her. He moved away and another woman appeared. This one held an infant. The baby cried, but the mother did little to soothe her child. Her eyes were red and the hand that patted the baby's back was blackened with bruises.

Anger, hot and heavy, coiled in her belly as her demon twisted and writhed.

Let me free. Let me save them.

Ember's muscles tensed. *I've got this. We don't need you.* Why the hell hadn't Julian sent the text yet? As soon as he did, they'd fire at the glass and she and Kara would go after the women with Julian and Harrison providing cover. The other DDC agents here would cover the exits and ensure none of the buyers escaped. Everything had been planned. Timing would be everything and her and Kara's job was to get the women out as fast as they could.

Everything would be fine.

The plan was simple.

Too simple.

Who was in charge of fighting off the men who followed each of the women in there?

What if her demon took control again?

The next woman wasn't well. Both her eyes were blackened, her nose swollen. The way she favored her right side gave the impression of broken ribs. She seemed to stare straight into their booth, begging silently for aid. Her face was so swollen it took Ember a moment to recognize the woman as the agent who'd said hello to Harrison and patted George the first morning she'd gone to DDC Headquarters. Oh, God in Heaven, that was Kara.

"Shit." Harrison leapt to his feet.

The handler following Kara crowded behind her.

Kara's eyes widened.

Harrison drew his weapon and fired once, shattering the glass separating them.

Ember rose as Harrison broke through the window.

In one swift move, the daemon jerked Kara's head around to the side and shoved her at Harrison.

Harrison sidestepped and tackled him.

Ember blanched. "Oh, my God." She dived through the opening, onto the glass-covered catwalk, and checked Kara for a pulse or breathing or something. She wasn't sure what type of daemon Kara was, but when she got close enough to look in her face, Kara's lifeless eyes stared back at her. Kara was gone. She closed the female's eyes and sent out a quick prayer for her.

"Ember, go!" He slugged the daemon in the face. "Get out."

She took the gun out of her shoulder bag. She stood, backing away from Harrison and the daemon he fought, and put the purse strap cross-wise over her neck. Harrison's weapon was on the floor well out of reach from where he straddled the daemon, but he appeared to be winning. He knelt over the daemon and the daemon's legs kept turning into long writhing tentacles before snapping back into human-looking appendages.

Beyond them, back toward the ballroom, people screamed. Something loud crashed and gunfire erupted. God, she hoped that was the DDC arriving.

Ember turned around, heart lodged somewhere north of where the organ should be. They said to follow the hall away from the main entrance to a staging area. She kicked off her heels and ran along the brightly lit catwalk.

The door at the end opened.

Ember slid to a stop as a big brute of a daemon walked in. One of the handlers—he'd shadowed the first woman paraded in front of them.

Where the hell was Julian?

She lifted her gun and fired. Her shot jerked his head back and he dropped.

That seemed way too easy. Was he a Lycan? Harrison had said the bullets were silver.

With her weapon held out in front of her, she sidled closer, watching his chest for movement. Once close enough, she nudged him with her foot. She didn't think he moved, but she couldn't seem to take her gaze of the jagged black hole in his forehead. Her stomach roiled. She glanced over her shoulder at Harrison. He'd ashed the daemon and was jogging toward her. Braver now with him at her back, she started to step over the body and looked down—straight into blood-red eyes.

The daemon's hand clasped her ankle and she screamed.

Her elbows locked tight, she pulled the trigger, firing her

weapon into his face.

———◆———

Harrison wrapped an arm around Ember from behind. "Stop. He's gone."

There wasn't much left of the daemon's face. Nothing could survive that many bullets. She fired the last shot and even after the magazine emptied, she continued.

"Stop, love." The clicking of the firing mechanism ended and she tried to look. He palmed her throat, his hand preventing her from witnessing the damage she'd wrought. "You're all right, honey. Keep walking." He nudged her through the doorway, righting her when she slipped in the daemon's black blood.

"He scared the fuck out of me."

In the sudden silence, her heart slammed an erratic beat in her chest. He needed to get her calm. "I know. Remind me not to surprise you, okay?" She shouldn't be here. He and Scott needed to have a long talk about her involvement when all this was done. As soon as they got far enough away that she couldn't see the daemon any longer, he stopped and pulled out his weapon.

"Ember, I want you to take my sidearm and the extra ammo."

"What about you?"

"I learned to fight from a Guardian. They don't use guns."

"Where's Julian?" She stuffed his gun and the three clips in her purse. "He was supposed to come through the glass."

He had a feeling his partner was in deep shit. This whole setup reeked of one of Adia's games and that gave him hope. Adia wouldn't destroy Julian. Not if there was a possibility she could ash Julian in front of him. If he played this smart, he might still come out of here with both Ember and his partner.

"It's a trap, Em. They knew we were coming." He glanced both ways along the hall. All clear. "We're gonna to find Julian and get out of here."

"But the women."

They were either dead or had already been moved. Likely, the two they'd seen were the only ones here. "If we come across them, fine, otherwise our mission is compromised and our new goal is to get us all out in one piece." He forced her to look at him. "You understand?"

She gave him a jerky nod and he leaned forward to give her a quick peck on the cheek. "You're doing great." She really was. He took her hand in his and led her deeper into the house.

They found nothing in the next room. Nor in the next.

They sidled into another hallway leading to what looked to be a second ballroom or music room. Carpet surrounded a polished wooden floor.

A massive fish tank took one entire wall along the length of the room. The creatures swimming in the crimson water were not of this Earth. They were from Machon—the daemon world. Razor-finned, spindle-toothed, spiked and clawed—they resembled nothing living in this world's aquatic kingdom.

Gods, this place was a regular house of horrors.

The shadows shifted, catching his attention and making him squint until he made out the form of a tall woman. She stepped into the reddened light from the tank.

Adia.

She flashed him a grin and slipped through the door.

Harrison took off at a dead sprint.

———◆———

Ember started to follow Harrison when something big and black fell into the water.

She slowed, unsure what she saw. Bubbles obscured her view, but it looked like a man. She stopped and walked closer, putting her palm on the glass.

Black pants. Black shirt. He had a hood over his head and his arms and legs were bound. An eye patch floated nearby.

"Julian!"

Stepping back, she raised her gun and unloaded the weapon into the tank as the strange fish inside brushed past Julian, spinning him one way and then another. The thick glass cracked but didn't break.

She dug into her purse for the other magazine. Loaded, and fired. Each round echoing, ringing in her ears.

The glass shattered and red-tinged water burst into the room, knocking her off her feet. One of the creatures brushed against her and she screamed as razor-sharp scales abraded her leg. She scrambled to her feet, found Julian and waded over to him, avoiding the fish squirming and splashing in the dissipating water.

Alive, he thrashed for all he was worth, trying to unbind his wrists. She hauled the hood off his face and he sucked in a deep breath.

Once she got him into a sitting position, she cupped his cheeks. "You okay?"

"Jesus, you're too bright." He winced away from her, squeezing his injured eye shut, peering at her through the other. "There were . . . four of them . . . waiting in the booth." He hauled in a deep breath. "Adia, two brutes, and the Asian lady who led me there."

"They killed Kara." She slipped her blade from where she'd secured it on her thigh beneath her dress and cut his hands free. "It was a trap."

"Damn it. How the hell did they know?" He glanced around and wiped the crimson liquid from his face. "Where's Harry?"

"He went after Adia."

His attention focused on something over her shoulder. "My feet, Em."

She cut him loose and he stood, pushing her behind him. "Get out of here. Now. And Em, stay away from that Asian lady."

As she backed out, two male daemons came through the remnants of the aquarium. These must be the assholes that meant to let Julian drown.

The bigger of the two glanced at his partner. "What now, we gotta catch him again?"

"No. We did what she asked. Not our fault she showed herself too soon. Ash him."

She hesitated, torn between helping Julian who was outnumbered and going after Harrison who faced his worst nightmare.

Julian waved her away. "Go on. I got these two."

He was a mesmerist. He'd be okay. She slipped through the door and into another hall. She paused to look both directions out of the room. The lights flickered. To her left a window overlooked the back of the property. Red and blue flashed against the glass. She ran to the window and saw scores of DDC patrol units. Many of the well-dressed people she'd seen earlier were being hauled into vehicles for transportation.

This may have been a trap, but the DDC had pulled through.

She continued on, listening for any sign of Harrison.

A woman's scream came from somewhere past the end of the hall and her heart stuttered in her chest.

CHAPTER 15

October 13, 2:56 AM

A SCREAM RENT THE SILENCE OF the house as Harrison split off a couple copies as he ran. Adia must have gone straight—where that scream had come from—but he refused to take any chances. Each of his copies scoured the rooms on either side of the hallway while he continued on.

He doubted the woman he chased was the real Adia. Most likely, he followed one of her copies, but he had to know.

He entered a long room at the end of the hall. Once it may have been a living or dining room in the family portion of the house. Now the space provided a holding area. The whole place stank of human musk. Cages, three occupied, lined one wall. There were maybe twenty women in all. The woman with the infant curled against the wall of one, panting. Was she the one who had screamed? He caught her gaze and gave her a nod, hoping she realized he'd come to help.

He stalked down the wide aisle, staying to the center of the space, pausing between each of the cages to make sure Adia hadn't hidden between them. A woman in nothing but a camisole and panties motioned to him. She jerked her head toward the back of the room. Lifted two fingers.

There were two.

Harrison flipped his knife so the flat of the blade pressed against his wrist and withdrew a second, doing the same with it. He crouched, edged into the room. His gaze never still. Watching.

Waiting for the first strike.

Behind him, a woman screamed. He spun on his heel.

Two males entered. *Great.* Now there were four and he was surrounded. The eyes of the two males reflected the dim light. Vampires.

Harrison backed toward the nearest cage, enabling him to watch the newcomers while keeping an eye on whatever might come at him from behind.

He checked his watch: 2:15 AM. He'd been alive for twenty-four years, ten months, three days, four hours and eleven minutes, and these two were not going stop him from seeing that twelfth minute.

They strolled forward, taking his measure.

He glanced at the darkened end of the room. Someone was there, but still no movement.

Looking back at the vampires, he caught a twitch from the one on the left.

Harrison smiled. Oh, he knew that twitch. It had taken years of Duncan's constant nagging for him to overcome the reflex. That one was a splitter, like him. The daemon hadn't learned yet to control his ticks; he must be a neophyte.

The other gave no hints.

Ember barreled into the room, right into the tension. Both vampires swung toward her and Harrison took advantage. He leaped forward and sank his blade deep into the splitter's neck.

The vampire crumbled to ash.

The other spun around, slashing out with his blade.

Harrison backed away, circling to keep himself between the vampire and Ember.

Behind him, metal clanked on metal as Ember released the women.

The vampire padded toward Harrison, transforming as he moved. A black-leather hide shot out from his feet, rising to envelop the vampire within its kindred form of a hellcat. The size of a lion, the creature had razor-sharp talons instead of paws, a muscular frame, and nine whip-like tails that swished and snapped behind it. A raptor-like hood surrounded the feline's neck, dotted with reflective scales. When extended it would garner and reflect light onto its prey in a disorienting display.

The big cat roared and leapt at Harrison.

He threw himself to the side, lashing out with his blades, but doing little more than nicking the hellcat. When he hit the ground, he rolled, coming to rest on his feet once again.

Ember froze with two captives near one of the cages. The hellcat eyed them.

"Inside!" Harrison sprinted forward, trying to draw the hellcat's attention from the women.

Ember fired one shot at the hellcat, before opening the door and slipping into the cage. She slammed the door shut, the metallic ring echoing in the room.

The large feline cocked back on its haunches and pounced at Harrison.

Harrison dropped to his knees, letting his momentum carry him across the slick floor, intending to slide past it with his blade extended, but the cat lashed out with one of its tails, encircling his throat and dragging him to an abrupt halt. Two other tails wrapped around his wrists, holding him immobile.

Shit. He couldn't breathe. He dropped one of his knives to claw at the barbed tail but did little more than bloody his fingers on the tiny spikes.

A shot rang out in the room. The hellcat's tails flexed, dragging Harrison around, and putting him between it and Ember's weapon.

The cat pawed the ground, talons clicking against the marble.

Its other tails whipped and sliced into Harrison's skin. He struggled against the hellcat's tails, straining to raise his arm higher. He slashed at the tails holding him, slicing through the one around his neck and the other two let go.

He stumbled back, gasping.

The hellcat circled around, whimpering and trying to lick its wounds. It limped.

"Here, kitty, kitty." He got to his feet.

The hellcat's eyes narrowed. It hissed, sprinting toward him. Its talons clicked across the floor.

He waited, muscles tensed.

The hellcat's hood shot up, gathering the light in the room and reflecting it out to blind its prey.

Harrison closed his eyes. As soon as the clicking stopped, he dropped to his knees with his knife overhead. His arms jerked back as his blade sank deep into the big cat's flesh and ash rained around him.

"Harrison?" Ember swung open the cage door. The hinges protested, partially covering another sound. She froze. She must have heard it, too. It wasn't his imagination.

He waved her back into the cage, frowning when she shook her head. She closed the cage door, but she stood on the wrong side.

Damn it. He scowled.

Ember didn't notice. All her attention was focused on the dark end of the room, her brows drawing together.

A small, bobbing orb of light dangled from the ceiling, almost like a Chinese lantern. He squinted. That hadn't been there before.

He got to his feet.

Adia had disappeared down there. Her and one other. He passed Ember, and whispered, "Get them out." The cage door swung open again as he made his way along the center aisle.

"Go. Go."

At the sound of Ember's voice, he glanced back. Well, shit. The damn woman should've led them out, not shooed them out, while sticking around to open the rest of the cages.

He should give her hell; his attention, however, returned to the orb. About six inches in diameter, it swayed in a hypnotic motion. A shiver ghosted over his skin. Whatever that was, he didn't like it on a primal level.

He drew in a breath and gagged on the stench of rotten meat. What the hell was down here?

As he approached, the orb sank lower, hovering overhead as if teasing him to touch it.

Forcing his gaze away from the orb, he peered into the shadows beyond. At first, he couldn't decipher what he was seeing. It almost resembled some evil Tiki mask. Huge and etched into a blackened medium, the image blended with the shadows. Except the faint light from the orb gave it depth. Showing in relief the deep, sunken eyes. The wide spindly-toothed mouth.

He froze.

Gods. Was that a Diwe?

Trying not to make any noise, he backed away.

Behind him, one of the cage doors slammed shut.

Two large, glowing eyes opened.

Shit. Swinging around, he shouted to Ember, "Get out!"

He sprinted back the way he came, motioning to Ember to run. The whole room shook under the Diwe's heavy footfalls and somewhere nearby, a woman laughed.

Adia. Goddamn her to hell.

Ember's eyes widened, her lips parting. She jerked into motion and ran. *Finally,* she listened.

Metal groaned behind him as the creature rammed into cages, trying to squeeze past the tight confines of the room.

He grabbed Ember's hand as he passed and yanked her through the doorway before stumbling to a halt.

The women milled about like they had all the time in the world. What the hell were they thinking?

"Run!"

Their eyes widened and they bolted down the hall, the woman with the infant struggling to keep pace.

Harrison shouted directions as he ran. "Last door on the left. Go. Go."

The infant wailed. He caught up to the woman, forced her to pause long enough for him to take the baby. "Run faster; I've got him."

Mom ran.

Behind them the Diwe crashed through the door, her size and bulk taking out part of the wall, too. Pieces of wood and plaster pelted his back and zinged past. He pulled Ember in front of him, urging her faster so he could protect her, cradling the baby to his chest. "Through the room and another right."

The whole building shook as the Diwe tore through walls to chase after them. Chunks of plaster dropped from the ceiling. Walls cracked on either side of them. *Gods,* she was gaining on them.

Harrison let go of Ember and pulled out his phone, hitting the speed dial for Scott.

The Diwe roared, sounding like the typical dinosaurs or dragons from the movies.

On the phone, Scott answered with, "What the hell is that?"

"A fucking Diwe. Get the suit out." He hung up as they turned into the fish tank room, slipping and sliding through the crimson water. He slowed, glancing at the infant to make sure he was all right.

Julian was kneeling over a body and paused to stare at the women running past.

Harrison waved him on. "Move your ass, Jules!"

His partner's eye went saucer-wide as the wall behind them exploded under the force of the Diwe. The women screamed.

Julian leapt to his feet, shooting an accusing glare at Ember. "I told you to stay away from the Asian chick."

Ember gasped. "You should've told her to stay away from us."

The walls shook. The windows rattled in their frames, fracturing under the strain.

He couldn't see all the women, but shouted out the next direction. "Left at the end, through the broken window, and left past the door."

Ember shot him an amazed look. "How do you remember this shit?"

"This shit is saving our collective asses."

They kept running, over the dead daemon Ember had aerated with bullets and past the shattered glass.

"Straight past the door and keep going until you're outside." He glanced at Ember. "You, too, Em."

"No."

"Fuck's sake, we are going to talk about this later."

Her eyes narrowed. "Good."

They slowed in the ballroom. DDC agents lined the front wall of the ballroom, automatic weapons raised. The baby's mother returned and took her child from his arms with a tentative smile of thanks.

"Get ready, Em."

She nodded, breathing hard and shaking like a wet Chihuahua. She dug another magazine out of her purse. It must have been the last because she pulled the bag off and tossed it to the ground before facing the wall with her weapon at the ready.

His mate was amazing.

The noise increased. The Diwe was making its way like a wrecking ball through rooms too small and halls too narrow, making the ground shake. Deeper in the building, it sounded as if whole sections of the building were falling.

Where the hell was the suit? He spied Deno standing at the end of the row of armed and ready DDC agents. Nearby, the robotic exo-suit he'd requested sat in a useless, unmanned heap. Harrison's furious gaze shot to Deno and he stormed across the room. "Why aren't you ready?"

The Oni scowled. "It's a stupid idea, that's why. Fucking suicide."

The Diwe rammed the wall behind him. Harrison swung round, shielding his head. Cracks spider-webbed through the plaster, but the wall held.

For now.

"Everybody, back. That wall's coming down!" Julian yelled the order as he walked toward Harrison.

The agents let out a string of curses. Oh, they all hated these things. The Diwe's hide was thicker than an elephant's and they didn't stop until they were dead. They all backed away as large sections of dry-wall shook loose. The crack expanded as the Diwe slammed the wall again.

A small section between support beams gave way. Plumes of dust erupted from the debris, lowering visibility.

Gunfire erupted in the enclosed space.

Harrison glowered at Deno and raised his voice over the Diwe's roars and gunfire. "What the hell else are we going to do? Have Jules mesmerize her? Maybe I could feed her some of my copies? We can let you bleed on her." He glanced over his shoulder. The Diwe hadn't broken through the support beams yet.

"Do you get how thick that hide is?" The Oni's mottled skin flared brighter, almost glowing in his agitation. "This'll be like digging out of Newgate with a spork."

Julian elbowed the Oni out of the way. "Christ, Deno, they should leave you at the fucking desk where you belong." He nodded to the suit. "Get in, Harry. You've piloted before."

"Once." Harrison crammed his fingers through his hair as Julian lifted the suit. Once, in a fucking training exercise, he'd manned an exo-suit. Never in combat.

More of the wall crumbled. The mammoth creature appeared through the drywall dust and sparking electrical wiring, moving in ungainly lurches as it tried to clear the rubble. Looked like one of her rear legs was stuck. Beyond the Diwe's angler-fishhead, the body resembled an emaciated elephant, with a thick hide shrouding its cumbersome skeleton. No meat or muscle softened the sharp shoulder blades or curved pelvis and in one place in the middle, the hide hid nothing but lumpy vertebrae.

"What's your plan?"

Harrison climbed into the metal exoskeleton and pulled the shoulder straps on, buckling them between his thighs "I go for the eyes and blind it." The softest part of its body were the large glowing eyes. He needed to figure a way past that gaping, toothy maw.

Julian pulled a face. "Jesus. You've gotta be kidding."

"Flip the switch."

Julian walked around to the back of the suit and turned the contraption on. The exo-suit lifted Harrison three feet higher as the legs activated. He slipped his hands into the arm controls and wrapped his fingers around the grips. The exo-suit's arms raised, one a grappling tool, the other a long sword. While he tried a few different maneuvers, getting a feel for the suit, he glanced at Ember. She'd adopted a battle stance, legs braced, arms outstretched and hands locked tight around her sidearm. All things considered, she seemed steady as hell and, gods, he admired her.

He flexed the arms into a fighting position and took his first step toward the Diwe.

The gunfire stopped.

The Diwe struggled, tangled in the debris, splintered wood, and wiring. He wanted to be within striking distance now, to get a few good hits in while she was immobile, but the exo-suit moved slow as a drunk snail. Or maybe the lack of speed was due to his lame-ass newbie piloting skills. He arrived within striking range as the Diwe pulled her leg free from the rubble.

She lurched forward amid a cascade of sparks. His first blow with the sword glanced off her head. The force of her momentum pushed him several feet. The exo-suit's metal feet scraped across the marble floor making him wince.

The Diwe didn't like it either, she reared back, heaving onto her rear legs and forcing him to dodge her spiked front legs. He twisted to the side, raising the sword arm and drawing it across her chest. Even with the force of the robotic suit behind the blow, the blade did little more than nick her thick hide.

Eyes. He needed to stab her eyes.

The Diwe dropped back to all fours and she lashed out, snapping at him with long, crooked teeth. She was too damn close for him to get any momentum in his hits. Trying to put enough room between them, he retreated a step. Then another. And another. She stalked him. Snapping. Biting. His blows doing nothing more than glancing off her thick hide. He curled into himself so the suit took the worst of her next bite. One of those yellowed teeth scraped down his leg.

"Harry!" Ember's voice.

"Fuck." Fire lanced through his leg. He ground his teeth together. He'd be damned if he was going down in front of his mate.

As the Diwe pulled back, he grabbed hold of one of the teeth with his grappling tool. She reared and bucked. The only thing keeping him from being thrown onto his back under her assault was the grip he had on her.

He slammed the sword down on her. He couldn't fall, that would be the worst possible scenario. The exo-suits were slow, he'd be vulnerable while regaining his feet.

A shot went off behind him and the Diwe backed off a bit. He released her, and when she bowed her head and shook, he seized the fleshy stalk protruding from her forehead with the grappling tool.

She roared.

Finally, a soft spot. He pulled. The dangling orb bent to the ground, forcing her head low. Leaving her eyes within striking range. He twisted the suit. Pulled the sword arm back.

Someone took a shot. The orb burst and a milky phosphorescent substance spilled out, splattering him and the exo-suit. Pooling on the floor beneath the exo-suit's feet.

The Diwe reared. He stepped back and the suit's feet slid, leaving him hanging onto the creature for balance.

She tossed her head, throwing him flat on his back. Dazed from the rough landing, he struggled for precious seconds trying to right the suit. The motor's whirred and the suit rocked, but like a damned turtle, he was stuck. Gunfire erupted in the enclosed space, the DDC agents trying to give him some cover.

His head swam and the phosphorescent liquid dripped into his eyes, burning. He kept rocking the suit, fighting the limits of the controls while he wiped the acidic liquid from his face with his arm.

The Diwe roared again. When Harrison opened his eyes, it was to see the Diwe's leg coming down on top of him. He couldn't move out of the way, strapped into the broken exo-suit as he was. Had to lay there and get trampled.

A hoarse shout ripped from his throat. It felt like a goddamn two-by-four pierced his shoulder.

The exo-suit sparked. The grappler arm went dead.

The Diwe's head lowered, eyes closed, toothy maw wide. He used every ounce of energy to raise the sword arm. Braced against the floor, he didn't need to do much besides put it into her path. As she lunged down, the large blade pierced the Diwe's eye.

The Diwe's scream was deafening. She backed away, lifting her leg, and he relived the agony all over again. The whole room spun. He fought to remain conscious.

Someone was dragging him, suit and all and then a lavender, scaly body slithered over him and the exo-suit. Jesus. Em.

He strained to see what was happening, but couldn't lift himself out. Couldn't get the straps off either, not one-handed.

DDC agents shouted, cheering. That meant she was winning, right?

The Diwe roared and the building shook as it slammed into one of the walls. He had to get back on his feet. Had to help Em.

"Jules!" Why wasn't anyone getting him out?

What time was it? He tried to glance at his watch, but couldn't move that arm. *Shit.*

Julian's face appeared above his. "Guess that was a crap idea." Julian helped him out of the harness. He tried to look back where the Diwe was roaring, but Julian tugged him forward. "How 'bout we sit this one out, whaddaya think, big guy?" He hauled Harrison out of the suit and put an arm around him to keep him upright as the whole room spun. "Holy shit, she is pissed off."

The other agents were still shouting and cheering.

Julian forced him toward the door as fast as he could move, but he kept trying to look back. "Where's Ember?"

"Kicking ass." They'd made it to the entryway and Julian paused to let him look back. "Man, I thought Diwe's were mean. Damn things got nothing on a succubus who's seen her mate hurt."

He was right. Scott and the others held their fire, no doubt to keep from hitting his mate, but they were cheering her on. Ember's demon had taken control. Her violet hair whipped around her scale-clad curves as she slashed at the Diwe with those long black nails. Everywhere the Diwe brushed against Ember came away blood-soaked as she got a feel of the razor-edged scales covering Ember's body.

"She's fucking magnificent, isn't she?"

"Yeah, she is." Julian patted him on the back and set his whole shoulder ablaze in pain. He clenched his jaw and leaned harder on the wall. Gods, he was turning into a fucking wimp. His shoulder couldn't be all that bad. Julian would've wrapped it if he'd had a hole there like he first thought.

Ember's demon hauled back her arm and struck the Diwe in her injured eye.

"And you, my friend, get to explain why you kept telling her to get out as if she were defenseless."

Julian's face blurred in front of him. "Like you've never had that argument with Kat." He tensed as the Diwe took a threatening step towards Ember, jaws wide, but Ember's demon grabbed hold of the teeth on either side, holding her jaws apart.

"Oh, we have that argument. I never win, but we have it."

Harrison looked back at the fight just as Ember's demon tore Diwe's jaws several inches wider than they were meant to go. The snap of bone and the tearing of flesh accompanied the Diwe's roar of pain. The Diwe had taken too much damage between the bullets, the blades, and Ember's demon. The Diwe's body began to shrink, changing in shape. The Asian woman bled from multiple wounds, her jaw hung askew. She wouldn't survive, but Ember's demon wasn't taking any chances.

She broke the Diwe's neck.

"You'd better sort her out before she goes after the others." Julian jerked his head toward the DDC agents.

Yeah, Ember's demon had no love for men. Harrison pulled himself away from the wall and walked over to Ember. Walked, stumbled, what the hell, he was moving. Every step made pain shoot down his arm and across his back. Fuck's sake, he was losing his grip. Everything started to blur and he shook off the vertigo. He took off his jacket as he neared Ember, pulling his good arm out and then dragging the sleeve off the other.

"Em?"

Ember's demon whipped around, her face twisted into an angry sneer.

He swallowed. She looked ready to finish him off. "It's over now, honey. Everything's all right."

Her thick, snake-like tail flexed and rolled. Her arm cocked back with her nails poised to slash.

Gods, what if she didn't recognize him? His gaze slid to the crumpled body of the Asian lady. "I'm your mate." He wet his lips, unease lifting the hair on his arms. "You won't hurt me."

There was no hesitation in her expression. If anything, his statement seemed to make her more furious. She clasped her hand around his throat. Her sharp scales abraded his skin. Her nails dug into his throat.

Shit. His breath stuttered as his throat tried to close on him. "Ember . . . honey. Help me out."

Finally, her brows furrowed. "No." She shook her head, but her fingers squeezed tighter. "*No.*"

A shudder ran through her. Her eyes cleared, returning to that familiar emerald green. She released him and he staggered back, his hand going to his tender throat.

Gods, that was close. She needed to mate. Her demon was growing stronger.

The scales faded from Ember's body, and her skin and hair took on their normal hues. He stepped in front of her, shielding her from the others as she shifted back and wrapped her in his jacket. The damn thing covered her ass, but left her long, gorgeous legs bare. His jaw clenched as he noticed the other agents looking their fill. "I need to start wearing longer coats."

Her gaze dropped to his throat and she lifted her hand to touch him.

He captured her hand and gave it a squeeze. "Glad to have you back, love." He tried to smile, but her image blurred in front of him.

CHAPTER 16

October 13, 3:29 AM

"**H**ARRY!"

Ember steadied her mate. He swayed on his feet and his skin had turned pale. Tiny cuts and red welts ringed his neck from where her demon had grabbed hold of him. Her gaze traveled lower, noting a tear in his shirt. She grabbed the material in both hands and ripped it wide. She blanched. "Oh, God."

Below his collar bone, to the right of his shoulder was a jagged wound. Not a tiny bullet hole, more like a two-inch round crater. "You're hurt."

"Nah, I'm good."

Ember's gaze locked onto the gaping hole in his shoulder. He was *not* good. "What happened?" He staggered like a drunk and she pulled his arm over her shoulders.

"You need to mate, Em."

For crying out loud he even sounded like a drunk. "Oh, you think so?" She spied Julian talking to Scott. "Jules, I need you."

Julian ran over. His brows drew together. "What happened?"

"Are you blind? His shoulder."

Julian cursed. "You damn fool, why didn't you say anything?"

"Figured if I was hurt bad you woulda taken care of it."

"I thought you hit your head." Julian pulled off Harrison's shirt and ripped the fabric down the middle. He wound the material round Harrison's shoulder and knotted it tight. "All right, let's take off before we find more trouble."

"Adia's here." Harrison tried to force Ember to turn around. They almost went tumbling when she lost her balance.

"Was. She gave us one hell of a distraction while she made her escape." Julian urged Ember away and pulled Harrison's good arm over his shoulder. "Scott and the others can finish this. We got the women, that's what's important."

"The women." Her gaze locked with Scott's.

He waved her on. "Next time. Go get him sorted."

Julian got him walking toward the exit. "We've been doing this a long while, Emerald Eyes. We can handle everything one more time, before you show us how it's done."

Right. Good. She couldn't stomach the thought of leaving Harrison while he was wounded. She followed behind like a worried mama hen. Julian was great. He kept an ongoing if somewhat nonsensical conversation, as if the two of them were hanging out, shooting the shit.

"What time is it?"

Julian snorted. "You don't need to know the time."

"It's important."

"Nope. Nothing momentous is happening tonight. Keep moving, dickhead."

They made their way through the wreckage of the club. Outside, DDC vehicles waited. Julian motioned to Deno. "Give us a lift."

At the car, Deno pulled out her bag from the trunk and handed it to her. She went around the side and pulled on a pair of jeans and a tee-shirt before sliding into the back seat.

Ember didn't say much during the ride. She was too worried. Harrison wavered in and out of consciousness. What concerned her most was that even when conscious, he didn't seem to notice, much less mind her touch. His head rested in her lap, one of her hands splayed wide on his chest, the other stroking through his hair. She was touching him and he didn't care.

Despite the roads being deserted, getting home took almost an hour and a half. Julian and Deno talked about what happened at the auction, speculating on how Adia discovered their plan and if she had a spy at the department, but she couldn't concentrate on the conversation. After a while, she quit trying and just watched over Harrison as if her vigilance would keep his spirit from attempting to sneak away.

She couldn't lose him. Didn't want to die if he did and didn't want to go on without him. She just needed him to be well. They'd been together less than a week and they had a lot of problems—she shouldn't feel this strongly for him but she did. She needed him in her life. Would rather face a mountain of problems with him that live peacefully without him.

Oh, God. She was falling in love with him. Even knowing he may never return her feelings, she couldn't stop. Didn't even want to.

She leaned down, curling her body around his and pressing her lips to his forehead. "Don't you die on me."

Lucas jumped to his feet as soon as she and Julian walked in with Harrison supported between them.

"What the hell happened?"

Harrison amazed her when he opened his eyes, plastered a smile on his face. "All good, kid. Don't worry. Be good as gold for Friday." No sooner had he spoken than his head fell forward and he became dead weight.

Ember staggered. Julian turned into Harrison and hefted him onto his shoulder in a fireman's carry.

Lucas' eyes widened. "Jules?"

"He's all right, kid. He's a vampire remember? He needs some R-and-R, that's all."

Lucas slipped his hand into Ember's and squeezed. "I'll be here, okay? You need anything, let me know and I'll help out."

He was always trying to play so tough, seeing all his bravado slip away because of his concern was almost too much. She smiled and swallowed past the burning lump in her throat. "Thank you, Lucas. You're very sweet to offer. Can you get the elevator for us?"

Lucas ran ahead and punched the button, shifting his weight while he waited for them. "He doesn't look real good, Jules."

"Comes with the territory." Julian winked at Lucas. "I promise, he'll be fine by Friday."

Lucas stuffed his hands in his pockets. "It's Wednesday."

"Yep. You'll never know he'd been injured by Friday."

As soon as the elevator doors slid closed, she turned to Julian. "He's passed out, right?" Passed out, not dead. Not dying.

Julian nodded. "It's a good thing, Emerald Eyes. His body's forcing him to conserve energy, that's all."

When the doors opened, she followed Julian into the apartment and then ran ahead to open the bedroom door and pull down the sheets. Julian deposited him into bed.

She'd never seen Harrison so pale. So still.

Julian touched her shoulder. "You okay for a little while?"

She dragged her gaze from her mate to Julian. "I don't know what to do for him."

"Keep him comfortable and make sure that wound stays covered. Kat will be here before sunrise and she'll heal the worst of it."

She stopped him when he started to walk away. "He's going to get better, right?"

"Yes. It's bad, but it's not *that* bad." Julian smiled and squeezed her shoulder. "I'm going to go clean up. Are you hungry? I can make you something to eat first."

Just the thought made her stomach sour. She shook her head.

"Okay. Yell if you need anything."

Once alone, she pulled off his shoes and socks, went to her side of the bed, and sat next to him. She stroked her fingers through his hair. The long, unruly blond locks were soft, thick. They'd been mated for six nights, had made love, and she couldn't remember touching his hair once before tonight's car ride home. How could that be?

He seemed to like the attention. He rolled over, planting his cheek on her breast, throwing an arm across her stomach and nudging his thigh between hers.

Tingling heat pooled low in her belly and her nipples tightened. She clenched her teeth. He was hurt and her demon only cared about sex. She inhaled a deep, cleansing breath and tried to focus on something other than the arousing weight of her mate sprawled on top of her.

George provided the perfect distraction.

The minion skulked into the room with his fur sticking through his scales. A low growl reverberated through him.

Did George think she did this? Would he retaliate? She pulled her legs higher on the bed. Would've moved altogether, but Harrison had her pinned in place.

George leapt onto the mattress and crawled on top of his wounded master, his inky eyes focused on her.

"George, no." She tried to wave the small creature away. "George, out."

He hissed, swatting at her

She snatched her hand back, her heart slamming in her chest. George flattened out over Harrison's hip, his head hanging. He rubbed his face against his master and whined.

"Do not eat me." Odd that her voice was so calm, as if the rioting emotions inside her had pushed her into a false peace to prevent her from going mad. "He'll be fine. I'll take good care of him until Kat gets here. I promise."

The minion gurgled, his stare remaining steady on her, giving her the impression he intended to make sure she did.

After a while, exhaustion overtook her fear of George and her worry for Harrison and she dozed until Julian returned, balancing a large tray in one hand. "I've got food for you. Figured you must be hungry by now."

She shook her head. "Not really."

He paused, searching her face. "How 'bout tea? At least have some of that." Julian waited while she wriggled upright and forced a cup of steaming tea into her hands.

"Thanks." Her attention remained on the man sprawled across her. "Shouldn't we take him to a doctor or something?"

He grinned. "No insurance, remember?"

Her lips twitched. All of the stress and horror of the last few days bubbled out of her in stifled laughter. "I shouldn't. I don't know why I'm laughing."

"It's the stress, Emerald Eyes." He tugged her hair. "Laugh or cry, right?"

She nodded, sobering as she looked at her mate.

"How are you, Em?"

"I'm fine." She stroked her fingers through Harrison's hair. "Worried."

"Right." He nodded. Jerked his head toward the bathroom. "Why don't you go clean up?"

"I don't want to leave him alone."

"I'll stay. George and I can handle this." His mouth twitched. "Trust me, you don't want Harry to see you like that."

After everything that happened tonight, she must look a fright. "All right, point taken. Can you help me move him?"

Julian helped roll Harrison onto his back and adjusted the bandage. When she still hesitated, he shooed her with a wave of his hand. "Shower. Go on. I'll be right here."

Ember grabbed a change of clothes from the other room and closed herself in the bathroom. She turned on the water and peered in the mirror as she removed her jeans and tee. Yep, Julian was right. She had no desire for Harrison to see her looking like a zombified clown.

Her hair stood in tangles all over her head. Her make-up smeared, she had a bruise on her cheek and a cut on her lip.

Once under the hot spray of water, she couldn't stand the constant state of arousal anymore. The need had built for days now. Her demon writhed under her skin. While she washed and rinsed her hair she ignored it, but as soon as she soaped her body, she lost the battle.

She closed her eyes and pictured Harrison. His broad shoulders, tight abs, and those brilliant blue eyes of his staring into hers. Imagined his voice urging her on. His scent surrounding her. She slipped her fingers between her thighs, shivering.

His name whispered past her lips. "Harry."

Recalling the thick, slick glide of his cock, the way his fingers entwined with hers when he held her hand, she came. With a gasp, her whole body shuddered as pleasure coursed through her.

There. That should shut her she-bitch demon up for a while, at least long enough for Harrison to heal.

She faced the spray of hot water and finished washing. She dried off, combed her hair and re-dressed in jeans and a tank.

As she turned to leave, desire rocked through her with staggering force.

She braced her hand on the wall as she bent forward. Her nipples drew into hard points and her pussy clenched tight.

Oh, God. She'd made her need worse.

When she could straighten, she leaned against the door and stared at her reflection. Her image shifted in the steamy mirror. She swiped her hand across the remaining condensation and peered closer.

A blue-tinged, ghostly replica of herself stretched away from her as if her spirit wanted to escape. Except this version of her had reptilian eyes and long, razor-sharp claws on the ends of her fingers. Its arms strained out in effort to grasp hold of the sink to anchor itself outside her body.

Her demon.

As it glared into the mirror, its face changed. Altered from one she recognized as her own, to something fanged and scaly. It hissed. *Let me free. I will ensure we are sated.*

Ember closed her eyes, clenched her fists and visualized her demon getting sucked back where it belonged. When she opened her eyes. The ghostly image had disappeared.

She smoothed her shaky hands along the seams of her jeans.

She didn't have time for this.

Ember returned to the bedroom to find Julian sprawled in the armchair near the bed. His hooded eye zeroed in on her. "What's wrong? You look worse than before."

She pulled a face. "Gee, thanks."

He got to his feet. "You're pale as an albino bunny. You okay?"

"Yeah. I'm just worried. How is he?"

"He's—" His head cocked to the side and his whole body stilled while he listened. A wide grin spread on his face. "Kat's home."

Ember trailed behind as Julian strode into the living room.

A woman with bright red curly hair was setting her bag on the counter. Julian didn't say a word as he hauled her into his arms and kissed her.

Ember grinned. Never had she doubted that Julian loved his mate, but she also had never quite been able to picture him with her. He spoke so softly, Ember couldn't make out the words, but the way he pressed close, the way he touched her face and stroked her hair while he whispered to her spoke volumes.

She returned to the bedroom to give them privacy. Sat on the edge of the bed and pulled Harrison's hand into her lap. "One of these days, Harry, that'll be you and me."

"Ember?"

Ember turned to the door and smiled.

Julian grinned, his hands planted on his mate's shoulders. "This is my mate, Kat."

"Hi."

Kat walked straight to her and gave her a hug. "It's so good to meet you." She stood back at arm's length for a moment, and nodded. "You're right, Jules. She has a lovely aura." Her brows drew together. "Are you all right?"

"I'm worried about him."

She let out a heavy sigh. "I'd tell you this doesn't happen very often, but I don't like to lie. Karma can be a real bitch when you owe and these two tend to be chronically injured."

Julian tugged on Kat's bright red curls. "We want to make sure you know you're needed, butterfly."

Kat scoffed but she leaned back against Julian and in turn he rubbed his cheek in her hair. They were a beautiful couple. She'd always thought her and Harrison would've been like that if they'd gotten together.

A sliver of jealousy made her glance away. "Jules tells me you're a healer?"

She motioned to Harrison. "Do you mind if I examine the wound?"

"No." Ember helped unwrap Harrison's shoulder and stood back while Kat inspected the jagged flesh at the edges of the puncture. After a moment she straightened, and smiled. "He'll be fine." She turned to Julian. "Go on, Jules. We'll take care of this and I'll be out in a minute."

"You sure you don't need anything?"

Kat gave him a quick kiss. "Nope. Ember will help me."

Julian left and she closed the door behind him.

Kat turned around and winked. "He hovers when Harry's hurt, just as bad as Harry does if Jules is. Drives me nuts."

Ember tried to smile. "You said I could help? What do you want me to do?"

"Undress and get into bed."

Her feeble smile faltered. "What?"

"He'll need your body heat after this. I'll be able to close the wound completely, I think, but he'll need a full day of rest to be back to his old self. Keep him warm and let him sleep it off."

"Okay." She unbuttoned her jeans. Maybe this was a good thing, him waking and discovering her in his bed with no adverse results might aid her cause. Being so close to him would be hell for her, as aroused as she was, but maybe the closeness would be good for Harry. Or maybe he'd feel betrayed.

Didn't matter. He needed her body heat. She needed him healthy. She got into bed, wearing the tank and her panties.

Kat leaned over him, holding one hand over his shoulder. With the other, she clutched a deep red stone hanging from a chain around her neck. The air between Kat's hand and the wound shimmered like when heat rose from the streets in summer in Arizona. The edges of the wound melted together.

He moaned, restless in his sleep and she slipped her hand into his lax one. George echoed his discomfort with a menacing growl.

As soon as the skin knit itself together, Kat stopped. "Help me get him on his side. I want to make sure the exit wound healed."

Ember took hold of the arm farthest from her and pulled Harrison toward her while Kat pushed one of his legs over. George hopped to the floor long enough for them to get him settled and then went right back to his spot to keep watch.

Kat repeated the procedure. After a few moments, she straightened, put her hands on her lower back and stretched her back muscles. "The wound healed shut. His body will take care of the rest."

Everything was going to be okay. He was fine. She needed every ounce of control not to sob in relief. "Thank you."

"Get some sleep. Tonight, you and I can get to know each other." She paused. "Lights on or off?"

"On, please. In case he needs me."

Kat closed the door behind her.

Ember pulled the covers over them both and eased Harrison onto his back. She cuddled next to him, resting her face on his good shoulder and shut her eyes.

Take him.

Her eyes snapped open as her nipples hardened and desire wound deep in her belly. Tears filled her eyes. She hated her demon. Hated what she'd become.

She folded her arms over her breasts and squeezed her legs together. She closed her eyes once again, ignored the demanding voice in her mind, concentrated on her mate's steady breathing. On the man she loved.

The low rumble of George's purr helped lull her and exhaustion won out.

CHAPTER 17

October 13, 5:12 PM

HARRISON LAY ON A SATIN-CLAD bed in Adia's arena. Unlike last time he was there, he was wearing jeans.

This wasn't right.

The walls were dank and stained, but didn't smell the same as he remembered. He inhaled a fresh, clean scent. The sheets were warm and soft and as he rolled over he realized he wasn't alone.

Ember lay by his side, her lush body stripped bare and tied down. He tried to untie her, but his hands jerked away. He didn't have control of his limbs.

As if they had a will of their own, his arms lifted until the rest of him had no choice but to follow. Wire wound around each of his wrists. Other wires circled his feet, his knees, elbows, and his hands. The wires pulled him to his knees and then to his feet.

His gaze traveled higher and he saw Adia standing in the viewing booth, watching, manipulating his actions with a marionette's wooden control bar. With a flick of her wrist, he hopped across the bed and knelt between Ember's thighs.

Ember stared at him with wide, terrified eyes. She shook her head. "Don't touch me. You're dirty. You're a child killer."

She wouldn't say that. She didn't think that. Not anymore.

This wasn't right.

The wires dragged him forward and down. He tried to resist, to pull out of the tangle of wires, but he had no control. He lay on top of her, nuzzling her neck. Grinding his hips against hers. His cock thickened with his arousal and he pressed the bulge of his erection to her warm slit.

She tried to arch away from him. "Stop."

Gods, he had to stop. Ember was right. He was a murderer. Adia was right. He'd never be any good for anyone but her. He'd allowed himself to be used. Worse, he was a male—if he hadn't liked the things Adia did, his body wouldn't have reacted. If he didn't like what Adia forced him to do to Ember, it wouldn't feel so good.

He was wretched. Used. Still being used.

None of this was fair. The only reason Ember was with him was because Adia forced her hand. The only reason he'd mated Ember was because Adia forced his. That night he'd found her in the hotel was rape by proxy from both sides. How could Ember ever love him after that? How could they ever have a future when their past was controlled by his enemy?

The wires jerked and his hand dropped to Ember's breast. Squeezed and kneaded, plucked and tugged until Ember writhed beneath him, moaning. Her body responded despite her protests.

His knees dug into the bed as he pressed his jean-clad cock deeper against her belly. Rotating his hips, he rocked against her. Bursts of shivers broke out across his lower back. His balls drew tight. He fought the growing need to come.

Damn it, *no!* He refused to allow Adia to manipulate him again. He was the male. He had control. If nothing else, he had authority of his body, damn it. He'd decide when and how and where he'd love his mate. Not her. Not ever again.

Despite his resolve, Ember was soft and warm beneath him. He wanted her to love him. Needed her to respond. The wires jolted and his mouth lowered to her breast. He dragged his tongue over the puckered, jutting tip. Ran the uneven edges of his teeth across her nipple.

Ember moaned.

Or had she? Maybe Ember's response was nothing more than a flick of Adia's wrist, too.

He rolled his hips against the warm cradle of Ember's body.

Her hand stroked his back, her nails sinking into his flanks, pulling him closer. Gods. His body shuddered over hers as he came. Pleasure pulsed through his pelvis, radiating across his lower back and gripping his cock.

When he opened his eyes, he lay in his room. In bed. On top of a sleeping Ember. She moaned and shifted under him. He had her shirt lifted over the rise of her breasts.

What the fuck had he done?

Slowly, he tugged her tank back into place and eased off her.

Harrison rolled out of bed and glanced down at himself. Fuck's sake, he'd come in his pants like some fucking tween.

He dropped his head into his hands. What the hell was wrong with him?

She didn't want him. He'd offered multiple times, and she kept saying no. Now that she'd been sated, now that she was out of Adia's control, she didn't have any use for him.

And why should she? This whole mess was his fault. Hell, the whole situation was fucked up and he had no idea how to fix it. Worse, now that he'd had a taste of his mate, he *wanted* her. He'd been fighting his own need, determined not to put her into a position where she'd feel like she needed to accommodate him. Where he didn't have to acknowledge Adia or Ember or his own damn body had any control over him.

But he *wanted* Ember.

And he didn't.

He raked his fingers through his hair and went into the bath-room, closing the door. What he wanted didn't matter. What mattered was she needed him.

She'd need him again.

Then he could touch her. He could sate his own need without feeling like he was submitting to Adia's whim.

Or his body's.

CHAPTER 18

October 14, 5:15 AM

EMBER STEPPED OUT OF THE bathroom feeling awkward as a teenage boy who'd discovered what penises could do besides pee.

This was getting ridiculous. The brief respites she got from masturbating were hardly worth the effort. Each time, the arousal returned stronger than before. She needed to mate, but wanted to give Harrison time. Time to ensure he healed. Time to get comfortable with her. Time to trust her.

She was going to go back to their room and try to sleep it off, but Kat spotted her and grinned. The red-haired lady bounded up from her spot next to Julian on the couch and linked arms with Ember. "You don't mind if I steal you away, do you?" She tugged her along, strolling off into the Crowley side of the household. While masculine, with large pieces of furniture and heavy rugs over the wood flooring, Kat's touch could be seen everywhere. The soft throws folded on the back of the couch. The romance novel on the side table. The his & hers slippers tucked under the edge of the bed. Flowers graced the nightstand and mantle. A small alter decorated with stones, dried flowers, and a statue of a pregnant woman with the Earth as her belly.

Another sliver of jealousy turned her stomach. Harrison had

allowed her into his bedroom, but had yet to offer to let her bring her things into his space. She tamped down the unwanted emotion.

Two armchairs sat in the corner in her and Julian's bedroom, and Kat guided her toward them. "I thought we could get to know each other where our mates with scary good hearing can't overhear."

"Your rooms are beautiful." She glanced around again, her gaze catching on a landscape painting of a river running through a valley. There was something odd about that picture—

"Oh, thank you. Please have a seat." Kat patted the seat and she had no choice but to turn away from her study of the painting.

Gingerly, Ember sat, hating her inner demon with a passion.

Kat frowned. "Are you sure you're doing okay? You're moving a little stiff."

"A little sore, nothing to worry about." She smiled, pushing aside her discomfort. "I can't tell you how much I appreciate your help—" She stopped as unexpected tears threatened. He was safe, there was no reason to cry. She was just so damned grateful to Kat.

Kat leaned over and patted her knee. Then, changed the subject. "Julian mentioned you haven't asked to make any phone calls. Do you have friends or family you need to contact?"

For the first time in years, she wished she did have someone like that. She'd turned herself into a loner and was starting to regret it. Wished more than anything her mother was still alive to talk to.

Kat's expression turned sympathetic at her hesitation. She forced herself to smile. "I will, but right now I don't know what I'd say."

"Sometimes hearing their voice is enough."

She didn't have anyone like that, except Nancy. Her parents died long ago. She'd only lived and worked in Bellevue for three years and while she'd gained plenty of acquaintances, she found she liked anonymity. Liked that no one knew her story. In order to keep things that way she'd never taken any of her friendships beyond the superficial except with Nancy. The thing was, right now, she didn't know what she should or shouldn't say to Nancy. The last thing she wanted was to make more mistakes with Harrison. "They'll have lots of questions and I'm not ready to answer them yet."

"How about you and Harry. Is everything working out okay?" Kat frowned. "Your aura went all kinds of wonky just now. What's going on?"

Ember closed her eyes. She'd never considered being friends with a witch before. Sounded like there wouldn't be much use in trying to hide things from her new friend. *So talk to her. Ask for advice.* "I messed things up."

"Already?"

She met Kat's gaze and they both laughed. "Okay, Miss Perfect, how long were you and Jules together before you felt like you messed up?"

Kat took a deep breath. "Well, right from the start, if I want to be honest. I kidnapped him."

Ember gasped. "No." She couldn't picture anyone getting the better of Julian, much less someone as small in stature as Kat.

"Yep. Kidnapped him and held him against his will." She looked at Ember askance. "This is Jules we're talking about. How else could I to get him to pay attention and fall in love?"

Ember tried to stifle her laugh under her hand. "You're as bad as he is."

"I'm sneakier." She huffed out a burst of air. "So, Harry's being stupid."

Oh, God. She didn't want his friends thinking he wasn't a good mate. "No, he's been great, all things considered. He's . . ."

"Not falling in love with you?"

Wow, she was blunt. "No." Ember grimaced. "Not even a little."

"See? Stupid. We've all been hearing about you for ages. Now he's got you and he's messing it up."

"I'm being impatient." Ember shifted in her seat, trying to get comfortable. "He needs more time. If you have any suggestions on—"

"Oh, I've got suggestions all right." Kat grinned, drumming her fingers on the arm of the chair. "I think we need to remind him how well the two of you got on together."

She made it sound so stinking easy. "How do you suggest I do that?"

"Come on." Kat stood, pulled Ember to her feet and led her

into the living room where the men were playing cards.

<hr>

Harrison did a double-take when Kat sailed into the living room with Ember in tow. She plopped next to Julian but all her attention was on him.

What the hell?

Ember eyed the spot next to him, then chose the armchair adjacent to him.

He leaned back in his seat with a frown. Somehow, he was doing something wrong. What if she hadn't been asleep this afternoon? Maybe she knew about the whole debacle and pretended to be asleep to keep from embarrassing him. What a mess.

Kat cleared her throat, drawing his attention. "Ember tells me you two were childhood friends."

"Yeah." Kat was up to something. He'd told her about Ember years ago. "We went to the same school."

"His parents pretty much adopted me." Ember smoothed out a long blond lock of hair, twisting the strands around her finger. "They always invited me to dinner and on outings."

"Huh." Kat knocked her foot against his leg. "Must have kind of sucked for a teenage boy, getting stuck hanging out with a girl all the time."

His gaze sharpened. Even Julian's gaze was bouncing between his mate and Ember. "Why would you say that? Ember and I always had fun."

"Oh?" Kat's eyes widened. "What did you guys do?"

"I don't know." He shrugged. "Went swimming."

"Really?"

Oh, for fuck's sake. Had she never heard of swimming before? He tossed his cards face down on the table. Obviously, the game was done.

Julian leaned forward. "You're folding?"

"No. I'm not folding." He motioned to Kat. "Your mate is distracting me."

Julian grinned. "You folded." He tossed his cards on the table. "I win."

Harrison dragged his hand through his hair. "We lived in Arizona, Katherine. It's hot. Everybody swims."

"Well, how should I know? I've never been there." She stood long enough to fold one of her legs under her, and then sat back down. "Did you go to a community pool?"

Harrison shot Julian a 'What the fuck?' kind of look. "Is this some weird interrogation?"

"This is small talk, *Harrison*." The look she leveled at him suggested he not fuck about with her.

Julian snickered behind his hand and Kat jerked her elbow into his ribs. "I want to get to know your mate."

What the fuck was going on? He glanced at Ember, who appeared to be trying to disappear into the armchair. Her cheeks were tinged red and she was taking great interest in studying the ends of her hair. He turned his attention back to Kat. "Then why are you asking me?"

Julian quit trying to hide his mirth as tears welled in his eyes. "Give in, man, it'll be less painful for all of us."

Bastard. It'd be nice if Julian at least clued him in on the joke. He slumped back in his seat. "Private. My parents had a pool."

"And you swam?" Kat nodded her head slowly.

He glared at her through hooded eyes. "Yes."

"All the time?"

"Oh, for fuck's sake. What's gotten into you?"

Julian looked like he was going to piss himself he was laughing so hard. Kat whacked him.

Ember leaned forward and blurted out, "We played Star Wars."

Everyone stared at her. Julian stopped laughing, his brows raising high on his forehead.

He moaned. Of all the things she could say, why that?

Julian shot him a side-eye glance before turning his attention on Ember. "Oh? Who did you play, and wearing which outfit?"

Kat gasped. "*Jules!*"

"What?"

Well, hell, this conversation was in a fast-downward spiral.

Ember lifted her chin a notch. "I always played Leia, of course, but Leia from the third trilogy. You know, like in the books, after she'd trained as a Jedi." She shrugged. "I wanted a light saber."

A stupid grin spread on Julian's face. "Okay. I'm impressed by your geekiness."

"We'd climb onto the roof." Ember tucked her feet under her

and leaned against the arm of her chair. Gods, she was getting comfy for a nice long story. No stopping her now.

Kat's brows drew together. "I thought we were talking about swimming."

"We are." Her eyes grew brighter than he'd seen them in days. He didn't have the heart to stop her, though he knew Julian would tease the hell out of him later. "We'd climb onto the roof and when one of us took a mortal blow we had to jump off into the pool."

"How close was the pool?" Julian asked.

Ember shrugged. "I don't know, what like ten feet?"

"Nah. We jumped from the corner eave, more like three or four."

Julian grinned. "And who did you play, *Harrison?*"

"Shut it."

"Nuh-uh. I want to know. Ember said you fought with light sabers, but if I remember right, in those books, Leia married Han and you don't strike me as a Luke. . ." Julian waggled his brows.

Harrison turned his glare on Ember, whose lips twitched with mirth. A wise woman, she kept her mouth shut, but she'd said enough. "You know what I liked to do when we were kids?" He grinned. Oh, paybacks were a bitch. "Going to Canyon Lake."

She pulled a face and shook her head. "Why? We only went that one time . . ." The furrow between her brows eased and her eyes widened. Ember gasped. "You wouldn't."

He leaned forward. "Trout. Shark."

Ember pointed at him. "Do. Not."

Like hell he wouldn't. "She'd gotten a little spoiled swimming in pristine, chlorinated pool water so when we—"

She yelped, launching herself over the arm of her chair to clamp her hand over his mouth. She shook her head. "Please don't."

He licked her palm.

As soon as she jerked her hand away he continued, "—went to Canyon Lake—"

She cupped her hand over his mouth again. This time, he pulled her onto his lap and wrestled her into a position where he could restrain her. "She was afraid to get in the water."

Julian and Kat were both grinning at them like idiots.

Ember slumped back against him. Her tone was pouty. "The

lake had leaves and bits of stuff floating around, and something brushed my leg."

Harrison chuckled, remembering a young bikini-clad Ember standing rigid in knee-deep water with a disgusted look on her face. "It took me an hour to convince her to get in the lake."

She whipped her head around to glare. "There were fish."

Julian snorted. "It was a lake."

Ember stuck her tongue out at him.

He closed his eyes, picturing the desert beach, the wide expanse of water and the high canyon walls on the other side. Everything echoed in that corner of the lake, bouncing off the red rocks. Especially her screams. "There was this little island about a quarter mile out, I talked her into swimming out there."

"It was close to the canyon wall and I wanted to jump off '51/50'—it's a ledge halfway up the canyon—we'd talked about doing the jump all summer."

He still had his forearm locked around her shoulders. She rested her chin on his arm and gods, he was feeling nostalgic. "I reached the island first and I looked back to find out what was taking her so long. Em kept stopping and peering into the water."

"Something brushed against my leg," she spoke through gritted teeth, her arms folded over her chest.

He grinned. "Yeah, well, for whatever reason I got a wild hair up my ass and decided to tease her."

"A wild hair?" Ember wriggled out of his grasp and turned, kneeling on the couch so she faced him. Her eyes blazed. "You had a bit of the devil in you, Harrison Cayce." At the last moment, she added, "Sinclair."

"I cupped my hands around my mouth, and yelled, 'Watch out for the trout shark.'" He couldn't stop smiling—remembering the look on her face. "For a few seconds, she bobbed real low in the water as if the fish might not notice her if her eyes were above the surface. Then. . . ." He cleared his throat. "Well, you remember on Looney Tunes how they could run on water?"

Both Kat and Julian giggled. Even Ember wore a rueful smile. "I swear to God there were bubbles in the water."

Harrison shook his head. "I've never seen her swim so fast and every couple of strokes she kind of leapt out of the water and screamed." He couldn't take his eyes off her. She was so damn beautiful right now, wearing a bemused smile with her cheeks tinged pink. It almost hurt to look at her. He brushed his knuckles against the curve of her jaw. "Gods, we always had a good time together, didn't we?"

Her voice lowered to a whisper. "I woke every morning wanting nothing more than to discover what kind of trouble we'd get into."

Yeah, he had, too. "After I left, I thought about you every day. I can't begin to describe how much I missed you." He glanced away and chuckled. "They ducked out on us."

She sidled closer. When she put her warm palm on his chest his body reacted with the same enthusiasm as if she'd stripped naked. She bit her bottom lip, leaving a tiny indent in its lush curve. "I guess they wanted to be alone."

He couldn't pull his gaze away. He wanted to strip her bare, pull her beneath him and sink deep into her heat. Her gorgeous green eyes filled his vision as she leaned in until her warm breath fanned his lips. Gods, he couldn't seem to get enough air. Adrenaline shot through him, leaving him struggling for control. Struggling for air.

This wasn't a good idea. Every time she touched him his body went into overdrive. What if he lost control? What if she did? He knew too well what could happen. What if he hurt her? Or if she…? He slipped out from under her palm and stood. Slowed his inhalations long enough to exhale. The pain in his chest eased. "We should get some sleep." Gods, he was sucking air like he'd run a marathon.

Her brows furrowed.

"You okay, Em?"

She looked away. "Yeah, fine."

He offered his hand to help her to her feet and led her to their room. Once inside, she turned to him and flattened her palm on his chest again.

Gods, he'd just gotten his breathing back to normal. With a smile, he covered her hand with his, gave her a little squeeze, and removed it. Easing her around, he hugged her from behind, pulled her silken hair back from her neck, and trailed his lips along the downy curve of her throat. She shivered in his arms and pressed into his embrace, her bottom nestled against his erection.

"Are you sure, Harry?"

"Mm." This he could do. As long as he was in control. As long as she didn't touch him. He ran his tongue along the delicate shell of her ear. She needed him, so he could do this. Her hair smelled of his shampoo. Twisting the long strands around his hand, he tipped her head to the side and brushed her cheek with his. "How is your skin this soft, Em?"

She sighed, resting her head against his shoulder.

He eased her top off and removed her bra. Turning her, he took her hands in his. Backed her against the door and pinned her arms to her sides. Her heart thrummed in his ears as he kissed his way to her chest. He loved her full breasts. The dark, rucked nipples. He laved one with his tongue before sucking the tip deep into his mouth.

Her breath caught. The erratic pulse of her breath brushed his face. She must be watching him suckle her. She arched her back, offering him more. The sweet smell of her skin, the earthy scent of desire filling each breath was driving him insane. He tugged at her breast and she shivered. The scent of her desire laced the air.

He released one of her hands and opened the fly on her pants with a quick tug. She helped him slide them off those long, lush legs and stepped out of them. She cupped his cheek and he pressed his face deeper to her palm. Gods, he wanted her hands on him. Soon, but not tonight. He pulled her hand away as he stood and guided her to the bed. Urged her onto her hands and knees.

He cupped her breast in one hand, found her slick slit with the other and circled her clit in teasing strokes until she shook beneath him. He found her entrance. Tried to slide his finger into her, but her inner walls were locked tight. Hot to the touch. "Em, honey, are you all right?"

"Now, Harry. Please." She moaned, pushing back against him.

"I don't want to hurt you. Try to relax." He slid his slicked finger in past the flexed inner muscles and she shivered. Gods, she must have needed him for a while now. Needed him and hadn't said anything. Why had she waited so long? Was she embarrassed? Did she not want him?

She pushed back against his hand and he stoked her, thrust into her until she shuddered beneath him, crying out. Her inner walls eased.

"Are you sure, Em?"

"Please, Harry."

He undid his pants.

CHAPTER 19

October 14, 7:32 AM

ADIA GLARED AT THE HALF of the cuero she kept caged on her nightstand. The two lovers displayed on its slick skin.

This wasn't how she planned things.

Adia's nails bit into her palms as she watched.

Harry covered the succubus from behind. He pinned her down and they both cried out as he entered her. His long, muscular legs kept her thighs spread wide and his ass flexed with every plunge. His hands held hers down on the comforter. The succubus tipped her hips back to meet each of his powerful thrusts.

She hadn't meant for him to enjoy that bitch.

"Harry." The succubus fisted the sheets in her hand. Arched, shuddering through an orgasm.

His forehead pressed into the succubus' back. He wrapped one arm tight around her body, holding her close through his own orgasm. They lay together as their breathing slowed. He kissed her shoulder, nipping at her skin, caressing her.

The succubus rolled over and smiled.

He rose, turned away, and pulled on his pants.

Ah. Perhaps the lovers weren't so happy after all. He found the succubus lacking. Good.

"Harry?"

"Em, please don't take this wrong, but could you not call me that?"

Adia smirked. Of course he didn't want the succubus to call him Harry. *She* called him Harry.

Content, she went in search of her latest conquest.

———◆———

Ember sat up and dragged the sheet over her chest. "You prefer Harrison?"

He nodded, glanced away. "I know it's stupid."

"No, it's fine. I like it. Suites you better."

He shot her a rueful smile, and scrubbed his hand over the back of his neck. "Thanks for understanding."

She didn't. She had no idea why his nickname bothered him, but he was talking. He'd told her something he wanted and she'd be damned if she was going to interrogate him about it. "You just need to talk to me, tell me what you want. On occasion. I can be pretty reasonable."

He came back to sit on the edge of the bed. "What's going on, Em? You needed me and didn't say anything."

She still needed him. Beneath her skin, her demon writhed, curling in her belly, but he wasn't ready for more. They way he'd practically lunged out of bed to tuck himself back into his pants told her he still wasn't comfortable with her. How would he react if she asked for more time? More intimacy? "I wanted to give us time to get reacquainted."

"I'll buy that as part of the reason." He pressed his palm to her chest. "But I can hear your heart, Em. I'm a bit of a walking lie detector. You're hiding something from me."

The desire unfurling in her belly made thinking impossible. She didn't want to hurt him and he'd never trust her if he thought she was lying to him all the time. She folded her arms over the tingling tips of her breasts and crossed her legs beneath the sheets, pressing her thighs together. "I want to give you time to get comfortable with me. You seem uncomfortable and—"

He trailed his fingers along her arm and arousal surged through her with such force she doubled over. She couldn't restrain the moan that ripped from her vocal chords, nor the shudder wracking her.

"Em?" He gripped her arms in his hands. "What's wrong?"

She jerked away, unable to stand his touch on her over-sensitized flesh.

Give him to me. I'll make him sate us.

She flung herself to the far side of the bed and as the next wave of need tore through her she pressed her face to the mattress. She could feel her demon trying to claw her way out, trying to take control, and she couldn't let that happen. She didn't trust her demon not to hurt him.

What the hell? Her demon had gotten what she wanted. He'd made love to her. Had brought her to orgasm twice. How much more did she need?

"I'm getting Kat."

"No!" She forced herself into a sitting position. "I'm fine."

He wiped his hand over his face. "What am I doing wrong, Em?" He walked around the end of the bed, rubbing his chest with the heel of his hand. "I'm trying to make you happy. I'm failing, but I'm not sure how." He reached for her.

Give him to me.

She scooted away. "Don't touch me." The hurt in his eyes broke her heart but he had to go. She was afraid for him. "I need a few minutes alone. Can you give me a minute or two? Please."

Jaw clenched tight, he strode out of the room, pulling the door shut behind him with a soft click that seemed to echo in her mind.

You're weak. Her demon roiled and surged and she needed every ounce of concentration to keep the sex-hungry bitch locked within her body. After a few moments, she regained control again. The arousal settled into an annoying background static and she sat up.

This was insane. What she was experiencing didn't mesh with what he'd told her to expect. He said she wouldn't crave sex after he sated her, but she did. She didn't have full control of her demon. She grew more aggressive every day. What happened when her demon became stronger than her?

Part of her wanted to talk to Kat, but what would she say? That she'd become a nymphomaniac craving sex with the one man who wanted as little to do with her as possible? That even after he made love to her and gave her wonderful orgasms, arousal returned with painful intensity?

How humiliating was that? And she refused to tell Harrison. He'd feel horrible and none of this was his fault. The last thing he needed was for her to add more pressure to the situation. The problem must be hers. Some defect she'd always had but never noticed until her demon drove it to the surface.

Something was wrong with her.

Ember grabbed the pillow with the intent of throwing the thing, but knocked everything off the night stand in the process. She pressed the pillow to her face and screamed to release her frustration. What did her demon want?

What did Harrison want from her? Anything?

She shouldn't be angry with him, but her demon and Harrison seemed to want opposite things from her, which left her struggling alone in the middle, trying to satisfy them both.

She was furious with him and irate with her daemon.

There was no way she could satisfy them both.

She grabbed her nightgown off the bed post, pulled it on and flung the sheets to the side to survey the damage. Where did all this stuff come from? None of these things had been here before. She picked up a decorative box of tissue and smacked it onto the nightstand. Same with the little trivet and the now empty glass of water.

Crazy man couldn't even drink water and here she was cleaning the mess. And tissues? He didn't need any of this stuff.

Pausing, she glanced over the items again. A tissue box, a glass of water on an emerald green trivet, and a small vase of flowers.

He'd made a place for her.

And she'd made a mess of it. Like everything else.

She slid to the floor and sat with her back against the bed, grabbed the box of tissues and plucked one out. She folded the soft paper in half, running the seam between her fingers. This must be hard for him. When she did her internship at the shelter, some women who came through after being abused or raped didn't seem to ever want a stable relationship. They refused to allow intimacy—whether physical or emotional. Is that what she faced with Harry? Had he been hurt so much he'd never recover?

Or maybe she wasn't the kind of woman he needed.

Perhaps that's why her demon and Harrison were at such odds. Where did that leave her?

The tissue box jerked.

Not a whole lot, but the damn thing moved.

She kicked it. The box tumbled over the carpet and slid, coming to rest near the door.

The box jumped.

What the hell? She crawled to it on her hands and knees, and pushed the small container around with her finger until the opening became visible. All she saw was tissue.

Carefully, she grabbed the box from the bottom—it was much heavier than it should be—and held it upside down, shaking it. A black goo oozed partway out, hanging for a second before splattering on the carpet.

What the heck? She'd expected a roach or a mouse. She leaned closer.

An eye popped out of the goo.

She reared back with a gasp.

Eyes erupted all over the blob. Some mammalian, others reptilian. A few even appeared human. Independently, the eyes scouted out their environment. The oily splotch shifted, rounding out into a bulb before splitting off tentacles.

"Oh, my God."

All the eyes focused on her. The creature scrabbled across the floor toward her.

With a screech, she scrambled to her feet and jumped onto the bed. "Harry!" Heart slamming in her chest, she grabbed the glass from the night stand. When the thing peered at her over the edge of the bed she hurled it.

The glass hit the edge of the bed just to the left of the creature and bounced off, landing on the carpet, and rolling under the dresser. *Shit.*

The creature leapt at her.

Ember threw herself off the far side of the mattress and landed in a tangle of hair and sheets and nightgown. Her neck and shoulder throbbed from the fall and before she freed herself, the black, oily thing grabbed hold of her upper arm. Pain sliced through her limb. She let out a full-throated scream.

Adrenaline slammed through her system as she tried to pry it loose.

The door flew open, slamming against the wall.

"Get it off! Get it off!" She got to her feet and ran to him. The creature bit down again. "It hurts!" Tiny teeth tearing into her flesh. Oh, God. She stopped and hit it with her free hand. Tried to pry the creature off, but tiny biting mouths appeared wherever she touched.

"Honey, you gotta hold still. Let me—"

Oh, God, she'd be missing half her arm by the time they got it off.

Finally, he grabbed the blob in both hands and pulled. The creature stopped biting but hung on, the tentacles tightening on her arm. Clinging before slipping away one by one. She was free! A couple good chunks had been taken out of her arm. Dear God, was that bone? She slapped her hand over the burning wound. Blood streamed between her fingers, staining the carpet. She bent forward. Squeezed her arm. Kept her eyes on the creature.

"Fuck." He threw the creature across the room.

He shook his hand, then paused to inspect a bite on his palm.

Julian walked in with George on his shoulder. "What's going on?"

The minion hissed and leaped to the ground, growling low in his throat.

The creature froze at the sound. Eyes erupted all over its body, scanning around before zeroing in on George. The eyes disappeared. Hundreds of tiny mouths sprouted. All of them started talking at once. "You don't like boats? Water. So, Harry's being stupid. Trout shark." The creature scrabbled up the wall. The voices mimicked theirs.

Harry's gaze shot to hers. Crap, it was repeating everything they'd said.

George whined, pacing below.

"—bust the auction over on Camano Island. I'm trying to get to know your mate. You're folding?" The creature climbed across the ceiling, making a beeline for the door. "Now, Harry. Please."

Ember's cheeks flamed.

"Get the door." Harrison motioned to Julian. "Shut it."

Julian slammed the door.

She looked at Harrison. "It's repeating everything we've said."

"It's a cuero."

They both turned toward Julian. "What?"

"A cuero. They're great little spies. Undetectable—they have no scent and can squeeze themselves into small spaces to hide anywhere. Whoever has the other half of this one can see and hear everything it sees and hears. We found our spy."

The cuero skittered across the ceiling toward the window, hiding behind the drapes, chatting away. "You don't want Harry to see you like that."

Harrison's assessing stare flashed to Julian.

Julian shrugged. "She was a mess after what happened at the auction."

"Right." Harrison motioned to the curtains and the two of them closed in on the creature. "Well, let's get the damn thing."

They were insane. "Didn't you see what it did to me? Use gloves or something."

"I'm going to trap it in the drapes." Harrison leaned close to the wall, peeking behind the curtains.

The cuero bolted across the floor. "This might hurt a bit."

Both men jumped back.

"There." She pointed under the bed. Got on her knees to peer under, like Harrison and Julian. Good God, she'd lost her mind now, too.

George dove under the bed, growling and snarling.

The cuero darted out with George hot on its tail. The creature raced up the wall, the tiny mouths appearing again, chatting away in her voice. "George, no. George, out."

George stopped at the sound of Ember's voice coming from the cuero. Paced. He growled low in his throat. Sniffed the air.

Harrison clapped his hands and pointed at the creature. "George, get it."

George growled, baring rows of wicked teeth, pacing closer.

The cuero shifted. "George, no."

"It's confusing him. Sounds like you, Em." Harrison swore. "Gods, Adia's a sneaky bitch. The daemon Lucas told us about must have let the thing loose in the building."

Hadn't Lucas also said the daemon was singing? She took a deep breath, and sang. "John Jacob Jingleheimer Schmidt—"

Both men turned and stared at her as if she lost her mind. She motioned to the wall where the cuero had gone still.

"—his name is my name, too—"

A slow smile spread on Harrison's face. "Brilliant, Em. Keep singing."

The tiny mouths disappeared.

"—whenever we go out, we can hear the people shout—"

The eyes returned. All focused on her.

Harrison clapped, directed George to the cuero. "Go on, get it."

The minion bounded up the wall and pounced. The cuero didn't stand a chance. George chewed with wet smacking chomps and swallowed the thing in one gulp. His forked tongue licked away the remaining traces of cuero from his muzzle as he strolled back down the wall.

"Em's hurt." Harrison strode across the room. "We need Kat"

"She was running a bath, must not have heard us past the water." Julian opened the door. "I'll go get her."

Ember tightened her hand over the bites. "They hurt like hell." Part of her wanted to see how bad the damage was—had she really seen bone?—but feared if she moved, the air hitting her raw flesh would burn even more.

Harrison brushed her hair away from her arm. "Let me see. Do you feel sick? Faint?"

"It kinda burns."

"Let me see."

"I don't want to let go."

He shot her a fierce scowl. "Ember Elaine Moon, you move your hand right this instant."

"God, you're bossy." She moved her hand.

"And you're brilliant." His concerned gaze traveled from her wound to her eyes. He pressed his palm against the bite marks to slow the bleeding. "Jules and I would've been chasing the damned thing around half the day."

They shared a tentative smile.

"Listen, Harry—Harrison." Geez, she had to quit tripping over his damn name. "I'm sorry about earlier. I'm frustrated. I want this to work out and—"

Julian ran back into the room with Kat in tow. Her gaze swept both men before settling on Ember's arm. "What'd you say did that?"

"A cuero." Harrison released Ember's arms and moved out of

the way.

"Gaia, you're lucky to have your arm. It must have fed recently if this is the worst of the damage." Kat winced as she examined the bite marks. "This'll hurt a bit." She gripped the blood-red stone hanging between her breasts in one hand and held the other over Ember's arm.

Warmth radiated from her palm and into Ember. The heat, soothing at first, soon started to burn. She gasped. Harrison wrapped his arms around her from behind and she gripped his arm in her free hand. "I've got you." His cheek pressed against hers. "She's almost done, honey."

She didn't understand him. How could he be so loving now, but dislike her touch when making love? He laced his fingers with hers, pulling her hand away from his arm.

Her eyes widened. He didn't seem to mind touching her when they made love, it was *her touching him* that seemed to be the problem. Even now, as he held her and let her lean on him, he wouldn't allow her to hold on to *him*.

The heat started to fade, leaving an itchy patch in its wake. She let go of Harrison to scratch the spot, but he stopped her.

"All done." Kat smiled. "You leave that alone, though. New skin is sensitive."

The arm was healed, not even a scar marred her flesh. She couldn't imagine having the kind of power Kat had. "Thank you."

"No problem." Kat's gaze traveled over both men. "Did either of you get bit?"

"Harrison did when he pulled the cuero off me." Ember grabbed his hand and turned it over. Her blood covered his palm, but the skin was smooth and whole. She took his other hand, but no bite marks marred the skin there, either. "I thought the cuero bit you."

"It did." His chin rested on the top of her head. "I'm a vampire, Em. Blood heals me."

"But I'm not human."

He shrugged. "Blood is blood."

"You three need some rest." Kat shook her head. "You all look ready to sleep where you're standing. Come on, Jules. You boys can chat about this tomorrow. Goodnight, Em."

Ember smiled. "'Night."

"Let's get you cleaned up." He led her to the bathroom where they both washed their hands. He wet a wash cloth and wiped down her arm. "I'm glad you're okay."

"Thanks." She smiled. "And thank you for making a place for me. I appreciate the thought."

He pulled away. "What?"

"The glass of water and the tissues." When he continued to stare at her she added, "The rose? You know, the stuff on the nightstand."

He shook his head. "Sounds nice. Wish I'd thought of it, but I didn't." He went through the bedroom to the door and flung it open. "Jules."

Bare feet padded along the wood floor, coming closer. "What now?"

"Did you and Kat leave gifts for Em?"

"No. Why?"

He turned his attention back to the table. "Em, where did the cuero come from?"

"It was inside the tissue box."

"I didn't notice anything there earlier." He ran his hand through his hair. "The daemon Lucas told us about must have left this stuff."

"He said the elevator didn't move." Julian leaned against the doorframe.

Harrison wandered the room, opening drawers and cabinets. "Maybe he was a ghost type."

Julian kissed his teeth. "Lucas said he wasn't a vampire."

Ember had never seen Harrison like this. His breathing was growing strained and the more he searched the more upset he seemed to get. "What are you searching for?"

"Maybe a wraith, then. Adia must be behind this, right? Who else would want to spy on us? Whenever she does something, there's always a clue." He continued his search, growing more agitated by the minute.

"Adia didn't leave a clue at the hotel."

"*You* were the clue. You told us about The Knot Works. At the club, the incubus had the invitation to the auction. They'll find something at the auction. Mark my words."

She stepped into his path. "Okay. Whoever she sent might have left this stuff for the cuero. Or maybe this is unrelated. Couldn't this be the result of another case?"

His lips thinned. "Everything has always been so planned. . . ." His attention fixed somewhere over her shoulder and he cursed. She turned, searching behind her. The dresser didn't appear any different. A bottle of cologne stood on top along with a couple pairs of folded jeans. He had some books stacked in one corner and a picture.

The picture was new.

Harrison lifted the photo. His hand shook. Ember and Julian both went for a closer look.

The photograph showed Harrison and his parents in front of their home in Tucson. "Em, did you put this here?"

She shook her head.

He stared at the nightstand. The tissue box, the green tile, the glass, and the rose. His eyes closed. "Aqua Verde and Rose Street."

Those were the cross streets of the house he had lived in with his parents. "Oh, my God, Nancy. Give me a phone."

Harrison hesitated, so Julian tossed her his and she dialed Nancy's number. She paced while it rang. What if they were too late? What if—

"Hello?"

"Nancy?"

"Well, who else would I be? Is that you, Ember Moon?"

"Yeah." She let out the breath she'd been holding and nodded to Harrison. "Is everything all right? No one weird hanging around your place or strange calls or anything?"

"Ember, have those DDC agents been bothering you, too?" A rueful smile tipped the edges of Ember's mouth. Oh boy, Nancy was vexed. "They want me to leave my house. Can you believe the nerve?"

Ember sat on the edge of the bed. "I think that might be a good idea. For a little while."

"I thought about it, perhaps. . . ." Nancy sighed. "The way I figure it, if I'm not in enough danger for them to continue watching my house, then I don't need protective custody. They wouldn't even tell me who'd made the threat against me. I'm staying put. Until someone is willing to tell me the truth, I'm not moving. Did they give you any particulars you can share with me?"

"Um, well, the thing is, I'm here with—"

Harrison snatched the phone out of her hand. "Don't."

"She won't move unless she knows why."

"Make something up." He scowled as if he thought he could intimidate her with the force of his displeasure.

She stood. "You're being stubborn as an ass." She wrested the cell out of his hand and pointed to him with it. "I'm not happy with you." She put the phone back to her ear. "Nancy?"

"You can tell whoever you're talking to I'm not leaving my house. Period. Now, I've got to go, Em, but you come visit soon, okay?" Nancy's voice shook and Ember had a feeling she'd guessed she was with Harrison.

"Nancy—"

"Love you." Her voice cracked. "'Bye-bye, Em." The line went dead.

This couldn't continue. She scowled at Harrison. "You need to talk to your mother."

"And tell her what?" His fingers made to tug his collar from his throat, but he was wearing a tee-shirt with a V-neck. His hand fisted. "Did you stop to think she's better off not knowing anything more than she does?" He glanced at his watch and she wanted nothing more than to rip the damn thing from his wrist. She was sick of him looking at his watch as if he didn't have *time* for her, for his mother.

"Focus, Harrison, this is important. No. I've thought about this a lot, and that has never, ever crossed my mind." Ember stepped closer. "She's your mom. You should go to her."

He shook his head, the muscles in his throat straining with every breath he took. "I *can't*."

"No one's watching her. The DDC pulled the surveillance you ordered and tried to put her into protective custody. She wouldn't go, so they left her."

Harrison stared at Julian while he strained for a breath. "Convince . . . her." He was breathing way too hard. The veins in his neck were protruding, standing out in stark relief against his bleached skin.

Julian slouched against the door frame. "Em's right, if she'll listen to anyone, it'll be you. She might not even open her door for me."

Maybe she shouldn't push him so hard. He was starting to hyperventilate. She wanted to comfort him, help sooth him, but feared the rejection that would follow if she tried to touch him.

"No, but . . . she'll . . . open for . . . Ember. You can . . . use your talent."

She gasped. He wanted Julius to mesmerize his mother?

Julian ran his hand over his face. "Jesus. Listen to yourself, man."

"Just do . . . this . . . for me."

"Whatever. Fine." Julian walked out.

Harrison cursed. He paced to the end of the room and back. His hands bracketed his hips and he stared at the floor.

She didn't want to push him, but she couldn't let this go, either. Nancy deserved to be reunited with her son. "Would you at least think about seeing her? It doesn't have to be right now, but she's been waiting a long time."

His eyes closed and she didn't think he'd agree. Then, he nodded.

"Thank you."

She busied herself tidying the room, giving him time to control his breathing without her staring.

After a few minutes, he made his way over to her and wrapped his arms around her from behind. His body pressed close to hers, his scent surrounded her and her demon writhed. Twisted. Renewed desire washed over her with the force of a tidal wave. She required every ounce of restraint she possessed to keep her hands loose at her sides. She took a deep breath. "I'm tired and . . ." *pissed off you're treating Nancy like this.*

His chin rested on her head. "I'm worried about you, Em."

"I'm okay." She leaned back deeper into his embrace, she couldn't help herself. "I'm gonna zone out on some TV."

"Want me to join you?"

"No." She winced. That had come out more forceful than intended. "Get some sleep. I'll come to bed when I'm tired."

He lifted his arm to look at his watch again. Was she really so boring?

His arms fell away from her, leaving her cold. He didn't say another word as she slipped from the room.

Ember settled onto the sofa and flipped the TV on. She didn't recognize the show, but didn't bother changing the channel, either. The noise was more important than the content. She pulled the blanket off the back of the couch and wrapped the soft material around herself.

What was she going to do? She couldn't change him. The tiny glimpse he'd given her into his past was devastating. She didn't want to push him or demand what he couldn't give. None of this was his fault and God, she loved him. If still human, she'd give him all the time and patience he needed. She could adapt and let things progress naturally. Coax him into trusting her. Loving her.

She wasn't human, though.

And her demon terrified her.

What would happen if she couldn't restrain her? Her demon was getting stronger the more unsatisfied it became. Angrier. All her rage seemed to be directed at Harrison.

Maybe if she went home for a little while her demon would settle down. Then they could try being together again.

The bedroom door opened and she tensed, eyes fixed on the TV screen. She wasn't ready to talk to Harrison. Didn't think he'd be receptive to her concerns.

He didn't come out, though. George did.

The small minion peered at her over the back edge of the couch with his big inky eyes.

"What do you want?"

She wasn't as afraid of the creature anymore. She had woken a couple times yesterday to find the minion snuggled between her and Harrison. Still, they weren't on the friendliest of terms.

George gurgled. His diamond-shaped head tipped to the side.

With one finger, she stroked him from the top of his head to the tip of his nose.

His mouth spread into a grin and his black, forked tongue flopped out one side. He seemed to like that.

"I'd much prefer if I could make your master do that."

The minion crawled over the edge and onto her chest, nuzzling her neck. "Good God, I'm a mess, George." How bad off was she when a little affection from a minion she wasn't sure if she even liked brought tears to her eyes.

"I've always had an idea of how a relationship would be between us. Even after he was gone, I hoped he'd return. And then, watching how Jules is with Kat made me so damn jealous. I always thought Harrison would be like that with me."

The minion flattened his body over her chest. His head butted her chin and he snuggled down for the day. It felt a little like a hug. She stroked him from head to tail, amazed by how soft he was. His scales were smooth as marble and the tufts of black fur poking between were soft as a kitten's fur.

Yeah, she'd admit it. She was jealous of Kat. She didn't want Julian, she wanted a bond like they shared to grow between herself and Harrison.

She closed her eyes, letting George's heat and the soft vibration of his purr lull her to sleep.

CHAPTER 20

October 14, 8:44 AM

SHE DREAMED OF JULIAN.

Sound asleep with the sheet slung low on his hips, she saw far more of him than was decent. He was scarred from the base of his neck to his wrists and all the way to where the sheet stopped her wandering gaze. Not an inch of exposed skin wasn't roughened by scars, as if he'd been tortured for a very long time.

What was she doing? She had to leave. She had no business here. Kat was curled at his side and they both seemed so peaceful, content.

Her view shifted as she rose to float above him. Ghostly strands of her hair hovered around her face as if the room had no gravity. Afraid she'd float right out of the room, she reached out to Julian. Except her hand was gossamer—her skin translucent with a blue tinge. *Her demon!*

She tried to pull her hand back, but her limb wouldn't listen. Instead she stroked over Julian's muscular torso in a gesture so obscene her face heated. Whisper soft, she pleaded with her demon. "Please don't do this."

He has what we need.

Julian moaned in his sleep. Shifted positions and stretched. "Mm, butterfly."

His eyes opened and, when he saw Kat sleeping next to him, they widened.

His gaze snapped to her. The eye he kept hidden behind the eye patch wasn't grotesquely damaged, but crystalline, faceted. "Holy shit."

She eased her palms down his body. She tried to open her mouth to warn him, to tell him to run, but nothing came out.

He can sate us.

"Ember, don't." He scooted higher on the bed, pulling the sheet with him.

She shook her head. She didn't want to do this, but she wasn't in control. Her demon was.

Her demon writhed as she stroked his cock through the sheet. This was wrong! So wrong.

His gaze slipped to Kat and then back to her. "Ember can you hear me?"

"I'm in control today." That wasn't her voice, but her demon's.

"Ember, you need to wake up." He swallowed and her gaze followed the bob of his Adam's apple.

She squeezed her fingers around his cock.

He slapped her arm away.

Everything shifted as her vision turned red.

Kill it.

Her fingers curled and her nails elongated. Her heart raced. She needed to wake up. She needed to get out of here. Her clawed hand lashed out.

His whole body tensed. He lunged up, slapping his hands together in a loud clap. "Wake up."

— ⬥ —

Ember woke with a gasp, and sat up. George clung to her, whining and nudging her chin.

A door opened on the Crowley side of the apartment. Julian and Kat ran into the room. Kat had thrown on a robe and had a book clutched in her hands, but Julian wore nothing but a sheet. Pink stained his cheeks and for a moment he seemed to flounder.

"You all right?" he asked.

Her gaze dropped to his chest. Four long lacerations streaked his chest amid scars always covered by clothing. She couldn't have known about them unless. . . .

"That was real?" She tightened her grip around George. "I didn't mean to." Her gaze shot to Kat's. "I would never—! I don't know why, I—"

"I can see your aura, I know you wouldn't." Kat came and sat next to her and put her arm around her shoulders. "It wasn't you, Em. That was your demon."

Julian's gaze raked over her and he frowned. "Jesus, you're losing control, aren't you?"

"Jules, go on back to bed. Ember and I are okay."

He gave Kat a quick kiss, pausing to chuck Ember under the chin. "'Night, ladies."

As soon as he was out of sight, Kat flattened the book on her lap. "Are you sure you're all right?"

Ember shook her head. "I am freaking the fuck out." If Harry found out what happened . . . he wouldn't be half as understanding as Kat.

"Thought so." She gave Ember a lopsided smile. "I found some information on succubi. I thought you might like to see it."

Ember nodded. "Yeah. Anything to shed some light on what's going on with me."

Kat flipped open the book. "So, succubi have two forms. A full demon form"—she pointed to a picture of a snake-like woman—"and a seductive dream form." The opposite page showed a man asleep in bed. A phantom woman floating above him.

"I've manifested both those forms now and sometimes, when I'm alone, I can see my demon trying to pull away from my body. Why?"

"According to the text, succubi feed off intimacy."

Ember slouched back on the couch. "We *are* intimate." Sort of.

"I think this is referring to emotional intimacy."

All right, they weren't very intimate at all. Therein lay the problem. He wasn't ready for that kind of intimacy. He wouldn't even let Scott clue her in on Julian's secret, so why would he let his guard down long enough to trust her with his own?

"I think this is why so many of the succubi they've found have died. They're mated and having sex, but there is no intimacy."

"Then, why did my demon go after Jules?" She had a stronger history with Harrison. If she was going to build emotional intimacy with anyone, it would be him.

"Personally, I think, right now, your friendship with my husband is more intimate than your relationship with Harry." She sat back on the couch. "Jules trusts you. I think that's where the legend of succubi accosting men in their sleep came from. Think about it, only an incubus can create succubi and they have an uncontrollable need to do so. The succubi either mate the incubus who's emotionally ambivalent to them or go find a different mate who may or may not want more than a sexual partner. In instances where the succubi couldn't achieve intimacy, the demon would take over and go in search of it elsewhere."

Ember put her hand over her face. "I can't force him to trust me. I mean, if I demand emotional intimacy from him I'm sure he'd try, but it wouldn't be genuine."

"I could talk to him, or Jules can, but I think you're right. If Harry doesn't choose to open himself to you, I don't think the demon will be satisfied."

No, and Harrison had said her demon would kill to get what she needed.

"So where does that leave me? I spent my life trying to do some good in the world. I don't want to hurt anyone, least of all Harrison." She covered her face with her hands. "I could've injured Julian tonight."

Kat patted her shoulder. "Jules and I can handle this. We won't be caught off guard again."

"Yeah, but now my demon is angry with Jules, too. I doubt she'll go after him again. So, who's next?"

Kat clutched the book to her chest. "It could be any of the males in the building. Your demon will keep after them, trying to fill the void until they resist. Then she'll attack like she did tonight."

"I couldn't live with myself if I hurt anyone."

"Not for long, no." Kat put her arm around Ember. "Honey, the thing is, once your demon starts taking over, it won't be long before she self-destructs, taking you right along with her. Either you need to figure out a way to gain Harry's trust, or . . . ." Kat shrugged, looking worried but bewildered. "I don't know."

There was only one thing to be done. If she couldn't figure out a way to gain Harrison's trust, she'd have to do everything in her power to make sure her demon couldn't hurt anyone else.

CHAPTER 21

October 14, 5:23 PM

ADIA THREW HER BEDROOM DOOR wide and screamed for her assistants. Their feet slapped against the stone floors as they approached and she flung her arm out to indicate the bed. "He's broken." She pounded her fist on the door. "Why do you keep bringing me defective ones? Why do they keep breaking? I love them and I teach them and they lie there and die."

The wraith glanced at the bed. "Mistress, perhaps if you didn't rest all your weight on their faces."

"Who asked you?" She punched him. Slapped him. The twin chrono-deviants cowered away. "Get out. Get me another. A stronger one."

"Older?"

"No. Not older. Stronger. Go."

She turned back to the bed, her heart breaking. What a waste. This one had been so sweet. Eager to please with nothing more than a few kind words. He hadn't disobeyed her once.

Where was Harry? Why didn't he come home? The coven may have aged him, but on the inside, he was the same. He still matched her. Challenged her. Then again, when he returned, she'd have to punish him for making her wait.

He'd want to be punished.

He liked it.

He always used to like when she bit him. When she punished him, she gave him an opportunity to release his emotions, a difficult feat for most males.

She ran her hands over her breasts. *Yes.*

When he lived here, she'd bite him. Would sink her teeth in so deep she'd feel his flesh burst open.

She squeezed her breast.

Oh, the way he used to scream. His body thrashing and kicking and hitting which did nothing but make her teeth sink deeper.

A tremor ran through her.

He tasted divine, a mixture of sweet and metallic. She loved when she could force him to come as she sank her teeth into him. The smell and taste of his sex mixed with blood gave her the most amazing orgasms.

Yes. Oh, yes.

She'd gone a little too far that last time with Harry, though. She'd transformed him. She couldn't bite him now, but she could make him want her.

In a flash of brilliance, she knew exactly how to get him home. "Assistants."

The males lumbered back into the hall, eyeing her. "Bring me the boy you told me about."

The wraith's bush-red brows drew together. "The Asian lad? But you don't like—"

"Yes. Him." She motioned to the bed and the twin chrono-deviants came in to retrieve the body. "You can trade him for this one."

CHAPTER 22

October 14, 11:28 PM

"WE SHOULDN'T HAVE AGREED TO this." Ember glanced at Julian, then focused on the road. As soon as the sun had set, Harrison had started prodding them to go to his mom's.

"He'll come around. In the meantime, we can't let his mother become bait for Adia." Julian tapped his thumb on his knee in an erratic beat. "Are you going to tell me what the hell is going on between you and Harry?"

No wonder he'd been acting so nervous. She'd been given a reprieve this morning after her demon interrupted his sleep thanks to Kat, but she'd known he wouldn't let the topic rest forever. Luckily, there wasn't time to talk.

"We're here." She parked in front of a two-story cookie-cutter home. Nancy's house looked out of place in the beautiful neighborhood on Mercer Island. Some miscreant had spray-painted Go to Hell across the garage door and left torn-open garbage bags littering the lawn.

Nancy didn't deserve this.

Julian glanced at the other pristine homes. "So, this is the burbs, is it?"

"She's very vocal against segregation. I've started to wonder if she somehow knows about Harrison. It would explain her abrupt decision to move to Washington." A light burned in the living room. "Looks like she's awake."

Julian opened the car door. "Wait here. I'll be quick and we'll get out of here."

For several heartbeats, she did nothing but sit and stare at Julian's retreating back. She understood Harrison's fear. He wasn't ready to see his mom. Maybe he never would be and what then? Where would that leave her trying to maintain relationships with both of them? She slid her hand around the cold handle of the card door. She couldn't let Julian mesmerize Nancy. She at least deserved the truth.

Ember got out of the car and by the time she'd caught up to Julian, Nancy was opening the door.

"Julian, wait."

Both Julian and Nancy turned toward her.

She smiled at the older woman. "Hi, Nancy."

"Ember?" She took a step onto the cement porch in her floral-patterned robe and purple fuzzy slippers and smiled. "Oh, honey, how are you?"

Julian stepped between them. "What the hell are you doing?" He pointed at Ember. "I told you to wait in the car." He turned to Harrison's mom. "And you should never step out of your home at night unless you know who's at your door. What's wrong with you?"

Nancy stood shorter than Ember. She was on the thin side and next to Julian's imposing figure she seemed frail, but she lifted her chin until she was looking him straight in the eye. "You going to give me a hard time, young man?"

Ember was impressed. "Nancy, this is Agent Julian Crowley with the DDC."

Nancy's eyelids narrowed. "So, the DDC *is* dragging you into this." Her arms folded over her chest. "I'm not leaving."

Julian scowled. "Why not?"

"I'm waiting for my son and nothing you say will make me change my mind."

Julian kissed his teeth, cursed, and folded his arms over his chest. "Your son's my best friend. You've got five minutes to pack a bag."

Nancy's jaw dropped and tears welled in her eyes. Ember scowled at Julian for being so abrupt. "Come on, Nancy." She put her arm around her shoulders. "I'll help you pack."

"No." Julian took hold of her arm. "You stay with me."

"Jules—"

His one eye narrowed. "I have no doubt Adia's been here. I'm not letting you go into that house without me."

Nancy sniffed and motioned into the house. "Come inside, both of you."

Julian's grasp tightened. "We're fine out here."

"I'm not going anywhere with you until you explain." Nancy frowned. "Is my house contagious?"

Ember tipped her head toward Julian. "Julian is a vampire. He needs a formal invite."

Julian shot her a biting smile. "Which is why we're happy to stay here."

"Nonsense. As long as you're my son's friend you're always welcome here. Please come into my home."

Julian's grip on Ember eased. "A conditional invite. Smart lady." He guided Ember into the house, his gaze never still, taking in their surroundings.

"I've tried to learn everything I can about daemons." Nancy closed the door behind them. "I hoped someday Harry would come home and I didn't want to make any mistakes."

Julian turned. "You know he's daemon?"

"Detective Sinclair came to talk to us about—"

His laugher cut her off.

Ember stared. "Did you say Sinclair?"

Nancy couldn't answer past Julian's laughter. Great guffaws peeled out of him. "Oh, Jesus, Harry is gonna ash the son of a bitch."

"Who?"

"Detective Sinclair." He snickered, wiping at his eye. "That's fucking rich."

Nancy raised her brows. "You know him?"

"Duncan Sinclair is a Guardian. One of the best. The other Guardians refer to him and his buddy, James Pasquino, as Legendaries. He's also Harry's adopted father."

"Oh." Nancy drew the one syllable out.

Odd, if Duncan had contact with Harrison's parents why was Harrison so worried about their reaction—"Oh!" Ember's hand flew to her mouth.

"Detective Sinclair never told Harry?" Nancy asked.

Julian shook his head. "Not that I'm aware of."

"That's unfortunate." She folded her hands in her lap. "When can I see my son?"

Julian sobered. His one-eyed gaze pinned Ember for the answer.

Right. Nancy deserved an explanation and it was up to her to do so. "Let's sit for a moment."

Nancy's shoulders slumped. She led them into the living room where Julian paused by an altar. A statue of Hecate stood in the center. Small bowls of offerings mingled with candles. A picture of a sixteen-year-old Harrison lay at the goddess' feet. For as long as Ember remembered, Nancy had always loved the esoteric. No one in the community had minded until daemon kind revealed itself. Now her beliefs were yet another bone of contention between her and her neighbors.

"My wife favors Gaia."

Nancy smiled. "The beautiful and trustworthy Earth goddess. Your wife must possess a gentle soul."

The corner of his eye crinkled. "When she's near, her presence blocks out all the ugliness in the world."

For a moment, Nancy studied him as if trying to dissect and figure him out. "Me, I've always feared crossroads. Decisions are difficult. Hecate resonates with me."

Julian sat on the edge of an ottoman, Ember sat on the loveseat and Nancy lowered herself into the arm chair with a sigh. "He won't see me, will he? He must blame us for what happened. We weren't vigilant enough. Tom couldn't even look at himself in the mirror after we lost Harry." Her mouth curved into a shadow of a smile. "Oh, we'd tell each other we weren't to blame. We couldn't stand to see the other hurting so much, but deep down, as a parent who's lost a child, it's impossible to ever believe it."

"What happened wasn't your fault. Or his. Shit happens." Julian leaned over and took Nancy's hand. "Believe me when I say Harry would be horrified if he heard what you said. He does not now, nor has he ever thought either of you were to blame."

Nancy blinked back tears.

"Do you believe me? He's got a lot of concerns, but never has he voiced any related to your ability to parent. Okay?"

She wiped her eyes. "He was always a good boy."

"He's a better man." Julian stood. "Look, since we're having this little break, you mind if I make Em something to eat?"

Nancy pointed him toward the kitchen. "Help yourself."

Ember's belly churned at the thought of food. "I'm not hungry."

"You'll eat every bite. Harry's always taken good care of Kat when I needed him to." He stalked out of the room.

Ember met Nancy's intrigued gaze and explained. "Kat is Julian's mate."

"You know, it's odd." She glanced toward the kitchen, then leaned forward and lowered her voice. "Out on the porch he terrified me, but he's not so bad."

"No, he's an F.A.O. Schwartz teddy in a grizzly suit, but don't tell him I said so."

Julian's voice drifted in from the other room. "I can hear your heartbeat, Emerald Eyes. Do you think I can't hear your whispers?"

They shared a smile.

"So, am I to understand, since he's comparing you to Kat, you're Harry's—how did you refer to Kat? His mate?"

Ember nodded. Harry should be here, giving his mother the news. Then again, maybe that was part of the reason he didn't want to be here. "I wish I could say he chose me." Her eyes filled with tears.

Nancy rushed over to her side and sat on the couch next to her, putting her arms around her. "Honey, are things as bad as all that?"

"He's a good man. You'd be so proud of him. He works for the DDC and he does his job well. I've seen him work. He's brilliant and brave." She shrugged. "I'm starting to think I'm not the right woman for him."

"Look at me, honey. Tom and I always assumed the two of you would be together. You were meant for each other. If he's as brilliant as you say, he's going to come to the same conclusion, and love you as much you love him."

"God, I hope so."

"Here." Nancy stood and walked to the china cabinet. In most homes, the cabinet might house the good dishes, but never in the Cayce household. Here, the china cabinet protected stones and crystals of every type. "Amazonite helps a person focus through chaos to find their personal truth. Slip the stone into his pocket."

Ember accepted the small, pale-green stone accented with dark green swirls. "Thank you."

"Tell me about him." She sat next to her.

"He's tall, six-three or -four. Broader than Jules, with an athletic build. Not too thin, and solid muscle. He's too handsome for his own good." Ember sat back against the couch. "He's on the quiet side, unless he's sparring with Jules and then their language would make your ears burn."

Nancy grinned.

"He checks his watch all the time, as if he's the White Rabbit and always running late. I have no idea why. The quirk makes me crazy because he does it at the least opportune times. He's too protective. He can be bossy. Dominating. Unbending."

"He doesn't sound very nice. Perhaps it'll be good if things don't work out between you."

Ember frowned. "He's wonderful. He's got a great sense of humor. He's considerate. He never complains and he goes out of his way to make me comfortable."

"Then you tell him I'd like to meet him again." The corner of her lips trembled and she blinked hard, glancing away.

Her heart was breaking for Nancy. She had to find a way to get Harrison to see reason. "He'll come around." Julian entered the room with a three-decker sandwich that would make a master chef salivate. "Good God, Jules. I can't eat all that."

He scowled. "Eat it all. Or I'll make you eat it all."

Her eyes narrowed as she accepted the sandwich. She didn't trust him not to use his talent, so she took a big bite under his watchful stare and choked the food down. Ever since her transformation she couldn't seem to eat. Food didn't taste good and her stomach protested every bite. Maybe it was just part of being a daemon. Maybe it was because her demon wouldn't let her think about much of anything aside from trying to sate her lust.

"Good. Now, we need to get moving. Harry's gonna wonder why we've been gone so long and I'm not planning on telling him we didn't do what he asked."

"What did he want you to do?" Nancy's gaze bounced between them.

"He's worried about you." She picked at the edge of her sandwich. "Especially after Adia got to me. He wants to make sure you're safe."

"Adia?"

Ember swallowed. "The woman who . . . kidnapped him."

Nancy searched Julian's face. "He's not planning to go after this woman, is he?"

He nodded. "She's getting desperate. Sloppy. Things are starting to happen. We'll get her."

"To what end?" Nancy sat back and fiddled with the tie to her robe. "What does the DDC do with such daemons? Where do you take them?"

She'd wondered the same thing. No one ever spoke about a daemon jail or daemon trials.

"Harry and I—" He huffed out a breath. "The daemons we hunt aren't candidates for rehabilitation." His one-eyed gaze zeroed in on Ember. He pointed to the laden plate.

She brought the sandwich to her lips, but as soon as he turned to Nancy she set the plate aside.

"They don't return to the DDC for hearings, I take it?" Nancy asked.

He shook his head. "Never. Not the ones we hunt."

"That must be a difficult responsibility to shoulder."

"Ma'am, Harry and I . . . ." He paced away, came back and knelt in front of her. "I'm not saying this to hurt you, but you need to understand. We've both been in places so hopeless, so painful and demeaning that we feel like we regain a bit of our humanity when we destroy those we hunt. It's not nice. You might even say it's a special brand of madness, but it's what we have."

"Okay." Nancy cupped Julian's face in her hands. "I'm glad he has you. It must be a comfort to have someone who understands."

"Mrs. Cayce. We need to go. Harry's got this thing about time, and—"

She nodded and as soon as Julian backed up, she stood. "I don't want you to get in trouble. I have an emergency bag I always keep packed. I'll grab it and we'll go."

"Thank you."

CHAPTER 23

October 15, 2:13 AM

AFTER THEY GOT NANCY SETTLED into the safe house under DDC protection, Ember sped the whole way to the apartment trying to make up for their lost time. Julian spent the time on the phone with Scott, sorting things out for Nancy. She almost made the whole trip without having to talk to Julian, but once parked, Julian grabbed her arm, preventing her from getting out of the car.

"I heard you talking to Nancy at her place, about you not being the right woman for Harry."

"Oh." She slouched in her seat.

"I'm worried about you." Julian frowned. "Have you been sleeping? I know you haven't been eating. Don't think I didn't notice you didn't take more than one bite of that sandwich. I keep thinking about it and I can't remember seeing you eat much of anything else while you've been with us."

She leaned her head against the headrest. "I'm not hungry. I don't know what's wrong with me. I don't feel right. I'm afraid to sleep now, and . . . ."

"How are you and Harry?"

"Fine." She traced the logo on the steering wheel with her thumb. "Considering he didn't get a choice in any of this, he's been wonderful."

"But is he taking care of you?"

Her cheeks flamed. "Yes, Jules. He has sex with me. He makes sure I'm sated."

"He has sex with you?" Honest to God, he sounded shocked. His brows rose high on his forehead.

Ember sank lower in her seat. "Do you always initiate such personal conversations?"

"Due to circumstances out of my control, I was unable to practice my social skills for a long time."

Had he been in prison, then? Was that why Harrison had to "check him out" like a freaking library book? Was that the deep, dark secret Harrison feared her knowing?

"Look, Em. I've been mated awhile now and spend quite a bit of time with the coven and one thing I've noticed is that there is a huge difference in mindset between 'he had sex with me' and 'we made love' where women are concerned. The first tells me you're not connecting with him, which isn't good."

Her throat closed and her eyes burned. How bad was their situation that even Julius could see the problem?

"Oh, for Fuck's sake, don't cry." Despite his harsh admonishment, he pulled her into a rough embrace. "Come on. What's going on?"

"He doesn't trust me."

"Now, I know that isn't true."

"He won't let me touch him. Never when we have sex. And while he's very attentive and tender, it still feels cold 'cause I'm there being taken care of as if it's a duty and he can't stand anything more. I want to be patient with him, but my demon's tearing me up on the inside. I've tried to give him time to get used to me, to keep a grip on this need I have for sex, but I'm losing the battle, considering what happened last night, and I don't know what to do. I'm stuck between satisfying my demon and hurting him, or giving him more time and maybe hurting someone else."

"Fuck's sake."

She pulled out of his embrace. "What does that mean? You all say it."

"It's a British thing, think 'for God's sake' minus taking your higher power's name in vain." He smoothed her hair back from her face, cupped her cheeks and wiped the tears away.

For such an ass, she could see why Kat was head over heels for him. He was a really nice man.

"So, this is a problem."

She frowned. "Of course it is. I can't continue like this forever."

"Well, that, too, but the problem is bigger than that."

"What do you mean?"

"I mean, he's claimed you and kept you alive by sating you sexually, but he hasn't sated you emotionally, which equals a long, painful, wasting away for a succubus."

"Kat told you."

He nodded. "It's been less than a week and you're losing weight. Losing your healthy glow. You can't control your demon and if this continues, you'll be seeing more and more of her. Your demon will become stronger than you. Control you. Eventually, she'll self-destruct."

"Oh, God. I don't know what to do."

"Yeah. Look, Harry does care. He does want you. He's always talked about you. Maybe you need to push him a little harder."

She shook her head. "When I touch him, he very politely and very succinctly removes my hand from his person." She ran her hand through her hair. "He's uncomfortable with me when he's not in complete control."

"His person?" He grunted. "Considering what he's been through, I'm not surprised." He sighed. "Honestly, what I find amazing is him allowing any sort of intimacy."

"What happened to him, Jules? If I understood more, my demon might be more patient, too."

"You saw his face when he walked into the interrogation room, Em. I shouldn't have told you as much as I did. Wasn't my place."

This was proving to be a useless conversation. She still had no idea how to get around Harrison's defenses. Nor did she learn anything new to aid her cause. If only there was some magic potion that. . . . Ember leaned back and stared at Julian. "What if you mesmerized him?" Jules shook his head but she kept going, latching onto the idea. "You could make him relax long enough to let me show him how things could be between us. Get him to give me a chance."

"He'd ash me the second he was free." He snorted. "Might

even kill you, too."

"So how else? How can I get him to give me a chance?"

"I don't know, Emerald Eyes, but your last idea isn't going to happen." He sighed. "Look, I'll talk to him. Maybe I can get him to be reasonable since we've somewhat similar pasts."

Oh, sure that would work. They'd just explain that her demon needed intimacy right now and all would be well. Just like that Harry would change. She scoffed. More likely, he'd torture himself trying while being consumed with guilt. Nothing good could come of that. Her heart sank. "No. Any other ideas?"

"Nah."

That was it, then. Her worst fear was confirmed. She wouldn't allow her demon to take over. The thought of hurting Harrison or Julian or anyone else was too much to bear. She didn't have five years to wait for Harrison to come around like Duncan had.

"I think I'm ready to go home."

"Home?"

"Yeah, Jules." She keyed the ignition. "I'm going home. Alone."

There was only one way to protect those around her. To ensure her demon didn't hurt anyone she cared for.

"I don't think—"

"Get out of the car, Jules or I'll let my demon loose."

He cussed. "This is a bad-fucking-idea, Emerald Eyes."

Once Jules got out, she drove to her place in Bellevue in silence. Considering what she was planning to do, she felt strangely calm. The incubus' last words kept rolling around in her head. *She's not fully sated. She'll tear you two apart.*

Like Harrison had said, it was a choice: Either she had to shoulder the burden of taking one life, or accept the responsibility for all those lives ruined due to her inaction.

Unfortunately, the life she had to destroy lived inside her.

CHAPTER 24

October 15, 2:38 AM

THEY'D BEEN GONE TOO LONG.

Harrison scratched George under his chin. The minion butted his head against his and gurgled.

"They left over three hours ago, George, and they should've returned in two." He must've been insane to send Ember out at night with no one but Julian for protection. Not that Julian wasn't capable, but something was wrong.

Or maybe Ember was stalling before coming home.

Gods, she'd been miffed earlier. Maybe he should've gone and spoken to his mother.

No. He'd turned out nothing like the man his parents tried to raise. The places he'd been . . . the things he'd done. . . . Mom might understand, he'd been away since he was sixteen, after all. No. He let them think he was dead. He hadn't been there for her when his father died. Adia was still on the loose. His mother had plenty of reasons not to want him around. He wasn't ready to risk her rejection. Not now.

He considered Ember's willingness to stay with him a goddamn miracle. Then again, she had no choice. His mom, though. . . .

His mom didn't *need* him.

Unable to resist, he checked his watch again. Gods, he needed to stop with the time thing. He'd started doing it during his time with Adia. Maybe he'd been waiting to be rescued or for death to claim him. He didn't remember, but his obsession with time had stuck.

He froze mid-pace as the elevator pinged. He should be relieved. They were here, but the knot in his gut wound tighter.

The doors slid open. Julian pulled himself away from the back wall of the lift and entered their flat. He wouldn't meet his gaze.

Oh, gods. He tugged at the collar of his shirt. "Where's Ember?"

"She took her car." Julian shifted his weight. "She went home, man."

Out of everything he conceived of Julian saying, the possibility of Ember leaving him hadn't even crossed his mind. She needed him.

He glanced at his watch. He'd been mated to Ember seven days, twenty-two hours, and thirty-two minutes. Fuck's sake, he must have hit the land speed record for fucking up a relationship.

"Don't worry, I've got her address for you." Julian held out a slip and Harrison snatched the paper out of his hand to read it.

Bellevue was at least thirty minutes away. He didn't have a lot of time if he wanted to get her back here before the sun rose. The drive took about a half hour round trip, plus he needed time to convince her to come home. He started for the door.

"We need to talk first."

Talk? "Now? I need to go get Ember. You know damn well she's not safe on her own with Adia on the loose."

Julian put his hand on Harrison's shoulder to stop him.

He came around swinging. "I don't have time." George flattened out, prepared to fight.

Julian dodged the blow. "Why? Why are you going to bring her back?"

The fuck? "She needs me."

"You're an idiot." Julian shook his head. "You might stop to wonder why she went home."

"I don't have time for this." He punched the button to recall the elevator.

"She's bending over backward trying to gain your trust. She and George have bonded. She and I. She and Kat. She and Duncan. What's it gonna take, Harry? What's she got to do for you to let her in?"

He didn't understand any of this. "I trust Ember. I allowed her into my bed. She went with us to the Knot Works and the auction. What makes her think I don't trust her?"

"You haven't told her about me. That I'm the Harbinger she's so scared of." Julian wouldn't even look at him now. "You haven't told her about *your* past. You refuse to risk yourself and let her all the way in."

Harrison shook his head. "Some things are better left unsaid. We're doing fine."

"No, you're not. She needs intimacy. Her demon's demanding it."

This was ridiculous, the solution was easy enough. "I'll apologize." *And make love to her.* He stepped into the elevator and punched the button. "Don't leave without an escort, Jules. You know the rules."

Julian cursed. "Ember was right." He shook his head looking almost . . . resigned. "You're not leaving me any choice, man."

The doors slid closed.

He almost hit the button again to find out what Julian meant. It seemed a strange thing to say. An odd way to say it. Not angry—you're not leaving me any choice other than to stay here. More, defeated—you're not leaving me any choice, man. I gotta do what I gotta do. The son of a bitch better not leave the apartment unescorted. They'd all be up shit creek if he got caught.

"Fuck's sake. I don't have time for this shit." He'd get to Ember's, apologize—say whatever she needed to hear—and get her to come back.

He was starting to get used to her being around. He liked the way she bantered with him. Craved the sight of her smile and the challenging gleam lighting her gorgeous eyes when he teased her. She made him feel normal. Whole.

The doors slid open and he strode into the parking garage, pressing his key fob to unlock the car. She'd come back. She had to, damn it.

Didn't she realize how much she needed him?

CHAPTER 25

October 15, 3:27 AM

TURNED OUT SUICIDE WAS HARDER than she'd thought. Simple enough. Load the gun. Click off the safety. Put the barrel in your mouth. Tip it to the right angle and then squeeze the trigger.

It was the last part she couldn't complete. Had, in fact held the gun in her mouth so long the barrel had stuck to her lip. Now she had a little sore spot from when she pulled the gun away too quickly.

She'd covered the curtains with an old sheet. Bathed. Did her hair and make-up—though she wasn't sure why, because that would get messed up—and changed into easy-to-remove clothes for the coroner's benefit.

Oh, and she did the note thing, so they wouldn't worry that she'd been murdered.

The thing was, she kept thinking about Harrison, wondering how much this would devastate him. He'd blame himself, and she didn't want that. By killing herself she'd remove the danger her demon posed, but she'd still hurt him.

She pulled the gun out of her mouth again and took a generous sip of wine. The alcohol burned the corner of her mouth where the gun had rested too long.

Had she smeared her lipstick?

A startled laugh burst from her and she swallowed her sip of wine the wrong way, making her sputter. "Well, I guess if I had to be inept at something, I'm glad it's this." She lifted her glass to the empty room in a toast.

Though was she? If she didn't off herself, what then? What would happen to Julian? Harrison? Her neighbors? What would *she* become?

The possibility of her demon hurting anyone wasn't something she wanted to live with. Waiting for her demon to self-destruct didn't sound like much fun, either.

Her demon clawed at her, trying to pull away from her body. *Let me free. I can fix everything.*

"Yeah, right." Ember closed her eyes, fisted her hands, and called her demon back. "If I go, you're going with me."

The thing was, she was afraid she didn't have it in her to pull the trigger.

Someone knocked.

What now? Was Julian here to try and talk her into coming back? Maybe Kat?

Ember set the gun aside and went to the door.

When she opened it, Harrison scowled at her. For a moment, he didn't do anything else. Just looked her up one side and down the other and frowned even harder.

Her body didn't care about his obvious displeasure, reacting with fierce need to his proximity. She swallowed and took a deep breath. "Hi." Her gaze flicked to his shoulder where his minion perched. "George."

"Can we come in?"

She glanced over her shoulder. This was the last thing she needed. She pressed her thighs together trying to squelch the sudden throb. "Now's not a good time."

"I won't stay long. I want to talk."

Whoever said history repeats itself was spot on. She sighed. "Please come in, Harrison. You're welcome in my home."

A ghost of a smile curved his mouth. "You remembered I needed a formal invitation."

All she wanted to do was to wrap her arms around him and hold him tight. Instead, she turned and went back to her chair, grabbed the glass of wine and took a deep gulp. As surreptitiously as possible, she slid the gun and the old picture of her and Harrison she'd been looking at behind a short stack of books sitting on the table.

He wandered in, checking out her place. Her house was sparsely decorated. She'd taken a hit on the property she'd sold in Arizona and prices were high in Washington. She never entertained, so she had no dining table. She had a small, cozy sitting area with two oversized chocolate-colored armchairs and one cream-colored divan. Shelves stuffed with books lined her walls which added plenty of color to the room.

His gaze locked onto the sheet draped over the curtains. His brows drew together and he shook his head. "Look, I wanted to apologize." He swiped his palm across the back of his neck. "I didn't mean for any of this to—"

Good Lord, he looked as uncomfortable as if he stood in line to have his balls tattooed. She giggled. Shook her head at his quizzical expression. "Remember the afternoon before you left for England?"

His mouth was still poised to continue his sentence, his jaw snapped shut, and he nodded. "Yeah, sure. Look, I know you think I—"

"I knew better than to let my temper show with my stepdad. The bastard was always drunk, but I was desperate to go with you and your parents."

With an exaggerated sigh, he sat in the armchair next to hers. George hopped to the carpet and roamed off to explore the house. "Everyone has the right to lose their temper now and again. That wasn't the problem. The problem was him."

She flashed him a smile. "Took me awhile, but I did figure that out. The reason I brought it up, was because of what happened after."

With a snort of disgust, he shook his head. "I put you in harm's way. I shouldn't have taken you out to that dry riverbed."

Ah, Harrison. He carried the weight of the world on his shoulders. "I remember different."

"You're remembering wrong."

She tipped her head to the side. "When I was training for Social Work they taught me something I've since found quite valuable—there is no right or wrong memory—just different points of view."

His gaze traveled to the door.

"Coward."

His jaw clenched. He glanced at his watch.

Tick, tock, time is running out for me.

"Fine. I'll bite. What do you remember?"

"Leaving my stepdad's trailer with a bloody lip." His gaze dropped to her mouth and her insides clenched. "My ears were still ringing and my neck hurt. My best friend and the people I'd come to know as my family were leaving the next day and I couldn't see the sun."

He cocked his head to the side, studying her. "That's saying a lot in Arizona."

"Yeah, it is. I was done. I was headed to our fort." She leaned her head on the high-backed chair and pictured it. They had built a fort out of dried saguaro and plywood, tucked into a deep wall of the ravine. People dumped their garbage farther up, closer to the barrens of the Sonoran. They'd often made pilgrimages out there and had collected quite the cache of goods. Their fort had a cot, a nightstand, and a three-legged kitchen chair they'd propped on a cinder block. "To our emergency supplies." To get the old rusty hunting knives they'd spent an afternoon sharpening.

"You wanted to move in there?" But no sooner had the words left his mouth than he scowled. His next words came out as an accusation. "You weren't planning on living anywhere."

Ember shook her head.

"That's why you kept telling me to go away. You were gonna kill yourself."

"I was so mad when you wouldn't leave me alone. I dared you to walk with me out the Sonoran end of the ravine because I knew if your parents found out you'd be toast. I think I hoped you'd get into so much trouble they'd cancel the vacation."

He sat back in the chair. "And by agreeing, I put you in harm's way anyhow."

"No. You gave me something to look forward to." She reached out to take his hand, thought better of it, and sat back again without touching him. "You remember the old car? My imagination went nuts when I saw it."

The old blue Pinto. The thing had rusted out. One door was missing as well as most of the glass from the windows.

He dragged his hand across his face like he wanted to scrub away the memory from behind his eyes. "It was stupid. Anything might have been in there. A derelict. A body."

She slanted him a You-can't-be-serious expression. "That was the point." Remembering back to how startled they'd been when a Javelina lunged out of the backseat, she laughed. The wild pigs were ugly creatures with a stout body covered in wiry brown hair and wicked tusks jutting out from either side of their snouts. "I'll never forget your face when you saw those Javelina."

"At least *I* didn't scream like a little girl."

"I *was* a little girl, you beast." She shook her head. "I don't know how we made it to the fence line without getting gored on his tusks."

"I'll never understand why that fence was even there."

A giggle bubbled out of her. "You're right. There was miles of chain-link, but it hadn't connected to anything—it was just one long fence. Lucky us, it was." She grinned. "After you pushed me up you jetted over the fence like your ass was on fire."

He'd fallen over the other side without a smidgen of grace and she'd tried to catch him. She had no idea what gave her the idea she could. She'd lost her balance and he'd knocked the wind out of her when he fallen on top of her.

"Yeah, well, getting close and personal with those damn tusks will give you wings. Shit's better than Red Bull."

They both chuckled.

"I still remember that pig butting against the chain-link, snorting and pawing the ground." She gave him a tentative smile. "I should've been scared, but I wasn't."

He scoffed. "You were dazed from when I landed on you."

"I was lost in those eyes of yours."

His smile faded. He shook his head.

"And then I was lost in your kiss."

His lips parted and his eyes softened. "Em."

Then, those damn shields of his snapped right back into place. "You can't call that awkward lip-mashing a kiss."

"To my sixteen-year-old-self, you were perfect. I fell in love with a scrawny boy with an untamed mop of hair, and the most brilliant blue eyes I'd ever seen. In that moment, you saved my life."

He stood.

Disappointment flooded her.

Twice, he opened his mouth and twice he shut it again. He dragged his hand across the back of his neck. "I gotta go. I came by to apologize. For what I am. For getting you into this mess. For not being what you need. I—" He shook his head. "I am so damn sorry for everything, Em. And, I wanted to know if you would consider—" His hand stroked through his hair, leaving tufts standing on end.

Her heart beat hard against her ribs. Trying to be vulnerable with him when he wouldn't do so in return was an exercise in heartbreak. If he walked out the door, she knew what she had to do. She couldn't risk going to sleep and letting her demon loose again. Damn it, she didn't want to die. She wanted the future she'd always dreamed about with him. "I know that was a long time ago."

He headed for the door with long, carpet-eating strides, but not before she saw his longing. His need.

"I loved that boy back then." She stood, raising her voice. "And I'm falling in love with the man he became."

Finally, he stopped. Hesitated with his hand on the knob while he checked his damn watch.

She made her way over to him, wishing he'd confide in her, give her some hint as to what his fear was. She didn't know if he resisted her touch because he feared what she might do or if he felt he was too "dirty" for such intimacies, or both. "I admire what you do for the DDC."

"Em. Don't."

Her heart raced. At least she had touched on part of it. Why else would he resist a compliment to something he took obvious pride in? "I enjoy listening to you spar with Jules. Watching you with Kat and Duncan."

He leaned his forehead against the door.

"I'm even starting to make friends with George."

His body jerked when she placed her hand on his arm. "Turn around, Harrison." She waited, letting the seconds tick off in silence. When he did comply, her heart broke over the pain in his eyes.

"You came home because you were done with me, remember?"

"No, I came because I was done with me. Everyone needs a second chance." She took each of his hands into one of hers. "What if we each try giving ourselves another one?"

"Gods, Em—"

"You're a good man."

"Male."

She smiled. Good, he was relaxed enough to tease. "Fine. You are a good male. You have worth. To me. To Jules. To the DDC. To Madison and Lucas and everyone you've helped through the years."

He leaned back against the wall, letting his head rest on the plaster.

"Stay."

"You need me so soon?"

She wet her lips. "I don't want you to stay because I need you to sate me. I want you to stay because you want to be with me. Maybe you could let me love you, too." He started to shake his head. "Then why did you mate me?"

"I'm not denying the desire to stay, but this is not a good idea. I'm not right in the head. The things I . . . they left a stain. I'm not rejecting you. I'm worried I'll hurt you."

"That you'll hurt me, or that I'll hurt you?"

His jaw clenched tight. "Both."

She couldn't speak past the lump burning in her throat.

"I don't think you have any clue how beautiful you are." His knuckles grazed her cheek. "How hard it is to stay in control when you touch me."

"We're mated. You don't always have to stay in control. It's okay to lose yourself in the moment."

"No. That's how people get hurt." He pressed his lips together. "I want to be with you, but—"

"Perfect. We'll go super-sloth speed." She grinned.

A rusty laugh burst from him.

"You don't move. Tell me what you like and what you don't. If you don't like it, I'll stop."

"No experiment needed. I like you and I don't like being

touched."

"I'm touching you now and you don't seem to mind."

CHAPTER 26

October 15, 4:05 AM

HARRISON STARED AT HER HANDS in his. Her small, soft fingers laced between his. "I've held your hand before." How did she do it? She was so trusting. Open. All the things that terrified him. So much crap had built inside him, he was afraid of what would happen if he ever opened up.

"Would you at least try? Let me touch you and you can have all the control. I won't do anything you tell me you don't like."

How did he decide what that was? He was already torn between a raging hard-on and trying to keep his breathing regulated. Thing was, this seemed important to her and he wanted to try. Gods, he loved when he did something she liked. Loved the return on investment she gave him over the small things.

What if he could be a little more normal? She'd never need know how awkward he was feeling. As long as *she* believed he was normal, that's all that mattered.

He nodded.

"Mm. So let's try something a little different." She focused on his mouth, and he *felt* his lips as they tingled in anticipation.

Something burst in the pit of his stomach, letting loose a thousand tingly, wriggly bits. She made him feel like a rookie at all this. How was that possible when he was dirtier than a Mike

Rowe special?

She lifted on her toes, balancing herself with one hand on his chest. So close he tasted her words. "You haven't kissed me since that first night."

"Honey, I've kissed you so many times I lost count."

Her other hand slid into his hair. He closed his eyes, focusing on her fingers against his scalp.

"Not on the mouth. Not to where I could kiss you back." She bit her lip. "How many women have you made love to?"

She wanted to talk about that? "Come on, Em."

"How many?" Her voice was nothing but a whisper and she was so close each word brushed over his lips. "Be honest."

"One." It was the truth. Love had never had anything to do with the violence between him and Adia.

"Good."

His eyes snapped open at the pleasure infused in that one word, but slid back closed, as her lips met his.

This was no awkward melding of mouths, but a gentle sip. A warm lick. A naughty tug on his bottom lip with her teeth. Parting his lips, he let her show him what she wanted. He memorized every tingle, every hot glide of her tongue.

When he couldn't hold back a second longer, he gave everything back.

His hands tangled in her hair and he slanted his mouth over hers, swallowing her moan. He plundered her mouth, taking every sweet nuance of the experience and tucking them away in his heart. His cock pressed hard against the fly of his jeans. His breathing grew ragged and he forced himself away.

"S'okay, baby."

Had anyone ever called him that before? He couldn't remember being innocent enough for such an endearment.

"Easy."

Christ. His grip was too tight. He released her. "Fuck's sake, Em. This is no good."

"It's perfect." She smiled. "If you don't trust yourself, keep your hands on the wall."

He did. He flattened his palms on the rough plaster and leaned back on them.

Ember's hands slid along his shirt front, undoing buttons with quick flicks of her fingers. She spread the edges wide and tugged the cuffs until the shirt slid off his arms. "You tell me if I'm doing something you don't like." One finger trailed down his arm. Then her whole hand slid over his skin, returning to his shoulder. Spreading her fingers, both hands eased over his chest in a caress. Her hands were warm. Soft. Holy hell, did she feel good. His cock was as hard as forged steel and all he wanted to do was strip her bare, press her against the wall, and sink into her. He started to reach for her.

He fisted his hands. Tucked them behind him.

Her thumbs traced around his nipples. She dragged the pad of her thumbs over the rigid tips.

His chest tightened and he fought to regulate his breathing. Exhale. He had to remember to exhale before the next breath.

Her mouth pressed to his collarbone and she ran her tongue along his skin. His grasp on his control was slipping and he hated it.

That's when people got hurt.

When passion ruled, Adia had always lost control.

He refused to lose control. "Em, this is where you need to stop."

She pulled her hands away, her worried gaze met his. "You don't like this?"

Fuck's sake. Now he had disappointed her. No wonder she wanted to leave him. What reason did she have to stay?

"I do. I . . . I can't. I don't want to feel. . . ." He grabbed his shirt, but didn't bother to put it on. "George, come on." He nudged Ember out of the way, swung the door wide, took one step and froze.

Julian was stepping onto the porch looking for all the world like he'd lost his best friend. Gods, had something happened to Kat? He met Julian's gaze. "What's going on? Why're you here?"

"You have no free will."

All the blood drained from Harrison's face. He couldn't move. Adrenaline burst through his veins as he struggled to make his body work. To blink. To talk. To do anything.

George crawled up his paralyzed body and perched on his shoulder.

Ah, gods. After all this time, after everything he'd done to protect the son of a bitch, now Julian decided to fuck him over?

Ember slipped past him onto the porch. He wanted to call her back. To warn her, but he couldn't speak.

"What did you do?"

"I took away his free will." Julian looked away. "While he's under the effects of my talent, he can't voluntarily act. Don't worry, he's conscious. He's thinking, but he can't act on any of those thoughts."

"You told me no." Wringing her hands, her gaze darted to Harrison and back to Julian. "You said he'd never forgive us."

Ember was in on this? Of course, she was.

Pain always followed the gentlest moments.

"I started thinking—" Julian's gaze landed everywhere but on her. "You know, if he could have what I have with Kat—it'd be worth the risk." Julian frowned. "Stop it, Harry. No one's gonna hurt you. You're safe, man. Relax. Breathe."

Oh, sure. His best friend and his mate were plotting against him, but he needed to chill the fuck out.

Ember put her hand on his arm. "What's wrong with him? Why is he shaking?"

"I suspended his free will, not his faculties nor his bodily functions. He's aware and pissed as hell. He can hear us and will remember everything—so don't do anything you don't want to be accountable for later."

She inhaled a sharp breath. "Of course not."

Julian scoffed. "Yet here we are, Emerald Eyes." His gaze shifted to Harrison. "Give us a minute, Em."

She nodded. She opened her arms to George and the minion dove right in. Traitor. Cuddling him to her chest, she moved out of sight.

He stared at Julian through a frozen expression. He was gonna ash the fucker as soon as Julian released him. He couldn't believe this. How could Julian, of all people, do this? He knew, damn it. He had been through his own personal hell at the hands of another. Had been stripped of his will when he'd been possessed by that Watcher.

"I know you hate me right now."

No shit.

"I wasn't gonna. . . ." Julian's face twisted. He paced away.

"Fuck."

Oh, poor baby.

"I know this is shitty. She doesn't know what to do and frankly, neither do I." Julian's words ran together, as they did whenever he was upset. He hadn't seen Julian like this in years. "She's a succubus, man. You mated her, so I know you care. Thing is, you're so caught in your own shit, you're failing to see what's in front of your face. She's not eating. She's getting thinner. Having trouble controlling her demon. She's depressed. Why? 'Cause she's not connecting to her mate. Think about it, why does a succubus need to have sex with her *mate* to be sated? Because they need more than the physical act. Yeah. Yeah, you're hearing me. You gotta quit letting Adia and her fucked-up games control you, 'cause you and I both know you'd be gutted if anything happened to Em."

He was wrong. Ember would tell him if she was having a tough time. She'd tell him she needed him.

"Look, man, you know what I was like before. If I hadn't been trapped in that house with Kat, I never would've stayed put long enough to learn to care. I'd be ash, yeah? She saved my ass. Gave me a life. So don't think I don't get it. Thing is, you're out of time. I've watched you get more and more obsessed with finding Adia the last couple years. It's no way to live. And with Em running out of options—I'm not watching you go through losing her. So, here's the deal—I'm giving Ember authority over you."

Harrison struggled to speak. To break eye contact. To do anything.

"Jesus, breathe, damn it. She wants you to hold still long enough for her to show you she's not like Adia. She needs you to give her a chance. I'm giving you an out. She can restrain you and keep you relaxed—that's all. You understanding me? You'll remember everything and she can't do anything you don't want done aside from keep you in place."

Fuck's sake. He was about to live one of his worst nightmares.

"Here's your out—if your nerves register any pain—you're free."

Okay. His partner wasn't so bad after all. He'd let him live. He was going to beat the swagger out of him, but he'd let the son of a bitch live.

"Ember, come here." Julian waited until Ember came back to the door. "All right, he's pissed as hell, so you might want to make sure there's some distance between you two before you release him."

"Oh, God." Her hand pressed against her stomach.

"No, now don't worry. I'm sure he's beginning to understand we're trying to help. He'll follow your directions to the letter until you restrain him."

Her jaw dropped. "Restrain him?"

"You said you wanted to—Jesus." Julian walked away a few steps and came back. "Sit him in a chair and tell him his wrists are bound to its arms. Or a bed post, or whatever. . . ." He waved his hand in front of his face. "You get the picture, but once he's restrained, his free will is back full force. Understand? He can't break the binding until you release him, but he can do anything else. *Refuse* anything else."

She nodded, shooting Harrison a worried glance.

"When you're ready to release him completely, tell him something like—you must count from one to one hundred without skipping any numbers. When you reach one hundred you'll be free."

She blanched. "You think I'll need that long of a head start?"

Oh, she was gonna need a hell of a lot longer head start than that.

"Maybe a million would be better."

Her hand flew to her mouth. "Oh, God."

"I'm joking. It was a joke." He glanced at Harrison. "Sort of."

"Julian!"

He wiped his hand down his face. "Everything'll be fine by the time you're finished. Remember? You wanted him to be still long enough to show him what you're like—what things could be like if he could trust you. Right?"

"This isn't a good idea. I thought of a different plan, and—"

"No." Julian nudged her chin. "If your plan is what I'm guessing, it sucks worse than this one. Get the idea out of your head."

What the hell had she come up with that was worse than this?

Her lips wobbled and she pressed them into a tight line. She hugged herself and gods, she seemed so miserable, despite everything, all he wanted to do was hug her.

Julian put his hands on her arms. "You'll be fine." Patted her shoulders. "Everything is going to be fine." He glanced at Harrison. "The only other commands he has to listen to are commands to relax or calm down. Understand?"

She nodded, blinking away unshed tears.

"Good. I'm going home to Kat before I get caught being out on my own."

"You're leaving?" She reached out with both arms as if to grab him.

He turned around and walked backward while he spoke. "Look, sweetheart, I don't think he's into the threesome gig. I know I ain't."

Her cheeks flamed. "That's not what I meant."

"Goodnight, Emerald Eyes. Good luck."

Her gaze locked on Harrison and she bit her lip. She patted his shoulder like Julian had done to her. "Everything's going to be fine. You and me, we're going to be fine."

Yeah, fine. Fucked–up. Insecure. Neurotic. Emotional. That pretty much summed things up from where he stood.

CHAPTER 27

October 15, 5:19 AM

"**G**O INSIDE, PLEASE."

Harrison re-entered her house. What the hell was she planning?

She closed and locked the door and walked past him. "Follow me."

In the living room, she paused by the large overstuffed armchair he'd sat in earlier and something inside him calmed. She wanted to talk. Why she felt she needed to go to this much trouble was beyond him. Had he been that much of a bastard?

She bit her lip. Her gaze dropped to his pants. She took a deep breath. "In for a dime, in for a dollar, right?"

Ah, hell.

"Drop your shirt. Take off your shoes, socks, and pants, and sit in the chair."

His belly dropped somewhere south of his navel. This wasn't happening.

"Relax. Breathe, baby. I won't hurt you."

She was hurting him. He removed everything but his boxers. As soon as she had him restrained, he'd be able to speak his mind, and she was getting an earful. He couldn't wrap his head around the fact this was happening. Ember had always been so damn sweet. He sat in the big arm chair she'd occupied earlier, the cool cloth raising gooseflesh on his exposed skin.

"Do you remember the first morning in the hotel?" Kneeling in front of him, she started to touch his knee but at the last second snatched her hand back.

As if he might forget the morning he took her to mate.

"Of course you do. I pretty much ruined your life." She blushed and shook her head. "Neither one of us had many choices, did we?"

Pissed as he was, the expression on her face damn near broke his heart. Gods. Is that what she thought?

"I was so angry. I felt like I had no control." She shrugged. "Then I realized, even chained up, you'd given me all the control and you had none. The second morning with you brought home the message. Even though I had to abide by your rules, you never did anything I didn't ask for. I wanted to do the same for you. To show you, even while I'm touching you, even when you're not dominating the situation, you can trust me not to hurt you. If you hate it, if you hate me after this, I'll go away. You'll never have to see me again."

His chest tightened. She couldn't leave him, damn it. Even if she did, she'd have to return often enough to be sated. Didn't she understand?

"I meant what I said, when we were kids, I was in love with you. Even as angry as I was when you didn't come home, I still compared everyone else to you. I love you now, too. I'm sorry if that scares you or if you don't want it, but I do love you and because I love you, I need to know now if there's a chance for us. Do you understand? It's eating at me. Maybe because I've always been this way, or because I'm a succubus now, but every little rejection is doing something to me. Changing me. I can't wait to find out how things will end. I wish I could. If things were different, I'd wait forever for you, but they're not and I need to know now. My demon is . . . ." She gave him a tentative smile. "If we're not a good match, I have to leave before I lose myself completely."

Where the hell did she plan to go? His muscles locked tight. His throat squeezed. He wanted to speak, but she hadn't restrained him yet. How had he screwed this up so bad in a week?

"I'm going to touch your arms now. After this I won't touch you again unless you give me permission." She moved each of his arms so they lay flat on the large curved arms of the chair. His fingers hung over the edge and she curled them around the pillow-topped cushion. "I want you to be honest tonight. For both our sakes, do not let me do anything you don't want done. You can speak one of two words from here on—more or leave." She stood and backed away a few feet, wringing her hands. She gave him her back. "Okay, Harrison. You're no longer under my control, but you can't move your arms from those cushions."

Harrison blinked. Did she realize what she'd done?

Was he free?

He moved his wrists on the arms of the chair to confirm. Yep, she'd freed him from Julian's talent, prior to instructing him to remain restrained.

He could leave.

Nothing prevented him from doing so except he needed to know how far she planned to take this. Was she being honest with her intentions or did she plan to try to force him the way Adia used to? Part of him didn't want to know. The fact he even needed to ask made him furious.

He curled his fingers around the cushion until his knuckles paled. "More."

As soon as she turned back to him, he dropped his gaze to her sweater and her pants. He quirked his brow.

She nodded. "Right. I guess it isn't fair I get clothes and you don't."

He set his jaw and nodded.

With a quick jerk she pulled her sweater over her head.

Shaking his head, he held his fingers off the cushion and lowered them slowly.

"Slower?" She fidgeted with the sweater before tossing it aside, looking uncomfortable as hell. Good.

She pulled her long blond locks forward, trying to hide behind the gossamer strands and twisted the ends around her fingers. Her cheeks turned pink. Her actions didn't remind him in the least of the manipulative way Adia would go about seducing him.

"I thought maybe you'd prefer to watch, since you don't like it when I touch you."

What? When had he ever said that?

A ghost of a smile lifted her lips. "You never noticed? I wondered if you realized what you do."

He wanted to ask her what she thought he did, but damn it, he needed to see this through to the end. Needed to know what she planned.

"Anyway, I thought you'd prefer to watch for a little while."

"More."

She slid her hands over her lacy bra, pausing to circle shaky fingers around her nipples.

Then seemed to change her mind, turning away from him to unbutton her jeans and shimmy them off her hips.

His lips quirked at the sexy jiggle of her ass.

Stepping out of them, she let her hands smooth over those long, gorgeous legs, up the curve of her hips. Twisting her arms behind her, she grasped the two sides of her bra and waited.

"More." Had his voice gotten deeper?

Once undone, she held the cups to her breasts and faced him. Slid a strap off one shoulder, then the other. Her eyes closed and she squeezed her breasts, rubbed the rough, lacy material over them until the tips hardened.

What did she picture in her mind's eye? What caused her lips to part on that little sigh?

She tossed the bra aside to soothe herself with soft fingertips.

Did she imagine his hands on her?

She skimmed one hand down her body to cup her mound. Slipped her fingers under the lacy panties. Like an addict, he had a euphoric recall—felt her silken wet heat on his own fingers, squeezing tight around him. He breathed the words, "Gods, Em," before he realized he shouldn't. Louder, he said, "More."

Once she slipped her panties off, she lounged back on the divan. She faced his chair head on and, as she reclined back, she spread her thighs.

He couldn't drag his gaze away. Couldn't imagine ever being secure enough to put himself in such a vulnerable position. The tiniest bit of pink flesh peeked out from her blond curls, her back arched, thrusting her breasts out. Green eyes stared back at him. No one should be so beautiful and sensual.

He moaned, unable to tear his gaze from her wandering hands.

His cock tented his boxers and pre-come dampened a spot on the front. His muscles bunched in his arms and chest, but not from stress. Not from a desire to run. From the need to get up. To go to her.

She let her hands wander over the inside of her thighs, spreading her folds for a second. Just long enough for him to catch a glimpse of pink perfection glistening with arousal. His breath hitched as she arched her back again.

Her gaze locked onto his face while she stroked herself off. Sweet tension wound deep in his belly. His balls drew tight against his body. He wished he were this engaged, this relaxed when he loved her. He'd kill to be more like other males.

Her muscles tightened and she cried out. "Harrison."

Furious as he was, he wanted her. He leaned forward, his feet flattening on the carpet, but at the last moment, he remembered.

He sat back. "More, Em."

Rising onto shaky legs, she crossed the short distance and knelt in front of him between his legs.

He tensed and had to close his eyes. He wanted to be wrong about her, but all evidence was to the contrary. He had no idea what to do with the conflicting emotions rioting through him.

That pissed him off most of all.

He'd spent so much time manipulating his relationships for minimal impact, for distance. Ember had blown all that to shit. He couldn't *not* feel when she was near. With every interaction, his heart softened more. Made him crave something from her he couldn't name.

When there was no touch, no kiss, no nothing, he opened his eyes. She held her hand an inch or so from his knee, watching him. Waiting.

If he gave her permission, then what? Would she take it as approval to do whatever she wanted? His whole body shook and he hated it.

Ember stared at him through those perfect emerald green eyes. "Breathe, baby. I won't do anything you don't want me to do. I promise."

He clenched his jaw. "More."

She lowered her hand to his knee. Her skin was too warm, almost feverish, and he frowned. Succubi didn't get sick, they were as immortal as vampires. They only became feverish if they hadn't been sated. If Julian hadn't showed up, he'd have walked right through the door and left her unsated. Damn, he was a selfish bastard.

He studied her face while she glided her hand over his leg. Dark circles smudged under her eyes and she *was* thinner—her cheekbones a little sharper, her collar bone more pronounced. Now that he was thinking about it, he didn't remember ever seeing her eat.

That wasn't possible, was it?

Maybe Julian had been right. What if sex with a chosen mate wasn't enough to sate a succubus? What if mating needed to be more than a physical act?

Gods, she needed the one thing that terrified him most.

She lifted her hand from his leg and rose to a kneeling position. Her gaze met his, hands hovering over his abdomen. Though she hadn't touched him yet, heat radiated from her palms, seeping into his skin.

So far, she'd stayed true to her word. She'd allowed him complete control. Damn it, he *wanted* to trust her. "More."

Her hips forced his thighs wider as she leaned in to stoke her hands over his chest. Her touch inflamed him, crowding away his residual anger and chipping away at his control. His cock pressed against her belly. His breathing hitched and he had to fight the urge to pull her hand away and take over.

It all clicked into place. Why she refused to tell him she needed him. Why she thought he didn't like her touch.

He *had* been rejecting her.

Not on purpose. He enjoyed her touch and yet giving her free rein with his body made him nervous. She made him *feel* and that was dangerous. She made him lose control and he couldn't allow that.

She jerked back and lifted her hands away. "Harrison, you will be calm and breathe. Slow down."

He inhaled, exhaled through his mouth. Gods, he had to pay more attention.

Her demon stretched away from her, a perfect gossamer twin. Ember's eyes closed and her demon snapped back within her. Her hands shook and she fisted them, resting them on her lap.

How long had that been happening? She needed him. For the first time tonight, he almost wished she'd take what she needed. "More."

She shook her head. "I don't think—"

Was she crazy? She almost lost control of her demon. "More."

Her hands shook as she skimmed them up his torso. She leaned into him until her mouth was a hair's breadth from his. "What do you want?"

He closed the distance. Stroking his tongue over her lower lip before sealing his mouth to hers. She tasted of sweet wine with a strange underlying metallic note. She started to pull away and he leaned forward, keeping her close, plundering the recesses of her mouth and sucking her bottom lip, desperate to keep her with him.

She dragged her mouth from his, breathless as he. She nipped at his stubble and scraped her teeth along his neck.

He hissed in a deep breath at the exquisite pleasure, his chest expanding under her palms.

She paused. Waited.

"More."

She peppered his chest with kisses. Stroked the flat of her tongue over his nipple. Lower, she nipped and licked her way along the ridges of his abs. He loved the way she'd smile each time his muscles flexed under her mouth. She trailed her lips along the edge of his boxers and her long blond locks tickled the insides of his thighs. Her hand hovered over the open seam in his boxers. "Can I taste you?"

He couldn't drag his gaze away from those luminous green eyes of hers. They were too full of hope.

What had she said earlier, in for a dime, in for a dollar? He could do this. So far, everything had been fine. Not fine, pretty damn wonderful. She'd been arousing and patient. There was no way she could possibly fathom what she was asking.

"It's okay. I don't have to."

"More." She wouldn't hurt him. He trusted her.

She eased his cock through the slit in the front of his boxers, holding his gaze. His jaw clenched as she swirled her tongue over him to catch every drop of pre-come. When she licked him from base to head with her warm, slick tongue his knuckles whitened where he gripped the armrests.

"Breathe, baby."

The breath he'd been holding burst out of him. His fingers flexed on the cushioned arms of the chair.

"I can stop."

"More." She wouldn't hurt him.

She took him all the way into the warm satin of her mouth and he arched off the chair. She stroked him with her tongue and suckled.

Her teeth didn't graze him once. He grew harder, thicker. He closed his thighs around her and his breathing turned harsh. She cupped his scrotum through his boxers. Squeezed him. Her other hand worked in time with her mouth. It was perfect. She was perfect.

And it didn't hurt.

With one hand, she dragged her nails down his chest while she pleasured him. His muscles flexed. A moan wrenched from him. "Gods, Em. Don't make me come yet."

Not until he'd sated her demon.

Mid-suck, she released him with a smack. Her gaze met his.

"More." He nodded. "Something else, but more."

She smiled and slipped her fingers into his waistband and began tugging them off. "Lift up, baby."

"Em, I—"

"No. Only two words. Too much of your past sits between us. Tonight, we're taking out all the shades of gray. Tonight, it's more or leave."

Not that. She wouldn't touch him if she saw. He shook his head. He was starting to lose control of his breathing. Needed a minute to think.

He kept inhaling and his chest tightened until a dull ache filled his ribcage. He clenched his jaw, forcing himself to slow down.

In. Out. Breathe out.

Ember sat back on her heals. "It's okay. I promised I'd stop if you didn't like what I'm doing and that's what I'm going to do." The corner of her lips curved and she looked so damned earnest.

He needed a minute. He glanced to the side where she'd tidied up when he first walked in. Her glass of wine sat on a small stack of books behind which lay a framed picture of them as kids.

They grinned as if they didn't have a care in the world. He didn't remember when the photo was taken. His mom must have taken a thousand just like it. They were smiling. Just two happy, innocent kids.

Beneath the photo, the barrel of a 9mm stuck out.

Why the hell did she have her sidearm out? The damn thing was pretty much useless against him or Julian or Adia. He doubted she had the silver bullets required to kill a Werewolf or Oni.

Out of the corner of his eye, he caught a glimpse of the white sheet draped over the curtains.

His gaze shot to her. She had her eyes squeezed shut while she struggled with her demon.

Everything clicked into place.

And his temper boiled over. When he first saw the sheet, he'd thought she'd been trying to prepare her place for sunrise. He'd almost told her the sun wouldn't hurt her and that the material wasn't thick enough to block out the sun anyway. But no, she wasn't worried about sunlight. She was too concerned about making a mess on the goddamned curtains.

Gods, the metallic taste—she must've had the goddamned pistol in her mouth right before he interrupted her grand plan. No wonder Julian thought her other plan sucked. Why he risked everything to travel across town unescorted to mesmerize him. Now, her odd mood earlier made sense. Her *story* made sense.

She must be going through hell trying to accommodate his eccentricities against the demands of her demon. Damn it, why hadn't she said anything?

They needed to have a long, detailed conversation about all this, as soon as he calmed her demon. "More."

She shook her head. "No. It's fine. Everything's okay. This was a bad idea." She gave him a tremulous smile. "You don't like when I touch you and that's okay. I know you don't do it on purpose. I'm not angry, baby. I can't express how happy I am we had this morning."

No, she wasn't angry. She looked sad. Devastated.

She was breaking his fucking heart.

This touching thing he had was nothing but a personality quirk. He could change. "More."

She shook her head, giving him a wobbly smile. "No. No

more." She tucked his cock back into his boxers. "As soon as the sun sets, I'll release you. Don't worry, I'll stay awake today. I won't let my demon get control." She rose and picked up her sweater. "After that you won't have to see me again. We won't have to worry about my demon any more. I promise."

No, he wouldn't need to worry about her demon anymore.

Not after today.

But she damn sure should worry about his.

CHAPTER 28

October 15, 6:04 AM

BLINKING AWAY THE BURN BEHIND her eyes, Ember concentrated pulling the sleeves of her sweater right-side out. She gave it her best shot and so had Harrison. She couldn't even get angry over the situation—she wouldn't trade the time she had with him for anything.

"I have had enough."

Ember swung around at the sound of Harrison's too close voice and bumped right into him. "How'd you—?"

She took a step back and another. Bumped into the end table and skirted around it. Had Julian lied to her?

All his muscles bunched tight as he stalked her.

Her heart slammed in her chest. "I thought you—?" She motioned to the chair.

"You released me from Julian's talent before you told me to stay in the chair."

She had? Then why . . . "Oh." Her hammering heart seemed to have lodged itself in her throat. He'd been testing her.

He glared, those blue eyes flashing. "Are you trying to emasculate me?"

"No."

"You seem to think I can't take care of you."

She shook her head.

"Are you going to stop telling me what the fuck I do or don't want?"

Oh, God, he looked angry. She backed away. "I didn't mean—"

"Oh, but I think you did."

"You seem a little . . . pissed." If she ran like hell, she might reach the bedroom with enough time to lock the door.

His lip curled. "Livid."

She turned and bolted but at the end of the hall she had to slow to get the door open. His arms snaked around her. She let out a squeak of protest as he pulled her back against him. After a moment of struggle, she realized he wasn't hurting her.

He nuzzled the side of her neck as he pushed open the door. "First emasculated, then thrown into the role of the villain. You're killing me here, Em."

She choked on a sob of relief.

One hand spread wide against her belly, keeping her body flush with his, the other skimmed her ribs and cupped her breast. She inhaled sharply, trying to catch her breath. "I'm not thinking very clearly, that's all."

"No, you're not." He nipped her earlobe, walking her into the room. "Why is that, do you think?"

She shrugged, shivering as the hand on her belly dipped lower. Oh, God, she wanted him so much. "If I promise not to touch you, can I turn around? I want to at least see you even if I can't pleasure you."

He moaned, walking her forward before turning her and forcing her to sit on the bed. He pulled his boxers off. His jaw set and he looked off to the side, waiting.

His posture, the tensing of his muscles told her there was more to his behavior in the bedroom than his desire to not be touched. Oh, God. Did she want to look? She'd never seen him naked. The idea he might be hiding something hadn't occurred to her. Not until now.

Her gaze roved his chest, over all the scars that had so disturbed her their first day together. Not that she minded the marks—it was the pain he must've endured in their making that upset her. She steeled herself and despite her best intentions, she blanched when she saw the damage he kept hidden beneath his boxers.

He'd been bitten. Repeatedly. Dozens of oval-shaped bite marks crowded around his pelvis. In some places, the webbed scars were so bad no hair grew around the bites.

Her face heated as a healthy dose of adrenaline released into her bloodstream. She forced her lips into a thin line to keep them from trembling. How hard had it been for him to let her take him into her mouth? To trust she wouldn't hurt him.

"Damn it. I know I'm disgusting. This is why—"

She grabbed him by the hips to keep him from moving away and kissed him, right over one of the worst scars.

He sucked in a harsh breath. "You don't have to—"

She kissed him again, the damaged skin rough and puckered under her lips. His hand stroked through her hair and his returning erection brushed her cheek. "I love you, Harrison." She let her lips linger.

He crowded her back onto the bed, knelt between her thighs and stretched out over her. His whole body shook and the ferocity of his gaze held her captive. His breathing grew erratic. He wasn't exhaling as he drew in more air, and she removed her hands from him. "Baby, you don't have to do this."

Slowly, he nodded. "Yeah." He drew in a breath and then his throat strained. His lips pressed together. "For us."

Oh, God. She wanted to ease him, had her hand almost on his cheek before she realized she almost touched him again. Fisting her hand, she let it fall back to the bed.

He'd noticed, though, and dragged her hand back, pressing her palm to his face. He closed his eyes and sucked in a shuddering breath. "Stop . . . treating me . . . like I'm . . . gonna break."

God, he was starting to hyperventilate. She wanted to help him, but had no idea how. "I don't know what to do."

His expression shuttered. "Do you still want me? Despite—"

"Yes." Her cheeks heated as the one word burst from her lips. Tears filled her eyes. Here he was having trouble breathing past his anxiety and she was pushing. "I'm so sorry."

A bemused expression crossed his features. "For wanting me?"

"Yes. No. I don't know." She covered her face with her hands. "I feel like some sex-crazed cartoon character lusting after someone uninterested and out of my league."

"Ah, gods, Em." His lips brushed her throat. "I'm interested and I'm the one not in your league. This worries me."

"Why?"

"What if I lose control and hurt you?"

"Stop treating me like I'm going to break." She smiled.

He lowered his face and brushed her lips with his. "Spread those lovely thighs for me, sweet Em."

She parted her legs, shivering as his cock nestled against her. A delicious shiver coursed through her, leaving her shaking as much as Harrison.

Her hands fisted in the sheets. "Thank you for not leaving me, baby."

He lifted onto his elbows and his whole body trembled with renewed vigor. She couldn't tell if he was angry or reacting to her nearness. His jaw clenched and his eyes turned so fierce they appeared lit from within. "Tell me about the gun."

She swallowed. If she played this cool, there was no reason he ever need to know what she'd almost done. "It's a nine-millimeter M-and-P Shield."

His eyelid twitched. "And can you explain why you taste like Smith and Wesson?"

Heat coursed through her cheeks and she tried to slide from under him.

He refused to budge.

She didn't want to talk about this. Not with him. Out of everything she'd done tonight, this was what he wanted to focus on? "You shouldn't be mad at Jules. Everything was my fault."

"I'll deal with Julian later. Right now, I want you to tell me about the sheet."

The sheet? "I don't know what—"

"Try again." His legs spread, pushing her thighs wider. He pulled her arms over her head, pinning them there. "Try the truth."

"I didn't want to make a mess."

"You didn't—" His mouth twisted and he pressed his lips into a straight line. "And what about me? Didn't you consider how much you'd have messed me up?"

The pain in his expression made her feel so ashamed. She wanted to hide, but she couldn't move at all. "I couldn't do it because of you. Because of your mom, and Jules and Kat."

"What were you thinking?"

"You told me." Her voice rose. "You said I could either shoulder the responsibility for taking one life or shoulder the responsibility for all the lives adversely affected. I know what I'm becoming. I don't want the responsibility of knowing I hurt others."

"What are you becoming?"

"My demon's taking over. She's tried to go after you. She's always trying to get out. She went after Julian."

He blanched.

"Nothing happened. I swear to God, baby, please, believe me. Julian woke me in time and Kat was…God, I can't believe how understanding she was."

"Kat knows?"

"She was there. We weren't trying to hide it from you, I just hadn't found a way to tell you."

"So instead of taking me into your confidence, you decided to blow your head out of shape."

"I didn't want to hurt you anymore."

His expression severe, he leaned in until his nose touched hers. "You. Need. Me."

He shifted his weight and thrust into her. She gasped at the overwhelming fullness.

"Ah, Gods, Em, you gotta relax. All your . . . muscles are locked . . . tighter than last time. Am . . . I hurting you?"

She shook her head. She didn't know what he wanted. On the one hand, his need to dominate was obvious. He couldn't have put her in a more vulnerable position. She was spread wide beneath him, pinned by his weight.

At the same time, he was worrying about her.

"Maybe I should turn over." It was easier for him when she wasn't facing him.

He flexed his hips against her, sinking deeper. "You need me."

Why did he keep saying that? Her breasts tightened to aching points and her hands twisted in his grip. The feel of him was too much, too intense, and she wavered between wanting to pull away and wanting him closer. Deeper.

The sight of him mesmerized her. He was a study in contrast. His features were set in hard lines, yet each touch was gentle. His lips flattened into a determined line, but he shook like a wet dog. He couldn't seem to catch a breath.

Taking one of her hands in his, he pulled it to him, flattened her palm against his chest while he flexed his hips against hers. "You need me." His hand cradled her head, forcing her to face him.

And then she saw it, there in his eyes. He loved her.

"Damn it, say it."

He wanted her to say she needed him, but she refused. They knew she needed him. Wanted him. Loved him. "*You* need *me*."

He reared back as if she'd slapped him, as if he'd found a snake in his bed. His hips stilled, so she flexed her own, sinking him deeper into her heat, surrounding him. Loving him.

She pressed her cheek to his palm, kissing his thumb. "You want me."

He started to shake his head. His lip curled into a feral expression and she couldn't fathom why she continued to push. With everything he'd been through, he might snap. He was so much bigger than her. Stronger, and in this position, there wasn't a damn thing she could do if he turned on her.

She widened the cradle of her thighs, and arched against him. Holding his gaze she inhaled deeply, exhaling through her mouth.

Without a word, he mimicked her.

She did it again. Again. Coaxed him into a calmer place, making love to him the whole while. His expression calmed.

"And you love me."

He kissed her, wrapping her so tight in his embrace she couldn't tell where he ended and she began. She loved his thighs between hers, holding her wide. His weight, grounding her to the bed. His muscular arms caging her close. His mouth drove her to distraction, plundering one moment, skimming her lips the next.

He made love to her with a slow, languid grace, a melding of bodies and spirits. When he couldn't seem to catch his breath, she breathed for him—holding his gaze and reminding him what to do. With each prolonged drag of his cock, tension built deep in her core. Shivers blossomed in her pelvis, tremors fluttered through her belly. An orgasm quaked through her in shattering undulations, leaving her gasping.

He pumped into her once more, shouting as he came. His grip tightened around her, his groin flush with hers.

Her demon settled, curling up like a contented viper to sleep.

CHAPTER 29

October 15, 7:47 AM

EMBER SNUGGLED CLOSE TO HARRISON under the covers of her bed. It was too late for them to risk returning to his place, so they'd covered the windows with heavy blankets to keep him safe from sunlight and holed up in her room.

She opened her eyes, studying the firm set of his stubble-covered jaw. "Can I ask you a question?"

"Yeah."

"Why don't you like me calling you by your nickname, but it doesn't bother you when the others do? I don't mind. I'm used to saying it and I prefer calling you Harrison. I'm curious."

He frowned. "I never noticed anyone did."

They lay in silence for a while and she didn't think he'd say more.

"I think I need you to be as different from her as you can be."

"Adia called you Harry?"

Damn. She shouldn't have asked. She'd refused to answer his questions about her stepfather their first morning together and here she was questioning him. She stared at the ceiling for a long moment, wondering how to fix the breach. "It was prom night, junior year."

His gaze shot to hers. Too much pain filled his expression for him not to have understood what she meant. "Who'd you go with?"

She smiled. "No date. I'd planned to meet some friends."

He turned on his side and propped his head in his hand. "I'd have taken you, Ember Moon."

"I know it, Harrison Cayce Sinclair." She gave him a saucy smile and stroked her lips across his chin.

"Tell me about the dress."

Lord, she used to torture him with tales of what she'd wear to dances and how her wedding gown would be cut. In her defense, they were usually digging in the dirt or building forts while she did, but he never complained. Did he remember? "Guess."

He traced the shell of a strapless V-neck on her chest.

She giggled. "What color?"

"Emerald green."

Her smile faded. "I always told you my dress would be pink."

"And I told you emerald green would match your eyes. Who won?"

She had to fight the burn behind her eyes. "You."

"Ah." He caressed her trembling lips with his thumb. "So, even though I wasn't there, I took you to prom anyway."

"Yeah." She sniffed. "You would've hated it. The theme was Masquerade Under the Stars."

"I would've worn a Phantom of the Opera mask." His lips quirked and his brow arched. "I'd have been the coolest kid at the dance. Afterward, you would've come home with me and we would've watched movies all night. Scary movies, so I'd have an excuse to put my arm around you."

She nodded. "It would've been perfect."

He frowned. "Tell me he was too drunk to get it up."

She shook her head.

The corners of his mouth dipped. "At least say it didn't go on too long."

"He passed out in a stupor pretty quick and I went straight to your parents' house. Nancy and Tom were great. I hadn't seen much of them since your disappearance, but they took care of everything. The police arrested him that night and there was enough evidence they didn't need me to testify in court. He went to jail and I never saw him again."

"Good." His finger stroked her cheek in an almost compulsive motion. Did he realize he was doing that? "I kept telling them you should come live with us."

"I did." She winked. "I stayed in your old room."

His eyes narrowed. "Tell me you didn't find my porn stash."

She smacked his arm. "You didn't have a porn stash. However, I may have stumbled over a different kind of collection."

Moaning, he rolled over onto his back.

"You had fifty-two pictures of me."

Both his hands covered his face. "Fifty-three, but I'm not listening to this."

"Fifty-two." She leaned on her elbow. "I counted them a couple times. You had photos from school and some your mom took. Others that I never figured out where they came from. Let's say, I don't remember them being taken." Pictures of her sunbathing in her back yard. Photos taken through her bedroom window.

"Gods, Em. You're making me blush."

She laughed. "That'll be the day." She dragged his hands from his face. "I thought your, uh, preoccupation was sweet."

"Harrison Cayce—the sweet stalker." He turned his head to the side and studied her. "Why didn't you turn out different? I mean you're still so open, trusting."

"I didn't let it eat me." She turned on her side. "Didn't you ever talk to Duncan?"

He shrugged. "Bits."

"I've got quirks, too." She smiled.

"Like what?"

"It wasn't normal for me to pound you to the ground after you rescued me."

A reluctant grin broke through his stern expression. "I had a beating coming."

"When I moved here, I found peace in anonymity."

His gaze sharpened. "How so?"

"For the first time since I was thirteen, no one knew me as the girl whose mom died. Or the girl whose best friend went missing. No one knew me as the girl who sent her drunk-ass stepdad to prison."

"Mm." His gaze searched her face. "Sometimes I think I'd like that—for no one to know."

"It sucks." She sighed. "I loved it at first. My self-imposed isolation turned into a kind of addiction I needed to feed. I kept people away. After a while, I realized I'd made my own prison. I was lonely as hell and I couldn't seem to change my behavior. I think I'd prefer a healthy balance. There's nothing wrong with having the people closest to you know about your past."

"You don't worry they'll treat you different?"

"I am different."

He turned his gaze to the ceiling. "There was this place on Tully Street in London called the London Dungeon. I bugged my parents about going from the time we got on the plane in Seattle through the first two weeks of vacation. They finally caved. Mom refused to go, thought it would be bad karma to enjoy something like that."

"What was it?"

"The whole thing was kind of lame, but I thought the gore was great. You would've loved it. The whole time, I kept thinking of how I could've gotten you to scream."

"You have a mean streak in you and you still didn't answer my question."

He chuckled. "They had wax statues acting out scenes of violence and death. The plague, Jack the Ripper, torture scenes. This one part of the museum was real dark and everyone was facing the guide and everything froze."

Ember leaned on her elbow. "What do you mean everything froze?"

"All the people. Dad, the guide, the other visitors. Everyone froze. The creepy music stopped. The animatronics. Everything seemed suspended in time. I stood there like a lemon, gawking, thinking the whole thing was a prank. Then I saw these eyes in one of the walls. At first, I thought they were knots in a piece of plywood, but they were so perfect. As I stared, I realized I could make out a whole face."

"The wraith."

He nodded. "When I walked closer to get a better look, he peeled himself off the wall and grabbed me."

"Your dad, he kept saying he'd been looking right at you. That you'd been talking and he blinked and you disappeared. I refused to talk to him for ages, I was so furious. I thought he was lying, trying to cover for not paying attention. We got past it. I got past it."

"He didn't do anything wrong. We didn't even know daemons existed back then. There were three males, one was the wraith, I never got a good look at the other two. It wasn't my dad's fault."

Ember lay back against the pillows, waiting to see if he'd say more.

"When I first met Adia, I thought she was a prisoner, too. The guys, they took me into this room and left me there. A little later, the door opened and they tossed her in with me." He shook his head. "She played the damsel in distress and I did my best version of a big, brave man who would take care of everything."

All she wanted to do was pull him into her arms and hold him. No one should ever have to go through what he went through. "Pedophiles find a way to be on the same level as the child and gain their trust so they can catch them doing something they can blackmail them with or find a way to fulfill a need the child has. The courting phase can go on for months."

"Adia was a pro. Took her less than ten minutes." He turned his face away. "She wasn't wearing anything but an open robe. I was sixteen and curious as hell. She had me by the balls before either of us had spoken one word."

"So you saw her body." She slipped her hand into his. "You didn't do anything any other teenage boy wouldn't have done."

"I know, but back then I was terrified of my parents finding out I was so depraved."

"You were a healthy, normal teenager. You did nothing wrong."

He gave her hand a little squeeze before flattening her palm on the center of his chest.

"How long were you there?"

"Six months, twelve hours, and fifty-two minutes."

She propped herself on her elbow. "You know to the minutes?"

"The watch was all she let me wear. I became a little obsessed with time. I marked the time whenever something happened."

That's why he was always looking at his watch at inopportune times. It was a compulsion.

"At six months, thirteen hours, and twelve minutes Duncan arrived. Less than thirty minutes before, I murdered nine boys. I hadn't even planned on fighting them. After she transformed me, I refused to feed. When she put me in the arena with them, I wanted them to kill me, but as soon as the first one put their hand on me, my vampire instincts took over."

From the bits and pieces she knew, she didn't think the fate of those boys would've been any better had they survived. "What would've happened to them if you hadn't killed them?"

"They were dead one way or another." The corners of his mouth turned down. He shook his head. "They just didn't know it yet."

"Did she transform all the boys she took?"

"Nah. I think I may have been the only one. I know I'm the sole survivor. The others, they never listened. For a while, I tried to . . . to teach them so I wouldn't have to watch them die, but they never . . . " He drew in an unsteady breath. "They'd get scared . . . and they'd forget . . . what I . . . told them to do, and—" He stopped. Took a few slow breaths.

"It's good for you to talk. You don't have to tell me, but you've got to get it out."

He blew out a deep breath and threw an arm over his eyes. "You remember Sidney Rathbalm?"

Her brows drew together. "The school bully?"

"Yeah." He grinned. "That little prick is the reason I'm still alive. I overheard him once in the boy's bathroom talking to some other kid. He was telling him the best way to give oral sex to a woman was to write the alphabet with your tongue."

"What?" She pulled a face. "You don't seriously—"

"Well, not now, no." He laughed. "I'm not telling you my tricks now. To a sixteen-year-old me, tracing letters made sense."

Her gaze traveled the length of his body to where the sheet pooled around his hips, covering his scars. She shuddered. "She liked oral sex?"

"Adia liked everything." His mouth thinned out into a line. "But yeah, especially oral."

"And when the boys didn't perform she'd get angry."

He shook his head. "They'd freak out . . . and as soon as they started . . . thrashing about she'd get excited and—" His mouth twisted and he shook his head.

She brought his hand to her lips and kissed his knuckles. He'd had enough for today. She wasn't certain she could stand to hear anymore right now. "Did you like living with Duncan?"

His mouth curved into a wobbly smile. "I'll never know why he didn't ash me. I made his life a living hell for the first year. Tried to ash him. Tried to escape. Broke his stuff. Hell, I damn near burned his place to the ground. He's a fucking saint as far as I'm concerned."

She smiled. "He loves you."

"Yeah." He sniffed and cleared his throat. "That he does."

"I love you, too." When he met her gaze, she held it, willing him to understand her love didn't come with conditions. Wasn't contingent on whatever he did or didn't do in the past, or what he may do or not do in the future. She just loved him and more than anything, wanted him to love her back.

He rolled over until he lay on top of her, nestled between her thighs. "Tell me again."

She smiled. "I love you, Harrison Cayce Sinclair."

"Put your hands on me, Ember Moon."

She placed her hands on his narrow hips.

He kissed her nose. "More."

Giggling, she caressed his lower back, glided her hands lower to cup his bum.

His breath hitched.

Ember bit her lip. "I'm not trying to rush you. We can go slower."

He shook his head. "You threw down the gauntlet. I'm picking it up." He latched onto her nipple, stroking his tongue across the tip. Lavishing attention on both her breasts, he didn't stop until she writhed beneath him.

She spread her legs, encouraging him to press deep, but he rolled with her, until she lay on top, straddling his hips. He pulled a pillow under his head and grinned. "Have your wicked way with me, sweet Em."

He trusted her. Her chest squeezed. Somehow, during the mess she'd made of today, she'd managed to earn his trust.

Her gaze darted over his body and she bit her lip. "Mm, I don't know what I want to do first." She spread her fingers wide over his skin, easing them over his six-pack and over his chest and shoulders. Leaned in until her body stretched over his and kissed him. His lips were soft, demanding, and his jaw rough with stubble. The hard length of his cock pressed against her slit. She couldn't get enough.

His hands cupped her head and pushed her back. His gaze searched hers and his breathing turned ragged. "I know . . . I'm not what . . . you expected." His jaw clenched tight. "But don't . . . leave me, Em. Not . . . to go home. Not to . . . eat lead. Don't . . . ever leave me."

"Sh." Her heart broke a little, seeing how much the request cost him. "I'll stay. I didn't want to leave, baby. I wasn't thinking clear, but I couldn't. I kept thinking about you and I couldn't do it. I'll stay."

He cupped her face and pulled her down to meet his lips. His mouth was wild under hers. He swept his tongue in to mate with hers. Nipped and sucked at her lips. Dragged his stubble-roughened chin along her neck as he sat up, spreading her thighs wide over his.

Prodding her to her knees, he took her nipple into his mouth. Suckled and tugged until she wanted to scream from the pleasure. She gripped his hair in her hands, holding him tight to her breast.

He fitted himself to her opening and drew her down as he pushed into her. Each thrust spread her wider, sank him deeper and with each teasing nip and arousing tug, her slit clenched tighter.

She squeezed her thighs around the hard male beneath her, reveling in the solidness of him beneath her. Her fingers sunk into the skin pulled taught over slabs of muscle.

"Harrison."

His hips flexed, giving her a solid foundation to thrust against and each deep drag of his cock sent her higher. He surrounded her. The taste of him lingering on her tongue. His breathing was harsh in her ear. His scent filled each breath and his skin was warm beneath her hands as she stroked her fingers through his hair, grasped his shoulders, his arms.

His respiration changed, growing short and strained. She pushed him back against the pillows, held his gaze and breathed deep until he followed suit.

"Gods, Em. Make me come, honey."

She increased her pace, rotating her hips and squeezing her

inner muscles around him.

He moaned. His hips rose to meet each of her thrusts and her gaze zeroed in on the bunch and release of his abs, the sight of him pulling out and disappearing into her.

It was too much. Her body clenched tight, pulsing through her release. He tensed beneath her. Gripped her in his arms as he shuddered through his orgasm.

She was drifting off to sleep when she saw him glance at his watch.

This time, she didn't mind.

"At twenty-four years, four months, four days, nineteen hours and twelve minutes, I made love to my mate for no other reason than I wanted to."

She smiled, snuggling deeper into his embrace.

CHAPTER 30

October 15, 10:12 PM

Harrison pulled open the door to their apartment building and ushered Ember inside. "Lucas is never going to let us hear the end of this." They were late.

"I got extra snacks as an apology." George was leaning over, peering into the grocery bag, and she moved the bag to her other arm, out of reach. "What movie did he decide on?"

"No idea. Probably something gory and scary." He stopped, scanning the empty lobby. There were no mysterious boxes. No thrumming heartbeat. Lucas wasn't here. "He must be upstairs already."

They rode the lift to the apartment and when the doors opened, Julian was coming out of the kitchen. His one-eyed gaze dropped to where Harrison held Ember's hand. "You both look better."

Ember released his hand. "I'm going to put the stuff away and start the popcorn." She gave the minion a scratch behind one of his horns. "George, make sure these two behave."

George gurgled.

Harrison waited until Ember was out of sight. Once she turned the corner, he hauled off and punched Julian square in the jaw.

Julian staggered back.

"You had that coming."

"Which is why I'm not hitting back." He opened his mouth and stretched his jaw. "You're a fucking bastard."

"Cunt."

Julian cracked a smile. "I take it things are better?"

"Yeah." He scratched George, unable to hide his grin. "Where's Kat?"

"Claire has a cold, so Kat's covering for her tonight. She'll be back in the morning."

Ember came out of the kitchen. "Where's Lucas?"

Julian shrugged. "I haven't seen him since we came home from the auction."

Ember slipped her hand into Harrison's. "Do you think he got grounded or something? Maybe his parents haven't let him out the last couple of days."

"Maybe." He shook his head. "Nah, I've never known him to get grounded."

"He was pretty worried about you." She squeezed his hand. "Think he might be nervous about coming. Worried maybe that you didn't heal?"

Julian walked over and hit the button for the elevator. "Let's go check. Lucas gave me their apartment code. We should've asked his parents before inviting him instead of sending an invite for the whole family through Lucas. Maybe we upset them."

They piled into the elevator and went up to the top.

The elevator opened into a foyer similar to theirs, and he stepped into the apartment. "Mr. Zhang? Mrs. Zhang." He waited for a response. "Lucas, it's Harry."

An entryway table sat directly across from the elevator and there was so much unopened mail it had spilled off the table and onto the floor.

A sense of unease slithered up his spine. He glanced at Julian.

They both pulled their weapons.

"Lucas?" Julian's voice echoed in the foyer. "Dude, don't play games, man. We're armed. Safeties are off."

When they'd first moved in, they'd come up once to introduce themselves. The apartment had been meticulous. Now, it looked like a college dorm room. Had the Zhang's gotten divorced? "Hao? Sada? Do you need help?"

Julian stopped at the kitchen counter. Pizza boxes, juice containers, and soda cans littered the surface. Dishes were piled high in the sink. He lifted a piece of paper off the counter, read it, and held it out.

NEPHILIM STRIKE TERROR INTO SEATTLE AREA

He didn't need to read the article. Three months ago, Nephilim hit the area after almost a year of nothing. Humans had gotten brave. They hadn't been outright ignoring the curfews, but they'd been pushing them, staying out until twilight or a little after. A lot of humans had been killed that night.

"You think . . ."

Julian nodded. "Haven't seen them in a while now. Lucas kept saying they were working extra hours, but—" He motioned around the apartment.

Ember took the news clipping from his hand. Gasped. "Oh, God. He's been here alone all this time."

Alone. *Shit.* They should've asked more questions. He should've come up to check on the Zhang's when he hadn't seen them. He strode down the hall to the bedrooms, pushing open doors as he went.

Bathroom. A mess, but empty.

Master bedroom. Dusty. Empty.

Bedroom. A whole wall was covered in monitors.

George hopped from his shoulder to the floor. Julian and Ember stepped in behind him.

Some of the monitors were black-and-white, some color, but they were all the boxy, heavy kind no one used anymore. A laptop sat open nearby and he stroked his finger over the mouse pad. The webpage for an online high school application popped up on the laptop and all the monitors came alive. He even had infrared linked to each of the cameras. Vampires weren't photographable, but they put out a heat signature. "Lucas has the whole damned place wired. No wonder he always knew when we arrived. He saw us coming from two blocks away."

"Harry." Julian's tone was serious, his voice shook.

For a moment, he couldn't make himself turn around. He continued to stare at the monitoring equipment as his gut twisted. Lucas shouldn't have been alone. He should've checked—

"Harrison."

At the sound of Ember calling him, he forced himself to turn around. Zeroed in on George, who paced over a sheet-covered heap on the bed. "Fuck."

He couldn't hear a heartbeat. The body didn't move.

Why hadn't he protected Lucas? He'd been so focused on protecting the people from his past he'd forgotten the most vulnerable person in his life. He shouldn't have accepted Lucas' explanations for his parents not being around. Sweat broke out on his brow. His gaze locked onto Julian's. *Gods, why?* "I can't."

Julian didn't move.

Ember walked over and jerked the blanket away. "Oh, God." She let out a shaky breath. "It's not Lucas."

He let out a shuddering breath and the scent of old, dried blood, and sex tainted the next.

"There's a note." She lifted a slip of paper and held it out to him. "It's addressed to you."

He took the note which reeked of Adia's perfume and unfolded it.

Dearest Harry,

How's mommy? I assume all is well. While you were off chasing false leads, I may have found the male of my dreams. He's quite resourceful, making his own way in the world. Living alone without his parents all this time. Lovely boy, Lucas. I think this one will be strong enough. Not like the last.

Love,

Adia

P.S. I won't touch him for one day. Come home soon, Harry.

Julian nodded to the note. "What's it say?"

"She's got him." He handed the letter to Julian and joined Ember by the bed. The boy had been dead a few days. Old, dried blood crusted around his crushed nose. "Jules, call Scott. Get a crew here. We gotta figure out who this kid is, who he belonged to." This had to end. He couldn't stand to fail any longer.

George climbed his body, curling around his shoulders and

cooing.

Ember pulled the sheet over the child. "She beat him."

He shook his head. "She gets off by—" Memories of boys long past flashed through his mind. Adia sitting on them, grinding her pelvis down while their arms and legs flailed. Listening to her gasps of pleasure as the boy's screams changed into gurgling wheezes as she suffocated them. He tugged his collar away from his throat. Gods, he couldn't breathe. "She . . . sits on them." He met Ember's horrified gaze. He didn't know how else to explain. "She sits on their faces."

CHAPTER 31

October 15, 10:48 PM

"DAMN IT, I SHOULD'VE PAID more attention." Harrison turned away from the body. What was he missing? Adia said to come home.

Home. She'd always talked about the place she'd held him prisoner as home. Duncan had checked the place out not too long ago and it was deserted. Hell, DDC agents had been there earlier in the week. She'd been in Washington a couple days ago at the auction. Even if that had been her copy he'd seen, the real Adia couldn't have been far away.

The magnitude of his epic failure closed in, suffocating him. He knew what Lucas might be enduring. He had to stop her.

He couldn't run anymore.

He had to go home.

Gods, he'd been there twice. Once when Adia kidnapped him, and once when he went there with Duncan to rescue Trina and neither time did he see where the building was located. He couldn't get there on his own.

Julian would know, but he needed someone to stay with Ember. He didn't want her anywhere near Adia. Anywhere near *him* when he did whatever was needed to secure Lucas' freedom.

Ember hugged him.

"Don't." He pushed her away, turning away from the hurt on her face. "Get down, George." The minion clung to him, growling. "Down!" George moved to his back, but continued to cling. He needed to get out of here; he couldn't breathe. He reached behind him and dragged George off, handing him to Ember.

"Harry." Julian's voice was sharp.

Harrison stopped and pointed to Julian. "Call Scott . . . and stay with . . . Ember. I'll be . . . right back."

He ran upstairs, struggling for breath, dialing Duncan as he went.

"Yeah."

"Duncan, I need . . . you to . . . come here. She's . . . got the boy . . . and . . . I need to . . . go to London."

"Slow down—"

"I don't have time . . . to explain. *I need you.*"

"Where are you?"

"In front of the . . . apartments." He strode through the lobby and into the brisk night air.

A bright white light lit the darkness and he shielded his eyes even as he strode toward it. "You remember . . . where you went . . . when they sent . . . you . . . to destroy me?"

Duncan's brows drew together. "What's got you wound so tight?"

"I need you to take me . . . now."

Duncan shook his head. "Where's Jules?"

Harrison gripped his shirt in his fists. "I don't . . . need Jules. I . . . need . . . you . . . to take . . . me . . . now."

"The place was empty, pup. You think I wouldn't've checked?" He inhaled deep and blew the breath out through his mouth.

He grit his teeth, but followed suit. He couldn't pass out. Not now.

"That hidey-hole of hers was covered in dust. No one had been there in years."

"She opened . . . it."

Duncan drew in a slow breath. "You can't go off all half-cocked, pup. That's a quick way to—"

"She's got . . . Lucas."

Duncan's gaze flashed to the apartments. "You sure?" When he nodded, Duncan added, "Get Jules and we'll go."

"No. Need him . . . to stay with Em. Don't want her . . . alone if this . . . is another trick."

Duncan scrubbed his hand across the back of his neck. "I don't like this."

Since the day Duncan rescued him, he'd been telling Harrison he'd find a way to help him confront Adia. "You promised."

Duncan nodded. "Yeah, I know it." His gaze dropped to study Harrison. "You packin'?"

"Yeah."

"Let's go."

He put his hand on Duncan's shoulder. He hated this form of travel. As soon as Duncan started the Traveler's Spell, his body turned buoyant. He closed his eyes, refusing to look at the disorienting way his and Duncan's molecules separated, making them appear like one of those pointillism portraits. Something hit his shoulder as the spell took effect.

Seconds later, water pelted his shirt and hair. The scent of the air had changed, turning muskier. He opened his eyes. They stood in Cavendish Square in London and, as usual, it was pissing rain.

George butted his head against Harrison's chin.

Shit. "Damn it, George." He hadn't wanted him along, afraid of what Adia might do to the minion.

"It's done, pup. Ember let him out of the building while we were chatting. Come on."

He hopped over the short, wrought-iron fence surrounding the park, following Duncan. They angled down one of the mews lined with ancient four- and five-story buildings huddled together. "These are all houses."

"Surgeries, mostly. We're off Harley Street near the Circus."

He followed Duncan along the Mews to a home with a bright green door. Wide pillars stood on either side with goats' heads perched at their peaks. In all his time in London, they'd never been to this area before.

Duncan pulled out a key and let himself in.

"Where the hell are we?"

"You've been here before, lad. Just never by the front entrance."

He glanced around an old, dusty waiting room. A gaudy burgundy-and-gold scheme accented the white walls. Old magazines surrounded white lilies, long dead, that moldered in a cut-glass vase. "Come on."

He followed Duncan through a darkened hallway and into an elevator. Duncan pushed the button for the very bottom.

"How much farther?"

Duncan held his finger to his lips. "Once the doors open, game's on, pup. She could be anywhere in there, but I expect she's in her old lair, two levels below where we'll get off. We'll take the service stairs into the old cisterns."

Harrison nodded. "Get ready, George." George sleeked out on his back. Harrison palmed one of his knives, gripping it so the flat of his blade pressed against his wrist. He was ending this tonight. One way or another, he'd get Lucas out of here.

The doors slid open, revealing a large, round foyer. Someone had lit the wall sconces, and the dust on the marble floors had been disturbed. Someone was here, but they hadn't been here for long.

They exited the lift. On the other side of the foyer, double doors hung askew on their hinges. He knew this place. The Vampiric Council used to operate here. He'd come here with Duncan and Kat to confront the old Council after they'd kidnapped Trina. He'd fought Adia that night, but she'd slipped away.

She wouldn't slip away tonight.

Duncan pointed to another doorway leading into a long corridor. They paused at each intersection to sweep the rooms before moving along. None of the rooms appeared lived in. Dust and cobwebs coated the old furniture.

There was a hole in the wall at the end of the hall. Brick and plaster lay in heaps on the floor.

"This was solid wall last time I came." Duncan led him through the ragged opening and down two flights of stone steps. "I helped brick the entrance meself."

Adrenaline pumped through him and he forced himself to take long, slow breaths. When they reached the bottom, wall sconces lit the area bright, highlighting the old, rounded brick walls. Duncan took a left into a narrow hallway, pausing by an arched entryway.

Beyond, three large arches curved under a domed ceiling, leading in three different directions.

The thick, dank air made every little sound echo. The drip from a pipe. A rat skittering between the walls. Cockroaches buzzing their wings.

Harrison turned to Duncan, and whispered, "Why don't we split up?"

"Nah. We stick together, pup."

Time was running out. He glanced at his watch. 11:23 PM. "We need—"

A faint scrape made him spin around. He wasn't sure what it was, but Duncan reacted. George, too.

They spread out, searching the darkness beyond the cistern. A chill prickled on the back of his neck.

A hand clamped his shoulder and jerked him around.

The glint of light on metal flashed in his vision. Harrison brought his blade up, deflecting the attacker's knife. The blades slid together and Harrison kicked his attacker back.

George attacked. The daemon knocked him away, sending George tumbling to the floor. The minion rolled, regaining his feet, and stalked the intruder.

The dark-haired male, a little shorter than Harrison, bared his teeth. He rolled his wide shoulders. Circling. Keeping both him and Duncan in his sights. He backed all the way into the dark recess of one of the tunnels, disappearing for a second. He reappeared with a copy.

A splitter. No problem.

The splitter and his copy rushed them. The copy came straight for Harrison. He backed away, throwing off the force of the copy's slash. Harrison deflected the blow, brought his arm around and cut a shallow gash in the copy's arm.

The copy gasped.

His eyes narrowed. The copy shouldn't feel anything. Not unless the original's consciousness had shifted. The male Duncan fought wasn't wounded yet. This must be the Splitter, then. Not the copy.

The Splitter attacked.

Harrison's block was too slow and the blade sliced through his skin, burning a trail across his forearm. He punched out with his other hand, landing a blow to the Splitter's neck. The Splitter staggered back, touching his neck with his hand, gasping.

Harrison's gaze shifted to the male Duncan fought. He hadn't lost any momentum, his blade clashed and slid along Duncan's in a dance for dominance. The copy…if he was a copy, favored his right side.

This wasn't right. Something was off. Neither of them were behaving like copies. They were both favoring wounds now.

He pulled out his sidearm. The one he'd thought was the Splitter howled a war cry, sprinting toward him.

He fired.

Everything stopped.

Both Duncan and George froze.

The daemon Duncan had been fighting turned as the male he shot crumpled to the ground. Black blood trickled from the wound in his head.

He wasn't a copy.

He wasn't even a vampire.

The daemon Duncan had fought shouted in anguish.

CHAPTER 32

October 15, 10:56 PM

HARRISON BLINKED AND SHOOK HIS head.

At the end of the hall, an archway led to a large, round chamber. Three large arches curved under the domed ceiling, leading in three different directions.

The air was dank and heavy and every little sound seemed to echo in the round chamber.

He turned to Duncan, and whispered, "Why don't we split up?"

"Nah. We stick together."

Time was running out. He glanced at his watch. 11:38 PM. For some reason, he'd been expecting the time to be 11:23. "We need—"

What was that? The sound had been faint. He wasn't sure what it was. But Duncan had reacted, George too, so he knew he hadn't imagined the noise.

"Christ, pup, I've got the worst feeling of déjà vu."

So did he. Had he dreamt this scenario?

George whined low in his throat, crawling off Harrison and onto the floor.

They spread out, searching the dark corridors beyond the cistern. He heard nothing now. No sound. No movement. Still, a chill prickled the back of his neck.

His boot butted against something. A body lay on the floor. The man was ancient. White hair sprouted in tufts around his liver-spotted head. Black blood oozed out from a hole in his forehead.

Harrison withdrew his sidearm. That was a fresh kill. The blood hadn't had time to congeal, yet he didn't remember hearing a gunshot.

He *did* feel like he'd been here before. He touched the muzzle of his gun to his jean-clad thigh—still hot. *Shit!*

A hand clamped on his shoulder and jerked him around. He lifted his blade, barely deflecting a stab.

George attacked the male from behind. The daemon spun around, arms flailing as he tried to dislodge the minion from his head.

Harrison waited for a clean shot and fired his weapon.

The male staggered back.

George jumped to Harrison.

The male's eyes went wide with shock as black blood bloomed on his shirt front. His thick, dark hair receded, turning gray, then white as his skin paled and wrinkled. He fell to his knees and then dropped to the floor.

Duncan stared at the fallen male. "Fucking chrono-deviants." He wiped his hand over his face. "Some nights I wonder if we didn't do more damage by opening the portal to Machon."

"It was the lesser of two evils. Least now we know how she's been taking kids without any witnesses." How they'd taken *him* without anyone seeing. "These two probably halted time during the abductions." Harrison scratched George under his chin. "You did good, buddy."

"All right, pup, which way?"

He pointed to the direction where the other body lay. "Let's try that one."

They made their way into the next darkened tunnel. In some areas, his night vision couldn't even penetrate the absolute darkness. George shivered on his shoulder, mewling.

Harrison increased his pace, eager to be out of the tunnel. Finally, a light. The tunnel opened into another large cistern. Here, the brick walls had been charred black in some places.

Gods, he remembered this place. The scent of mold tinging the frigid air. The chipped mosaics on the domed ceiling. As a kid, they'd reminded him of what Hobbit holes might be like. The brick walls leaked, creating little rivulets of water streaming along the sides of the floors.

He selected a tunnel to the left and spotted a door he recognized. Adia's room.

His steps quickened and when he reached the end of the hallway, he kicked the door wide. Gods, nothing had changed. Thick rugs lined the floor. The big bed pushed against one wall. A vanity, with her image etched into the glass still sat against another wall. The bed. The chains. Adia's boudoir even smelled of a fresh kill. The scent of blood hung in the air. *Not Lucas. Please, not Lucas.*

Harrison swallowed the burning lump in his throat.

There was no movement in the space. No beating heart nearby.

Duncan nudged him into the room, pointing.

At the end of the bed, a sneaker poked out from the bed skirt. Oh, Gods.

The angle of the shoe indicated someone wore it, but there was no heartbeat.

He glanced at Duncan, who nodded toward the bed.

With his sidearm pointed ahead of him, his blade clutched in his other hand, he walked toward the shoe.

Please, don't let him be dead. Not Lucas. He couldn't survive such a failure.

As he came around the bed, the rest of the young boy came into view, sprawled on the ground. Blond. The dead boy had blond hair. A jagged bite had been taken out of his neck, but no blood flowed from the wound.

He drew in a shuddering breath. Glanced around and—

Lucas hunkered low near the bed, trembling. His thin arms covered his head and he clutched a Guardian blade in his hand. All the little-big-man-bravado was gone. Jesus. Where were his clothes? His heartbeat?

He had no heartbeat. He focused on that because he *had to.* Couldn't think of the other—why he wasn't wearing anything.

The bitch had transformed Lucas.

The tragedy of the scene tore at what was left of his soul. He'd failed.

At least Lucas had fed. Lucas would be more rational than he'd been the night Duncan rescued him.

He knew how Lucas must feel—the shame, the horror, the *loss*. If he allowed his anger to show, his crushing disappointment that Lucas had been transformed, forced to kill, and gods only knew what else, he knew damned well the kid would think those emotions were directed *at* him. Harrison had never seen either of those emotions from Duncan, not the night he rescued him and not for months afterward. It wasn't until this moment that he realized how difficult that must've been for Duncan to hold all those emotions at bay.

He forced himself to relax his posture. "Hey, dude."

Lucas jerked, his gaze darting up, before he curled himself even tighter into the corner.

He needed to get rid of the body. Harrison put his weapons away, glanced at Duncan and motioned to the body.

Silently, Duncan lifted the body and moved out of sight.

Harrison pulled the sheet from the bed. "You're late for movie night, man."

Two big, brown, blood-shot eyes peered at him over his knees. At certain angles, the light gave his eyes a silvery shimmer. "Harry?"

"Mm-hm." He dropped the sheet on the floor within Lucas' reach.

He snatched the sheet and wrapped it around himself.

"Jules and I have been searching for you."

Harrison let himself slide down the wall until he sat on the floor, closer to eye level. He gave George a rub to gain the minion's attention and pointed to Lucas. "Hell of a night, huh?"

George slunk to the floor, and approached Lucas. When he didn't shy away, the minion butted his head against his thigh before crawling onto his shoulders. His diamond head rubbed Lucas' hair, prodding and nudging until Lucas pulled him down and wrapped his arms around George.

Lucas' eyes cleared a bit.

"I'm sorry you had to meet Adia."

The boy curled George into the crook of his arm, rubbing his belly. "You know her?"

"When I was about your age, she stole me from my parents."

"Oh."

"Well, she had some guys do the kidnapping. When I first got here she pretended she'd been captured, too."

For the first time, Lucas gave him his full attention. "Was she wearing anything?"

Damn. He'd hoped, maybe, she'd left him alone. *Focus on Lucas. Tell him what you needed to hear back then.* Harrison shook his head. "A flimsy robe with no belt. I remember thinking how she must've been really scared to not notice." He grimaced. "And of course, I was curious as hell, right? I mean what guy at that age wouldn't be?"

Lucas' gaze slid away. "Did she catch you looking?"

"Caught me with a boner."

"Me, too." He rested his cheek on George's scaly head.

"Ah." Harrison shrugged. "Nothing wrong with that. She's a beautiful woman. Thing is, back then I thought I'd done something wrong and she was quick to take advantage."

"Oh, yeah?" Lucas leaned forward a little, but he wouldn't meet his gaze.

"Told me she'd keep my dirty little secret as long as I played a game with her."

"Her game is kinda fucked-up."

"Yeah, it is." Harrison shrugged. "Someday you'll find a nice woman and you'll enjoy doing all that stuff with her. I hated it with Adia, though. I didn't like her."

"She wears too much perfume."

Harrison nodded. He'd always thought she drowned herself in perfume to hide the smell of her rotting soul. "So, Lucas, I was thinking, since you're one of us now, Jules and I, we'd like to take you up on your offer."

Lucas' gaze sharpened.

Gods, he looked so suspicious it damned near broke his heart.

Harrison tugged at his collar. "Yeah, you know, if you don't have anyone else waiting for you."

"My parents died in one of the Nephilim attacks. They were late from a meeting or something."

Harrison nodded. "We went to your apartment. I figured it might be something like that."

A shudder ran through the boy. "I did more than look."

Damn her. He cleared the burning lump from his throat. "Yeah, me too."

"You still want me at your place?"

"Yeah." Harrison sniffed, coughed, and blinked his eyes a few times to chase away any trace of emotion. "Yeah, I think it'd be good. Guys like us need to stick with other guys who understand."

"Is that why you hang out with Jules?"

"Mm. Yeah, he gets it." Harrison shrugged. "Kat and Em, too. You won't have to worry about any weirdness with us."

"I don't know." Lucas bit his lip. "Sounds like your place is kinda crowded."

"You kidding? We've got the entire floor. You can have one of the guestrooms all to yourself. Bathroom, too."

Lucas shrugged. "Maybe I could try it out for a little while."

"Cool." He glanced around the room. "You don't happen to know where your clothes are, do you?"

Lucas shook his head.

"All right. Why don't you wrap yourself in the sheet until we can find you some?" He looked up to find Duncan watching him with an expression he hadn't seen in years. "Do you remember my dad?"

Duncan walked over and dropped to his haunches. "Hiya, Lucas."

A fierce blush colored his cheeks upon realizing they weren't alone.

"You know, I carried Harry out of here in a sheet when he was your age."

"Oh?"

"Mm-hm." Duncan jerked his thumb toward him. "He was a bit of a bugger about it. Squirming around and trying to bite me."

The corner of Lucas' mouth curved.

"You think you might be a bit nicer to me?"

Lucas nodded. "Am I in a lot of trouble?"

"Nah." Duncan shook his head, his bottom lip popping out. "You'll be staying with Harry and Jules. That's punishment enough for whatever ya think ya did."

Harrison shared a rueful grin with Lucas. "What do you think? You ready to go?"

Lucas allowed George to curl around his neck as he pulled the sheet around himself and got to his feet.

Duncan gave him an assessing once-over. "Have you traveled by spell before, Lucas?"

He shook his head.

"You're gonna have to hold onto me, lad."

Lucas turned to Harrison.

"You can trust him, Lucas. He's always been good to me and George can stay with you." The minion appeared conflicted, perching on the boy's shoulder as if he wanted to jump back to Harrison. "George, stay. Protect." The minion gave a little growl of displeasure, but curled himself around Lucas again.

Duncan held his arm out. "Hold real tight to my wrist and don't let go until I say so." Lucas did as instructed and Duncan met Harrison's gaze. "I'm sending Julian back."

"Don't." The last thing he needed was to worry about Adia getting her hands on someone else he cared about and use them against him.

"Come with me, then."

"I gotta finish this. I can't wait for her to take someone else I care about." He backed away. "Take Lucas home. I'll call you when I'm ready."

Duncan cussed, but light filled the room and they disappeared.

Harrison drew his blades. He'd get her this time. Halfway to the door, the vanity caught his eye again and he paused. He remembered the small box sitting on the golden surface. None of the boys had ever been allowed to touch that box. He strode across the room and flipped the lid.

Bric-a-brac filled the box to bursting—little army men and knotted string, gaming dice and some rocks. Her trophies.

She must have kept whatever treasures she discovered in the kidnapped boys' pockets. He turned the box over, dumping the contents on the vanity. Damn it, where was his? He didn't want her to have it. He pushed the bits and bobs around until he uncovered his prize.

He lifted Ember's picture with a trembling hand. Until Ember reminded him of his hoard of pictures, he'd forgotten about this one. It had the name of their old school on it and she'd signed the back. That was how Adia had found Ember. He tucked the picture into his pocket. Good. Now all fifty-three pictures were accounted for.

Adia no longer had any part of him.

He turned to leave.

Something heavy and hard as hell slammed across his face. Pain lanced through his skull. A frigid coldness slipped through him and he tried to hold onto consciousness. Fought to keep his eyes open even as the floor rushed to meet him.

CHAPTER 33

October 16, 12:40 AM

EMBER JUMPED AS LIGHT FLASHED in the apartment. Harrison was back! But when the light faded, Duncan and Lucas stood in the living room. "Lucas." She rushed to him, but stopped when he stepped behind Duncan, his gaze firmly locked onto the floor. Her gaze flicked to Duncan's and the devastating concern on his face said everything. She folded her hands in front of her. "I'm glad you're back, Lucas."

His voice carried out from behind Duncan. "Thanks."

"Where's Harrison?"

Duncan scowled. "Hunting."

"Alone?" Her heart thrummed so hard, she put a hand to her chest as if she could still it by touch. "Take me."

"I'm not taking you alone. She's got all types of minions that make George look like a sweet little kitten."

"I'm going." Julian strode into the room armed to the teeth and carrying extra holsters with him. "Since I need a DDC-approved babysitter, she's coming with me." He knelt in front of her and began strapping weapons on her. "You can drop us off and come back to get Lucas settled."

"He said not to."

Julian spun around. "You're listening to him?"

"Nah." Duncan shrugged. "I'm letting you know he won't be happy to see you."

"Like I give a shit."

They were going. Thank God. The idea of Harrison alone with that woman made her skin crawl and her stomach twist. By the time Julian finished, she wore a belt with ammo and a sidearm, a leg sheath with a blade, and an ankle sheath with a small revolver. He patted her on the leg. "You good, Rambo?"

She nodded.

He paused long enough to kneel in front of Lucas. "How you doing?"

Lucas shrugged. "You're going to bring Harry back, right?"

"It's Friday. We're watching a movie before sunrise, buddy." Julian nodded to the couch. "You sit your ass down and don't move until Duncan gets back."

Lucas pressed his lips together and his chin lifted. "How long?"

"Sixty seconds. Hundred and twenty tops." Duncan pointed to the entertainment system. "You watch the seconds hand on that clock over there."

Lucas slouched onto the couch. When his gaze flashed to Ember, she smiled and asked, "What movie are we going to watch?"

He shrugged. "You pick."

"Yeah?" She smiled. "How about *Star Wars*? I always liked how black and white that one is." There was something simple about the movie. Comforting.

"Yeah, all right."

"Let's go." Duncan held his hand out to Ember. "Take hold, love."

She slipped her hand into his. Julian grabbed his shoulder. Duncan palmed a stone that hung around his neck. All the sudden, she was floating. Her body seemed to be expanding and when she looked at the others she saw why. Their bodies were breaking apart into billions of tiny dots.

When she would've pulled away, Julian tightened his grip on her hand.

Light filled her vision and when it faded they were somewhere else. Whole. She smoothed her hands over her belly and hips to make sure.

The thick musty air made her sneeze. So much for sneaking up on them. "Sorry." She sniffed. "Where are we?"

Julian answered. "This is where the Vampiric Council once reigned supreme. Adia's got balls coming back here."

Duncan snorted. "Yeah, she does. You remember the training rooms?"

"Two levels below."

"Yeah. Harry and I came in through the front door, but upstairs was clean. This level, too. In the cisterns, we ran into a couple chrono-deviants, but no one else 'side from Lucas. Looked like she decided to come back recently."

"Thanks, man." Julian slapped him on the back. "We'll call when we're ready to come home."

"I'll be sending Kat."

"No."

But Duncan was gone.

Julian cursed and paced away. When he came back, he was all business. "You'll listen to everything I say and do it, no questions asked. Got it?"

She nodded.

"Even if I tell you to shoot something that your first instinct is to protect. Kat got fooled by someone projecting an image of me once. That's how she became a vampire. If I tell you to shoot Harry, you fucking shoot him."

Ember blanched. "How would you know?"

"I see auras. I can tell real from fake at a glance." He tugged her arm. "Come on."

They walked in silence for a few minutes. "Hey Jules, thanks for not arguing about me coming."

He paused, his brows snapping together. "We're partners. I can't go anywhere without you or Harry, remember?"

Actually, she'd forgotten.

"Besides, I figure you saved my ass. Harry's, too. Why wouldn't I want you at my back?"

She couldn't help the little smile that crept up on her as she followed him into a long corridor and onto a staircase.

"Oh, and Em? If I take the patch off, stay behind me."

"Why? What's under the patch?"

"My eye." He grinned. "It's sensitive. Your aura is damn near as bright as Kat's. Gives me a fucking headache if my eye isn't covered."

She gave him a little push. "You talk to your wife like that?"

"Hell, no."

They went down two flights and as they neared the bottom, he lifted his hand.

Ember slowed and when he pulled his weapon, she did, too.

He glanced back and held his finger to his lips. For a big guy, he could move with absolute silence. She studied the way he crouched, the way he stepped, and mimicked him as best she could.

The cisterns were dark. Flickering light came from flaming wall sconces spaced along the wall every thirty feet or so, which made for a lot of dancing shadows in between.

Her heart lodged somewhere north of her chest, pounding out her anxiety in a frantic tattoo. She wiped her slick hand on her trousers, switched her weapon to the other hand and wiped that one, too. When she gripped the 9mm this time, she thumbed off the safety.

She couldn't hear a damned thing above her own breathing. Water trickled down the red brick walls creating a little stream that rambled along the edge where the curved wall and floor met.

They came to a dome where three round tunnels splintered off the one they were in. Two skeletal remains littered their path. Gray, long, scraggly hair protruded from their mummified skull. Dried flesh clung in bits and pieces to their fragile frames while cockroaches burrowed their way to the bones. Were these the chrono-deviants Duncan mentioned?

"Which way, Emerald Eyes?" Julian spoke under his breath, so low she had to strain to hear him.

None of the pitch-black tunnels looked inviting. She didn't want to go into any of them. Julian's eyes might gather filaments of light allowing him to see in dark places, but hers didn't.

She shook her head and shrugged. Nothing gave them a definite clue of which way Harry had gone. One of the bodies lay in the center of the cistern, the other at the edge of one of the dark tunnels. Maybe he'd been the last to be killed as Harrison went into the tunnel. She pointed past the body as her demon slithered under her skin, wanting to join the hunt.

He nodded and took her hand, placing it on his shoulder. She curled her fingers, grabbing hold of his shirt for good measure as she gingerly stepped over the body, dodging a brave rat scurrying past to his newly discovered meal.

Don't scream.

In they went. Not an iota of light penetrated the tunnel as far as she could tell. Inky blackness as thick and fierce as a physical entity enfolded them. She couldn't see Julian. Couldn't even see the hand where she held onto his shirt. She was blind. Her breath came in erratic gasps and her chest began to hurt. She couldn't hear anything beyond her breathing, her heart. Anything could be in here with them. Some creature could leap out at any—

Julian pushed her against the wall, his hand covering her mouth. He spoke in a whisper against her ear. "I've got you, Ember. Everything's fine. Breathe out. Long breath out, good girl. Breathe in and hold it. Good. Out."

Neither of them moved for several seconds. They stood silent and still until her heart calmed and her chest eased. Every moment they waited was a wasted minute. She breathed in deep long breaths until her pulse slowed. Why hadn't he simply mes-merized her into a calmer place? *'Cause it's too dark to see.* When she'd regained control, she nodded against his hand.

"If I see anything, I'll tap your hand."

She nodded.

"Trust me, Emerald Eyes."

When he pulled his hand away, she whispered, "Thank you."

Julian put her hand back on his shoulder.

This time, knowing he'd alert her to any danger, she had more courage. After several minutes, a light came into view, flickering outside the opening at the end.

CHAPTER 34

October 16, 1:22 AM

HARRISON ROLLED OVER AND CLUTCHED his head. Great gods, that hurt. He hadn't even gotten a good look at the son of a bitch that knocked him out.

Cautiously, he slit open his eyes.

He lay on a hard, ash-covered stone floor surrounded by curved, blood-stained walls.

He was in the arena.

How the hell did she expect to trick him into fighting this time? And who did she want him to fight? He was older. He had control now.

Slowly, he stood, covering his groin with one hand while wiping the soot and ash from his naked body with the other. He almost laughed when he noticed she'd left his watch on. It took some effort, but he refused to look. He wouldn't mark the time. This was nothing. Unimportant compared to the rest of his life.

"Oh, good. You're awake."

He lifted his gaze. The booths weren't quite as high as he remembered. If he could find a good foot hold in the wall, he could launch himself up there.

"Don't get any ideas, dear boy." She wagged her finger. "The rest of our guests should arrive soon."

His chest tightened. "What guests?"

"Your mate. Your partner." She clucked her tongue. "Why did you mate her? She's nothing. She's in the way now."

He sucked in a hard breath. "Leave them alone, they've got nothing to do with this. You and me, we can talk. We'll work things out."

Her eyes narrowed. "I don't believe you."

"Come on, I'm DDC. Did you think I'd let her die?"

"Yes." The single syllable echoed in the arena. "You've taken no lovers until now. You stayed true to me this entire time. Why wouldn't I expect you to let her die? How was I to know you'd grow unfaithful?"

Gods. She was crazier than he remembered.

She glanced over her shoulder and then stared at him again. "Now you shut up. You don't speak unless you're spoken to. You remember what happens when you misbehave?"

Oh, yes. He remembered. He nodded.

"People get hurt." Adia disappeared.

Ah, gods. He had to get out of here.

———◆———

Ember breathed a sigh of relief as the tunnel opened into a large chamber. A sooty substance coated the floor, muffling any sound their shoes may have made. The moss dusted red-brick walls appeared scorched as though they'd seen fire at some point; thick black swirls were burned into the cement.

She started to turn away, but something about the pattern captured her attention. She focused in on the wall once again. The way the wall had burned, it almost looked like a face. The sooty marks outlined big owl-like eyes and a round face. A twisted, screaming mouth.

The Wraith.

Ember took a hasty step away.

The eyes blinked opened.

She stifled her scream. The image peeled itself off the wall. She raised her gun and fired, kept firing, even as it engulfed her entire body. Enveloped her in an icy grasp. Freezing darkness passed through her and when she opened her eyes she stood in a new room.

The space was small. A fire burned in a grate on one side of the room. One wall was nothing more than a waist-high railing, as if this were a loft of some sort. Shadows darkened most of the area. A single sconce near the door lit the room.

Awareness prickled along her spine. She wasn't alone.

She turned, lifting her arms to fire her weapon, but her gun was gone.

A male glared. Big, with fair skin and red-tinged hair. A long shaggy beard covered his square jaw. His arms flexed as he folded his thick arms over his chest. His eyes narrowed into warning slits.

Heart slamming against her ribs, she lowered her arms and backed away. She reached for one of the other weapons Julian had armed her with. The holsters were empty.

"They're gone."

Ember's gaze whipped to the sound of the female voice, searching the shadows near the railing. "Adia."

"My assistant disarmed you when he brought you in." Adia rose from where she lounged against a railing, coming into the light. "He's a wraith."

Her demon coiled deep in her belly, clawing to get free. Ember closed her eyes, urging her demon to the surface.

"Uh-uh. I have Harry."

Ember's eyes snapped open.

"I'll have him destroyed before your demon makes it halfway across the room."

No, Adia wanted Harrison too much to destroy him. Still, the bitch could hurt him. The scars on his body were proof of that.

A shudder wracked through Ember as she willed her demon away. She refused to do anything to risk Harrison.

Adia's gaze flashed to her assistant. "I think the succubus and I understand each other. Fetch the other one."

Julian.

"Where do you want me to drop 'im, Mistress?"

"Here. I have plans for him."

The burley male turned to a sooty mist and breezed out of the room.

Ember swallowed. "What do you want, Adia?"

"It's not about what I want. I have what I want. Harry came

home." Adia leaned back against the rail and her golden robe slipped open, revealing far more than Ember cared to see.

"When I transformed Harry, I promised him we'd be together forever. I promised him he'd always be in that perfect adolescent state." She frowned. "But his behavior forced me to call the Guardian." Adia crossed the room and glanced over the edge of the loft. "Harry has punished me all this time for failing him. He stayed away and made me wait." She turned and smiled. "Now, he's forgiven me. He's returned, and I'm going to give him what he wants. What he needs."

She was crazy. Harrison hadn't returned, not in the way she meant, but Adia sounded so sure of herself, so taken into her own lie, Ember half expected him to walk in and give Adia a peck on the cheek like a doting husband.

"What do you think he wants?"

Adia reared back. "Why, to be punished, of course."

October 17, 1:22 AM

Julius stared at the small arsenal of weapons lying in an untidy pile on the floor. Ember had been right behind him, damn it. He hadn't realized she hadn't followed him into the next room until she screamed. By the time he returned, he'd been too late.

Damn, she'd disappeared fast.

He glanced back the way they'd come, not real keen to travel into that tunnel again. Despite what he'd told Ember, even he'd been blind in some sections of that tunnel.

He'd have to hope to hell Adia didn't have Harrison, too. Damn it. The bitch would keep Ember alive until the opportunity to kill her in front of Harrison presented itself.

Onward, then. With a little luck, he'd run into Harrison and together they would make quick work of this place.

A frigid breeze blew past and Julian threw himself to the side. Rolling, he came to rest back on his feet. He scanned the room. Nothing moved. Christ, did he have a chameleon following him?

His gaze searched the darkness of the tunnel, the floor, and the walls.

There. The almost indiscernible, stretched-out features of a man on the wall. Not as if someone had drawn the image, but as if he'd been squashed flat—the features were off—pulled and twisted.

Come on, asshole, open your eyes and look at me. He only needed a second of eye contact to mesmerize him.

He withdrew his Guardian knife, gripping the blade between his thumb and fingers. In one quick movement, he hauled his arm back and threw the blade.

The image in the wall came to life, the smoky, shadow-like creature expanding as it flew away from the wall. The blade zipped past, clattering to the floor.

The wraith condensed into human form once again. A big son of a bitch with a copper beard. He kept his beady black eyes fixed on Julius' chin. The wraith flexed his meaty hands, grinning, but he wouldn't meet his gaze. The wraith knew what he was. He was being careful.

Julius withdrew another blade. "You looked better splashed against the wall."

"An' you'll look better sprinkled on the floor." He lunged forward, his body taking on that grainy, shadow-like consistency as he expanded.

Julius dove to the side. No way in hell would he allow himself to get caught in that thing's grasp. He could end up anywhere. The Sahara at sunrise. The Mohave at high-noon. In a cage in Adia's basement.

He stood and pitched himself to the other side. This time, he turned as he fell, lashing out with his arm as the wraith solidified again. The blade left a deep laceration across the back of the wraith's knee.

The wraith pulled out his knife. Not a Guardian blade, just a six-inch serrated blade, but the way he moved suggested he claimed a Pro-status in knife-fighting.

Julius backed away as the wraith circled him. If the motherfucker would meet his gaze this would be over. "So, does Adia let you do her?"

A deep rumble came from the wraith. "No one touches the mistress." His arm whipped out with the blade, making three succinct slashes.

Julius met all three strikes, blocking them with his own knife, but it was a close thing. For such a big bugger, he was quick as hell. *Come on, big boy, look at me.* "She tell you that? Doesn't seem to mind when Harrison touches her."

Again, the wraith slashed out. This time in a z-formation, ending with a sweep up the middle that nicked Julius' chin.

Julius withdrew his other blade and turned it to shield his wrist. "You can't touch her. You're stuck here in this hole. Running around, playing gofer. Are you getting anything out of this gig?"

"I get the woman."

"Ah, was starting to think you got off on watching Adia play babysitter." He paused. Waiting until the light dawned in those small, black, rat eyes. Until the wraith's mouth pulled down into a fierce scowl. Julius struck with both blades. He put all his weight behind each lash, nicking and slashing through each block, striding forward until he backed the wraith against the wall.

With a shout of frustration, the wraith turned shadow-like.

Julius leapt out of the way.

The wraith solidified behind him, the bite of steel leaving a burning gash across Julius' shoulders.

Julius whipped around, but the wraith disappeared. Again, the bite of a blade scored his back.

This time, he didn't move.

The wraith appeared right in front of him. His little rat eyes widened as Julius thrust his blade into his heart. "Fool me once, motherfucker."

The wraith faded, leaving nothing but his rumpled clothing behind. Julius stared at the pile of clothes while he waited for his breathing to calm.

The jacket moved.

What the fuck?

He crouched and used the point of his blade to lift the garment. Nothing lay underneath. The tee-shirt the wraith had worn slipped to the floor. He set the jacket on the floor and used his blade to lift the pocket open.

The black, oily skin of a cuero flexed and pulsed inside. Tiny mouths gnashed and gummed at the edges of the material. The little beast was hungry.

He remembered how the other cuero had responded to Ember's

singing and gave it a shot. "John Jacob Jingleheimer Schmidt. His name is my name, too." Eyes sprouted.

Julius stood, sheathing his blades and put the jacket on with the cuero snug in the pocket.

As he continued through the tunnels, he hummed.

"I have a present for you, dear."

Ember eyed Adia. This woman didn't have anything she wanted. Unless she was offering Harrison. She kept her mouth closed, though. Until she knew where Adia had stashed Harrison and who might be with him, she didn't dare attempt to play hero.

Adia slipped her hand into her robe pocket and withdrew something shiny. She glided around behind Ember and lifted her hair. "Hold still now. Harrison will love seeing this on you."

The tiny hairs at her nape stood at attention and as soon as the cool metal touch her throat, Ember tried to pull away, but the collar pinched until tears pricked her eyes.

"Now, I told you not to move. See what happens when you don't listen?" Adia moved around to stand in front of her, admiring the cold, heavy metal around her throat. "Lovely." She held a silver chain her hand.

"You put a fucking leash on me?"

Adia smiled.

Ember had never seen her smile before, not fully. She would've remembered. "You have the teeth of a horse."

Adia yanked on the chain.

Spikes sliced into her throat. The resulting pain brought Ember to her knees. She opened her mouth to scream, but only a strangled gurgle emerged.

"Stop!"

Ember sighed at the sound of Julian's voice. She couldn't show her appreciation, though, she was too busy trying to loosen the collar around her neck. The spikes were stuck in her skin. Reflexive tears blurred her vision while her fingers slipped along the cool metal. Her fingers came away wet with blood.

A healthy dose of adrenaline spiked though her, urging her to flee. The spikes felt short, but what if they were long enough to hit an artery? She tried to crawl away, but Adia wound the chain around her hand, shortening the leash.

"Mr. Crowley, I'll warn you now, if you attempt to mesmerize anyone in this room, she's ash. You'll drop your weapons now. All of them or I'll rip her fucking head off."

Ember's gaze jerked to his. She shook her head. "She's—"

Adia jerked the chain in warning. "Get up."

Ember rose onto legs unsteady as Jell-O. She couldn't stop the tremors wracking through her. Where was Harrison? She was starting to doubt if he was still alive.

Julian dropped his blades.

"Where's my assistant?"

A slow smile spread on Julian's face.

Her eyes narrowed to slits. "On second thought, don't move. We'll get the rest."

He stared hard at Adia. "You gonna bag my head like everyone else?"

Adia laughed and the sound made Ember shiver. "Why? Perhaps, if you were your brother. Julius' abilities were the stuff of legends, but we both know he had a master tutor in the Watcher that possessed him. You on the other hand. . ." She clucked her tongue. "Rumors abound about you. Tell me, are you nothing more than a projection cast by Julius' love-sick mate?"

Ember frowned.

"What's a matter, dear? Didn't you know Katherine was mated to the Harbinger? They say she stood there and watched him die. That she lost her mind and used her Vampiric talent to create a projection of her mate so she wouldn't have to live without him."

She shook her head. No way. Kat and Julian were a beautiful couple. The kind of people she knew down to her marrow were meant to be together. No way was he a projection.

"Personally, I prefer the rumor that he's Julian—the Harbinger's brother. Still, that means he was stuck in Machon for three hundred years. Alone." She pointed at Julian. "Which means you don't have the skill to command another body without speaking your desire out loud and maintaining eye contact."

That didn't sound right either. When Julian mesmerized her at DDC headquarters he'd only spoken some of his commands out loud. Even after she broke eye contact, that sneaky little voice stayed in her head, eroding away her will. Did this have something to do with the Julian's secret?

Her attention flashed back to Julian and this time he stared back at her.

Everything's fine, Ember Moon. Relax. Trust us. His mouth hadn't moved. He glanced away from her. *Follow her directions. We'll take care of everything. You concentrate on not pissing her off.*

Instead of the brutal demand she knew him capable of, Julian's talent was a gentle nudge in her mind, coaxing her to calm. Her chest eased. The rush of adrenaline slowed.

Maybe if she summoned her demon, she could make quick work of Adia.

Adia's eyelids narrowed. "That goes for you, too, succubus. In the time it takes for your demon to take control, Harry will be ash."

Don't do it. Listen to us, Ember Moon. That's not Adia, it's a copy. We can't mesmerize her. Nod to us, Ember Moon. Trust us.

Without thought, Ember gave a nod.

"So what's the plan, Adia?" He folded his arms over his chest.

Adia glanced at Ember. "Strip him."

Shock rocked through her. She started to shake her head.

Do it. Trust us. All will be well, Ember Moon.

Ember approached Julian. He'd locked his jaw tight, his muscles ticked out his irritation. What the hell did Adia have planned?

She clasped the edges of his jacket and he lowered his arms to allow her to remove it. *Toss the jacket close to her. Listen to us. Heed us.*

"Slowly." Adia gave the chain a tug. "No quick moves."

She slid the jacket off his arms, turned and dropped it on the floor behind her as close as possible to Adia without raising suspicion. When she turned back to Julian, he gave her a slight nod.

"The shirt."

He seemed worried now. Tension radiated from him but she didn't know if it was because he didn't like anyone seeing his scars or for some other reason. She unbuttoned the front of his shirt and the cuffs at each wrist, with trembling fingers. She tugged the material away, trying to touch him as little as possible. She tossed that behind her next to the jacket.

"The pants. Don't try to touch any of his weapons."

The shoes, Ember Moon.

Ember knelt and untied his shoes first. The last thing she wanted was for him to get stuck with his pants around his ankles, tripping him if he got an opening. If he attacked, though, what would the real Adia do in retaliation? Did the real Adia have Harrison? Maybe that's why Julian hadn't made a move. He might save her, but he might also be signing Harrison's destruction warrant.

She pulled off each of his shoes. Undid his belt. Popped the button free from his jeans and unzipped them. Damn it, she'd just made friends with Kat and already her demon had tried to seduce her mate, marked him, and now she was undressing him. Kat would never forgive her.

At her hesitation, that sneaky voice returned. *Finish it, Ember Moon. Trust us.*

She hooked her fingers in Julian's waist band and started to drag his black jeans off.

"All of it."

Oh, God. Her face flamed. She hooked her fingers over the waistband of his Calvin Klein's. "I'm sorry."

The collar tightened, pinching her raw throat.

Easy. Relax. Breathe, Ember Moon. Julian shushed her out loud. "What's a little nudity among friends, Emerald Eyes?"

She smiled, because she thought doing so might make him feel better. Then, she stared at the floor while she finished undressing him. He made the task easy, shifting his weight as she stripped each leg, but she was miserable.

What did Adia want? Did she plan to force them into a compromising position and have Harrison walk in?

"Get up."

Ember stood, staying as close to Julian as her leash allowed.

Hum to us, Ember Moon.

Her mind went blank like back in middle school when the teacher called on her. She knew hundreds of tunes but she'd be damned if she remembered even one.

"I knew your brother." Adia's gaze raked over Julian. "I'd have to say Julius was the handsomer of you two."

Julian scoffed. "We're twins."

Hum to us, Ember Moon.

A low vibration burned in her throat, but she resisted. Why did he want her to hum?

"But nothing alike." Adia walked closer to Julian, tightening Ember's leash as she went. The woman might be crazy, but she wasn't stupid. She stayed well out of striking distance. "I always liked your brother. He saved me once."

Disgust twisted Julian's lips. "Like hell."

"I was young. My father sold slaves back in Kenya. When my mother was alive, he sold them as workers. Then, one day, he caught my mother cheating. Decided to make an example of her. He made me watch while all the men under his employ and all the slaves took turns with her. She died before dawn the next day, and I took her place in his life."

Ember shivered at everything implied in that, at the pride in Adia's voice.

Hum, Ember Moon.

She fought the need he instilled in her to hum, afraid to draw Adia's notice.

"After that, he sold only women. It was a good business move, they sold for higher prices. His mistake was selling me when I turned twenty."

"What's that got to do with my brother?"

"André, the male he sold me to, was the first white man I'd ever met. A vampire. A monster. Vicious. Cruel. He bought lots of women, but he sold them as food instead of whores. Eventually, the Guardian came."

That sounded plausible. From what she understood, the Guardian had policed daemon kind.

Julian shook his head. "You've got Julius confused with someone else. He never went to Africa."

Ember fisted her hands. He hadn't even been there, so why argue? What if he pissed her off?

"The male who bought me, brought me to London."

Still, he shook his head, though to Ember, he didn't seem so sure of himself.

"When we arrived, André's ship was packed with six hundred women. He sold them right off the boat. About halfway through, Julius Crowley arrived with his partner."

"Kioshi Lee." He wiped his trembling hand across his mouth. "Shit. André ashed him."

"Yes, but Julius ensured I survived. I escaped with the women who hadn't been sold yet and eventually I returned to Kenya and killed my father for giving me to that bastard. He should have kept me. He said I pleased him but threw me away with that brute. I took over the business and it thrived under my direction. It bought me a place on the Vampiric Council."

He closed his eyes. "The rest, as they say, is history."

"Harry's history, yes." Aida turned her head and shouted over the railing. "Did you hear, Harry? You and I were fated long before your great-grandfather was born. Your best friend's brother saved me for you."

"God damnit." Julian let out a deep sigh and closed his eyes.

What was she missing? Why did he look so guilty for what his brother had done? Then again, he always looked guilty as hell whenever Julius' name came up. She'd always assumed it was because he still paid the price of being related to him, with the press and needing constant supervision. . . .

Then, *bam*, everything clicked into place—this was the secret they were keeping from her, why Harrison lashed out at her for disparaging the Harbinger, why Kat and Julian seemed so perfect for each other even though *Julius* Crowley was supposed to be her mate.

He *was* Julius Crowley.

Good Lord, she was standing next to the Harbinger himself. Everyone thought he'd died. Ember took a step away, her eyes widening. The daemon responsible for loosing Nephilim upon humanity. The daemon who'd forced daemon kind to reveal themselves. *He* was responsible for millions of human deaths. The reason the world had become such a different place. Because of him, Adia lived. Because he'd saved Adia's life, she'd survived.

Don't speak of it, Ember Moon. For Harry's sake. For Kat. Trust us. Don't speak it out loud. Not here.

She shook her head. Even without his suggestion swirling in her mind, she wouldn't speak her epiphany out loud. Everyone associated with him would be crucified right along with him if word got out. She liked Kat. Duncan. She loved Harrison. She'd never hurt them. She'd even come to care for Julian. To rely on him as both friend and partner. What she knew of him was nothing like the evil villain the media made him out to be.

Which is exactly what Harrison had said—they used Julius as a scapegoat. She couldn't begin to comprehend the *how's* or *why's* of the situation. However, she wouldn't repeat the mistake she made with Harrison. Not with his best friend. Her stance relaxed as she stared into Julian's hazel eye. This male had mesmerized her and Harrison. He had her in his grip even now, but he'd never hurt them. Not even when her demon went after him.

Ember nodded, retaking her place next to him, trying to let him know without words that nothing had changed. She trusted him.

His eye warmed, a tentative smile curling his lips.

Adia nodded to the rail she'd been leaning on earlier. "Both of you, go see."

Ember gripped the rail in both hands, terrified Adia would push her over the edge, hanging her by the leash around her neck. She leaned over and peered into a small, round arena. Stone gates were spaced along the far side, all the doors were closed tight. Relief made her lightheaded as her gaze settled on Harrison—the whole side of his was face one big bruise, but he was alive. He was as naked as Julian and she had no doubt he'd heard everything. Would he be angry with Julian? If he hadn't saved Adia all those years ago, none of this would've happened.

Next to her, Julian's whole body jerked as Adia kicked him. Ember screamed as he went headfirst over the rail and dropped into a heap on the floor.

Adia tugged on the leash to gain Ember's attention. She cried out as the spikes dug into her raw flesh. Her blood trickled down, wetting her skin, her shirt. "Sit on the rail."

Ember shook her head. She wasn't a vampire, her bones would break in a story-high fall. The collar tightened around her throat until tears pricked her eyes. Pain lanced into her neck, stealing her breath and making her stomach roll. Bile rose and she forced herself to choke it back. She couldn't get sick, not with this thing around her throat. She climbed onto the rail on unsteady limbs, swung her legs over, and perched herself on the narrow railing.

As soon as Adia released the tension on the chain, Ember pulled the collar as far from her throat as possible. Ah, God, it hurt like hell. Was like pulling tiny shards of glass from her flesh.

They weren't going to survive this.

Beside her, Adia giggled. "See, my dear, this is what Harry wants."

Below, the two men confronted each other. Harrison's muscles were bunched tight. His hands fisted.

Julian held his arms out in a placating gesture. "Think of Kat, man."

Harrison loosed a vicious curse. "It's not your fault. It's—"

"Hindsight's twenty-twenty, right?"

"Yeah." Harrison's muscles, his hands relaxed.

Ember sighed. Harrison didn't blame Julius, thank God. The last thing they needed was to be fighting amongst themselves.

Hum, Ember Moon. Hum for us.

Ember blinked. He still expected her to hum?

Finally, a song came to her mind. She hummed the "Fiddle and the Drum."

Adia turned to stare at her.

Both men stopped, glancing up.

Harrison winked.

October 17, 2:19 AM

Adia's voice echoed in the arena. "Here are the rules, boys. Listen carefully."

Harrison turned his back to Adia and faced Julian. "What the fuck is around Ember's neck?"

"A pincher collar. Like the ones they use to train dogs." Julian put his hand on his naked hip. Tipped his head down and to the side to hide his face from Adia. "The fucking thing broke her skin."

Yeah, he could smell her blood.

"Are you ready to listen?"

Harrison swung around to stare at Adia. "I swear, if you touch her—"

"Oh, dear boy, I'm going to do much more than that." Adia wound the end of the chain leash around the rail, hooking the clasp onto one of the links. "Now listen before I tire of this game and push her off."

He fisted his hands at his sides and shifted his gaze to Ember's wide, terrified eyes. Blood stained the front of her shirt, creating a bright red bib on her pale blue sweater. Her knuckles had whitened where she gripped the railing. Still, she hummed "Fiddle and the Drum" to let him know she'd be displeased if they turned against each other.

Adia threw two blades into the arena. "You will fight to the death. I don't care who wins, as long as one of you is ash, I'll let her go."

Shit. He glanced at Julian.

"Pick them up." Her voice echoed off the dank walls.

Slowly, they each took a knife. Not Guardian blades, which would've turned them to ash as soon as the wood in the center of the blade punctured their flesh, of course not. Adia didn't want this to be quick, she wanted them to suffer. She was all about the mind fuck.

"If you try to leave the arena before you destroy your opponent, I'll kill the succubus instead. One way or another, one of you dies now."

Harrison stared at the floor. "How do you want to play this?"

"Carefully. I released a hungry cuero. When we hear Adia's screams, I'll boost you up."

He stared at Julian. Was he insane? "That's a copy up there with Ember."

"It's a fucking cuero. The damn thing isn't going to know the difference."

That's why Ember was humming, to try to get the cuero to engage. Did she know the plan? He backed away from Julian and checked on her, still perched on the rail above. Julian's little surprise better happen quickly.

They circled each other with all the enthusiasm of vegans forced to slaughter a cow. Julian made a weak thrust, Harrison knocked his hand away. Oh, they tried to make the fight look good, but seriously, did she expect them to slice each other to ribbons for her entertainment?

Adia's voice carried, echoing off the walls of the small arena. "One."

Harrison glanced at Adia. What now?

"Two." Adia's brows lifted. "Three." Ember let out a squawk of protest as Adia nudged her, not enough to push her over, but the threat was implicit.

"Fuck's sake." He thrust forward and pierced Julian's shoulder with his blade.

"Better."

Julian scoffed, fingering the gash. "So glad you approve."

"I'll keep counting in my head. Someone had better get cut before I reach three each time."

Harrison lunged. Julian blocked it, drawing his blade along Harrison's arm in a shallow cut. "How long?"

"Seemed hungry." Julian hissed as he nicked him again. "I'm starting to feel like a pin cushion."

Their blades crossed, Julian's slipped, slashing the back of Harrison's knuckles. They both hissed, him in pain and Julian with a sympathetic wince. Harrison switched hands. When Julian came at him, Harrison punched him and stuck him in the shoulder.

Julian grinned. "Gets easier once the adrenaline starts pumping, huh?" He bounced around on the balls of his feet as if in a training exercise.

Ember cried out as Julian struck. Gods, he'd forgotten to count.

He stepped on Julian's foot, grabbed his arm and pulled him into his knife.

When he released him, Julian wasn't grinning anymore. "Careful, now."

"Watch the time." He reversed his blade and went for a slash across Julian's chest. He dodged it, stabbing Harrison in the back. He stumbled, gritting his teeth against the pain and the world turned red.

One.

Instinct began to take over.

Two.

The impulse to survive glazed Julian's eye, too. He charged Harrison. They collided.

Three.

Julian's blade sank into Harrison's arm.

He hated the fucking survival instinct vampires were cursed with.

Panting, he stepped back. Where was the cuero? When would the creature attack?

Julian thrust forward and Harrison sank into a crouch. He grabbed Julian's wrist and twisted. Brought his own blade down hilt-deep on his thigh. "*Fuck.*"

One.

He'd always hated the feel of a blade sinking into flesh.

Two.

The silent pop. The slick glide.

Three.

Harrison dodged a blow and rammed Julian back against one of the stone gates. A fierce burn bloomed in his belly.

Julian's eyes widened and he shook his head. "Shit."

Harrison backed up, un-impaling himself from Julian's blade. He drew in a shuddering breath and pressed his hand to the wound low on his belly. "I'm good."

He blinked. Glanced at his watch. Damn, he'd lost count. Julian pricked his arm with his blade.

That must've been three.

One.

Above them, Ember leaned forward, her troubled gaze locked with his, humming her tune of peace.

Two.

Julian circled, limping. Damn it, he shouldn't have gone for his partner's leg.

Three.

Julian rushed him.

Harrison side-stepped. Clutching his belly, he turned in time to slice across Julian's hip.

One.

Julian backed against the wall. "Now."

Two.

"No." Adia would push Ember if they tried to attack now.

Three.

Adia screamed.

Everything slowed.

Julian braced himself, raising the hilt of his knife for Harrison to grab on his way up.

Harrison ran toward him. Keeping his eyes on Ember, he snatched the blade and bounded off Julian's leg.

Ember screamed as Adia backed into her, bumping Ember off her perch.

He dropped the blade, with one hand he grasped the rail and

caught Ember's wrist with the other.

"Grab my waist, Em." He swung her close and she wrapped her arms around him. He pulled them both up, straining from the added weight, gritting his teeth against the searing pain in his gut. Once they climbed over, he eased Ember away from him.

Adia's copy was running around the room, the cuero clinging to her. Biting. "Get this disgusting thing off me!"

This was his chance.

He wouldn't get another.

He split off a copy, sending it after the real Adia. Doing so was dangerous. Duncan drilled the rules of vampirism into his head from their first day together—never use your talent when you're wounded.

There was no other choice. Not if he wanted to end this.

He spied Julian's clothes, his weapons lying in a heap on the floor and dove for them.

Adia's copy stabbed at the cuero, nicking herself in her efforts to get the creature off. He lifted his blade, ready to immobilize Adia's copy as she swung around.

They both froze.

The copy's eyes widened as pain lanced through his chest. He glanced down.

Her blade stuck hilt-deep right between two of his ribs.

Worse, the real Adia saw him get stabbed through the copy's eyes, too. He had to make her believe him a copy. Had to play the game through. If she realized how close he was to death, she'd take her wrath out on Ember and Julian.

Adia's copy touched his cheek. "Harry?"

"You wish." Good, his voice was still strong. Stronger than he felt, by far. He pushed Adia's copy to the floor and pinned her with his blade through her neck. He crouched over her. "I'm coming to you, mama. You leave Em and Jules alone and I'll stay. Forever. Just like we planned."

The copy smiled as she faded away.

"Drop a rope or something."

Ember glanced around, but found nothing of use in the room.

"Hold on, Jules." She pulled herself off the ground and reached behind her to unclasp the dog collar. The simple task seemed to take forever as hard as she shook and every time she pressed to undo the latch, the spikes sank deeper into her neck. Finally, the clasp released and she pulled the collar from her throat. She threw the chain over the edge of the rail and checked to make sure Julian could reach.

Julian had already climbed halfway up.

She turned as Adia's copy faded. She must have recalled her copy. Harrison lifted his blade and stabbed into something on the floor. He stayed crouched over where the copy's body had been.

Ember approached him. His knife pinned the cuero to the floor. At first, she thought he was watching the creature's struggles, but his eyes remained unfocused, staring out into space. "Harrison?"

When she got no response, the hair at her nape stood on end. She touched his shoulder.

He fell forward, rolling onto his back. "Harrison!"

A knife stuck out of his chest on the right side. Lacerations and stab wounds covered his body. Some so deep she could see the darkness that kept him alive. Ember leaned over him and cupped his face. "Baby, can you hear me?"

He was awake, his eyes stared at the ceiling unblinking, but he gave no indication he heard.

Julian threw on his pants and grabbed his shirt to throw over Harrison's waist. He knelt on the other side. Snapped his fingers in front of Harrison's eyes. "Jesus, Harry, stop it."

"Why isn't he moving?" She was already worried, but Julian's urgency was starting to freak her out. "What's going on?"

He ignored her, leaning over Harrison's face. "Don't do this, Adia's not worth the risk. We'll get another chance."

Harrison didn't even blink in acknowledgement. If not for the slight rise and fall of his chest beneath her hands, she'd think him dead. His lifeless eyes stared straight up without recognition of either her or Julian. No expression enlivened his features.

"I know you can hear me, damn you. Call the copy back."

Ember went cold. What had Duncan told her about that? *I could get stuck, unable to stop expending energy to hold the form. I'd perish.*

He sent a copy after Adia when hurt this badly? "Help me cover his wounds." She put pressure on the two stab wounds closest to her, taking her hand off one to whack Julian. "Now, Jules!"

That seemed to snap him out of his daze. He pulled the knife from Harry's chest, and pressed his hand over the wound. "Kat's coming. Duncan was going to call her. She's got to be here by now."

Harrison moved under her hands and for a second she thought he was getting up.

No. He was convulsing.

Harrison needed every ounce of energy he had to keep his copy moving. He held one arm out to the wall to help steady his balance. He had to end Adia's games now.

At the end of the hall, he caught a flash of her gold robe as a figure darted past. Keeping tight to the wall, he flexed his grip on the Guardian blade and increased his pace. He turned the corner and stopped short. Candles lit the whole area. Adia was sprawled on her satin-clad bed in the center of the room. The dead boy had been moved and he wondered, briefly, where Duncan had put the body.

She smirked. "It's been a long time, Harry."

He took in the rest of the space. The door he came through was the only exit. Someone had tidied the vanity, tucking her little trophies back into their box. His gaze returned to the female on the bed. That wasn't Adia. He was almost certain he faced another copy. He needed to get the real Adia out of hiding. Fast.

He tossed the blade onto the bed next to her and leaned heavily on the wall.

Her almond-shaped eyes widened. "That was unexpected. It's not like you not to fight until the bitter end."

"It is the bitter end." He glanced at the multitude of deep gashes crisscrossing his naked flesh.

"Don't be melodramatic." She eased into a sitting position. "You'll heal well enough."

"I want to come back." He forced his body to relax. Maintained steady breathing with a force of will that sapped his energy.

"Prove it." When he didn't immediately move to obey, her eyes narrowed.

He took a step toward her and his knee gave out on him. He staggered back to his feet and approached the bed.

"Perhaps you are worse off than I first thought." She frowned.

"Isn't that what you wanted?" He kept his hand pressed to the stab wound in his belly. His right arm pressed tight to the one between his ribs, hiding the worst of the damage from her. "Me low and begging."

"Begging, yes, but I'd much rather bring you low in private."

She stood and stepped away from the bed. He knew what she wanted. How she expected him to prove himself.

His gut rolled at the idea of being intimate with Adia. Even Adia's copy.

There was no choice. Not if he wanted her to come out of hiding. His throat was closing on him. He went to pull at his stifling collar before remembering he was nude. If he didn't do this . . . If he didn't end this now, her sick games would start all over.

He sat on the edge of the satin-clad bed and lay back.

Gods, he'd thought being near her would be easier with his copy, but he was hurt too bad. His consciousness was slipping from his body into that of the copy. Instead of the cold cement below his body in the other room, he felt the fur rugs beneath his feet here. No longer did he feel Ember's warm hands on his face, or the shirt Julian had tossed over his hips. He couldn't even hear them anymore.

His copy's body shook.

Copies didn't shake. They didn't feel.

Adia's copy knelt on the bed. "You are coming back to me." She crawled higher on his body, but when she raised her leg to straddle his face he grabbed her ankle in a fierce grip.

She swiped at his arm with her blade, slicing deep. Her eyes blazed. "You've forgotten the rules, stupid boy." She slapped him and he let his head loll to the side from the force of her strike. "You don't ever touch me unless I say you can."

Her words echoed inside his mind. He'd forgotten.

Hadn't he treated Ember the same way?

He'd learned to be like that from her.

Dominating and oppressive.

Emotionally defunct.

Apathetic.

Cold.

No.

He wasn't that bad off. Not yet. Ember would keep him from sinking that far into desolation. He forced himself to look at Adia's copy. "Not with you. If you want me to prove myself, I'll do so for the real Adia only." When she tried to swing her leg over him again, he grabbed her, squeezing her ankle.

She lashed out with the blade, this time slashing his face. At first, he thought she'd cleaved clean through his copy's cheek, but the gash didn't quite go that deep. She raised the blade again. This time, she didn't strike out. Instead, she backed off the bed.

Movement by the door caught his attention. Adia walked in.

"Recall your copy so I know it's you."

She smiled.

The copy's blade fell to the floor as she turned vaporous and returned to her creator.

With a shrug of her shoulders, Adia's robe slipped to the ground revealing a thin, well-toned body and lithe curves. The bed dipped when she planted her knee on the sheet next to his hip and straddled him.

The scent of her perfume was stifling.

Adia leaned over him, dragging her taut nipples over his chest. She licked him from chin to forehead. Ground her wet slit on his disinterested cock. His stomach rolled and his breathing hitched, forcing him to acknowledge his consciousness had merged further.

He *felt* her.

Smelled her.

Harrison's chest ached as he struggled for air. Not now. He didn't need to have a panic attack now.

Adia's perfumed-laced skin filled each gasping breath.

His mind started shutting off. Tuning out. He was disappearing into his mind like when he was young. He fought the almost overwhelming desire to disappear into that dark, numb place he used to go.

CHAPTER 35

October 16, 2:18 AM

JULIAN STUFFED A JACKET UNDER Harrison's head. Ember pressed on his stomach, straddling his legs and trying to keep him from hurting himself as his body seized. If he survived this, she'd kill him for being so stupid.

"How long?" Julian spoke into the phone pressed between his shoulder and ear. Kat had arrived. She'd be here soon. "Jesus. His face."

Ember followed Julian's gaze. The deep laceration scoring across his cheek hadn't been there before.

"He found her." Her stomach churned. *Oh, God.* Right now, he was fighting Adia. Alone. Wounded.

"His consciousness is merging. Should I try to find him?"

She couldn't keep pressure on all these wounds by herself and they had no idea where Harrison's copy was. "No, this whole place is one big maze."

Frustrated tears blinded her. She leaned over Harrison, whispering words of encouragement, trying to call him back. "Come on, baby. This isn't the day and that's okay. We're safe. Lucas is safe. We promised him you'd come home with us." No response. This was useless. All she'd succeeded in doing was bathing him in her tears and blood.

"Em, your blood." Julian swallowed, nodding to Harrison.

The blood dripping from her throat had pooled in the little cup her thumb and forefinger made against his skin on his belly. Underneath, Harrison's skin appeared smooth, healthy. Hadn't there been a cut above the stab wound?

She remembered the other night when she'd inadvertently healed his hand. The cuero had bit him, but when he had covered the bite mark on her arm with his hand, his wound had healed because of her blood.

Julian spoke into his phone. "Yeah. Down both flights of stairs, Kat."

"Can't she spell travel to us?"

He shook his head and covered the phone with his hand. "She can't waste her Magic on getting here, when we need her to heal him." He spoke into the phone again. "When you get to the cistern, take the tunnel straight ahead and to your left. Hurry."

Dipping her fingers in the blood, Ember smeared the thick liquid across another shallow gash higher on his chest. The cut disappeared.

She eased her hand down a little on the wound her hand covered, and let her blood pool at the edge of the stab wound on his belly. Inched her hand along as each section of the wound as stitched itself together under the dark red pool.

All the while, Julian painted the smaller lacerations by dipping his fingers in her blood and smearing them across Harrison's wounds.

His convulsions stilled.

Harrison took a deep, steady breath.

Julian smiled. Nodded to the deep wound under his hand. "Now this one."

The blade.

He needed her to stay distracted long enough to get his blade.

Adia palmed his lifeless dick. "You showed far more interest in that succubus bitch." She squeezed.

He slid his hand across the satin sheet as she slipped lower on his body. Gods, she was going to bite him. She was going to . . . No. She couldn't. He was a vampire now. If she bit him, they'd both be ash.

"I don't understand how you could mate her."

The pressure in his chest built until he couldn't seem to drag in another breath. His finger touched the hilt, which managed to push the knife a hair's breadth farther away. "She lets . . . me have . . . control." This wasn't his body. If he remembered that, he'd be all right.

He was safe with Ember and Julian.

He wasn't really here.

Adia wasn't really touching *him*.

His chest eased and he sucked in a deep breath.

The burning pain in his belly lessened and faded altogether. He checked his wound, but the puncture in his gut had disappeared.

Somehow, he was healing.

"She *lets* you have control?" Adia laughed. "Did you never learn anything? If she allows it, you're not in control. *She is*." She licked him, a long drag from balls to head. He saw her do it, but he didn't feel the wet glide of her tongue.

He threw an arm over his eyes, using the motion to cover his reach with his other arm.

"Are you going to cry?" She let out a sound close to a purr, crawling higher. "I always loved when you'd cry for me."

His fingers closed around the hilt.

Harrison sat up, grabbing her by the throat. "I never cried for you."

Adia's eyes widened, she grasped his wrist in both her hands. "Harry. I love you."

Bullshit. He swung her around to pin her on the bed. "No. You don't know what that is. You don't get to say those words. Not you." He clenched his copy's jaw, fighting himself for control. It would be so easy to do the things she had done to him. To show her real pain. To degrade and humiliate her.

He was bigger.

Stronger.

And because of Ember, he was better than that.

Adia shook her head, trying to squirm away.

He brought the blade down, sinking the knife deep into her flesh.

His nightmare faded to dust.

CHAPTER 36

October 16, 2:54 AM

HARRISON OPENED HIS EYES.

A watery, emerald eyes gaze met his.

He was free. Gods, he was finally free. Adia couldn't hurt the people he cared about anymore. She couldn't hurt him anymore.

He drew in a deep breath and sat up.

"She's dead." His whole world had changed. He glanced around, nodded to Jules and Kat and returned his gaze to Ember. "You'd think something spectacular would happen now, right?"

Julian snorted. "Oh, it gets better, brother. Give yourself a couple days. You'll start realizing the one being you always thought would be the death of you is gone and you'll start noticing all the other threats to you and your loved ones that you never gave much notice to before."

Kat swatted him. "Jules, that's horrible."

He shrugged. "It's the truth." He met Harrison's gaze. "It does get better. With time." He put his arm around Kat and pulled her close. "Especially when you've got a nagging female around, always making you talk, and name your emotions, and shit."

Kat rolled her eyes. "You're lucky I love you."

"Yes." He kissed her on the nose. "Yes, I am." He cleared his throat and stood. "We'll go find your clothes. I want my shirt back." He turned to leave and Harrison stared at the spot low on Julian's back where "VINCE" had been etched into his skin long ago. Proof that Julian understood everything. He didn't know the whole story, but he knew Julian had been owned much like Adia had owned him.

"Hey, Jules."

Julian turned around.

"Thanks, man."

Julian nodded. His gaze flashed to Ember. "She knows. You know, about me. Figured everything out." He shot Ember a wink and they left.

His attention returned to Ember. She hadn't moved. Still knelt by his side wringing her hands with worry. For him.

"You're okay with Jules?"

She gave him a shaky smile. "I trust you and I know someday, you'll tell me his story. For now, he's our partner. He's your best friend. That's all that matters."

He breathed a sigh. Two of his biggest concerns had disappeared in a matter of moments.

"How are you feeling?"

Her question struck him as funny. What had Julian said about having a woman around wanting to talk about emotions? He laughed, thinking how similar he and Jules were. As similar as Ember and Kat. He laughed so hard something inside him broke open and then he wasn't laughing anymore.

All the shit he'd kept buried, broke free with the intensity of a dam burst, rocking him with its intensity.

Ember started to reach for him and paused. "Can I touch you?"

He hauled her into his lap, into his arms, and buried his face in her hair. "You don't need to ask." He must be squeezing her too tight, but he couldn't seem to stop. "Don't ask. If I'm having a bad day and start to pull away, hang on tighter. Can you do that for me?"

"Okay." Her fingers stroked though his hair. "If you're sure."

"I don't want to go back to how I was. I don't want to be like her."

"Oh, God." She forced his face up, thumbing away his tears. "You're nothing like her. Don't think that."

"I grabbed her ankle when she . . . ." He wet his lips, dragging his arm over his eyes only to have fresh tears wet his face. "She said I forgot the rules. That I couldn't touch her unless she said I could and I realized I do that to you."

"No." She smiled through her tears. "No, baby. You're not like that. You were protecting yourself, not being mean. Not being controlling. Remember what I said, you always gave me control even when you wouldn't let me touch you."

He sucked in a deep, shuddering breath, wiping his face in the crook of his arm. "Gods, I'm sorry about this, Em. Don't know what's wrong with me."

"Don't be a sexist pig. You're a healthy, strong male who's been through hell. You've had to face pretty much every one of your demons tonight."

Now, he'd done it. She was vexed.

He aimed for placating. "Okay."

She scowled harder. "There's not a damned thing wrong with you. Why on earth would you say such a thing?"

"Okay, honey. Go easy on me. I've had a rough night."

She pulled away to search his face. Finally, her frown eased.

"I love you, Em."

She shot him a cocky grin. "I know."

He moaned. "Gods, Em. You stole the best Harrison Ford line ever. That was supposed to be my line."

She laughed and he had to check his watch because he'd never heard anything quite so wonderful.

EPILOGUE

January 16, 11:12 PM

HARRISON LEANED BACK IN HIS chair, thinking today was damned perfect. Kat had gotten in yesterday and he, Ember, and Julian had the night off. Duncan and his mate, Trina, had taken Lucas to visit the daemon school in Machon. If he liked the academy, he'd start classes there in the fall.

The boy was doing well. He spent a lot of time with him and Julian, but he'd started warming to the women. Ember had even coaxed him into talking about what happened. Lucas was healing. So was he.

He compared his cards to Ember's, and George's head popped between their shoulders, trying to see, too. Harrison pulled the minion out of the way and set him on his shoulder.

He and Julian were attempting to teach their ladies the fine art of piquet. A card game long out of fashion.

Ember snuggled in his lap, giggling as he whispered their strategy in her ear. He raised his voice, eyeing Julian over his cards. "Jules always goes for the bluff, 'cause he's so full of shit."

"I heard that, Sinclair." Julian shot his mate an expression of mock hurt. "I told you what he's like, butterfly. That male is plain mean."

Kat kissed him, raising her cards to shield them.

Harrison scoffed. "Kat, you need a bigger hand for that, Jules' head is too damn big."

Laughing, she reached across the table, grabbed a fistful of Ember's popcorn, and hurled the buttery fluff at him. "He's right, you're a beast."

Behind her, Jules pulled a mocking face.

The doorbell rang.

"I'll get it." Ember bounced out of his lap and headed for the door.

He glanced at the couple across from him. "You two expecting someone?"

Julian shook his head. Suddenly, they both seemed extremely interested in their cards.

A female was speaking to Ember. She sounded like . . . . *Gods.*

Harrison stood so fast his chair hit the floor. His panicked gaze shot to Julian, to Kat, but neither of them could help him now.

As if in a dream, he floated through the living room and into the entry. George curled around his hip, gurgling softly. Ember's back faced him, and the door blocked the other woman from his view.

He checked his watch, 11:16 PM. Today he was twenty-four years, six days, three hours, and twelve minutes old. He slipped his hand into his pocket and palmed the small, smooth stone Ember kept sneaking into his pocket. This was what he'd waited for. If he stepped into the foyer, he'd never have to count the minutes again.

Or he could go back. He didn't have to risk rejection.

As if sensing his conflicted thoughts, George nudged his arm. He walked around Ember until he stared into brilliant blue eyes that matched his own.

She'd gotten older. Gray streaked her curly blond hair. The laugh lines he recalled had etched themselves deeper into the corners of her eyes. At rest, her mouth tipped downward a little more than before. She'd lost a lot of weight.

Gods, she seemed tiny. Hadn't she been taller? In all his memories, she'd been larger than life.

This woman was different from the one he remembered and he'd missed everything between then and now. Did he want to miss more?

The whites of her eyes reddened as tears filled them. Her lips parted, but instead of speaking, her hand flew to her mouth to stifle a sob.

Gods, he hadn't realized how hard this must be for her, too. He glanced at his watch.

What did he say after a little over eight years, six months, five days, eight hours, thirty-one minutes? Should he try to explain? Apologize? He needed to find the right words. An irresistibly witty comment or some emotional appeal she wouldn't dare turn away from.

Hoping for inspiration, he glanced at Ember. She smiled, her eyes filling with tears, too. "Aren't you going to speak, baby?"

He looked back at the older woman weeping in his doorway and his vision blurred. He opened his mouth, wanting to say something inspired. Something profound.

"Hi, Mom."

ABOUT THE AUTHOR

CARA CRESCENT CURRENTLY LIVES IN the Pacific Northwest with her children and three overly dramatic ferrets. When not writing, you can usually find her curled up with a book, engrossed in a movie or playing video games with her best friend.

Please visit her on the web at www.caracrescent.com

OTHER BOOKS BY CARA CRESCENT

The Beacon
The Shadow
The Knight
Don't Let Me Forget You
The Last Marine